DEEP BLUE

DEEP BLUE

David Niall Wilson

Five Star • Waterville, Maine

Copyright © 2004 by David Niall Wilson

All rights reserved.

This novel is a work of fiction. Names, characters, places and incidents are either the product of the author's imagination, or, if real, used fictitiously.

No part of this book may be reproduced or transmitted in any form or by any electronic or mechanical means, including photocopying, recording or by any information storage and retrieval system, without the express written permission of the publisher, except where permitted by law.

First Edition
First Printing: May 2004

Published in 2004 in conjunction with
Tekno Books and Ed Gorman.

Set in 11 pt. Plantin.

Printed in the United States on permanent paper.

Library of Congress Control Number: 2004100365
ISBN 1-59414-142-8 (hc : alk. paper)

ACKNOWLEDGMENTS

I would like to thank, first and foremost, the love of my life, Trish, for standing by me during one of the hardest periods of my career and helping to make this book possible. I'd also like to thank Lisa Snelling, whose artwork inspired the anthology where DEEP BLUE first took root, an unknown sax player in the Washington DC subway, the people who created the Holocaust Museum in DC for helping to make sure we never forget the horrors of the past, the movie *PI*, and Vince and Leslie Harper of Bereshith Books, all ingredients in the birth of the novel. This book is dedicated to all the blues men from Robert Johnson to Jimmy Page who gave me the music, and to my brother Bill—enjoy it, bro.

INTRODUCTION

The novel *Deep Blue* originated from the novelette by the same name published in an anthology titled *Strange Attraction*. In *Strange Attraction*, all the stories were inspired by the "Kinetic" Art of Lisa Snelling, each author choosing one of the characters on an intricately detailed Ferris wheel sculpture. I chose a harlequin, hanging by a noose from the bottom of one of the Ferris wheel's seats. I took the image, made it the wallpaper on my computer, printed it out and carried it around with me, and let it sink in. I could have written any number of stories that would have sufficed, but somehow I knew there would be more to this work, and so I waited.

The publishers of the anthology, Vince and Leslie Harper, invited me to have dinner with them one night when my job took me to Washington DC. We met for Mexican food and went together to see the movie *PI* which, at the time, was newly released. On the way to meet the Harpers, I walked down into a shadowed subway, and I was assaulted by some of the most haunting saxophone music I've ever heard. It bordered the blues, walked down old jazz roads, and I never saw the musician. That set the mood for what was to come.

I reached the restaurant without further incident, and we spent a pleasant hour scalding mouths and stomachs with jalapenos and washing them down with beer. Then came the movie. I won't go into detail about *PI*, but I'll say it's a black and white film, very surreal, filled with symbolism, and it left me visually and emotionally stunned. I parted company with Vince and his wife, found my way back to the subway and my hotel, and called it a night.

The next day, a friend of mine and I set out to visit The Holocaust Museum. I have always wanted to see it, but I was not prepared for the intensity of the images, the displays, and the words I would find in that short hour visit. I purchased a book of poetry written by the victims, and left with so much bottled up inside from those two days that I thought it would be the end of my sanity.

That night, I started to write. I started to write about The Blues, and how deep they might really get. I wrote about pain, not my pain, but the pain bottled up inside the world, as the pain had been bottled up inside me, and I wrote a way out. That was Brandt, his guitar, and his blues. The story, like the pain, refused to be bottled up in just the few lines of that novelette, and so I released it into the novel you now hold.

Everyone comes to their crossroads eventually—the defining moment of life. As Old Wally, one of the novel's main characters tells us—"Crossroads, or the crosshairs." Forward or back, but you can't stay stagnant—that way lies madness. I give you . . . *Deep Blue.*

ONE

(The Fool)

The lights flickered on. The stage, moments before a dark world of surreal sound and chord-soaked images, became a snarl of patched cables, scuffed speaker cabinets, and half-assembled equipment. No one spoke to Brandt as he passed, white makeup blurred with dark lines from the black that lined his eyes and lips, a melting harlequin image of angst and insecurity. He had his guitar case in one hand and his escort for the night, Jose Cuervo, clutched tightly in the other. The doors would close in thirty minutes. No leeway. Sid paid well enough, and he did right by the band, but at closing time he wanted everyone, and everything, out the door.

One of the waitresses, Katrina, let Brandt out the door, leaning to whisper as her enamel-tipped fingers worked the ponderous deadbolt. "You look like a fucking dead clown."

Brandt brushed past her, his shoulder sliding against her breast as he slipped into the night and turned down the road toward his apartment. He walked away slowly, not even thinking about looking for his car. No way he was driving. The guitar case slapped comfortably against his leg as he walked, taking his mind off the last set. Too much tequila. Too much apathy. Summed up in two words: too much. He'd forgotten the words to a song he'd written himself, repeated the previous verse and mixed that up with the chorus. No one had noticed. He thought maybe Shaver had caught it, just before launching into the solo, but he couldn't be sure. The audience didn't give a fuck what they played. Shaver only lived for the solo. Hard facts, but true.

Brandt thought about that for a long moment. He tipped the tequila bottle up, took a slug, and capped it again, moving off down the street. "Fuck them," he said out loud. "Fuck them all."

The streets were empty. The soft glow of street lamps pooled on the deserted roads, making each intersection a glowing oasis, and Brandt walked from one to the next, the tequila forgotten, words and music swimming through his mind. He hated nights like this. He hated the empty, nothing feeling of leaving a bar after a show where no one, not even the band, had cared. Nothing. Empty. He hated being alone and drunk. He hated the thought of his cave-like, nowhere apartment with the fading paint on the walls and electricity that only worked half the time. It reminded him too much of his father's home, and his father's life. It reminded him that no matter how many dreams he'd had, he was living in the image of his creator, minus the beer gut and the attitude.

His last private moment with a woman had been the landlady screaming about rent he wouldn't earn at all unless the nights got better than this one. More of the family scrapbook tossed in his face as the old bitch's features had melted to his mother's, the voice growing yet another octave more shrill, piercing his heart and his gut. Different voice, same message. Loser. Nobody. No future. Another swig of tequila, and he turned the corner to his block.

His building was one of many. Too many, all the same, layer upon layer of box apartments with doors only different because they bore separate numbers. Tiny worlds, each bleak and lonely, cut off from the others by walls too thin to block sound and too crumbled to hold paintings or coat hooks.

Brandt stumbled up the stairs, nearly fell, then recovered his balance just in time to keep from banging the guitar case on the dirty steps. The tequila bottle struck concrete with a loud *clink* and he cursed. Lurching up the final three steps, he leaned into the door and reached into his pocket for his keys. Nothing. He patted the tight denim, cursed, and shifted, letting the guitar come to rest at his feet and trading the Cuervo to his opposite hand. The other pocket was empty as well.

"Fuck!" he said, leaning hard into the door, his head cracking painfully into the wood and leaving a dirty white smudge. He leaned there, eyes closed tightly, blinking against the sudden attack of vertigo that assaulted his senses. The car. The keys had to be in the fucking car that he was *too* fucking drunk to drive, or even find. No keys, no door, and he wasn't about to wake that old bitch and tell her. She'd leave him on the street. She was ready to put him there anyway.

Brandt leaned for a moment longer, breathing slowly. Sometime in the soft void of that moment, sometime between thought and darkness and thought again, the sound started. It was hypnotic, dragging at his heart first and tugging his ears into service for the translation.

Music. It was the crisp, clear voice of a harmonica, floating to him through the stillness of the late-night streets.

He listened, then pushed off from the wall, trying to orient himself. Shaking his head, he considered taking another swig of tequila, thought better of it, and turned. He couldn't get in, and he couldn't stay on the stairs, either. Might as well find out where that music was coming from.

Brandt hit the street once more, turning the opposite of

the way he'd come. The music seeped out from the darker depths of the city. Not safe there, he knew. Not safe walking back for his car and chancing his alcohol-soaked mind to the streets, or the police, either. He stumbled ahead, letting the music lead him and blanking out everything else. It was beautiful, but sad beyond anything he could remember hearing, or experiencing. Tears welled in the corners of his eyes and he brushed at them, smacking himself painfully in the head with the tequila bottle and cursing softly.

He didn't recognize the tune, but it was blues, pure and sweet, blues so soul-deep that the voice of the instrument spoke in the place of a man's lips. The way it was supposed to be. The way he wanted to feel when he played. The way he felt when he kicked back, closed his eyes, and listened to T. Bone Walker, or Robert Johnson, or Billie Holliday. The way the blues had not been played in so long they seemed banished to some fantasy realm that never was, the recordings elaborate hoaxes, mocking him with things beyond his reach. Hot tears welled suddenly in the corners of his eyes. He ignored them. He knew they would run down, trickling trails through his ruined makeup, but he didn't care.

Brandt hummed the melody, trying to commit it to memory. He knew the classics. He knew the old masters. He did not know this song. It was intricate, dripping with simplicity that was belied by quarter-tones and shivering trills of sound that walked the tightrope between notes, hinted of notes that were missing, between the C Sharps and D Minors.

Ahead an alley opened to his left. He knew the place. It had once been a packing dock for a shipping company, long since gone to ruin. Brandt stopped. He did not want to think about that alley, had thought far too much about it already. A shiver transited his spine and he blinked once, unscrewing the lid of the tequila bottle and taking a long swallow.

The homeless gathered in that alley. He saw the flicker of trashcan firelight winking and shimmering from the darkened entrance. The music drew him, but his fears held him back. Stalemate. Brandt could see himself in that alley. He could see the downward spiral of his life spinning him into it like a giant drain.

As he slowly screwed the lid onto the tequila, he noticed for the first time that there was a huddled figure seated at the entrance. He tried to pierce the gloom and make out details, but he was still too far away, nearly a block. Breathing deeply, he stepped forward again, gripping both guitar and tequila as if they were talismans of protection.

It was a woman, old and cloaked in layer upon layer of tattered clothing. Spread out on the ground before her was a semi-circle of cards. Tarot. Brandt knew little of the brightly colored images, but he'd seen them often enough to know what they were. As he entered the mouth of the alley, he glanced down, and she suddenly raised her gaze to hold his, trapping him in the depths of yellowed, rheumy eyes. The music was louder now, captivating. The tune had changed, sweeping up and down minor scales, each note lingering, blurring into the next.

The woman did not speak, but held out the deck to Brandt, her mouth opening slowly in a toothless grin. He stared at her for a long time, not noticing the cards. He stared until he realized what he was doing, then turned, embarrassed, face flushed with tequila and shame, and staggered into the alley.

"Crazy old bitch," he muttered.

The alley was a chiaroscuro wash of shadows, contrasted

against the backdrop of trashcan fires, their dancing flames too dim to clarify those gathered around them. Brandt studied the darkened doorways and alcoves, but there was no sign of the musician. Brandt cocked his head to one side, listening. The notes were no less clear, but neither did they help him to narrow his search. The tequila wasn't helping either. He narrowed his eyes, swept his gaze over the alley a final time, and lurched toward the wall of a nearby building.

There were no fires too near, no future-of-the-nowhere-musician wraiths to beg or harass him. He spun, leaned against the dirty brick, and slid down to the ground with a soft thud. Somehow he managed to hold the bottle up so it didn't smash on the ground, and the guitar case so his instrument wouldn't crack or break. His ass was less fortunate, but the Cuervo numbed the pain.

Without hesitation, he slid the guitar case to his side, unhooked the clasps, and opened the lid. The polished wood glowed dimly in the flickering orange light. Brandt stared at the instrument for a long time. He wanted to play. He wanted to play so badly his fingers itched and his mind whirled. The whirling was too much tequila and not enough inspiration. Then he heard the harmonica again, really heard it, and his hand slipped down to grip the neck of the guitar. He pulled it free of the case, letting it rest gently and comfortably on his leg, and listened carefully to the melody of the lone harpist. Brandt might not be able to find the man, but he could hear. He could feel.

He remembered the barmaid's words: *You look like a dead clown.* He thought of Shaver's comment on his newest version of the makeup he'd worn since his first performance. It set him apart, erected a wall between Brandt and the band. They did not join the "show," or condone it. He could play, write, and sing, so they let him be.

"It's all such a drama to you," Shaver had said, watching him apply the white-face and the rouge, the exaggerated eyes, lined in pain and outlined in deeper black than the shadowy depths of the bar's corners. "That shit went out with KISS."

Brandt reached up gently, slowly tracing a nail through the smeared makeup. Drama. Shaver had no idea. Brandt's fingers slid to the strings gently. His eyes closed. He let his mind slide as well, let it slip to darkness, to thoughts of his bills, his landlady, anything to bring him down to those notes. He felt his fingers twitch, reaching for the strings. He held them back. So deep.

He wanted to blend with that sound, to feel the notes flow up and through him. He couldn't bring himself to try. Though the desire to play was a physical ache so powerful it nearly doubled him over, something even the tequila had failed to do, he held his fingers still. Heart thudding a dull rhythm in his chest, he stared into the darkness, listening, as the tears flooded his eyes and washed down his cheeks again. He couldn't fucking play.

The sound took him back, months back. The band had been on a rare road trip to the edge of town, opening for some skin-head local noise-mongers with a following and an attitude. The set ended early. Synthia had been drunker than Brandt himself, for a change, and had not been ready to call it a night. Somehow her wobbly enthusiasm and half a hit of acid had brought them further still from the center of the city, to the fringes of a small carnival. The Ferris wheel had been so short it seemed a toy, and the booths were lined with the seediest of the seedy. Lost men and women, boys and girls, eyes vacant of humanity and burning with a hunger that only the laughter, money, and dreams of the uninitiated could sate.

Syn had been oblivious to it all. She'd dragged Brandt, her small hand gripping his wrist, from booth to booth, through the fun house and its mirrors. Long faces and short bodies, endless legs and his mind traveling the length of her 'til they spun out and away again, ending in front of an old tent. The doors to that tent flapped loudly in the stiff breeze. The sign said simply, "Fortunes."

They'd stood there a long moment, and then Syn had lurched forward. Inside was a single table, a crystal ball resting on wooden feet in the center. Syn had approached it fearlessly, dragging Brandt like a faulty anchor. With a quick motion she'd spun him before her and pressed him into the chair, leaning over his shoulder gently, her lips so close to his ear as she whispered that he felt her hot breath, felt little sizzles of energy as the LSD sparkled through his senses.

"Find out the future, Brandt. Find out how famous we will be. Find out if you get lucky tonight." Her tongue had traced his ear then, and Brandt looked up.

There was an old woman seated across from him that Brandt hadn't noticed when they'd entered. She was cloaked in dark colors and slumped in her chair, eyes hidden by the deep folds of her robe. All Brandt remembered were those deep, piercing eyes. And the card. The woman had long, slender fingers, bony and blue-veined. Her nails were too long, curled under and yellowed. She had flipped the card, a single card, before a word was spoken. Before Brandt could protest that he did not want a reading, before Syn could cajole him into it, before reality could truly solidify in any real way, the fingers flipped, and the card turned.

The Fool. Inverted. Head down to the ground and ass to the stars. Brandt had stared, mesmerized. White-faced clown, idiot-savant, stepping into the void, long-fanged dog dangling from its grip on the fool's ass—and the cliff. Forever. Everything and nothing, cost and lost in a single false, clueless step.

    He'd staggered to his feet, turned to the door and fallen, Syn's hand on his shoulder. That had been all it took, that slight imbalance. He remembered her cursing, his feet tangling and the ground rising much too quickly as he threw his hands out in a futile gesture of denial. His chin had connected with moist earth, his eyes flashing with the strobed images of The Fool, and the ground, spilled drinks, and flecks of cotton candy filling his vision. He'd crawled forward, trying to drag himself free of the crackling grip of the visions, the melting images of reality and the sudden pounding of pain in his head that threatened to cancel consciousness absolutely.

    One hand at a time, fingers gripping the dirt and dragging him forward, he'd moved from the tent and rolled to his back, closing his eyes to clear his thoughts. Syn was over him in seconds, face too close, voice too loud, and slender fingers slapping him sharply on the cheek. She'd spoken to him, but her words were slurred, lengthening impossibly and blurring to incomprehensible noise. He didn't know if it was his mind, or hers, that was snapping.

    Brandt had opened his eyes then, and seen it. Far above him, looming like a monstrous insect. The Ferris wheel, so small and insignificant as they'd approached the carnival, loomed immensely, the image so powerful that it nearly stole his breath. Brandt had watched, mesmerized. Horrified. His angle allowed a clear view of the bottoms of the seats as they spun down—feet, legs, and then faces. He'd watched, and again, Syn's hand cracking into his cheek, leaving white-to-red splotched images of her touch as the odd, disjointed music of the carnival played in the background. The wheel had spun, and Brandt had seen the image clearly: the noose, dangling from the framework, and The Fool, dangling from the end in a St. Vitus Dance to oblivion.

Then it was gone, so many shadows, spinning up and away with the motion of the wheel, and spirits, LSD, and noise. He remembered Syn helping him clumsily to his feet, scolding him for being a "weird fuck," and the staggering return trip to the streets, to a dirty taxi neither of them could afford, and home, the images replaying relentlessly in his mind.

Brandt shook his head and the alley came into focus. Shadows shifted, emptied of nothingness to be filled with slowly moving figures, bright-eyed wraiths shuffling from the darkened corners, a single unit of disjointed members. There was no threat in their approach. As they drew nearer, Brandt was able to make out the central figure through the glistening salt-haloed lenses of his tears.

Darker than the others, arms elbow-bent and pressing the harp to his lips, the man stopped directly in front of Brandt. An old black man, his hair the gray of dark thread dipped in white paint, eyes not quite white any more, and glittering with captured firelight flickers. No words, necessary or offered. Music, and Brandt could not move, did not want to, and the tears flowed in a constant stream.

The notes flowed free and clean and when they stopped, they echoed through Brandt's mind. Brandt closed his eyes then, ignoring those who had gathered, guitar death-grip-clutched in straining fingers gone white from the effort of not failing. He wanted to memorize the melody. He wanted to make the notes his own, take them and dissect the pattern, find a way to bend fingers/mind/soul to that deep sadness.

They leaked through him and away, soaking into the grimy concrete floor of the alley and ringing in his ears, half-faded remnant of unrequited dreamsong.

    The alley slipped away again. Brandt was sitting in a room, clutching the guitar, a guitar, too fat somehow and clumsy. It was his old room, his fucking room in that nowhere life he'd left to launch a nowhere life of his own. He could hear Hank Williams Sr. wailing on the eight-track in the next room, could hear the lumbering thunder of his father's snores, punctuated now and then by the soft glass-clink of his mother's wine bottle dipping again to fill her glass.

    The guitar was a cheap, rough acoustic with the logo *Harmony* at the top of the neck. He had to press his fingers impossibly hard to bring the strings to the frets, and he frowned, concentrating through the pain. Hank was calling to him, calling from a far away pain and sorrow, reaching out with soft-twanging heart-notes, but Brandt couldn't quite concentrate through the other sounds. He frowned, pressing the strings harder, as if the physical effort could erase the empty *clink* of glass and the crash as his mother stumbled into a wall, cursing. He heard his father's even, labored breathing hesitate . . . glitch . . . and rumble. Then the snoring stopped, and there was a dead silence.

    Brandt gripped the guitar so tightly his fingers grew white with the effort and he turned from the door. He didn't want to think of his mother retreating to him, hoping for a reprieve from something Brandt could not save her from. He didn't want to think about his father, bursting through the door after her, turning to Brandt because at least Brandt still felt the blows, still screamed when slapped. He didn't want to think at all. His gaze locked to the twin clown portraits on his wall. Sad attempts at decoration, at parenthood. Deep-eyed guardians, impotent and leering, white faces glowing softly in the dim light of his bedside lamp.

Brandt shook free, so violently his head cracked back into the brick wall, and the images shattered, Hank Williams' bittersweet voice melting to the soft hiss of traffic beyond the alley. Brandt raised his eyes.

The old man squatted directly in front of him, head cocked to the side like an inquisitive dog, examining something intriguing. Brandt blinked and sat up slowly, feeling suddenly conspicuous. The harmonica rested easy and comfortable in the old musician's palm, soul extension of his pain. Brandt had a flashback to the pain behind that sound and blinked again. This time he controlled the tears with a deep gasp of breath, shaking his head.

"Damn tequila," he muttered, brushing the back of his hand over his eyes.

" 'Taint no damned tequila messin' wif yo head, boy," the man rumbled. His voice was deep, gravel spurted under heavy tires, or cigarette smoke dipped in whiskey.

Brandt didn't answer.

"Saw yo hands twitchin' son," the man went on, glancing at the guitar. "T'ought a minute there yo was g'wan play wit me. Me an' ol' Hank."

"I wanted to," Brandt whispered. Nothing more. He could read answers in the old man's gaze, and yet they formed in his mind as more questions. "What was the song?"

" 'Tweren't no song. Blue. *Key* of blue, boy, my blues. Last bit was yours."

Brandt's mind cleared a little. "It was a song. There was a melody, notes. Music is a pattern." The words rung hollow, and the old man laughed gruffly.

"Then why yo don' play 'em, ol' hoss?"

Brandt fell silent. He laid his guitar aside and opened the tequila bottle. Liquid courage. He took a long swallow and held the bottle out to the black man, who took it with a toothless grin. The bottle tipped up and Brandt watched in fascination as the old man's Adam's apple danced, an impossibly long dance that drained a full quarter of the golden liquor before it ended. The man smiled, but he didn't move to return the bottle.

"Who are you?" Brandt asked softly. "Where did you learn to play like that?"

Long stare and the man straightened slowly, gazing down at Brandt with a mixture of curiosity and sorrow. "Livin' is learnin' boy, so my pap said. Lived those notes, ever' one. Nary a chord I don' carry right here," and his hand touching his heart, palm flat, trapping the harmonica against the rough material of his shirt. "Carryin' a bit of you now."

That gaze was so still, so unwavering and serious. Pure, like the music was pure. The tears threatened again. Brandt smacked his head on the brick of the wall and cursed softly.

"Always the same, boy," the man said softly. "You let ol' Wally set you on the path. Crossroads, cross-hairs, all the same in the blues. Knowed both kinds, which're you? You want to learn, there's a price of years, lifetimes, damn worlds it costs, boy, all that and more."

"Teach me?" Words spoken and regretted the instant they left his lips. Fool drunk sniveling in an alley, drunk on his ass and begging winos for lessons. His gaze betrayed him, held steady.

"Cain't be taught," old Wally breathed. "Gotta be lived, boy, price gotta be paid. No blues ever come from a music lesson. None. Come from here," leaning down and stabbing an ancient, gnarled finger into Brandt's chest and holding, long second of contact, cold and dark, then away.

"How?"

Wally's eyes clouded. He stepped back, not speaking, the Cuervo gripped tightly in one hand.

Brandt rose quickly, reaching to his pockets. He didn't have much, a crumpled five and a handful of change the remnant of his worldly treasure. Cigarettes and coffee for a morning that was way too close already. No sleep, and the hangover would not be mild, or easily shaken.

"I'll pay," he said softly.

Wally slipped forward and slid the five from Brandt's fingers, ignoring the change, and then melted back in among his companions. "You'll pay boy, if you want the blues. No money g'wan do it fo you. Cain't be bought."

Turning, they left him. Spectral gallery of shadow-faces never clearly seen, slipping from shadow to black and gone. Brandt took a step forward, reached out to empty air. No one stood before him. No one walked through the nearby shadows, or gathered about the glowing coals of the barrel fires. Red-orange hints of dawn stained the alley's mouth, and the faint sounds of the city's day-time insinuated themselves, distracting him further.

"Gone," he whispered. He dropped his face into his hands, standing for a long moment and fighting the sick-drunk nausea that clawed at his system. No time for that now. He felt the fingers of exhaustion tugging at his eyelids, drawing him toward darkness, and he knew he had to get out of the alley. If he slept there, he'd wake with no guitar if he was lucky, and never wake at all if he was not. In future years the alley might be the only solution, but for the moment he needed his car, his keys, and his bed. He had to play again in twelve hours, and somehow he had to sleep without the images of long-trashed clowns glaring down at him from the wall over his head. Mocking.

Brandt leaned down, secured the guitar in its case carefully, then turned toward the alley's mouth and stumbled toward the sunlight. In the back of his mind, very faintly, the voice of the harmonica rose once more, mocking him and hurrying his steps. He stepped onto the sidewalk, but before he moved on, he glanced down, a sudden memory of yellow eyes and too-long, half-painted nails reminding him of the crazy woman. She was gone. Where she'd sat, a single dirt-streaked card leaned against the dusty wall. Brandt leaned down, picking it up slowly.

On the card, a young man in a jester's hat, face white-painted like a goth-boy death-mask rendered in porcelain, stepped off the brink of a cliff. A dog, snarling and angry, gripped the clown by the ass, but it did not seem to register. Brandt let his gaze slip lower and read the inscription. The Fool. Brandt memorized the lines of that face . . . the painted pretty-boy leer.

He turned toward the bar, and his car, the card released to float in a back and forth slip-dance through the early morning air. It landed upright, the boy's eyes gazing after Brandt as he stumbled away.

The sharp, too-loud clatter of the rusty Big Ben on Brandt's dresser dragged him half out of the bed to slap it to silence, head pounding from the motion and the moisture-sapped fringes of his brain. One thing about Jose Cuervo, he was always available for a date, but the fucker dressed and was gone before daylight every time. Brandt managed to shift so that a stray ray of sunlight caught the face of the old clock. Four-thirty. Three and a half hours before setup and sound check. No car in this condition, he was walking, and just enough time to hit the shower, then the coffee house, black coffee with a shot of espresso and an oversized blueberry muffin. Story of his life.

Images of the night before tried to work their way into his thoughts but he pressed them down hard. The steady pounding in his skull left no concentration for deep thought. He needed every ounce of juice he could muster just to make it to the club and back to this bed with a performance and a paycheck in between. Crazy old wino was welcome to the tequila; it was a damn good thing Brandt hadn't finished it.

He glared at the clock. Slow stumble to the shower and lukewarm water spiraling last night's funk and the clammy sweat of tequila hangover shakes down the dingy drain. Brandt stood under the steady stream, forehead pressed tightly to the tiled wall. His gaze locked for a long moment on the grimy water whirling tornado-like into the tiny round abyss and he pushed back a little too hard, nearly falling. He twisted the shower handles violently, staggered to his bedroom, and dressed, half-damp, in last night's jeans and a fresh t-shirt, sprinkling himself with an anointment of cheap cologne and sliding a Kool between his lips with a practiced flourish. He lit up and headed out, guitar slung over his shoulder.

The coffee shop wasn't busy. Thursday was a slow night everywhere, would be at Sid's too. Good damned thing. No one to throw beer cans when Brandt's half-numb fingers failed to draw the notes from the strings, or when his words wouldn't slip past the dry-clutch of the cotton in his mouth and throat. He watched the coffee in his cup swirling, and turned his gaze away, the memory of the shower drain too close to hand and heart.

"Fuck," he muttered.

The coffee ended too soon and the night began with

equal insensitivity to his plight. Fingers shaking, he tried to light another Kool and found he could not. Stopping and leaning against a dingy brick wall, Brandt took several deep breaths, squeezed his eyes shut, concentrated, then held the lighter still as he pressed the tip of the smoke into the flame. Biting menthol cut through the haze, nicotine battered it into place, and he was moving again.

Shaver glanced up from his tuning and effects pedals as Brandt entered noisily. Ignoring the shaven-headed guitarist, Brandt dropped his guitar case a bit too hard and cursed as he realized it, stumbling a half-step and righting himself carefully. Shaver watched for a pregnant moment that said more than any words might have, shook his head, and went back to adjusting his amp. Brandt cursed softly. No buffer zone tonight. His hands were still shaking, and he had a hard time keeping the glaring lights from blanking his vision with white-hot echoes of nothing.

Synthia glared at him in open hostility. Her bass was tuned and ready, leaning against its tripod stand like some massive, sheathed weapon. Her hands were on her hips, and her eyes flashed "don't you dare fuck this up, you drunken motherfucker" at him in bright blue. Syn was the one reason Brandt didn't fear too close a scrutiny from the audience. Most of the men and half the women's eyes would be glued to her short, taut frame. Brandt's own eyes had spent enough time there; he knew the spell she could weave.

Behind them, his drumsticks clattering noisily as he waited, impatient and primed, Dexter scanned the room, occasionally sending flurries of rhythm scurrying about the room. Dexter was oblivious to them all. He lived from set to set, and from all the time they'd played together, Brandt had learned only three things about the young drummer. He never slept, he never drank anything but black coffee, and he never missed a beat. Never.

Paying customers filtered in, lining the bar and taking their places at the scattered tables, but the band paid them no attention. Daylight retreated through the half-open doorway, banished from the windows by drawn blinds, and soft yellow pools of light formed beneath the dim lights. Waitresses in dresses so short they gave away the soft colored secrets of their panties sauntered about the room, taking orders, flirting, and killing time. Time was the one thing you had to kill at Sid's; if you didn't, it would never go away, and you would drown in the apathy.

Brandt accepted a Styrofoam cup of black coffee from a girl he vaguely knew as Shantaina. He carefully avoided meeting the gaze of anyone in the audience, or the band. The shakes were slowly abandoning his fingers, and for the first time since he'd sat up on his bed, he believed he might get a note or two out of the guitar. He didn't want to do anything to shatter that illusion.

The coffee clutched firmly in his hand, he headed backstage to the tiny closet they called a dressing room. He had only moments before they would be looking for him on stage. Fumbling under the counter, he dragged up his makeup kit. The mirror was dust-crusted and grimy, but Brandt had a very clear image of what he would do. The old card floated in the back of his mind, and the fool came to life, slow wash of mascara, deepening of the already deep hollows beneath his eyes . . . perpetual false smile, clueless and transcendent. He finished, meeting his own stare for a long moment, and then turned back to the bar. Something was in the air, rippling along his nerve-endings, but he couldn't place it.

Brandt didn't tune. The guitar had been in perfect tune the night before, and he knew if he engrossed himself in that ritual now, it would be over. He would fuck it up completely, be unable to get the pitch, and it would be bad. Better to be a half-note off from the start and compensate. His life was all about compensation.

Behind him he heard the soft shimmer of cymbals as Dexter determined the moment and the mood was right. They always let Dexter choose the moment. His timing extended beyond the drums to the surreal. Besides, it was easier to follow, flowing into the beat, than to anticipate it.

Brandt closed his eyes and let his fingers fall naturally to the strings. It was a slow number, slow and heavy, lots of sultry, hip-swinging beat for Syn to sync up on, but not too much for the rest of them right off the bat. Blues—it was all the blues, in one form or another, but this was pure. The melody was from a converted Hank Williams ballad, dissected, devoid of twang, but filled with deep, resonating tones and a heavy, slippery back beat. It was an arrangement that Brandt himself had come up with in a rare lucid moment, and he silently thanked Dexter for realizing it would draw him in. He had to get in quick, into sync, into the beat and the rhythm, into the sound, or he was lost.

He wasn't certain when he first became aware of the presence at his shoulder. He felt the moist-hot brush of fetid breath, caught the scent of dusty roads and sweat-stained clothing and in that instant, he heard the voice.

"You keep playin', boy," the old man whispered hoarsely, insinuating the rhythm of his words into the song. "You forget what you see, you forget what you know, but you don' forget to keep them fingers dancin'."

Brandt shivered and closed his eyes tighter, but he did not stop playing. There was a resonance to his notes, a fluidity that he had only felt small glimpses of in the past. Memories sifted up through his thoughts, memories he'd buried and left for dead. He shook his head, trying to concentrate on the music, to drive the invasion of pain away—failing. Phantom videos of all that had hurt him most deeply strobed before his eyes and drew the pain from him one note at a time, white-hot threads pulled through heart and skin in a long, slow, unraveling sound as tears flowed freely down his cheeks.

The song shifted subtly. Brandt no longer heard Dexter's drums, or Syn's bass, though he felt the rhythm shivering up from the floor to vibrate through his nerves. Softly at first, then with growing insistence, the voice of a second instrument rose. Brandt thought instantly of the old man's harmonica, but as quickly realized it was different. The sound trembled with emotion and vibrato, shivered with elegance. Violin. It was a single violin, the sound rippling against, then through Brandt's guitar, harmonizing, then stealing the center of the melody, then slipping up and away in a sublime shimmer of sound.

A tight, cold talon squeezed Brandt's heart. An old man stepped from the shadows, white hair billowing about his head, glowing nimbus wreath wrapped tightly about the very image of tragedy. Pain owned those features, rippled beneath wrinkled skin and forced expression after expression to play in a kaleidoscopic slide-show of angst. Brandt gasped. His eyes were still clamped tightly shut, but he could not erase the sight, could not look away from the sound as it wove around and through his notes. Brandt did not stop playing, but the tears rolled in soft trickles off and away, wetting his shirt.

The visions that tore at his nerve-endings shifted. He played, but the club no longer existed. His chair sat in the center of a dusty crossroad. The violin played in the background, but he could not see the violinist. The buildings that surrounded him were low to the ground and dingy, nothing distinguishing one from the next. There were few windows, and he saw no movement beyond them. The music took a subtle shift from the straight twelve-bar blues rhythm to a slow, torturous march. His fingers made the transition and the phantom violin slipped to a staccato beat, pounding through the notes and matching them to Brandt's suddenly speeding heartbeat.

There were footsteps as well. Marching. A small group of men rounded the corner. Brandt shrank back, melting to the chair as he recognized what he saw, nearly crying out in negation before the scene shifted again. He knew the uniforms, the black, over-polished boots. The distinctive, high-reaching steps.

Now he sat in the center of a different crossroads, gaze locked to a different set of doors. A line of people moved slowly and reluctantly through them. He felt their fear, their uncertainty and the voice of the violin pounded it deeper, made him part of it. A single set of eyes captured his and he trembled as the old man glared at him. The violin was nowhere to be seen, but Brandt knew who played. The musician shifted through the crowd, blended with the crush of bodies, and disappeared between the doors. There was a sickening ripple as he felt a part of himself torn free and dragged along, scenes shifting to shadows and confusion.

People crowded on all sides, too close, too many, all terrified, and there were men moving among them, barking out commands in a language that meant nothing to Brandt. Those surrounding him wore crude blue and white striped shirts—men, women, children—all the same. Brandt was jostled, and then shoved hard. He dropped painfully to knees that he knew were too thin, too arthritic to be his own. He tried to break the fall, failed, and fought to regain his footing.

Those around him stared mutely through humiliated, pain-soaked eyes at the invading soldiers, and terror so deep and dark it melted from them and dripped to the floor, filling the room and flooding Brandt's heart. They were stripping. Each of them, women, men, boys and girls, faces flushed in shame, peeling off their clothing as the men in their dark uniforms continued to command, and shove, and move from person to person without the slightest indication that they saw what happened around them. The clothing was grabbed, tossed, gathered, and gone, so quickly the moment was a blur. The terror that had been buried deep in the eyes of those surrounding Brandt seeped through his thoughts, imbedded itself in his mind and drove icy spikes into his spine.

Men were herded one way, no other word for it, moved like so many animals as the women split to the other side. The words were no clearer to Brandt, but seemed to calm the others slightly. The next thing he saw was a concrete room with walls lined in nozzles. Showers? They crowded in, too many, no way to be directly in the path of any particular spray. The shower nozzles themselves were strange, and then the soft hiss of something escaping from the nozzles, something less powerful than steam, more insidious.

The doors closed behind them with finality—with the essence of death. The room was immersed in a sudden dark, repressive fear. Breathing became difficult and those near to Brandt panicked, moving toward the entrance, and the exit, opposite sides of the dark, empty room, equally sealed. They pounded at the doors, more and more frantic with each passing moment. Nails broke as they scratched and dug at strong wood with fragile flesh, digging into grooves already worn in the surface, and Brandt slid down . . . deep inside . . . away . . . he felt the chair beneath him again, heard the notes of the violin so dark and empty and yet full of emotion, tearing at his world and shredding it.

Brandt's fingers moved of their own accord, ten-digit puppet controlled by the images, images controlled by the pain, beyond and behind it the song. Brandt's chords bent and shivered along with the lingering, trembling notes of the old violinist. He saw the man again, alone, staring with cold, empty eyes as the bow danced over cat-gut strings, crying its song to the night. Brandt's eyes clouded with salty, stinging tears and he clamped them shut hard, biting his lip and dragging his fingers harder over the strings, trying to control the uncontrollable song, trying to insinuate his own lesser darkness over the oppressive voice of the violin.

He glanced up, high on the dull gray walls and saw a face, white and leering, makeup bleeding from the corners of the eyes to stain the walls, fading to stone and brightening to brilliant blood red.

The song shifted. Brandt played through the hitch in his chest that threatened his breathing, played through the white-hot pain of fingers pressing too tightly to the strings, dragging so hard into bar-chords that skin nearly parted from the pressure. The notes softened. The mournful wail of the violin shifted down to the soft tearful voice of a recorder, or a flute, wood and wind, sound and sorrow. Brandt played, eyes still so tightly closed he felt he could push away the presence of a world gone mad.

He felt a warm breeze on his cheeks, and slowly, very slowly, he opened his eyes again. The sound of marching feet had faded to the soft shuffle of many feet, and the barking Nazi-soldier-voices were replaced by other whispers . . . no more comprehensible, but different. The first sight that met his eyes was a trail, crossing another trail. He stood alone in the center where the two met.

They came from his left, moving in a slow, straggling procession. He saw broken faces, eyes lowered and steps that were only half the length they aspired to. To one side of the trail a small girl stood. Her gaze was locked to his, and at her lips a long, tapered flute, hand-carved of soft wood. He tried to look away, to take in the panorama before him, but he could not. She held him with the depth of her eyes and the emotion in her song. He felt his fingers comply, twisting yet again and tracing unfamiliar chords as he accompanied in muted rhythm to her lead.

Then Brandt was walking. His steps were short and his breath wheezed in labored gasps through trembling lips. He wanted to voice a negation, but he could not form a word, could not waste the breath. He staggered forward, feeling the weight of years he had never lived and the frustration of a once strong body, a once proud mind, cowed and broken. He clutched a rough scrap of cloth about his shoulders, heavy and warm, but somehow gripping at his heart like a ball and chain.

Around him, others limped, staggered, and moved in a steady stream. Those who had failed to continue were carried/dragged/tended, continuing despite their physical limitations. Brandt shook in the grip of a fever, deep and dark, festering in his body and rotting his soul. He shivered and walked and shivered again, each step seemingly the last he was capable of and all that time the flute-like tones of the girl's song winding about him, coiling tighter and tighter. He watched bodies half-dead, long, dark hair trailing behind the wooden sleds, drawn on by hand, mule, and the occasional horse, skin red with fever and lesions, lips parted and tongues lolling, eyes wild and bright and all the while, the slow, constant movement toward . . . what?

He glanced down at the blanket, saw the crudely stamped letters, US ARMY, and dark, mirthless laughter bubbled up from deep within his soul.

The blanket weighed more heavily on his shoulders, and he felt the lingering evil that permeated the coarse material, even as he drew it more tightly about him. No way he could know, and yet he did know; the darkness of the smallpox lingered on each thread, weighed on his heart and mind and suddenly he realized, his fingers. He played the sickness, the nausea and the darkness as eyes puffed and hearts slowed, as the act of putting one foot before the next became the act of placing finger after finger on vibrating strings and the soft voice of the flute pounded through his head, feverish and full of the pain of betrayal and emptiness.

He saw the girl now. She did not stand beside the trail playing her flute, but trudged in the center of a pack of others, thin, emaciated to the point of either starvation or illness that rotted from the inside out. Her steps were not proud. They were defeated and monotonous, drawing her onward slowly and pointlessly. The voice of false promise permeated the air. The hitch in a trusting heart as sharp betrayal bit deep. Brandt played and he followed the trail of tears and notes from the girl's heart, to the soft dusty ground, to the bodies and the pain and back to his hands, always to his hands, drawing the music from the strings. His world shifted and he clamped his eyes closed once more.

Somewhere his own pain was lost in that flow, his world and his life petty beyond comprehension in the face of it. Dying, all but a few dying, and only the music to hold that pain. Her music, his music, deep dark river of anguish rolling on like the tide. He clamped his eyes tighter, and tighter still, and the music tilted one more time on an axis of surreality. He stood this time, guitar strapped over his shoulder, swinging against him in tight, pendulous motions as he drew the notes from the strings. It was the harmonica, sharp and bitter, driving through his rhythm and forcing his feet to move, one slow step at a time. Brandt opened his eyes.

The crossroads was no different from a thousand others. The trees were painted in the multi-hued colors of autumn and the wind whipped leaves about his ankles and sent them skittering across the road. In the very center, head down, the old black man, Wally, stood and played. His eyes were closed, his wrists quivered as he drew emotion in tangible threads from the small silver-metal harp. Brandt moved forward, playing the rhythm as he had never played it, feeling the bite in the voice of his instrument and bending it to support the solo. He wanted to close his own eyes and just stand and play. He wanted to let that pain flow out and through and away to some other place, to find his way back to safe notes and melodies with a trace of hope, but he could not.

His hands were numb from the effort, and his caffeine-fortified, life-ravaged system barely kept him upright, but he played. He was played. The music would not release him, and then the harp was silent, and he played alone. The old man vanished, glancing up and then sweeping away in the breeze, sifting to a wash of color that swirled among the dancing leaves and echoing deep pain in a last lamenting flurry of notes as he slipped away.

"Don't stop yet boy, you stop, you're on your own."

That voice, so close, so sudden, nearly ended it. Brandt felt his fingers tighten, felt the sudden weariness tear at him, but somehow he played. He clamped his eyes shut and concentrated.

"Blues can get mighty deep, boy. Mighty deep. So deep

you have to swim in them just to keep your head 'bove it all and think. Learned it a long time ago—a'fore you was born I learned, and I played. Can't never stop. That pain, their pain, it's yours now. It'll trickle into you slow-like, fill you from shoe to shaving cream a'fore you can stop it, and you just gotta play, gotta empty it back into the world where it belongs, or it'll eat you inside to out, heart first, until there ain't nothin' left but a shell—'til you wish you could go back to a happier time and share a drink with your damned drunken mom, or shoot pool with that prick you call a Papa.

"You don't want to be a shell; I reckon you'll play. Just remember, whatever you do remember, and don't let it get too deep. Don't fool yourself boy, you cain't keep it inside . . . cain't hold it all. You let it out.

"Crossroads, or cross-hairs, all the same. No way outta the pain 'cept t'rough da music, boy."

And the voice was gone. Reality rested on his shoulders like the final curtain of a stage tragedy. The notes sifted slowly about in his mind, a procession of eyes passing across his mind's stage. The old man, the children, the gas, and the violin merging with the defeated, helpless notes of the flute on that long trail of more than tears, trail of extermination and so many others, so many things that had festered in the back of Brandt's mind, pressed aside as unimportant in his private over-all view, now rising up to fill it.

He felt a soft touch on his elbow, and at last, he stopped. The ache in his heart shivered out and down his arm and he opened his eyes, glancing at fingers so red and raw he wondered that he could move them at all. He turned, and he found that Syn stood at his left shoulder, eyes wide, staring down at him.

"Brandt?" she said softly.

Brandt met her gaze evenly, only half-aware of the world he'd dropped back into so suddenly, trying to figure out what he would say to them, to figure out what they had seen, and heard. The rest of the band stood in silence behind Syn, watching him. Shaver held his guitar in one hand, and the only emotion in his eyes now was that of pain, as if something had been stolen from him.

"What was that, Brandt? What the *fuck* was that?" Syn said, her voice never rising above a whisper.

Brandt rose slowly, the guitar neck gripped tightly in his one good hand. He turned to the audience, the hangers-on and the drifters. None spoke. The girls did not wander from table to table, delivering shots of courage and charisma to the masses. No bottles or glasses clinked and no voice rose in praise, or in anger. Nothing. He presided over a silent church of pain, white-faced harlequin entertaining them with tragedies they could no more comprehend than he could deny.

Brandt placed the guitar in its case, took the case by the handle, and moved toward the bar without a word. Syn followed, for a few steps, and Shaver looked ready to burst into tears. Brandt wondered if the boy had heard the pain, or if he only wanted the notes. Brandt stepped behind the bar and gripped a bottle of Johnny Walker in his bloody hand. The pain bit through his haze and he managed to croak out some unintelligible promise of cash. Later.

Then he walked toward the door, and the night. Somehow he knew there would be no "later" for him here. He would have to move on. Things would have to change. Brandt didn't feel like the center of it any longer.

Just as he reached the door, Shaver caught him. The boy's hand gripped his shoulder a bit too tightly, and

Brandt turned to meet those intense eyes.

Without waiting for any questions he would not be able to answer coherently, Brandt spoke. "Be careful, Shaver, be very careful. They can get mighty deep. Soul-deep. You want to be careful you don't drown."

And then he was walking, the moon watching over his progress. Deep in his heart the music washed and eddied, swelling with each soft wave. He heard their voices, their music, and he hummed along softly. It ached, but he could wait, for the moment. Soon, though, he thought, stopping in an alley and tipping back the Johnny Walker, soon he would have to play.

In the shadows, the soft voice of a harmonica chased the discarded Tarot image down the gutter, dancing the white-faced harlequin in the clutch of a cold breeze.

TWO

Synthia didn't talk to angels, but she saw them. She never mentioned them. She didn't watch them directly, only out of the corner of her eye, and only because they were always *there*. It wasn't like she had a choice. They haunted the periphery of her vision, watched her world from the shadows, but they never watched her. Synthia saw the angels, but they didn't know she was alive.

When Syn had been ten, she'd tried to tell her mother. She'd sat down at the kitchen table and asked to share the oddly-scented herb tea that filled her mother's afternoons. She could still recall the heat of the cup as she wrapped her small hands around it, and the way the mint and herbs had sifted up through the mist to tickle her nose.

She'd felt very grown up that day, as if a page in her life had turned, or a cycle had shifted to the next ring. Her mother had had very deep, brown eyes, and long hair teasing down over her shoulders. Syn remembered the way the morning sunlight had filtered through the blinds, striping the refrigerator like a surreal, oblong zebra. She remembered her mother's odd little smile, the one that caused the shift. The one that made them friends, in that moment, and not mother and daughter. Deceptions were realities on all levels. That smile had drawn her in, and Syn had spoken her heart.

She had told her mother then, about the old woman on the landing of the stairs, white hair wisping about her face and eyes wide in pain, or fear. She told her mother about the two boys who mirrored her steps as she walked to school, books clutched tightly to her chest and eyes to the ground so that they would not catch her attention. She told her mother about the girl in the shower at school, the one who was there, always, naked and cringing in the corner, and the shadowy, half-seen figure who hovered over her. She even told her mother, for the first time, why it was that when they went to visit Grandmother's grave, Syn had clutched so tightly to her leg.

Throughout that dialogue, Syn's mother had not said a word. She'd nodded, sipped her tea, and listened. Silence is golden. Right. The liquid that had slid into the syringe had been golden. The doctor's eyes had been a deep, golden brown. Her mother's smile had been as sweet as golden honey. Nothing. Syn's mother had believed nothing. She'd called a doctor, and Syn had told her story again. The drugs had followed. One drug, another, and another still, in quick succession, each chemical attack trying to drive out the demons. Trying to drive out something that was just *there*, not illusion but frightening reality, made more frightening as the drugs robbed Synthia's control. There was no way to make them understand; only silence had helped. The silence had stopped the drugs, but by then two years had passed. Cynthia had passed to Synthia irrevocably, awakening as a junior in high school with barely passing marks and no friends with a future. Through it all the angels had watched the world in silence, and she had watched them in turn, never speaking.

Now they were multiplying. No matter where Syn turned, she saw them. When she closed her eyes, she felt them. When she slept, she dreamed dreams populated with their shadowy forms and empty eyes. She didn't even know why she called them angels. They looked more like ghosts, but that wasn't a place she felt comfortable. Angels would never hurt her . . . ghosts might not care. Ghosts might have laughed when Momma and the doctor brought the drugs. The angels had paid no more attention to the drugs than anything else.

Since the night Brandt had left the band, the ghosts had slowly overrun her reality. She knew it was foolish to dwell in the past. She hadn't spent enough time with Brandt when he was with them. She had teased him, promised him, but she'd never let him get close. Now he was gone, and that music—that last night. How could she reconcile herself to the reality that was the band and the memory that was Brandt and feel anything but loss and regret? How could she live her life walking through a mist of angels? Brandt had noticed her. Without that notice, the weight of his eyes and the soft sound of his voice, the nothingness of the angels' presence weighed on her like a shroud.

Syn rose, pulling the sheets up around her, automatically shielding herself from the prying eyes of those who didn't even watch. She blinked and shook her head to clear the cobwebs. She needed to hurry and shower. Shaver would call soon. He called her like clockwork, every afternoon at four. It gave her a minimum amount of minutes to shower, paint herself to perfection, and gather her wits. It gave her a chance to push aside the visions and focus on herself, and her life. Angels didn't pay the bills, and though the band wasn't breaking any records, since Brandt's drunken ass had carried itself so dramatically down the road, they had been doing well enough to get by. They might even break out of the bar circuit and cut a CD soon. If Syn could keep it together. If Shaver didn't lose his heart. If the new guy, the pseudo-Brandt they'd hired, Calvin, with his long, long hair and his long, long eyes, and his constant sniffing; no way to ignore the chemical base of *that* subconscious habit. Calvin could play. Calvin could sing. Calvin was barely aware that he could do either. He was helping the band in ways that Brandt never could have, but . . . he was no Brandt.

Synthia felt Brandt's loss in ways she'd not been willing to admit possible. He had always just been . . . *there*. Now there was the band, and her life, and the angels. Nothing else. Nothing that touched her on a deeper level than a mild sunburn. Not that Brandt had ever seemed so important. Synthia had spent more time cursing him than talking to him, and though she'd felt very comfortable in his presence, she'd not spent as much time there as she might have. No reason to. No reason to believe the opportunity would not present itself in its own time.

Now he had marched off down the road, right through the gathered ranks of angels who had actually watched him go, not ignoring him, as they did Synthia, as they had *always* ignored her. Brandt had left her to watch his receding back, looking somehow more appealing in the tight, faded jeans than she'd remembered him. And he'd left the memory of the music. Brandt had always been good. He'd always been just able to pull it off, no matter how drunk or out of it he might have been.

The music had meant more then, though it had taken the vacuum of Calvin and the "new" sound to drive that reality home. Even through the thick white makeup, dead-clown pretty-boy attitude, and sneering lips that sugar-coated a frustrated heart, Syn had sensed Brandt's talent. Each time Syn had been ready to kick his ass out on the street and demand he be replaced by someone who would at least show up for practice, he'd pulled something out of his ass and tugged at her heart strings with it.

Synthia remembered the night she'd convinced him to take her out, to the carnival. That night Syn had nearly told him about the angels. Then the old witch lady had turned over that card, and Brandt had flipped out. The moment, and the courage to speak, had slipped away.

Everything had been so right that night. Syn had felt so close to him, so special to be with him, though she'd have never said so. None of the others ever seemed to get it, but Brandt did. During his rare lucid moments, he was the only voice she trusted to answer her in the same language she asked a question. That night might have been the beginning of something special, but she'd seen that damned tent, and the past had intruded once more. There had been a single old angel, kneeling by the door in prayer, or sorrow. Brandt, of course, had seen nothing. The old angel's hands had scratched what seemed at first to be random lines in the dirt. The random lines had formed a word.

"Remember."

Synthia had read the word, turned from the angel, and her vision, and the only straight path had led through the doorway of the tent, toward the cards and destiny. Synthia's words, the whispered confidence she'd meant to share with Brandt, had slipped a notch back down her throat, and the night had done the rest. Stolen moments were often taken back. Rules of the road in the game of Life. Brandt had staggered out of the tent, drunk, tripping, and he'd fallen. Syn had followed, but the chemicals had robbed her of her strength, her ability to help him. She had tried, *God* she had tried, but the act of *trying* had pumped her blood more swiftly and the drugs more powerfully, and they had nearly *both* ended up lying together in the dirt, staring at the huge Ferris wheel instead of just Brandt. At what? She'd never asked him what he'd seen.

They never watched her. They never saw her. She saw the angels, but they ignored her. That was her pain. Her mother had seen her, but never really *seen* anything. Her father hadn't seen her at all. Boys, men, all had seen her body, her heat. None had seen beyond it. She had her own silent chorus of angels, mocking/accompanying her dirge-like song of life.

That was why Syn played the bass. The deep, droning tones. The vibration straight through to her soul and back again. Even the angels wavered when she played. When the deep intonations of rhythm and resonant power rippled through the air, it took on a deeper acuity. The angels did not listen to her bass, but they felt it. The universe was one giant chord, one universal vibration. Syn longed to find her niche in that unity. Her heart was a rebel . . . fighting her desire. Her playing was dissonant, deep, wild and passionate, but it seldom blended. Instead it forced the blend to her . . . forced her to become the eye of the storm, and every eye to seek her form. The only time she could forget that the angels ignored her was when no one else did.

She'd never asked Brandt why he staggered out of that tent, or what he'd seen, stumbling into the midway. She had stared into his eyes as he stared up at the Ferris wheel, far above them, and she'd seen . . . something, reflected in his eyes. She couldn't remember what, or who.

The phone's ring ripped through the silence. Syn gripped the blanket around herself more tightly, willing the world to silence. Failing.

She rose, the blanket trailing away behind her, gripping the phone's receiver tightly and drawing it to her ear, concentrating.

"Yeah?"

"Rise and shine, Princess." Shaver's voice was edged

with caffeine and fueled by that bright, inner fire that set him apart from every other being on the planet. Lead notes rippled through the tones of his voice if you knew him. The taut, corded muscles of his arms spoke of an inner fury, a driving need that only the guitar could sate, and then, apparently, poorly. Shaver had been, if possible, even more intense since Brandt's revelation and departure. His leads were faster. His eyes wider and more incomplete in the perfection of his motion. A technical marvel with etched tears tattooed on cheeks of granite . . . muscles drawn so tight they could turn bullets aside. The angels didn't watch Shaver either.

"I'm up," she said. "I'll be there."

"Coffee is on me," he said, and then the click/buzz/tone of the phone and silence again. Somehow it was less perfect, less intimate.

Syn let the blanket fall away with a sigh and rose, moving to the bathroom, the shower, hot, soap-scented mist and the grit of the past swirling away, sliding over the lip of the drain and into oblivion. The clock ticked. Rhythm of reality. She needed to get in and out of that steamy heaven and down the road to the coffee, Shaver, and the club. If things worked out, this could be their last night at Sid's. The "right" people would be in the audience tonight.

Calvin had managed it, somehow. Calvin and his drugs, his mediocre, good-enough-for-record-company-work guitar, his scratchy, cigarette-ravaged voice. His "Rod Stewart stars in the *Day of the Living Dead*" perfect look. Calvin had the package that sold. They should change the band's name to Pretty and Empty. The angels wouldn't care. The angels didn't even listen, no matter how hard Syn played, or cried, screamed, or lied. They stared into the nothingness of eternity and Syn was left to watch them as they watched. Alone.

Quick paint job at the mirror, pointedly ignoring the figure in the corner, a stooped old man staring out the window as if he'd been watching the city grow for a hundred years. Syn worked the mascara and blush carefully, practiced flicks of her wrist painting the hard, brittle edges of her eyes, first defense against the crowd. First defense against Calvin. If they didn't get the recording contract, she would have to do something with or about Calvin. The latter made her nauseous, and the former scared her like nothing in her life had scared her before.

The record execs had been around before. She'd seen them tossing back expensive drinks and slumping in corner booths, watching and smiling like they cared. They didn't listen any more than the angels, most of the time. Maybe recording contracts had nothing to do with what they heard. It didn't matter. Somehow Syn knew that if they didn't listen tonight, she was gone. No plan, nowhere to go, but she was out. Shaver would be fine. Caffeine and high E would get him a ticket anywhere he wanted to go. Calvin? Fuck Calvin. He would probably be signing copies of his tenth gold record within a couple of years, with or without Synthia. With or without Shaver. With or without a meaningful thought or moment in his long, tired existence. As he signed, the ghosts would stand around, oblivious. Synthia needed to hear them sing.

Brandt had done it. Fucking Brandt with his drunken-ass lyrics and his so-natural-the-fucking-alcohol-couldn't-blunt-it talent. His sad, out-of-date clown-face paint and words no one else had understood, but that everybody had loved. His beautiful guitar and tenement apartment. His voice, clear and transcendent when it didn't slur and spout the wrong words in long litanies that meant as much to the crowd as the real words—nothing at all. Brandt and that magic night he'd left, when the angels had played, and sung, and danced. The crowd and the band had watched Brandt. Syn had watched the angels, and on that single night, they had watched back, not just her, but Brandt, and the band . . . the crowd. They had spoken, and joined the song, making it something more than just Brandt's song. Brandt had flowed through the notes, but Synthia had felt them in her heart, and those of the others who heard. Brandt had played, and the world had gone still.

But Brandt was gone. Syn shook her head. Coffee. Club. Music. Those were the only things that could bring even temporary solace. If she closed her eyes, let her fingers draw the rhythmic, pulsing notes from the bass and her voice join with Calvin's, it formed a barrier. The angels didn't listen, but at least they seemed remote, part of the audience and the energy. They were less depressing as backdrop to the sound.

The coffee did less than Syn had hoped to raise her energy level. As she sipped the Americano, a tall iced-tea glass of black coffee with a shot of espresso, she'd been preoccupied by the young girl at the window. The girl's back was to the world outside, her gaze locked to the back of the bar. Not exactly a bar now but a bar in the past. Syn knew this as truth, though she had no way of knowing *how* she knew. She also knew that the angel . . . the girl . . . knew it. The world the girl watched was different. In that world, Syn did not exist. It hurt. Alone in the crowd and singing to nobody, that was Syn's story.

The coffee had burned her tongue, and it rolled around inside her, the caffeine waking her body, but the empty ache of no food and too much sleep fogging her mind. She couldn't get Brandt, or his angels, out of her mind. She drank the bitter liquid down quickly, hit the street, and headed for the club.

DEEP BLUE

* * * * *

Sid's wasn't too busy for a Friday night. There was a small crowd of regulars gathered near the bar and the pool table, but nothing to write home about. Synthia moved past them all, oblivious to the stares and soft catcalls. She was used to it. If she could stand the empty gazes of the myriad angels populating the vacant tables and leaning against the dingy walls, a few goth-punks and losers weren't likely to cause much stress. No sign of the record company, but no surprise there. Too early for anything serious. If they showed, it would likely be somewhere mid-third set, when the band was catching their stride, or stumbling to fall on their faces. Either way, it eliminated the gray areas.

Syn slipped through to the back, closed the dressing room door behind her, and leaned back against it to catch her breath. Something was different, something in the air, the taste of the evening on her dry lips. For once she was alone. None of the others was in the back room, and there were no angels. Syn turned to the mirror, watching herself watch herself and thinking.

When she exited the room, turning toward the stage in silence, her face was white. Ghost white. She'd found an old tube of Brandt's makeup. None of the black he'd used to darken his eyes and accent his lips, only the white, blanking out all that was unique, all that made her stand out from the crowd. She came to the stage as a blank page and lifted the strap of her bass over her shoulders with a quick shrug.

Brandt had always told her that the bass was the backdrop, the canvas across which the music was painted. If she faltered, the image was skewed. If she lost the rhythm, the lines would waver and the notes fall to discord. Shaver would shift off into a discordant shiver of steel-strung notes with no stable support. Face white, ready for the music, she became that canvas. Shaver stared at her for a long moment, his brow furrowed in concentration, then nodded and turned away, tuning. Always tuning, a nervous habit, fingers molded to the keys. Calvin's jaw dropped. He started to speak, started to make a bigger fool of himself than life had managed, then clamped down on his tongue.

What crowd there was grew silent. There was no one there who'd not heard the band before. There was no man in that bar that had not, in some way, come to share a moment with Synthia. To steal a fantasy from the supple curves of her body, the taut strength of her wrists and forearms as she played. The deep, purr-growl of her voice when the words were hers and the higher-pitched backdrops she laid for Calvin's throaty, grinding vocals. The white-empty face changed everything. Synthia's arms cradled the bass, but her face was . . . blank. No one knew how to react, so no one did. The angels didn't even notice.

The lights dimmed. Some bright-boy behind the bar found a single black-light spot and focused it on the stage, on Syn and her white-makeup, now brilliant and glowing. The eerie blue illumination removed even more definition from her features, a purple-haloed ball of captured moonlight floating above the glistening sheen of the sunburst finish on her bass. Energy. Synergy. Sound and motion blurred to wipe her from their sight and minds.

Syn couldn't see this. She felt it. The sound started, at first no different from a hundred other nights. Soft shimmer of cymbals, rippling to snare and back to cymbals. Dexter, the one constant in the band, the rhythm behind the rhythm. Dexter and his "skins," who never said word one to anyone but Shaver, who just showed up, played, and left. Syn's fingers moved to the strings of the bass, slipping into a slow, pounding thud of notes, overgrown-heartbeat rhythm rippling from the strings, winding down the wires and out through the speakers to shimmer through the air.

No one moved in the audience, no hips matching the swaying pulse of Syn's own, no feet shuffling. She knew they were watching her. They always watched her. It was different. She felt them seeking her face, her eyes, trying to pierce the black-light glare and the blinding white of the paint to meet her gaze. They seldom let their attention roam that high when she played. They were usually too occupied with their own fantasies to hear the lyrics, and too ashamed of them to let her catch their gaze. Tonight they were denied, so they sought the reasons in her eyes.

The band followed her lead. Calvin found a way to make his following seem like leading. That was his way, but everyone knew. The bass wrapped its notes around the music and wrestled it to submission, and beyond. The rhythm drove the melody. The lyrics hung from a backdrop of resonant harmony so deep and soulful that the air/floor/room shook with the power of it. The angels shimmered around the edges of the bar, stood nonchalantly in doorways, staring into eternity. Nothing. They were everywhere, and nowhere, and Synthia felt something inside her slip hard, falling away. A layer of—need, closer to the raw pain beyond. Her fingers had begun to ache, but she twisted the notes deeper. She played to the angels, the room slipping away and the band towed in her wake.

She played the usual songs. The band knew the chords, the rhythms. It wasn't like when Brandt had just taken over the stage and silenced them all with his pain . . . their pain . . . the world's pain. She didn't change the music fundamentally. It was the subtle shifts of emotion, the infusion of her frustration, and her hunger, that drove the notes deeper into the minds and hearts around her. Somewhere in that crowd were the record execs, or not. It didn't matter anymore.

Surrounding them, filling in gaps in the crowd, the angels stood, impervious, and the tears flowed down Syn's cheeks as she aimed her notes at their ethereal hearts.

She had never played to them before. She had watched them, all her life she'd watched them as they ignored her. Now she needed to know. Who were they? What were they watching that was so damned important they couldn't see her . . . hear her . . . comfort her? Who the *fuck* were they and why wouldn't they *hear?*

The songs shifted, one to the next. Syn caught short glimpses of Calvin's eyes, begging her to slow, to stop, to take a break. She turned to the side and saw that Shaver's fingers bled. He ignored it, as she ignored Calvin, but the music could not go on indefinitely. She felt as if she could play forever—close her eyes and drift into the music and not return. Syn didn't look at her own fingers, or think about them. The pain was there, but it didn't matter. The crowd shifted.

A figure wound slowly through the eerily quiet crowd toward the dance floor. Syn's eyes were half-blind from the spotlights, and the black light. She saw strobing, half-formed images, the one moving closer and the others that surrounded it. She concentrated. She couldn't tell if it was a man, a woman, or an angel, but she played to that figure. It was the last song of the set, maybe the last song of her life, and she played it with no remorse. The sweat and tears blurred her sight and she blinked, fighting to see, to know who would share that moment.

There was something achingly familiar in that swaying gait. Syn could make out long hair, but no features. She played. She felt the resonance of the bass through to her bones, felt the growing fire that was her fingers, and the strings, and the slickening of both, but the notes did not falter. No way. Not this time. There might never be another chance, and the face became clearer with each step, narrowing the gap between them, and the years. Syn's voice wavered, just for a second. Between verses, when she should have breathed, she spoke.

"Mother?"

For that eternal moment, the band sustained her. Those she had dragged swelled up behind her, Shaver's notes, still crisp and rippling, so technically perfect they seemed magical, and Calvin, his usually weak rhythm crunching suddenly, as he sensed her near-falter. Dexter, solid, bolstering the rhythm and jump-starting her fingers. They sacrificed themselves to that moment, held together, bonding and transcending the bar, and the mediocre, blues-cover melody to join in something more powerful. Syn breathed deep and sank to her knees on the stage . . . staring as her mother's form moved closer. Her fingers moved with the sound, her arm shifting, the bass a part of her, held close and tight.

The notes were winding down, but it no longer mattered. Synthia had no idea how she knew, but the thrumming of the notes slowly gave way to the thudding of her heartbeat, and the bass, still clutched tightly to her chest, grew silent. The room receded, sucked into a vacuum that left nothing but Syn, white-faced ghost girl and the angel/spirit of her past, faced off in a duel of eyes and silence.

Somewhere in the distance, the music continued. Syn knew it wasn't the band. The crowd was silent, staring. The magic of the band's moment was fading. She couldn't tell if they saw, finally fucking *saw* the angels, but they knew that she saw . . . something. Someone. Why now?

Her eyes raised to meet the milky-white, cataract-glazed

gaze of yesterday. Syn felt something lift free of her soul, but it did not make her feel better. She felt bare, naked before the crowd, nasty secrets and mother's love dragged to center stage in black-light synapse-strobed images.

The angel reached out dim-white hands, veined in deep blue, as if to stroke Syn's cheek, but falling short, always falling short. Syn nodded. Just like all those years before. Just that much short of all right. Syn held still, strained forward inside and gritted her teeth, rigid on the outside. No way she leaned into that touch. No way.

The moment passed, and a soft sigh escaped the angel's lips, first sound, only sound, Syn had heard from one of the apparitions other than the music, Brandt's music. That sigh, nothing more. No apology. No words could have mattered. No touch could have mattered. Syn lifted her gaze to her mother's, held it for a long moment, and watched through a sudden flow of salty tears as that face, so long gone from her life, melted once more, as the lights haloed. Syn's lip quivered.

Syn slithered back and away suddenly. Her head drooped and her eyes closed. She clutched the bass and she rose in a stumbling lurch. She felt the drums topple as she backed into them, microphones tilting and stands trapping her feet. Somehow she remained upright as her world crashed in a metallic heap. She was vaguely aware of the others, cursing, calling out to her, and touching her shoulders. She shrugged them off. She heard the voices of those who'd watched from the audience.

She moved through them, away from the stage toward the door. The crowd parted. Some of the braver among them stretched out their hands, brushing her skin, tugging at her clothes. One woman stepped into Syn's path and tugged at the bass, as if she would take it for her own. Syn

DEEP BLUE

rocked her hip forward quickly, and the woman stumbled back with a soft, surprised cry, coming to rest against the wall beside the doorframe as Syn slid sideways through and into the night, careful not to crack the bass on the wooden frame.

She knew they were calling out to her. The others: Shaver, Calvin, the bartender, maybe Sid himself. A hand grabbed her suddenly by the shoulder as she turned away from the club and started down the walk. Syn spun in a daze, meeting a set of too-bright eyes. Her own turned down to where his hand held her arm.

". . . wonderful," he was saying. "Exactly what we are looking for, what the scene needs, you know?" His voice was too fast, the words slipping from sincerity to business to sleaze in increments so obvious Syn could barely follow the progression. ". . . just sign, and of course the band, though they aren't a *deal breaker,* you know, because I can *see* who is the talent here. . . ."

Syn pulled her arm back violently, glaring at the man. "Get away from me."

The man held her arm a moment longer. He blinked, as if struck, as if there was no possible way in the universe he could have heard what he just heard.

"You don't understand," he said more slowly.

Carefully, not wanting to break his fingers . . . yet . . . she gripped his wrist and yanked his hand free of her arm. "Get the *fuck* away from me."

He started to say something. He even reached for her again, but something in Syn's eyes must have warned him away. The man stood, looking very foolish in his power suit and expensive jewelry, Rolex gleaming under the soft glow of street lamps and a small crowd gathering at his back, pouring from the mouth of the club in a slow, curious stream. Syn turned without a thought, bass sliding to her hip, dangling from the strap. She saw the angels, lining the streets. They did not ignore her, nor did they speak, or move. They watched, and she walked, steps as steady as her heartbeat.

Behind her she heard Calvin's shrill, whining voice, begging the idiot in the suit, selling what little soul he had left and trying to include hers as if it were his to sell. It meant less than nothing. So close, she'd been so close to letting the answers slip away. She wondered if the angels would have faded if she'd signed that paper, if she'd never seen her mother, and the music had carried her in a different direction. She wondered if Calvin would ever understand. She wondered where the music was coming from that dragged her on.

She moved through streets of dim light and scattered shadow. No one else moved, slow-traffic parade, coming and going in a rise-to-fade shimmer of sound and headlights. Synthia passed no living soul, but the angels lined the road, translucent sentinels tracing her motion with their eyes. She felt them as she never had before, and the sound, the music, swelled up around her, gripping her heart and twisting. It was her. The music was her song, her pain, and she felt the march of angel after angel, ghost after ghost, not speaking to her, but acknowledging, each moment where they'd slipped away silently brought back in a wash of images, and pain.

She reached 37th Street and turned, winding down Elm, knowing what was ahead and shivering. Her arm snaked down, drawing the bass to her like a lover. The music was louder, and she knew. Somehow she knew who it was. There were the sweet-soft strains of harmonica, the soul-deep song of a lone guitar. A thousand voices sang deep harmony in soft, half-whispered tones that led her on. Syn felt like the star in a bad horror flick, angel choruses leading her home.

Then the voice sounded, so close to her ear she couldn't understand why she didn't feel the warm brush of breath.

"Ain't no angels, sugar," the voice grated rough and sweet as the whiskey and honey cough remedy Syn's Grandma had given her when she was a child. "Just those dead and gone, and those just dead. You come to sing, you come to da right place, little one."

Synthia trembled, but she didn't turn. She knew that voice. She'd heard it once before, the night Brandt had disappeared. For the first time in as many days as she could imagine, she wasn't concerned with the angels. She followed the guitar, stepping through the entrance to the graveyard and feeling the gravel crunch beneath her feet. The gates were open. No security for the dead.

Syn wound down familiar trails, through a maze of white-stone markers and pretentious monuments to those beyond caring. White marble angels watched her progress, and the moonlight patterned the trail with crosses, shadows from the graves that lined the way.

She didn't stop until she reached a familiar plot and a dingy, off-white stone, rectangular and low-slung. Insignificant. One forgotten bit of granite in a garden where memories grew—this bit forgotten.

Synthia fell to her knees in the soft earth, letting the bass rest against her thigh. Tears trickled down her cheeks, but she wiped them away. The words were still clear, etched in stiff, final precision across the stone. Syn reached out, long black-painted nail tracing the final tribute to her mother's life.

She half-expected her mother's angel to appear again. Or

ghost. Or whatever. She expected to hear the scolding tones of her mother's voice. Out so late, and in a graveyard. It's what comes of hanging out with no-goods and playing *that* music. What happens to girls who talk about seeing things that couldn't be. Angels. The tears streamed, and the gravestone rippled, but she stared, stubbornly, blinking against the salty pain.

"She loved you, you know." The voice rippled with her vision, slipped through her senses, and gripped her heart. Brandt. His fingers still worked the strings of the guitar, the strings of her heart.

"Fuck you," Syn said through her tears, voice tearing roughly from her throat. "She didn't even know me."

"That is why it didn't work," Brandt said. "Doesn't change the love, only the outcome. She saw them too, you know."

Syn whipped around, finding Brandt lounging back over a mausoleum to her left. His fingers moved as he spoke, stroking the strings. The soft melody echoed the bittersweet march that had led her to the graveyard, to the stone and the memories.

"What do you mean?" she asked, knowing the answer but praying it would not come.

"She was afraid too," Brandt said. "She saw them, knew them. They even spoke to her. She knew one thing you didn't."

Syn gripped the bass more tightly, gazing into Brandt's eyes, searching now. For answers. For peace. "What?"

"She knew they weren't angels," Brandt said softly. "She didn't want you to know."

Syn's chin dropped to her chest, and her tears trickled down and off her cheeks, wetting her blouse, the ground, the white makeup running to a thin film. Brandt's fingers picked up the pace, drawing the moment around her and pulling tight the drawstrings on her soul. Her shoulders shook, her mind blanked, and deep inside, she drew her mother's angel tightly to her heart, holding and breathing apologies into the soft chorus of the blues.

THREE

Shaver stared at the wall. His fingers itched for the strings, for the rippling notes and patterns, but he could not play. He'd tried twice since the morning sun had slid through his blinds and dragged him into the day. The first time he'd screamed as the ruined flesh that had been his fingertips met cool metal. He couldn't press tightly enough to bring a clear note from the instrument, and the strings were still rough from the blood that had dried over and into them.

Cursing had not helped. Coffee made it worse. Wide awake, more aware of the pain than he'd been aware of any sensation in his life, Shaver had picked that guitar up again. A simple chord. Teeth gritted so tightly they ground together and challenged the pain in his fingers, muscles taut in his arms and his chest constricted with the effort of ignoring that searing, mind-blinding agony. A single chord, and only blind luck and the fear of losing the one thing close to his heart had kept the guitar from striking the floor. He'd caught it, managing somehow to avoid gripping it with his fingers. Clutching the polished wood to his bare chest, he'd lain beneath it, trembling on the floor.

The patterns raged through his mind, arranging and changing, shifting and drawing his thoughts one way, then dashing them back the other to shatter against his inability to seek release. Crawling from that heap, he'd slipped the Fender back into its case with a soft breath of relief and frustration.

Now he watched the walls, saw the patterns on the faded

paper winding and swirling, and soaked his fingers in Alka-Seltzer, bubbles long gone and the sting faded to a dull throb. Even that throb, his heartbeat in counterpoint to the motion behind his eyes, whispered of new progressions of chords to his fevered brain and hinted melodies, left still-born as he forced his thoughts away from them.

The phone rang. Shaver watched it, eyes narrowing. He didn't move to answer it at first. It would hurt. He knew it would hurt, everyone with his number knew it would hurt. The ringing continued, jarring and loud, and Shaver slowly slipped his fingers from their lukewarm soak, growling and swinging his legs over the side of the bed.

"Fuck you!" he growled at the phone. He staggered to his feet and lurched across the room. Leaning in with a curse, Shaver trapped the receiver between his chin and his shoulder and lifted. It rose half an inch, then dropped. The ringing stopped, and he stared at the phone, locked into that gray area between maniacal laughter and mindless rage. Shaver drew back his arm, already feeling the sweet release of slamming the phone into the wall when the silence shattered again, and the insistent ringing returned.

Shaver drove his palm down over the receiver, held, waited, and gripped, doing all he could do to keep the tips of his fingers from touching and finally he gained enough purchase to lift the plastic handle from its cradle. He slid his hand sideways quickly before the receiver could drop back over the phone and cut off the ringing, only to bring it again. Another pattern, this one broken.

He gripped the phone, gathered his thoughts, and lifted, letting the receiver slip to his shoulder.

"What?" he said sharply.

At first nothing. Silence.

"If this is a wrong number I'll hunt you down and kill

you like a dog," Shaver said, his voice regaining its rocking tone, the patterns of his thoughts shifting and merging into a coherent pattern.

Soft laughter and a quick snort, then words. Dexter. His words even and rhythmic. "Hey, man, how you feeling?"

"I was fine until you made me pick up this fucking phone," Shaver answered, unable to keep his voice as cold and distant as he wanted it and nearly laughing at himself for trying. "Fuck! My fingers hurt, Dex. They hurt bad."

"I told you to see a doctor, Shaver, your bad call," Dexter replied. Shaver could see the soft humor in his friend's eyes. No need to be there to know. Dexter always smiled when he spoke, especially when he was right and saying, "I told you so."

"Fuck you," Shaver said, smiling outright.

"I'm coming over," Dexter announced. "Be there in ten minutes."

Dial tone. No time for *no, don't you do it, leave me alone, my fucking hand hurts.* Just that. Coming over, ten minutes.

Shaver dropped the receiver into its cradle and turned, staring at his bed, and the wall, and smelling the half-burned coffee from the kitchen. He couldn't drink it, couldn't stand the thought of more energy, faster inner motion trapped without a release valve. He stared at his hands, at the wrinkled, pasty-white flesh he'd dangled so long—too long—in the lukewarm water and chemical bandage.

Shaver kicked a pile of clothing on the floor, dislodged a t-shirt, and grabbed it. Didn't matter that it had been worn once . . . twice . . . who knew. Didn't matter that it was one more interesting scent in the olfactory aura that was his new world. It was a shirt.

He slipped it over his head, grimacing at the necessary

gripping and tugging. As it slid into place, he glanced down. It was a black t-shirt, emblazoned with a brilliant white caffeine molecule. He laughed suddenly and moved to the kitchen, yanking the cord of the old, chrome-plated percolator from the outlet and turning back to search for shoes and a pair of socks he could bear to touch. Fucking Dexter.

The knock on the door found Shaver dressed and waiting. No way he was letting anyone in to see how his world was crumbling. Life was hell with no hands. Housework was out of the question. He pulled the handle and grimaced, fighting the urge to curse *loudly*, and forced a smile as Dexter's grinning face came into view.

"Hurt, didn't it?" Dex asked with a grin.

Shaver fought the urge to repeat his suggestion of monosexuality. "Not at all," he said, smiling. "Very refreshing after the normality of a sense of touch that didn't fucking *scream* at me every time I used it."

Dexter laughed, holding the door wide. "Fine, I'll close it, if you don't mind. I don't care if it hurts, but I don't deal well with close, soulful moments between men."

Shaver didn't say a word, just slipped past Dexter's slight form and into the hall beyond. The door closed with a decisive *click!* Swell. Lost in the world with no hands but Dexter's, Dexter who thought it was funny.

"So," Shaver said quickly, probably too quickly, "where are we going?"

"Coffee," Dexter said. No inflection, no emotion. Just that one word.

"No," Shaver replied. "No coffee. I can't." He was silent for a long moment, and then the emotion broke. "Dex, I can't fucking *play*, man, I can't do it. No coffee."

Dexter watched him carefully. "I have a bottle of straight Tennessee corn whiskey, if you think that would help more.

Might take the edge off, make those fingers comfortably numb. Either way, you have to come with me. I've been saving it. Meant to call you right after Brandt freaked out. Meant to call you after Synthia. Somehow, the bottle just sat there. Fucking *Mason* jar, Shaver, just like in the movies."

Shaver could barely keep from puking as it was, and the thought of the alcohol, the thought of sipping, then guzzling, his fingers tight and painful on the bottle, brought a quick shake of his head. "Not tonight, Dexter. No whiskey, no coffee." His resolve was slipping, but his voice remained calm.

"Trust me," Dexter replied. "You're going to need it."

They slipped down the stairs and out to the street with no further words. Shaver intoned an inner chant to his own recalcitrant mind. "No coffee." He knew he'd drink it if it were placed before him, and knew equally well that Dexter would do so without a thought. The patterns still shifted before his eyes, sidewalk cracks and road-lines, but as long as he moved, it didn't seem quite as nauseating.

Dexter didn't have a car. Shaver had a battered old Mustang, but he couldn't drive with no hands, and he let no one but himself touch the old Ford. They walked quickly, in step, down the street toward the Bean & Buzz. Dex was silent, habitually so, but this time it bugged the shit out of Shaver. Drag him into the world, order him toward coffee he couldn't handle, then just walk off down the street like nothing was different from any other day.

Shaver hurried his steps. He came even with Dexter, grabbed the drummer's shoulder, winced, drew his hand back, and stepped up even more quickly. "What the fuck Dex?" Shaver spoke sharply, suddenly angry. "What happened? You hear from Calvin? Synthia called? I've been in that house for a long time, man, sitting—watching the patterns on the walls run into guitar leads I can't play and emptying into the carpet. Alone. Nothing from you for a fucking *week*, man. Why now?"

Dexter kept walking, hands pressed tight and deep into his pockets. They moved on another block, and another, before he broke the silence.

"I found the song, Shaver," he said softly.

Shaver stopped in his tracks and just watched as Dex moved off down the sidewalk. His eyes narrowed. He didn't follow Dexter down the sidewalk. He didn't move at all, just stood, and watched, and waited.

Dexter moved half a block farther before he turned and looked back. He did not smile. "You coming?"

Shaver hesitated. His mind screamed at him to turn and leave. His room, another hot Alka-Seltzer soak, and his bed until oblivion claimed him for another day, and another, until his fingertips could feel again and his hands could grip the neck of his guitar. Shaver watched Dexter's face and frowned hard, brushing his fingers back through his hair in a nervous gesture that made him gasp in pain.

"Jesus, Dex," he said. "You find the fucking song *now?*"

Dexter didn't say a word. He turned and headed off down the street again, leaving Shaver to follow, or not. His steps were even and measured. Everything about Dexter was rhythm, syncopated animation with a subtle back-beat of unkempt, street-wise cool. Dex could carry that down-and-out prophet look that evaded others so easily, making them look like bums, or poseurs.

Shaver cursed, tried to stick his hands into his pockets, failed, and growled his frustration. He followed in silence, his feet subconsciously moving in subtly varied patterns, as if even in the act of walking he could play lead to Dexter's rhythm. As if his feet could make up for ruined hands and allow some warped release to the notes reverberating through his skull. He entered the Bean & Buzz on Dexter's heels.

"Hey!" Soft, feminine voice with a southern lilt floating from the left as a sudden wave of warm flesh and sweet perfume wrapped Shaver *almost* tight enough to remove the stench of days without a shower.

"Hey yourself, Liz," Shaver grunted, fighting to keep her tightening embrace from finding his hands and bringing an unmanly yelp of pain. "Long time."

She pulled back, feather-light blonde hair dancing around her face and her eyes bright. "Not because *I* have been hiding, lover. What's up with you, anyway? I haven't seen you since . . ."

"Not now," Shaver answered, reaching to hold a finger to her lips . . . hesitating as his hand came into sight, wrinkled from the soak and raw from the cuts. He tried to draw it back but she was too quick for him, slender fingers capturing his wrist neatly and turning it, inspecting.

The flash in her eyes moved from warmth to anger in seconds, mercurial and lovely. "You stupid bastard. Don't you care about *anything?*"

Before Shaver could answer, she was turning to Dexter. "Don't just stand there," she said sharply. "Didn't you see his hands? Go tell Maggie you need the first aid kit."

"I told him to go to a doctor." Dexter smiled thinly, obviously annoyed at the interruption. "Can't help it if he's dense as granite, now, can I?"

For the first time Shaver got a look at Dexter in the light and he gasped. His friend was gaunt and pale. The rock-star image had melted into the drummer's skin and drained away the color. Somehow, it seemed less significant that

Shaver's hands hurt, and he'd been alone for a week. Patterns shifted in the omnipresent cloud of billowing tobacco and clove smoke that slid up from the ashtrays lining the bar. The colored lights that lined the mirrored panels just below the ceiling shimmered through that white haze and Shaver took half a step forward, stumbling. If Liz hadn't had him by the arm, he'd have pitched headlong.

Dexter didn't move, and as Shaver regained his balance, something sounded in his mind, deep inside, where the colors faded and the patterns shifted to symmetrical perfection, sliding in spirals down and down. Into Dexter's eyes. The patterns shifted again, marring the perfection he'd glimpsed, and it was too much. The soft lilting strains of a song Shaver could remember clearly, and yet could not quite bring to the surface of his mind, dragged at him, holding his lips pressed tightly together, denying sound, denying him the output of any of it, drawing him inward instead, down the spiral. His hands/face meeting the floor never even registered.

The soft plastic of the booth was cool against his cheek and Shaver could hear voices close by, music in the background, the jukebox and Eve6 competing with snatches of—something—that he couldn't quite shake from his mind, cobwebs of memory and something more. He tried to sit up, first mistake in a slow reintroduction to pain. Nausea swept through him, and he turned his face to the side, but did not lose what he had not eaten, only gasped and clenched his lips/eyes tightly.

"Easy, Shaver." Liz's voice, calm, reassuring, and worried. Why was she so worried? It occurred to Shaver to mention to her that she'd not called or come by either. Then the rest of the pain reminded him where he was, and what had happened. His head throbbed in time to the beat as the band reached the break, the softly chanted words sifting through the speakers and his thoughts.

I am the one you don't know you need, 'til you can't feed your ego. . . .

He righted himself in a slow, lurching motion. As his hands met the booth, he flinched, but was surprised to find the pain much less than anticipated. Shaver stared dumbly at his bandaged fingers, each neatly bound in gauze and tape, the tell-tale seep of iodine reminding him of the dried blood, nearly sending him to darkness again in a vertiginous rush of *deja vu*.

"Fuck," he said softly. "What happened? I feel like I was clubbed in the head with a brick."

"Not exactly." Dexter's voice from across the table. "You clubbed yourself with the floor. Not the most graceful act I've ever seen, but it got you to hold still long enough for Liz to take care of your hands."

A sudden shift of air ushered three steaming mugs of coffee onto the table and Shaver groaned out loud. He waved feebly, but his hands were gently brushed aside, and the strong, pungent caffeine and steam magic wound their way up his nostrils and through his senses. Shaver cursed softly and sat back.

Dexter met his friend's gaze for just a second, and then stared down at his hands, and his own coffee, fingers drumming nervously. "You heard it." Not a question: a statement, blunt and matter-of-fact profound.

Shaver made no move or sound of acknowledgment. The truth floated in the air between them. Dexter knew. Liz knew, though she had no idea what they were talking about. Fuck, he couldn't even get the echoes to stop reverberating around in his head long enough to wonder *how* Dexter knew.

The silence thickened, and Shaver frowned. He curled his bandaged fingers around the coffee mug and lifted it slowly, already flinching from images of steaming liquid splashing off his lap. He had no confidence in the gauze-bound fingers, fingers that served him as no other part of his body, bringing the sounds and patterns together, now barely able to lift the cup and bring it to his lips. His eyes brimmed with sudden tears and he cursed softly as he realized he couldn't even hold the cup in one hand and use the other to brush them away. He felt Liz's fingers brush his cheek and the hot flush of shame at his helplessness.

Dexter still hadn't looked up, hadn't seen the tear, or the shame, and suddenly Shaver was angry. More angry than he could ever remember being. He slapped the coffee onto the table, feeling the hot sting as the dark liquid splashed over the back of his hand.

"Why Dex?" he asked, voice low and dangerous. "Why now?"

Dexter's head tilted back with a lightning quick motion, eyes wide, staring—empty. "It isn't my song, Shaver. I can hear it. Fuck, I might be able to *play* it bro, and my song might be there too, hiding in the background, but this one is you. What else could I do?"

Shaver stared. His heart was hammering, kicked into gear by the coffee.

"You know what I mean," Dexter continued. "That first night, when Brandt went off on that guitar like the Devil was working the strings. That wasn't my song, or yours. It wasn't even Brandt's, not at first. It grew into him slowly, and by the time he walked out that door there wasn't a lick of pain left in that boy that wasn't bared to the universe. Same with Syn. I wanted to ask her what she saw. I wanted to know who she reached for, kneeling on that stage, but the song . . . it wouldn't let me. Wouldn't let me do a thing but see things I was never meant to see, and I can still hear it. That never stops now. You hear it too."

Dex was silent again for a long moment, gaze dropping to his coffee once more. "You listen close, Shaver. That song is you."

"Excuse me," Liz cut in, breaking the sudden silence. "What the hell are you two talking about? What song?"

Shaver let out the breath he hadn't meant to hold and sank back against the booth. The anger melted away in a sudden flood of memory. He closed his eyes, trying to dredge up an answer that would make sense. Nothing came, so he opted for the beginning . . . fuck, where else would he start?

"Me and Dex," Shaver said, "have always had a theory. There are songs: good songs, bad songs, in between. More songs every day, and still they come. Each is different, even if only a little bit. Each is important. Like people. It works on a series of levels.

"One level, you got your pop rock, elevator music, mindless crap that sounds nice but gives you nothing. Lots of other levels. Sometimes it is so good . . . so fucking close. You were there." Shaver turned to Liz. "You were there when Brandt played. You heard it, just like we did."

Liz's eyes clouded. Her expression grew vague, and she nodded slowly. "I heard . . . something. It was good, damned good. I don't think I've ever heard anything like it, but . . ." She grew silent, and Shaver watched her, waiting.

"She heard it on a different level too, bro," Dexter cut in. "I've talked to at least a dozen others who were there, both nights. Everyone heard something. Everyone was blown away. No one gets it. First night they were feeling closer to God. Second night, it was . . . weird. Third night, now? They think it was one " 'kick-ass-fucking-concert' and 'it's too bad that fucking Brandt guy weirded out, man, you guys were *going* places.' "

"What are you talking about?" Shaver growled, anger bubbling up again. " 'Kick-ass-fucking-concert?' That? My gut hurt for a week after hearing that. And the . . . dreams. We talked about the fucking dreams, Dex. Who were those people?"

"I don't know, bro," Dexter answered. "All I know is, I heard what I heard, you heard what I heard, others heard what they heard. Not the same, and for them it fades. Some deal, huh? They get the experience, the pain, the music, and then they get their lives back."

Liz pushed back from the table suddenly. "You saying I can't hear what you hear?" she asked, angry. "You think you're fucking special for beating those damned drums senseless every night?"

"It isn't like that," Shaver said softly. He thought for a moment, sliding his arms clumsily around her shoulders, drawing her against his side and flinching as his fingers pressed to her shoulder. "You know how it is when you draw?"

Liz softened perceptibly when he mentioned the art. The murals that covered the walls inside and out at the Bean & Buzz were hers. She hadn't heard the music, but somehow Shaver knew he'd found a way to explain it to her.

"You ever wonder why you can give the same blank page and pencil to me, Dexter, and half the bar, draw a picture, and none of them can see it the way you do? None of them gets it. They might make something that looked vaguely like what you saw and drew. They might even have an image of their own with some power behind it. They can't draw what you draw. Most people can see things fine and can't draw

69

them at all. It's like that with the music."

"But lots of people can draw," Liz said.

"Not like you, Liz," Dexter threw in. "Not like you. You ever see something in your head and fight to get it out on paper, or a wall, and fail, and curse and try again, and again, and even though it is great, and everyone loves it, you can't get what you want . . . until it hurts deep inside, eating at your thoughts and stealing your dreams?"

Liz started, eyes shifting to Dexter's. She nodded, unable to speak.

"You are trying to draw the song," Shaver said. "That's what we're talking about. The one song behind it all. The one perfect pattern that blends each piece perfectly. Everything has a pattern."

"And no one can pin it down, no matter how clearly they hear it, or see it," Dexter added. "That was the theory, anyway. Brandt fucked that up, then Syn. You'd think it would make me feel better, knowing perfection exists, that it can be attained, but it doesn't."

Dexter glanced up, eyes deep and filled with pain that struck Shaver physically, quick withdrawal and reaching with throbbing fingers for the coffee, drinking in a failed attempt to hide the intrusion into his friend's mind. His own gaze dropped as he lifted the cup, locked to the swirling liquid and soft steam-stream that shifted over his cheeks. Hot burn of the cup through his gauze-bandaged fingers throbbing in time with the beat of his heart, winding down into other beats, soft and shivering quickly through his mind. He tasted the rich black coffee and quickly lowered the cup to the table.

The music Shaver had heard earlier shivered through him, deep burn searing through his soul but he ignored it, refused to grip the edges of the pattern. Madness. That was what insanity felt like. He knew it, sudden and sure, like the pain when he'd pressed that chord out of his guitar. Like falling and the hot scrape of palms on concrete, skin eaten and nerves exposed. Like staring into Dexter's eyes and knowing the pattern was not controlled, but controlling, eating Dex from the inside out.

"How can I help, Dex?" Shaver asked. "What the *fuck* can I do? I can't hum a tune to save the universe, and my fingers are so much chopped meat. Without my guitar, I can't even come close to that song."

"I know," Dex answered slowly, "but somehow it matters that you are here. I told you, bro, it isn't my song I hear. It isn't Brandt's or Syn's echoing in my head, much as I'd like to think it is. It's yours. I could tell you all the pain those other songs dragged out of me. I could tell you it was about us, but it isn't. This time it's you, Shaver. All you."

Liz grabbed Shaver suddenly. "Don't you freak out on me. Don't you dare fucking play some weird-assed song and head off into the sunset." She hit him then, a hard, pounding shot to the shoulder that shifted him in his seat, sloshing hot coffee over his bandaged hand and only a soft "O" of his lips to mark the passage of pain.

"Don't worry Liz," Dexter's voice, haunted, half-empty, half sharp-edged determination, "not going to let that happen. Not going to be left here either, not again. I don't have any reason to believe it, but I'm going on the possibility that I hear the music because I'm meant to. That it will mean something to me. That I'll understand why one night I'm laying down rhythm for a half-assed band with a drunken singer and the next I'm caboose on the blues train, headed out of town and into some fucked-up, magic place I can't even *see*."

"What do you want from me?" Shaver said, voice

whisper-thin and riding the edge of breakdown. His hands shook, throbbing pain of the torn skin joined with the steady burn from the hot coffee soaking the bandages.

"You tell me," Dexter replied, "what the song is about. Tell me what Brandt dragged out of you that night, what Syn chased through your memory and back again. Tell me what made you want to press your fingers through those strings so tightly that it robbed you of the one thing that gives you release."

Shaver pressed back into the seat of the booth, head shaking and eyes widening, then closing, hooded by lids striving suddenly and desperately to shut out the world. He shook his head, lips parting to speak and falling short of sound. He could feel those moments, those notes that had rippled through him: more than notes, images and dreams, memories and themes of pain and a childhood he had been running from full-tilt since his mother died. Since he was ten. Since the patterns had shifted, deep inside, and he'd begun a frantic quest to rearrange them into something sane.

"I can't," Shaver said at last.

"You can't *not,* bro," Dexter said sharply. "Hell, you think all this has grabbed us by the privates by accident? Time to move on, or go mad. I heard a whisper of a voice when Brandt was playing. Old voice, old and harsh and . . . deep. Wasn't talking to me, but just that one moment, I heard it. No way I was tellin' anyone about that, not as weird as things were, but I've been thinking a lot about what was said."

Shaver whispered, "There were a lot of people there. You could have heard any one of them . . . could have been fucking Brandt, for all you know."

Dex shook his head, but before he could speak, Liz

leaned forward, eyes too bright and hands clasped around her coffee. "What did you hear, Dex? What did they say?"

"Crossroads, or cross-hairs, all the same. No way outta the pain 'cept t'rough da music, boy."

Dexter's voice had deepened as he spoke, and the intonation, the inflection, and Deep-South drawl sent a shiver racing so quickly up Shaver's spine he nearly spilled his coffee again. He didn't. He grabbed it, fingers pain-tight, wrapped as if they might press through the porcelain of the mug, and he drew the cup to his lips, drained it, warm-bitter liquid washing down his throat and failing to drown the memories. The table, Dexter, even Liz, who had gripped his arm again as he leaned back, all fast-fading as he fought to bury the should-be-dead images.

"No." A single word to draw him back and his mind gripping it tightly, desperate claw-sharp concentration clutching tightly to sanity. Eyes closing trap-door tight on the visions and his palms flat on the table . . . muscles taut in his arms and throat constricted. Then it receded. Not gone. Not less intense, but the pattern solidified, long soft breath returning his mind to him and with it his voice. "More coffee."

Dex or Liz must have signaled the waitress, because the coffee appeared, clean mug and fresh wash of hot steam over his cheeks. Shaver never looked up. His thoughts whirled with the dark liquid. Walls were crumbling inside, memories shifting from archived never-open-even-on-Christmas nightmares to vivid present tense.

"Mom died when I was ten," Shaver said at last. "Dad died, at least the part of him that mattered, about the same time. I wanted him to live."

The room shifted. Shaver lifted and tilted the mug once more, but he barely tasted the coffee. His gaze was fastened on Dexter's face, or a point far, far beyond it and out of sight. He felt Liz's hand lying gently on his shoulder, but the warmth and closeness brought no comfort. It was a disassociated, random connection, lost in the moment, a moment puzzle-pieced together from memories and dreams.

The funeral parlor surfaced in his mind, a dark, surreal chamber filled with endless elongated shadows that were softened only by the eerie light of scattered candles. Men and women, some known, some dark phantom-masks as disconnected as the knowledge that his mother would not be coming home to cook supper, or breakfast, or anything—ever—roamed aimlessly about, their voices a low hum of white noise. Shaver had bounced from room to room, avoiding one set of eyes after another, searching, always, for his father's dark-gray suit and ruffled hair. Watching for the light at the end of a darkness that crept deeper and deeper into his heart with each passing "I'm so sorry" from uncaring lips.

There had been nothing of his mother in that place. No light. No laughter or soft, floral smells. There had been grim music and the cloying sweetness of lilies. The over-perfumed wakes of black-clad women who wept for their own pain. And in the corner, like a silent sentinel, the guitar case, leaning almost casually against an empty casket. He tried not to look in that direction, tried to move away and into another room, but the moment sucked him in like a vacuum.

Fingers gripped his shoulder and too-strong perfume washed over him in a nauseating wave. Hen-like voices clucked encouragement in his ear as others droned on about what a wonderful boy he was and how his mother would be proud and would see/hear him from a better place and his muscles straining to push him back, failing, as he was seated center-stage at the death-masque Ritz. They didn't want to hear him play. They didn't think his mother was listening, either. Most of them had barely known her. They wanted him to draw them back to life. They thought the cute little boy with the shiny guitar could revitalize their depressed lives, death staring them too close in the face for comfort, and his life stronger, just beginning.

Shaver searched the dark wash of faces for his father. He found only strangers, glittering eyes, and grim-tight half-smiles devoid of emotion. Frantically, driven, Shaver slipped his gaze from one to the next, back and on again. Someone had pressed the guitar into his hands, the sunburst finish catching the flickering light and licking at the periphery of his sight. His fingers gripped the neck of the instrument grimly. No comfort there, but the patterns coalesced, the candlelight and eye-flicker dance of life, and something inside shifted.

Shaver felt the strings beneath his fingers. He closed his eyes and smelled the lilies, the sickening backdrop of formaldehyde and salt-scented tears. The macabre strains of the organ had faded. Even the omnipresent backdrop of whispered comments had quieted. The world was silent, and only the squeal of Shaver's nails over the strings of the old Epiphone acoustic broke the silence, sliding up and down, up and down, trying to decide what to play.

He didn't want to play for them. He didn't want to do anything for/with/around them. He wanted his mother. He wanted his father to come to him and tell him it was okay, but it was not his father who moved closer. The crowd moved in, gathering close as if it would help . . . as if it would not be the most claustrophobic, breath-stealing thing they could do, and

Shaver gripped the strings more tightly still, eyes closing.

He let his fingers form the first chord, knowing halfway through that A Minor was what he would play, why, and to whom. He didn't know the name of the song. He didn't know where it had come from, when, or why, but it blossomed in his mind and blotted out the room and the stiff, white-faced mannequin that could not be his mother, laying ten yards away in a wooden box, and the image of his father's dead, uncaring face. It blocked out whispered regrets hung in the heavy air by voices trying desperately to prove they cared about someone they barely knew. It erased the memory of the priest's words, spoken in memory of someone Shaver had never known. Salvation was assured for that someone, but Shaver had known his mother, and it wasn't so cut and dried.

He slid from the A Minor into C and onward, each note flowing from his memory and blending with its predecessors, mimicking the strains of long-memorized melody. Late nights and his room, dark and empty except his toys, macabre half-shadows dangling over the edges of his toy box and slipping stuffed limbs from under his bed. Nights where amber bottles and wine goblets had stolen both father and mother, and the ominous squeaking of the springs in their bed had kept Shaver rooted in place, unable to go to them for protection, or comfort. The music was always the same on those nights: too loud, walls and floor and bed vibrating in shimmering counterpoint.

There was a shuffle of feet as the tune manifested itself. As the blues-based country twang shivered off his strings and into the dead-formaldehyde-soaked air. Appropriate? That was the question they wouldn't ask, but stared into one another's eyes. Now? Here? Why? No answer from Shaver but the notes, pure and clean, cleaner than he'd ever played them.

His eyes rose slowly from the floor and he searched. He shifted from face to face, figure to figure, and found the doorway and his father's eyes, windows within that doorway, open wide and staring. In that second, they linked. In that moment and that song, they understood one another as human beings and men and not mythical superhero father to son. Shaver drank in the pain and his father shared the music. For that instant. Then, with a snap that nearly tore out Shaver's heart, his father turned away, slipping from the room, and he was alone. Alone with the strangers, and the music, and he ran.

He didn't run away from the room, he ran to the music. He ran *through* the music. He dove through the notes, driving them before him like a frightened herd of cattle. The tempo raced with his thoughts, and the thoughts fueled his heartbeat. He wanted his fingers to fail. Wanted it to end in a tangle of bone and flesh so he could smash the guitar on the floor and run from the room, but it wouldn't happen. Faster, and faster still, chasing his mother's memory through the room, searching and seeking with flying fingers caressing and milking the strings in ways he couldn't even begin to understand.

His eyes were locked to the doorway. The empty doorway. He played, and he played harder, faster, and again, doubling and redoubling in his effort to bring his father back . . . to elongate that moment into a lifetime together. The white-noise rumble of the rest of the world intruded slowly, and he knew they would stop him, would take the guitar and the song and the moment, and none of the bastards even knew *why* he was playing. Hank Williams Senior two speeds above 45 and at least an eight on the Richter scale of his heart. Why wouldn't he come BACK?

Then hands gripped his arms, the guitar, drawing him

off the stool and away toward the back rooms, toward the food and the restrooms and the exit, mother left behind to be forgotten and twisted by the words of uncaring strangers, and his father fading into his own gray cloud.

Shaver looked up suddenly. His hands were pressed too tightly to the cup and the hot coffee had burned him. He did not release it. He gathered his thoughts, closed his eyes, then opened them again to find Dexter staring at him strangely. He felt a sharp pain, twisted quickly, sloshing coffee over his fingers again, and realized with a start it was Liz. Her nails bit deep into the flesh of his shoulder, and he felt her shaking. Even his twist failed to fully dislodge her.

"Liz," he said softly, then again, more loudly, "Liz, let *go* for fuck's sake. Are you trying to put my whole arm out of commission?"

Liz drew back suddenly, as if she'd been struck, or stuck her finger into a light socket. Shaking her head from side to side, eyes wide, she pulled back across the booth. "How . . . how did you do that?" she asked, trembling so violently that the coffee shook and spilled gently over the rims of their cups, pooling on the table top and shivering in endless ripples.

"What?" Shaver's mind was slowly clearing, but he had no clear recollection of anything past the delivery of the coffee he still held painfully tight.

"Where was that place?" Dex asked. "Shaver, where the fuck *was* that place?"

Comprehension dawned. They had seen. Shaver would have bet his life that he hadn't spoken, but somehow his thoughts had taken up the slack where his voice left off. Or had they? Maybe he'd told them the story after all . . . who the fuck knew?

"He never came back," Shaver said, rather than answering

directly. He lifted the coffee to his lips, tipped the cup, and grimaced as the still-hot liquid slid in and down. "Not really. He was there, bought me clothes, and paid for the food. Had a lady come in three times a week and clean up the mess. I saw him exactly one hour each day and sometimes on the weekends. He never talked much, never about Mom at all."

Dexter's eyes danced oddly, and his lip trembled. Softly, shaking from within, as if fighting against impossible pressure—failing—leaning back and chuckling.

Shaver watched him in shock, unable to react as the drummer rolled slowly into a ball, laughing, then harder, tears rolling down his cheeks. He felt his cheeks redden. "What? What the fuck is so funny?"

Dexter didn't answer, couldn't answer or speak, could only roll tighter on the seat, chin tucked to his chest and doing all he could to silence the maniacal laughter washing through him. Liz, mesmerized, somehow regained control of herself and slid back across the seat, pressing up against Shaver's side and leaning her head on his shoulder, gaze locked on Dexter's quivering form.

They watched. Silence on one side of the booth, assaulted by steady, helpless laughter from the other. The coffee cooled, forgotten, the mugs standing silent watch between. The moment diffused slowly. Liz's tension melted and she slumped against Shaver, who slid his arm carefully around her back, avoiding all contact between his fingers and anything, gripping her with his wrist and pulling her closer.

What seemed hours later, the waitress appeared, standing very still at the edge of the table. She was trying hard not to stare at Dexter, who was slowly uncurling, eyes red and wet with the effort of regained control. He rubbed his swollen eyes with his knuckles, grinding the salty tears in deeper.

"More coffee?" Her voice grated on their senses, dragging them through a vertigo-loop time warp to the present.

"What?" Shaver spoke softly. "What is so fucking funny?"

Dex glanced up, nearly lost it again, straightened. "Hank Williams," he said at last. "It was fucking Hank Williams. The song. Your song."

Shaver stared. His brain lagged, caught up, shifted. He tried to growl and failed. "You got a problem with that?" he said at last. "Fuck Dex, I pour my heart out to you and you make fun of my father's *music?*"

"Hey."

They turned. Three sets of eyes rising up the black-clad body of the waitress to her frustrated frown.

"You want coffee, or what?"

Shaver shook his head. He did not laugh, but it was not easy, and he felt Liz tense against him again, a pleasant tension, pressing to, not away from, his body.

"Not me," he said. Staring pointedly across the booth, he added, "And I doubt he needs much to stimulate his dumb ass either."

Liz giggled, and even the waitress lightened up a bit.

"I'll bring your check."

She didn't wait for acknowledgment, spinning quickly on too-high heels, skirt whirling quickly in the air, holding Shaver's gaze for just a second, and then releasing him to the moment. He glanced down at the table. Liz's free hand had been busy. The napkin that had lain before her had become her canvas. Shaver her subject. The hair was too long, the eyes so deep, so soulful and pain-wracked they snagged on Shaver's nerves and nearly dragged him back again. There was a thorn-crown circling his brow in the drawing: dark droplets, pencil-rendition-blood dripping over his cheeks.

Shaver reached out and touched the drawing, fingers sliding under and lifting the edge, tilting it so he could view it more fully. Liz's gaze dropped to his fingers, and her hand covered his . . . covered the image, stroking gently. Cutting off his line of sight did nothing to diminish the impact of that image. The eyes—his eyes—stared back at him from beneath his fingers, from beyond Liz's palm. Eyes that he had not seen in years. They were the eyes of a boy, the eyes of a motherless child. The eyes of a son watching his father fade into the shadows.

"You saw," Shaver said, voice accusing and credulous, amazed and filled with a sudden sense of awe.

"We were there," Dexter cut in, sliding his hand across the table, prying both Shaver's and Liz's fingers from the napkin and snagging it in a quick motion, turning it, and staring fixedly at the image. "We saw this boy . . . you. We heard the song. Brandt played Hank that night, too, remember?"

Before Shaver could answer, the waitress intruded again, another level dropped back, and they punted. Rising, Shaver reached for the check, realized his ruined fingertips could not lift the paper from the tabletop, grinned, and drew back his hand. Liz snatched the offending bit of paper quickly, before Dexter could move, scanned it, and dropped a couple of bills distractedly onto the table. Dexter clutched the napkin, Shaver's young/old eyes watching them all from the surface. Shaver tried to concentrate on the money, to calculate a tip. Failed.

He turned toward the door and started walking, Liz pressed tightly to his side and Dexter trailing after, bumping off people and tables distractedly as he stared at the napkin. Shaver wondered if his friend's mind was walking the familiar trail his own had taken so many times, if he was seeking Shaver's father, mourning his mother, or just lost in the notes of the song.

He pressed open the door and stepped onto the darkened street. In the distance, haunting and eerie, he heard the strains of a song, floating on the breeze. Humming, he inserted his voice into the melody, counterpoint, minor to minor harmony as he matched the rhythm with his footsteps, drawing Liz closer.

Dexter fell into step behind them, finally glancing up from the napkin image with a dark grin. He cocked his head to one side, moving up beside them and joining his own, deep, off-key voice to the refrain: "Why can't I free your doubtful mind, and melt, your cold . . . cold heart. . . ."

Shaver wanted to laugh. Dex's voice floated up from recent memory. "Hank Williams?" It didn't quite work. He couldn't laugh, and as the three of them turned the corner at Elm, heading for the cemetery, he knew it would be a long time before any of this seemed funny again. They rounded another corner, and the spiked, wrought-iron gates of the graveyard came into view. The music was smoother now, deeper and resonant. He could make out other tunes, melodies that haunted him with their tightrope walk around the edges of his memory, but that would not surface fully, and he stopped.

Liz had kept moving, nearly toppling them both as he dragged on her, human anchor to her caught-in-the-tide progress. Dexter was three paces gone before he, too, stopped, glancing back quizzically.

"I'm not ready to go there," Shaver said.

The music, as if sentient and hungry, drew up over and around them, seductive and strong.

Dexter glanced over his shoulder, back at Shaver, and then back to the graves again. "But . . ."

Shaver shook his head. The motion, half negation, half

to clear cobwebs of indecision, was all that it took. He turned slowly, drawing Liz with him. She dragged against that tug for a moment, leaning longingly toward the cemetery, then followed with a soft moan. Shaver leaned close to her ear, breath hot on her soft skin and whispered, "Not yet."

Nodding, she curled against him as he walked slowly away. Shaver sensed Dexter hesitating behind them. The moment was electric with energy, tension snapped taut between them like a wire. Shaver walked. The image of the wire tightened in his mind, vibrating, shimmering, so close to snapping back and slicing them both to the quick that he shuddered, but he didn't falter. It wasn't time. He knew it wasn't. That song had been his years before. That moment had been magic. It wasn't now. It wasn't him. It was his past.

"You still got that bottle, Dex?" Shaver called over his shoulder.

He didn't look back, but he felt the soft release of tension, felt the synchronization, like the music, like the band, melody and rhythm, drums and lead. Dexter fell in beside him, and Hank Williams faded into the soft voices of crickets and the hiss of tires on the road as the city's dark dwellers drifted past on their private missions. Even the throbbing in his fingers faded to a subsidiary of his heartbeat. At the corners of his mind, the song ate slowly and patiently, and he smiled.

"I'll get you, you bastard," he whispered. Liz turned, quizzically, as he spoke, but he met her lips with his own and silenced her without an answer. Suddenly, the night seemed too short and the options infinite.

FOUR

The soft, sad strains of the harmonica trailed off, fading as the footsteps of the three turned from death to life. Footscrape echoes trailed into the world and the moon bathed the old tomb in silvered luminescence. Brandt squinted, fighting to pierce the gloom, but there was no way he could see them. No way he could even understand how he heard them. Beside him, Synthia rocked slowly, her chin on her knees, which were drawn up tight against her breasts.

"Damn," Brandt said softly. "They didn't come." He shook his head slowly, disbelievingly. Synthia remained silent, brooding and glaring at the night as if she dared it to say anything.

"Not yours to decide, boy," a gravelly voice cut through the heavy silence. "Not your pain, nor mine. Changes nothin'."

Brandt turned slowly. "It changes everything. You said it had to be complete. You said that the music we needed, the answers that can make this all . . . sane . . . were tied up in the band. There goes the band, Wally. They are fucking walking away like they never heard a thing."

"Tonight t'aint forever boy," Wally growled, turning away and tucking the harmonica into a fold of his battered coat. "Not fer you nor me to say. Time does as time does. You had your learnin' to do, they got theirs."

Brandt opened his mouth, words resting hot and acidic on the tip of his tongue, but the notes crashed in his head, and he hesitated, regrouped. Nothing he could say would negate what he'd just heard. Nothing he knew could explain a single moment of time he could remember. Another step along the way, another short climb up the ladder toward the future. At least he hoped he was climbing.

"It's his father," Syn said quietly.

Brandt whirled, and even Wally turned to glance over his shoulder, dark eyes darker for that moment.

"His father," she repeated. "He has to find the song."

Wally nodded, turning away, but Brandt only stared.

"The song was playing just a minute ago," he said at last. "The *song* was supposed to fucking draw them here, bring us back together, and get this show on the road. Find the song . . . *fuck!*"

Wally ignored the outburst, and Synthia was still staring at the street, eyes bright with—something. Brandt turned from one to the other, noting the lack of impact his words were having, and his shoulders slumped.

"What then?" he asked.

"Nothin' then," Wally said. "We wait. You got some playin' to do, to get that outta you, boy, and I got things that draw me. Time will bring it together, or not. The world isn't a set pattern, much as we'd like it to be. Lot depends on your friend now, but nothin' you can do to make it happen. You play, and you wait, and you dream. You'll know when it's right."

Brandt turned toward the cemetery gates and stared into the darkness. He felt the notes itching at his heart, sliding down the sinews and veins of his arms, tugging at his fingers. Wally was right. He had to play, had to let the pain free, direct it up and out before it began to eat away at his mind and soul.

He spoke into the wind, the words gripped and twisted from his lips by the breeze and dulled by the mist-soaked air. "Figure it out, Shaver. Find that song. If I can't give it to you, you find that motherfucker and get back here where you belong."

The low hanging clouds killed any echo, and silence engulfed them in a clammy embrace. With no further words, Brandt turned, gripped the handle of his guitar case, and moved off into the night. Syn uncurled herself from the tombstone and followed without a sound. Wally was there, and then, he was not. Brandt didn't even care.

There was little discussion on where they'd go. Shaver was in no way ready to have his decrepit, rotting little world invaded by anyone from "outside," and Liz had food. Dex had the now-proverbial "bottle," and they scored that along the way, Liz and Shaver leaning in close beneath a half-lit neon sign proclaiming "LIQUOR" in brilliant green and pink as Dex slipped up a shadowed stair to his "loft," returning moments later, grin and corn whiskey accounted for.

The walk was completed in silence. Shaver had been to Liz's place plenty of times. The two were one of the hot-cold, on-and-off-again sensations of Sid's. Dex had only been there once, and under the irresistible influence of chemicals usually beyond their financial means. Liz led the way up the stairs, and Shaver noted distractedly that they were clean-swept and neat. That the door behind them actually closed and locked. That there were no loud stereos or crying children wailing into the silence.

Quick fumble of keys, purse nearly dropped, and a soft curse ushered them into her world. The air smelled faintly of incense, and the light flicked on soft and comfortable. Shaver stopped in the doorway. It was familiar, and new at once. He felt the smooth wood of the doorframe, sliding his hand up gently, not wanting to return the pain to his fingertips, but wanting to feel the solidity he sensed. He was about to try and voice this sense of peace when Dexter, tired of waiting behind him, gave a light shove to his back and sent him stumbling in, fighting for balance.

"What were you doing, meditating?" Dex asked with a grin.

Catching his balance, barely resisting the instinct to press his ravaged hand to the wall and catch himself, Shaver turned. "Don't know. Feels . . . good. Comfortable. I must have been here a thousand times, never felt anything like this. . . ."

And then a soft breath of perfume as Liz returned, catching them mid-conversation and stilling it. Shaver shifted his gaze to meet hers and knew she'd caught the last, caught her soft smile in return, quick lowering of her eyes and brusque words.

"In here. I want to look at those fingers again," she said.

Shaver followed, and Dex fell in behind, closing the door behind them. The magic of that first moment faded to a soft glow, and Shaver slid onto the couch, leaving room beside him for Liz and watching as she bustled about the small apartment, trying not to stare at him, getting caught and blushing.

No one said a word, but Dex produced the "bottle," and Liz produced clean bandages, a tube of ointment, and three glasses. Shaver almost laughed when he examined his and found it was clean. Hadn't been a clean glass in his place for weeks. He moved a bit too quickly and the motion sent a sudden breath of his own odor wafting about him. Shaver nearly retched.

"Mind if I shower?" he said.

"I thought you'd never ask," Liz grinned, tossing a towel at his head. "Take off those bandages first . . . the water will do you good. Going to hurt like hell, but serves you right."

Instinctive catch and thoughtless grip and the towel was in his hands, which throbbed from the effort. Biting his lip against the flood of abuse that washed through his mind, Shaver rose and turned toward the bathroom. He stopped at the doorway, staring at the shower, and Liz called out.

"You're going to need help, aren't you?" She wasn't teasing, but concerned, and Shaver leaned against the wall. It was true. He could barely get out of his clothing, and the bandages would drive him crazy. He wasn't sure how well he could grip the slick handles of the faucets, and he knew the water was going to hurt like hell. Sudden tears welled in the corners of his eyes, angering him again.

"Fuck!" he growled.

"It's all right, Shaver." Liz's voice, soft, comforting. "You aren't alone anymore."

She pressed into the small room behind him, leaving Dexter and his bottle to wait and wonder as the two slipped from sight. Shaver felt her pressing close, arms circling him. He wondered vaguely how she could stomach his stench, but eased back against her as nimble fingers gripped the lower hem of his shirt and rolled it slowly upward.

"Why?" he asked.

No answer, soft lick at his ear and the shirt rolling higher, arms raising slowly and the material sliding up. Shaver pulled his arms and hands free of the t-shirt gingerly, careful not to disturb the bandages, fighting for concentration as other sensations shivered through him.

"I'm glad you came," she said simply, tossing his shirt toward the nearest wall. "When you disappeared, I thought I might not see you again. Brandt never came back. Synthia took off after him and never looked back."

"It's different for them," Shaver answered, feeling her hands moving down again, to his belt, loosening by degrees and working the snap firmly, fingers slipping in and teasing before curling back and tugging the jeans apart, and down, drawing them slowly over his hips, impeded by her own pressed close from behind.

"How?" Her breath was hot on his skin, and her hands

lingered much longer than necessary as she lowered the jeans, holding them for him to step free and taking that moment to press her tongue to his spine.

Shaver spun slowly, clumsily wrapping her in a hug. "You know the answer to that. I've heard my song before, but I haven't lived it. Whatever happened to Brandt before he played that night, it was some serious shit. He never came back from it, and it was the same for Syn. They grew up, somehow, reached out and grabbed that fucking copper ring on the carousel."

"And you?" As she spoke, she slid closer into his arms, her lips so close to his that he could share her breath and her eyes wide, waiting, hungry in ways he could only sense, not truly understand.

"I'm not there yet," he answered simply. "I'm not there, and I'm not certain that if I was there, I'd react as they did. I have no way to know. I was always the one hoping the carousel would speed up, that if I got it going hard enough, I could shift up from the copper to the gold ring, just out of reach."

"Maybe you just never looked up at the right moment." It wasn't a question, and before Shaver could answer, his pants were dropping away between them and he felt himself stiffening at the taste of cool air and the soft brush of Liz's long nails. She smiled at him, turning away and reaching through the shower curtains to the faucet, releasing a stream of water that seemed to shift from cold to steaming hot in seconds as Shaver watched her back, the play of muscles as she moved. She spun back to him and he blushed, unable to conceal his erection and further embarrassed by her soft grin and the sudden brush of her nails down the length of him.

"Shower, hotshot," she said. "Hot water, clean fingers, then talk. We wouldn't want to give Dexter the wrong impression."

She was very close, fingers gently gripping his, working at the tape, and the bandages. Shaver flinched, but it didn't hurt, not really, not like it had hurt when he tried to play, or when Dex had made him answer the phone. Liz unwound the gauze and drew it away, tossing it into a small plastic can beneath the blue porcelain sink.

"In," she said, pointing to the shower. Shaver stepped over the edge of the tub and under the water, trying clumsily to reach up and pull the curtain shut behind him. Liz's hand slipped over his, pressing him in and tugging the curtain along its runners. She didn't close it all the way, leaving enough of an opening for her arms.

Shaver reached out, but, again his hands were pressed away gently, and the soap was suddenly sliding over his skin, steamy water running down and around her arms as she worked slowly, cleansing him, careful not to splash too much on his fingers, but not taking it easy on his weeks-old funk. He held himself straight, trying not to think about it, trying not to notice as she worked lower, as she teased, her nails slipping around the soap and scraping his skin, as the water swirled over and around the soap, drawing the fatigue and filth down, swirling away in a soft drain that encompassed much more than water.

Steam rose. Liz's fingers worked and slid, massaged and cleansed, and Shaver closed his eyes, overcome by the sensations, dull throbbing fingertips and skin so alive from the touch of scalding water and sliding hands. Too much, very suddenly too much, and he leaned into the wall, catching himself with one elbow, remembering for once not to throw up his hand to break the fall. Liz had grown silent, the only sound the rhythmic pounding of the shower and the pulsing, too-heavy beat of his heart forcing blood through his veins.

In the room beyond, oblivious, Dexter was pouring shots of corn whiskey, staring at them, sliding the glasses in odd patterns, emptying them back into the bottle and repeating the action, fingers nervous, almost frantic, with motion. The corner of his lip twitched, unconscious dance of energy defined and trapped. Waiting. Shifting his gaze to the door once more, he cursed softly and rose, moving to the window and staring out over the alley behind the apartment building. A drizzle had begun to wet the stone and brick, running in slow rivulets down and away, slickened and discolored by oil and chemicals, debris and long-dried blood. Quick rinse of the city's epidermis, growing slowly in strength as his fingers, never still, tapped Hank Williams backbeats on the window glass.

The rain began to fall more steadily, and Brandt leaned in close beneath the wide-spread wings of the stone angel perched over his head. He watched the slow drift of traffic up and down Elm, long-dead memory of a man and his family pressed behind him, seeping through the chill of the rain and the soft brush of Syn's thigh to his. In his lap, the guitar rested gently, held close as his fingers caressed the polished maple neck. He didn't play—not yet. He held the guitar, fingers slow-dancing with the strings, mind drifting with the mist. The notes rippled up the tendons of his arms, itched at his fingers, but he held them in check.

Synthia leaned closer, soft hair tickling at his neck as she laid her head on his shoulder gently. Brandt let his head cock to the side, resting against her and letting the scent of her seep through his senses, letting her proximity dull the pain that was the music before it could cut his heart. Too long. Too fucking long he'd waited. Brandt hadn't realized until that moment how much he'd been counting on watching

Shaver and Dex walk through those wrought-iron, spear-tipped gates. It was another emptiness, piled on the void that had been his life. It brought him that much closer to the pain, and the closer he got, the more he knew he had to play.

No audience this time. No wondering eyes or slack jaws slobbering disbelief into half-warm beer. No hungry, why-can't-I-have-that eyes dragging at his in pain. Brandt drew his fingers tightly to the strings and set his pick in motion slowly, rolling into the melody. No sudden jarring sound. No catchy introductory interlude. He launched straight down the center lane, closing his eyes, leaning into the stone angel's feet and letting the music flow.

He didn't think of the pain. He didn't think of those around them, though he could feel Synthia's gaze shifting, the soft motion of her head as she watched the *angels* gather. Brandt played, and he focused. He concentrated on Shaver's image, the cocky, too-quick grin and the sharp, questioning eyes. The bereft, tortured stare as Brandt had left him there on the stage, fingers white-knuckle gripping the neck of his Strat, oblivious to everything but the haunting-echo remnant of the music. The hunger . . . the raw need in Shaver's countenance haunted Brandt, and he let that emotion play out through his own fingers, drew it from the strings and sent it shimmering through the cemetery, over the *angels*, or ghosts, or whatever the fuck they were, willing it to his friend.

Those who gathered glared at him emotionlessly. They were not staring at him this time, but through him. The pain was not lessening, but growing. Still he played, keeping his mind set and his teeth gritted.

"Not for you," he managed, voice low and grating. "Not everything for you, you bastards," but his fingers burned. His eyes teared and the beating of his heart ran counterpoints that battled the flow of notes, skewing the harmony.

The crowding forms huddled closer and Brandt fought off a sudden blast of nausea, recoiling from it but holding to the melody, the stolen memory he knew only from old Wally's harp, from the song that had almost brought Shaver to him. He fought his way through the notes, as if sliding his fingers through heavy molasses, forcing his mind and body from the steady ebb of pain that surrounded him, flooding in and around and through his senses.

He felt the raindrops splashing off his face, his hands, felt the water warmer than it could be, steamy. The mist became steam, and still he played, unable to rid himself of that song, that single melodic chorus. Syn rocked gently on his shoulder and he used her strength shamelessly, fed off her, used her to press back against the crashing, battering waves of pain that were not his, but the world's, pain he knew he'd have to play and play and play to dull even to a soft throb. Voices murmured in his ears, soft brushes of more than air and water teased at his flesh. The sound became cyclical, swirling, notes whirling and whirling into themselves, quickening and shortening, dragging him in.

A low growl rumbled in Brandt's throat, and he forced his way through it all, forced the notes, one after the other as thought faded.

Shaver shivered softly. Liz worked the warm water and soap over his flesh slowly, and he leaned against the bathroom wall, eyes closing and steaming, rippling water working down over his face, over tired muscles and stinging sharply as it wound down to his fingers. He ignored that pain, concentrating on the soap, her hands, and the sound . . . the music?

"What?"

"Shhhhh." The curtain parted and suddenly, Liz was beneath the flow of the water with him, naked . . . smooth. The curtain slid back in place behind them and Shaver leaned more fully on the wall, head shaking gently back and forth, trying to concentrate. He heard the low wail of guitar, deep and resonant, shivering through the walls and aching down his spine. The warm water did nothing to raise the temperature of that wall, which felt more like cold, hard stone than tile, and very suddenly the steamy rinse of the shower chilled to the spatter of cold rain.

Liz's hands never left him, traveling over his chest, down . . . sliding in and cupping him gently. Shaver wondered through the haze how the *fuck* he managed to be erect as his brain swept away with the cold wash, as he shivered and arched away from that stone-touch, into her hands. He stood upright in the tub and clapped his hands over his ears tightly, fighting the sound.

His fingers itched again, not with the heat, or the pain, but with need. Raw, pounding hunger to play and play and not stop until the strings met bare bone drove through him and he cried out sharply, shivering now, chilled inside and out, and the notes continued to drag at his senses, fighting to control his thoughts.

Then the voices began. Slowly, softly, they slipped between the notes, finding cracks and holes, filling them like a rushing tide and expanding, each building on the last and forming a dull, droning roar that hid the beauty and pain of the notes with maddening discordance. Each spoke clearly, concurrently, words blending to other words and back to form a litany of pain that broke through the notes cleanly, though they rippled back each time, gripping Shaver's heart in a desperation both palpable and desperate, familiar and terrifying. The voices ebbed and the notes crashed, cold rain blended to steam and back and another sound leaked into Shaver's mind, working counter to the rhythm, jarring his thoughts free.

"Shaver? *Shaver!*" Liz's voice cut through the music and quieted the voices, gradually, her nails biting into his shoulders hard and shaking him roughly. "Damn you, stop it! You're scaring me."

Shaver shook his head dazedly, eyes focusing and skin warming suddenly, the water from the shower clear and very real, swirling over him, down between them and he leaned in close against her, feeling her soft breasts flatten to his chest, slickened with soap. He leaned in onto her shoulder and whispered harshly, "What's happening to me?"

No words, tight press of her body and undeniable heat, so sudden Shaver's knees nearly buckled as he wrapped her clumsily in his arms and held her, letting the hot, steamy water blend them, feeling her damp hair against his cheek, fingers pain-gripping her hips, ignoring it, letting other sensations claim him.

Her voice murmuring, "Thank God, don't go, Shaver, don't . . ." fading to the soft patter of the water, softer tracing of long nails over his back. No music, only the heady scent of moist heat, naked flesh, and floral soap.

Brandt felt the shift, felt the warming of the rain and reached out with the song, letting the notes cascade through the steam, reaching for Shaver's heart. He knew he was getting through, could sense the joining, the sync that had always clicked just before the music was perfect. It was hard, harder than anything he'd ever done. He knew the notes, knew what to play and how to make them do as he bid them, and yet it was difficult to concentrate. Each time one of the *angels* drew nearer, eyes wide and hungry, gazing at and through him, a shiver of notes rippled through him. Each time a vision invaded his mind, drawing him from the graveyard, and the shower, and the song, into some ancient, undeniable pain, it was a struggle to be free of it, to play his own choice and not theirs, to play Shaver's pain and ignore what gripped his heart.

Mercifully, Wally remained gone, doing whatever it was he did, leaving Brandt to fight his own battle. The rain warmed again, like a shower. He felt the tingling touch of another's hands, felt someone, not Syn, though he knew she leaned in tight to his side, but another, sliding sharp nails and seeking hands hungrily, his clothing melting in wet heat.

The voices swelled around him, the *angels,* each note drawing them closer, each defiant scrape of pick on string shimmering through them and agitating, blending the images, weaving the pain into a single blanket of misery that draped over and around Brandt, pressing him down.

"No," he whispered. He pressed his fingers tightly to the strings, and he screamed. Blistering, searing heat, pain like he'd never known rippled through his hands; only the death-grip rictus of cramped, ruined hands kept the guitar from spilling free.

He heard Syn's voice, felt her wrap herself tightly around him and draw him back. The *angels* hit them both like an icy wave, washing through, no physical touch but a psychic burn of outrage and frustration. Brandt knew in that instant that it was Shaver's fingers that could not play, Shaver's pain that drove Brandt's teeth through his lip and arched his body in such perfect agony. Brandt tried to regain the melody, to force his hands to move, to play. Nothing. He bowed double in pain, the guitar trapped as his mind gave a little snap to the wild side.

Brandt closed his eyes tightly, but it did nothing to ease the flow of images cascading through him. He tried to play them, to capture the music and set it free, but he couldn't shake that single moment of Shaver's pain. The strings lay pinned and mute, and the pain rolled about in his mind and gut, wrenching with cold talons at his sanity.

There was a rush of air, something/someone gripping his hair tightly and dragging him back, out of the huddled heap. His head whipped up too fast, too fucking fast, and there was a soft smack, wide "O" of lips as his skull struck the tombstone. The world shook again, but the images burst into fragments. Brandt turned his eyes down dumbly, staring. He felt the strings, the guitar, the cold rain that soaked his pants and shoes and beaded on the polished surface of his instrument.

He felt Shaver's pain acutely, deep within the achingly chilled fingers of both hands, but the pain that throbbed there now was his own. Calluses worn away, joints too cold and swollen to stiffness. Inside his head the pounding throb of pain he should have let go, of notes that rang from the rafters of his mind and shook his soul. There was nothing left of the warmth of moments before, only the dull echo of pain and the memory of failure, pounding to the rhythm of his pulse as it shivered through the growing knot on the back of his head.

Gradually his thoughts cleared. The pain receded, then focused. He shivered and found he couldn't stop, the cold rain and the shock of what he'd been through gripping him in paralytic rigor. Syn had her arms around him, and her voice droned in his ear. No words at first, sound, familiar sound, harsh and grating. Brandt shook his head and uncurled a bit from the guitar, aware suddenly that he was clutching it too tightly, that he could damage it. He stared at the rainwater dripping down the neck of the instrument and gasped, trying to rise and falling back with a lurch that smacked his head against the stone again.

"Fuck!" he gasped.

"Damn it Brandt, *listen to me!*"

The words focused through the haze and he leaned back into the stone. He felt Syn's hands gripping his shoulder tightly, shaking him, sending waves of nausea pounding through him. He held up a hand, wanting to tell her to stop, but unable to form the words, needing to be still, very still for just a second, just time to get his bearings and . . .

No way. His stomach rolled and the bile slipped up hot and acidic. He leaned to the side, away from Syn, away from the guitar, thrusting it feebly from the path of spraying filth. He hadn't eaten a good meal in days, but several gallons of coffee and half a cherry-filled donut spewed over the wet ground, washing down his leg, into the pooling rain and the oozing mud. He felt his insides clench, cold empty vacuum, and then gasped in air . . . holding back the second wave and drawing his knees up to trap the guitar against his chest. Tears rolled freely down his cheeks, but they were invisible, lost, futile in the wash of rain.

Syn's voice had softened. "Don't you fucking leave me again, you bastard," she whispered, drawing him to her more slowly. "Don't you even fucking think about it."

Brandt leaned into her shoulder, sighing. "We have to go," he managed, tasting the bile again and nearly retching all over. "Have to get out of the rain. Cold, so cold. My guitar . . ." He stared down at the instrument in horror. What had he been thinking?

Syn was up as soon as the words left Brandt's lips, tugging his sleeve, steadying him as he clumsily found his own feet and leaned on her shoulder heavily. He had no idea where they were headed as she started off through the mud-spattered grave-markers. His concentration was sapped by the effort not to gag, and the secondary effort of keeping his guitar from banging off of anything solid. He was vaguely aware that Syn carried his case. She was thinking. It was good one of them was.

They made their way slowly beneath the arched, wrought-iron gates of the cemetery and onto the street. The rain had slowed to a cold drizzle that clung and chilled, coating them with ice and soaking their clothing. Syn lived several blocks away. Brandt hadn't had a place to stay in a week. He hated to depend on her, clinging to her all the same, feeling her strength through the tight grip of her fingers and the bite of her nails. He was shaking, weak and drained, cold and the beginnings of a cough itching at the back of his throat.

"Dumb bastard," he heard her say. "Dumb fucking bastard, why couldn't you listen to the old guy? Why the hell couldn't you just play?"

"Shaver," he said. "I had to try."

Shaking her head violently, Syn dragged him to her shoulder and quickened her pace. Brandt leaned on her, watching the rainbow-haloed streetlights and shivering. He strained his senses, but there was no sound. No voices . . . no music in the background. His fingers felt like so much raw meat, though the pain was not his own, and his throat constricted slowly from the raspy ache of the cold.

He glanced behind them a final time . . . eyes downcast.

"I had to try," he whispered.

Synthia led him to a darkened set of stairs and the two disappeared quietly from sight.

FIVE

The door to the bathroom opened, steam and warm air washing into the room, drawing Dexter's eyes up from where he'd been constructing his thousand and twelfth pyramid of the crystal glasses. Soft clink of closure and coconut shift, now-you-see-it-now-you-don't arrangement and he was leaning back, as if he'd been that way all along, an expression of amusement painted across a sea of concern.

Shaver caught his friend's gaze, held it for a second, and then nodded. "You heard," he said.

Dexter turned away, reaching for the bottle, tugging free the cork almost desperately. He poured slowly, filling each glass to the rim, fighting the shaking in his hands. He slid one glass to his left, another to his right, and left the third planted firmly before him. No words. Shaver watched and waited, wrapped only in the warm towel.

Liz had taken his clothes. She'd threatened not to give them back without a wash, or a fumigation, or both. The hot scent of her filled his mind; cool air on wet skin tingled through his senses. Even his fingers, wrinkled from too much moisture, ached less obtrusively. Shaver eyed the glasses, shrugged, turned to kiss Liz on the cheek, and moved to the couch.

"He was calling to you," Dexter said, not looking up, fingers curling around his glass thoughtfully. "He wanted it more than anything I've heard him want, put it all in the song—your song. Never heard Brandt play fucking Hank Williams the *right* way before."

Silence folded over them for a long moment and Dexter lifted his glass, draining it in a quick toss and setting it thoughtfully back on the table, reaching for the bottle without hesitation and refilling.

Turning quickly, almost spilling his drink, Dexter fixed Shaver with a hard stare. "He wanted us all back together, man. What happened? He was calling us home."

Shaver reached for his own glass, suddenly self-conscious as the towel tried to unwrap itself. He felt Dexter staring at him, knew the stare had nothing to do with wet hair or shifting towels, felt that stare bite deep and concentrated, drawing the moonshine up and gulping it, quick grimace of distaste before the fire rose.

"Home? Where home is isn't for him to say," Shaver answered at last. "I'm not a child, Dex, and neither are you. Fuck, you act like it's all a done deal, walk off into a graveyard with a couple of lunatics and the world shifts to normal. I'm not ready for that. I don't know if I'll ever be ready for that. That mess is Brandt's world, let him live in it. Not long ago he was a drunken guitar player who could barely drag himself to the gigs, now he's the messiah?"

Silence reigned for a long, tense moment, then Shaver continued. "You want to help me find the song, man, let's just do it. We don't need Brandt, ghosts, Synthia, or anyone else. If the song is mine, or yours, then who else do we need to find it? *This* isn't Brandt's fucking world."

Just then, Liz popped back into the room, tossing a pair of men's jeans, *big* men's jeans, and a black t-shirt at Shaver's head. He watched them fly, nearly raising his hand with the drink to block the sudden assault, then remembering at the last second and taking them full in his face. Shaver slowly lowered his glass, cool drops of whiskey sprinkled over his wrist, and gripped the shirt first, turning it to read the inscription emblazoned across the front.

"Jazz is Life." He eyed it for a long moment, shifted it so that Dex could see, and turned to Liz, eyebrow raised.

She shrugged, eyes twinkling. "You aren't the only man who's been here, and Sid's isn't the only place I socialize. Take it or leave it."

Shaver laughed then, grabbing the jeans. "36/34? Big boy, that one," he called out, grinning. "What the hell am I supposed to do with these, make a tent?"

"They'll keep you warm until I sanitize yours," Liz giggled, slipping around to sit close at Shaver's side. She slid her hand over his still bare chest, fingers teasing soft hairs, and leaned in to whisper. "Easier to get in."

Dexter frowned. Shaver watched his friend staring into the tiny swirling eye of his glass, as though answers would shimmer to life on that glittering surface. Liz's entrance had shifted the moment subtly. For just an instant, the room changed; hard, cold rain splashed Shaver's face/matted his hair to his throat and he shivered, clutched by cold, sharp notes, ringing from scattered gravestones and echoing into the depths of his mind.

Reaching out, Shaver took his own drink, brought it quickly to his lips, and downed it, splashing a few drops on his cheek in his haste, bandaged fingers fumbling for a solid grip. He felt Liz leaning in, slender arm snaking around his shoulders to draw him gently closer. He held the glass near his lips for a moment, closed his eyes against the harsh bite of the corn whiskey, then lowered the glass slowly and watched as Dexter freshened it, sliding Liz's glass from the far side of his own.

"We don't need him, Dex." Shaver spoke very softly. "Just because he found a way to his music doesn't mean he could do the same for us. We have to do it for ourselves."

"Then why does it hurt so much?" Dex asked, spinning suddenly, eyes awash in pain. "Why is it that every time my mind replays that chorus, I itch like I've got the hives and my heart slows and skips. Fuck, some drummer, can't even keep my own body in sync."

"He stole it," Liz cut in. "Didn't you feel that?"

Shaver and Dex turned to her quickly.

"What do you mean?" Shaver asked. Something had tugged at his mind just then; her words had jostled it loose and tumbled him back. Exactly, stolen and claimed but not Brandt's. Brandt didn't play for Brandt anymore . . . that was the key. Brandt played pain. No way the fucker knew. The images, the funeral and the loss, Shaver's father, none of it. Dexter knew, and Liz, because they'd gone there . . . lived it through him . . . but not Brandt. Brandt had reached out and stolen that melody, those notes, bending them into some sort of psychic hook and trying to use it to latch onto Shaver's brain.

"Fuck," he said. "And I almost went. What would have happened to me? What would have happened to the song?"

Dexter seemed less than convinced, but he busied himself with the bottle and the glasses, lifting Shaver's and handing it to him, then Liz's as well.

"You better finish some of this," he said, voice low. "Don't leave it all for me."

Shaver nodded and held the glass, thinking. He could still hear the haunting strains of country-blues shivering through his mind, but he knew the answer wasn't that easy. It wasn't a Hank Williams cover tune they were after. It wasn't something you could sit back and figure out. It was something to be hunted and taken, discovered and overcome. He felt the old familiar burn slipping through his nerves, felt his fingers twitch, and quickly downed the whiskey. It was going to be hell not playing, but he knew now that he had to heal.

Dexter had lowered his own glass again, empty, fingers finding the surface of the table and tapping in gentle, nervous rhythms. His head was lowered, in thought or pain or both, and his eyes were closed. Shaver didn't break the silence, choosing instead to lean back against Liz's shoulder and rest. He tossed back the second glass of moonshine with a quick flourish, its white-hot bite and spreading warmth seeping through him and melting him back into the moist aftermath of the shower and Liz's embrace. Subtle shift and he felt her swallow, knew she had finished hers first, tensing against his back for an instant, then sighing softly.

Suddenly realizing that he was still wrapped in nothing but the towel, slipping off over his hips, he leaned forward, too-fast motion sending what still covered him sliding away. He dragged the jeans down and up, feeling the ridiculously large waist wrap about his thin frame, wishing for a belt, wishing he'd washed his own damned clothes and feeling more than a little foolish. Liz giggling behind him didn't help, and he dragged the t-shirt roughly over his head. Dexter paid no attention, busying himself making an art of refilling the glasses, his motions smooth and rhythmic.

Before he knew it, Shaver was leaning back again, barefoot in too-big jeans, chest proclaiming "Jazz is Life," to an uncaring world and downing his third drink. The soft lights of the room blurred at the edges and Liz's body became more comfortable and pliant, molding to him as she reached around and grabbed her own glass again.

Things shifted. The comfort Shaver had felt when he first entered the apartment seeped back in, but this time it wasn't his hand on the doorframe; it was the air, the sounds and sights, and the warm glow of the moonshine as Dexter continued to move his hands over the table, stacking and unstacking the glasses, tipping the bottle, crystal-drip fountain, now full, now gone, fire ebbing and flowing.

Too long since Shaver had had anything so strong. Last quick gulp and he settled back, closing his eyes, thoughts drifting to the rhythm of Dexter's motion and Liz's heartbeat. He floated, not focused on anything, caught up in a web of images that spun and wound about his thoughts. He slipped through memory to Sid's, back over the days/weeks—heard Brandt play, felt Synthia's resonating release, felt the cold rain wash his face and the music drain away. He saw his father's eyes, just for a second, raised his arm, as if to reach out and touch, found his hand filled with cool glass and sloshed himself and the couch with cool liquor, drained it without thought, cursing himself as the hot rush washed the images away cleanly, burning in and down.

"I'll find you," he whispered to the lost face, the untouched fingers. "I'll . . ."

Darkness slipped up and over, folding him tight and tugging him down. He felt Liz's arms draped lazily over his chest, her hair soft on his cheek as they leaned together. The last thing he heard was the soft clink of glasses being stacked, rhythmically, steadily filled, and drained.

Brandt and Synthia had crawled in from the rain and dark, stripped, and slid into her bed without a word, curling around one another and drawing the blankets tight and close. No question of anything but sleep.

Brandt's shivering had been hours in stopping, cold through to the heart, drained and his head pounding to the steady rhythm of pain denied. He'd not let them free, not let the notes pour out as they should, and all his strength had been spent on forcing his fingers to other notes.

Shaking, sweat pouring from him to dampen the sheets, teeth chattering and his mumbled apologies to Syn, whispered images. "This must be what it's like," he told her, "when you detox."

Her voice, soothing and soft. Shushing him like a child, long fingers stroking the sweat from him gently; more times than he could count or remember she had slipped away, only to return with a damp cloth, curling around him and holding him close. Some time in the night the world and the pain slipped away. Perhaps it was the first finger of light, crawling over the skyline and announcing the dawn, that released him. The pain slid and emptied back inside, compact and bearable, an icy ball of barbed-wire lodged in his gut. He didn't dream.

When he woke, Syn was curled over him, her hair soft on his shoulder and one arm draped around him protectively. He didn't want to move. His head pounded, his throat was dry, and his eyeballs ached. He had to piss so bad he was bent near-double, but he did not want to disturb her. His mind was clear enough to remember. She'd been there, taken care of him. He lay still as long as possible before slipping very carefully from beneath her arm. Syn rolled away with a sigh, the sheet drawing back to reveal the soft swell of one breast.

Brandt stood, naked, watching her for a moment, wondering. How they'd gotten to this point. Where they were going. Why he was such a fucking asshole. Turning, he left the room, moving to relieve the most pressing of nature's emergencies, his mind slipping ahead to coffee without shifting gears.

He was halfway into his second cup when Syn rolled over with a groan and called out.

"Brandt?"

He smiled, rising and pouring another cup. "Cream? Sugar?"

"Black. Strong."

Grinning, he picked up the cups and headed back into the bedroom.

"What time is it?" she asked groggily.

"No idea," Brandt replied almost cheerfully. He sat on the edge of the bed, holding her cup for her until she could orient herself and rise to a sitting position. Without a bit of self-consciousness, she slid into a cross-legged position, naked, accepting the cup gratefully.

Brandt stared openly as sensations he'd somehow avoided through a long night pressed close to her body manifested themselves. Syn watched him over her coffee, turning slightly, and smiling.

"Seems not all of you is dead," Syn said, sipping her coffee slowly and returning his gaze.

"No thanks to myself," he answered. Very softly, he added, "Thank you."

Syn's smile widened, and then she frowned. "It isn't like I have a choice."

The cups somehow made their way safe and empty to the floor, and Brandt was beside her, pulling her close. He drew her head to his shoulder, stroked her hair. He leaned down, breath hot and moist on her ear as he whispered to her. "We all have choices, whether it seems so or not."

She chose that moment to turn slowly and silence him with her tongue. She stroked up and down his chest with her long, tapered nails. For several hours, they managed to dull the pain. If any "ghosts" were watching, Syn's eyes were closed. If the pain was too much, it was numbed and redirected by a different sort of need, and release. They slept again, eventually, limbs entwined and sheets pulled tight, a soft, impotent shield against a world they were only just realizing as their own.

Brandt dreamed. He was walking alone down a narrow road, winding through tall trees. It was dark, and the moonlight filtered oddly through the branches, criss-crossing the trail like a pane of broken glass. There was a brighter light ahead, not silver-white like the moonlight, but deep and red, the coals in a long-burning fire, hidden in the pit where you could stare until the world blurred around you and disappeared.

Somehow, he knew he had to reach that light, but there was no time. He sensed eyes, thousands of eyes, glowing in the shadows to either side of the trail, staring out from beneath bushes and through the knotholes in logs, watching him from the low-hanging limbs of trees. He ignored them, quickening his steps. His guitar case dangled from his hand now, and he glanced down, surprised, tried to concentrate on it. Had he had it all along? Where had it come from?

The glow distracted him, glinting off the silver hasps of the case, and he stumbled forward, loping now, long, measured strides. The guitar case weighed him down, throwing off his rhythm and smacking painfully against his thigh. He heard his heartbeat echoing, thudding painfully, and his breath shortening.

Then it wasn't just his heart, but drums, huge, resonant drums, pounding faster and faster. Voices, hissing in and out among the slamming, nerve-jarring beats, licked at his senses. He couldn't make out the words, but images formed, blocking his view of the trail, and the light.

A young woman, withered, lying in her bed and wasting away. Drool dribbled from her lip, down over her chin.

A young black man rose, sweat glistening on his forehead and bare arms as he lurched, leaning into a leather harness, moving only a step before a long, leather lash bit deep into his shoulder blades, dropping him to his knees.

Knees, a multitude kneeling, voices chanting softly around a long, open trench, men in strange robes, eyes downcast, praying over a pile of naked flesh, arms, faces.

Brandt stumbled. The voices crashed in around him and he lunged, drawing the guitar up before him and falling, falling so long and far that he knew he'd reached the ground and passed through, guitar case clutched tightly, waiting for impact, waiting to shatter the instrument with his own weight. Waiting for the darkness to consume him and silence the pounding, the screaming, the searing pain burning him from the inside out.

Syn slapped him hard, shattering the dream world into tiny, brittle pieces, dropping away, leaving the light splintered, as the moonlight had been, drawing him to reality with a cold, focused snap of pain.

"Brandt. BRANDT! Let go, you're *hurting* me!"

The words sank in. Brandt shook his head, realized he was clutching . . . not the guitar. Not falling. Syn was wrapped in his arms, trapped beneath him, squirming to free herself. She drew back for a second shot at his head and he released her, rolling to the side and slamming his hands to his head.

Syn watched in consternation, letting her intended blow fall softly, stroking his cheek. He lay, head back on his pillow, eyes covered by his hands, which were pressed too tightly, fighting for release from . . .

"What, Brandt? What is it?"

He shook harder, turning away from her, and she pulled the sheet back over them, curling against his back and letting her arm wrap around him. No words were spoken, but slowly Brandt calmed. The shaking went first, hard fever-breaking tremors that wracked his entire frame, shivering through her. She heard his teeth chatter, and she held him tighter, wishing for blankets that were not there, knowing it was not the cold that made him shake. Slowly this stilled to uneven breathing. Syn felt the subtle shift to a different sort of tremor.

Brandt cried in her arms, wetting the pillow, feeling the icy pain diminish slowly, releasing his limbs, freeing his nerves, one by one. The voices echoed in his head, softer now, subdued, but constant. *Remember,* they said. *Always remember. Play.*

Wally's words echoed in the backbeat. *Crossroads, or the cross-hairs, one and the same, boy.*

When he was still, at last, Syn shook him gently.

"You have to play, Brandt. You have to let it out." Her voice choked a little. "It's killing you."

He shifted in her arms. A quick nod. No words, but he pressed back to her tightly.

Syn lay against him, sharing her heartbeat and her warmth, her hair soft against his shoulder. "Tonight," she said softly.

Coffee, as always, brought a different slant. Brandt cupped his fingers tightly around the tall "Red-eye," watching the swirling steam make mandala images on the surface. It was his second, and the caffeine was beginning to speak to his nerves and ripple through the tendons of his fingers. The voices were there, and the pain, but it was—different. The dream pain had smacked of retribution. This pain, the night's pain, was expectant. Potential energy versus kinetic. Energizing rather than numbing.

Syn sat across from him, a double-mocha latte steaming in her mug. Her leg was pressed tightly against his beneath the table, comforting and persistently—there. She gazed over his shoulder at an empty corner of the coffee shop. Brandt knew what she was watching, just not who. It was the same everywhere. He'd always wondered why she spent so much time concentrating on empty shadows and staring at blank walls. His own predilection for whiskey and self-destruction had prevented any serious inquiry. Now he was coming to take the *angels* for granted.

Syn watched his cup carefully, ready to signal the waitress if the level sank below what she deemed acceptable. They had had nothing else to drink.

"Where are we going?" Syn asked him at last, words formed to mock the question echoing in his mind.

Brandt started to tell her he had no idea, but stopped short. Bad enough that one of them worried. "Not sure. Everything seems to fall into place of its own accord these days. I thought I'd hit the streets, walk, and see what happened."

Syn's eyes sparked. He thought she was going to go off finally, good-old-bad-old days revisited, and scream him into submission in front of everyone in the place, but she kept her peace. Different times, different Syn. Everything different.

Brandt tipped the mug, letting the coffee drain down his

throat before it had a chance to grow cold or bitter. He rose, then, avoiding the same himself. His fingers itched, and the voices, always a low hum in the back of his mind, clamoring for attention. Five dollars on the table, a small trickle of change all that remained to slip back into his pocket as he turned toward the door and the growing darkness, Syn slipping in easily at his side. The bell over the door clanged as they slipped out.

The moon had risen, full and bright, lending an eerie illumination to the quiet streets. It was too late for business traffic, too early for the night to open its doors. Quiet time, and yet not quiet. Not exactly. From somewhere in the distance, against the fabric of reality, voices rose in song. Brandt stopped, cocking his head to the side, listening. It was coming from uptown, neighborhoods worse and worse as housing filtered away to concrete and high-rise corporate monuments to "progress." Nowhere Brandt would go, nor Syn. Nowhere where music would play.

Against the skyline, tall shadows danced, flickering with the wild abandon of images born of open flame.

"The park?" Syn asked the question, her words breaking the spell gently, not releasing Brandt, but including herself.

Brandt thought about it. Nodded. Without a word, he started forward, gripping his guitar case more firmly. No way to ignore the pull this time. They moved from street to street, sometimes waiting for the lights to shift, green "safeman" blinking happily at them, inviting them to cross, more often ignoring the lights completely. There was almost no traffic, and even less as they moved inward. There were no clubs in this part of the city, no night-spots or coffee-clubs, no college kids sharing wine and philosophy, or businessmen drowning depression and martinis in unison. There was concrete, darkness, glittering glass, and mirrored windows stretching to the clouds, graffiti-decked fences and alleys so dark they might have emptied into another dimension.

Syn slid closer as they walked, her arm circling Brandt's lower back and her hip soft against his, brushing as they moved. Neither spoke, but he saw her watching, always, followed her eyes more than once, but failed to see what she saw. He let his arm curl around her shoulder and pulled her closer.

The music grew steadily louder, shivering up and down Brandt's spine. It wasn't rock, not jazz, or anything he recognized at all. It was like being in church again, a small boy dressed to the nines in sharp-creased trousers and a bow tie, hundreds of adults gathering, raising their voices, harmony, discord, all at once joined in something that was not perfect, but was somehow very real.

They were two blocks from the park, and the shadows that had danced over the walls of the city loomed tall and menacing. There was a fire. Somehow, beyond city laws and safety ordinances, there was one *hell* of a bonfire in the park, and the music radiated from that point hungrily, drawing Brandt in, moth to that flickering flame.

Off to the right, softly, sound so faint Brandt nearly missed it, the song of a single harmonica broke through the pulsing beat. Brandt hesitated, nearly taking a tumble as Syn continued forward a step.

"What?" she asked, nearly snapping at him.

Brandt stared at her, shaking his head hard. The harmonica grew a little clearer.

"Wally?"

Syn returned his stare blankly, then turned again toward where 42nd Street would lead them to Main and the park beyond. Brandt didn't move to follow. He strained to extract the clean, crisp voice of the mouth harp from the reverberating insanity of the primal energy leaking from the dancing shadows ahead. Something was wrong. There were forces dragging at one another, a vortex of sound and energy. In its center, the eye of the proverbial storm, Brandt wavered, cursing softly under his breath as again and again Wally's song was stolen, or tossed aside.

Syn tugged on his arm insistently. "Come on, Brandt," she said. "It's time to play."

"Shhh." Brandt moved to shake her off, but she yanked harder, and that quick step put his legs in sync with the deeper song, washing the other away and down, burying it deep in his mind and dragging him ahead. Brandt's lips moved once, in a silent question, but there was no answer.

They reached the end of 42nd Street and stepped straight onto Main without a glance to the right or left. The park was alive, bodies shifting back and forth, leaping and turning, and the flames shivering up from the bonfire in the center.

"Just like in high school," Syn breathed.

Brandt turned to glance at her for a second. "What kind of fucking school did you *go* to?"

Syn glared at him. "Like the bonfires at Homecoming. You know, football? Rah rah?"

Brandt stopped again, pulling her closer. "Not like any fucking pep rally I remember."

Syn didn't answer that. The flames danced higher as shadowy figures ran in from the sides, tossing wood and broken furniture onto the blaze. It was a riot, out of control, and yet there were no sirens. The city shifted and blurred, flickering light from the blaze dancing off mirrored walls and endless empty windows. The moment cried out for police, for fire trucks and screaming megaphones. It cried out, and nobody answered.

From the shadows near the flame, long legs appeared, polished boots and a full-length trailing coat. Brandt stood, watching, Syn melting closer to his side. The figure tugged loose from the denser shadows, half-lit by firelight, half-dark. The shrouded figure half-smiled, flashing bright teeth and dark eyes glittering. Nothing humorous in that smile. Nothing warm, or inviting. And still, without knowing why, Brandt took a slow step forward, and smiled in return.

"Was wonderin' if you'd be stopping by tonight, or tomorrow, boy. All the same when you play the game, you dig?"

The voice was low, deep and resonant. The slang, bad movie drivel from days so long past Brandt couldn't place the year, dripped with authenticity. Brandt shivered. Like the dancing and the music, the impossible mid-city bonfire, it was wrong. Just wrong. No other word fit, and no modifier heightened the clarity. Wrong.

"What's the matter, son? Cat got that silver tongue?"

The man was close enough for Brandt to make out his features, long hair flowing back over the collar of his dark jacket, eyes gunmetal gray and flickering with a fire that challenged the heat of the bonfire beyond. The stranger's hair was either silver, or bright white. He walked with the grace and precision of a predator, stalking.

"Who are you?" Brandt asked, his voice weak and the words empty.

"Who don't matter none, son, and what . . . well," soft chuckle and hand extended slowly, diamond glint from the pinky and nails long and meticulously manicured, "that *what* might take a bit of talk-time we jus' don't have. You bring that guit-fiddle to play, or you just carry it around to balance a club-foot?"

Syn laughed nervously, and Brandt glanced down at his

guitar. He knew he had to play. Didn't really matter, he supposed, where, when, or even what. That would work itself out.

The man turned, expansive gesture of welcome as he waved one arm toward the fire. Brandt fell into step behind him, Syn stumbling along beside him.

The music surrounded them, a solid force that buffeted and directed motion. Brandt felt himself matching his steps to the rhythm, purposefully fought for discord, and nearly tripped Syn in the process. They moved from the shadows into the light of the fire.

Men and women moved around them in hot-flashes of motion and light. Laughter, dark and enticing, floated in from all sides, taunting and teasing, inviting them to join . . . something. The music.

Brandt turned to the stranger. "Won't hear a thing over that if I play."

The man whirled, his coat whipping up behind him with a flourish, and he smiled again. He pointed to one side, and Brandt turned to follow, nearly gasping as he saw the portable generator, and the amp. It had not been there moments before, of that he was certain . . . or fairly certain. He tugged free of Syn's embrace gently, taking a step forward.

"Brandt . . ." Syn called out to him, only a foot away, but her voice seemed to come from another world.

He turned back to her, but before he could speak, one of the shadow figures had stepped from the darkness and was pressing a bass into her hands. Not a Fender, like her own instrument. Not electric at all. It stood taller than she, glistening gold in the firelight. Brandt stared as Syn wrapped her slender fingers around the neck of the string bass. He'd not even known she could play one, but the fascination in her eyes and the easy way she plucked at the strings spoke of familiarity. Desire, even. The instrument followed Syn's own slender curves, as though made for her, and her alone.

Around them, the music slowed. It didn't stop, not exactly, but grew quiet and expectant. There was a buzz in the air, vibrant and quivering with promise. The moment before a storm, sky blue-green and filled with power, or that hushed instant at the beginning of a concert, half-whispered roar from the crowd settled in like white-noise.

Brandt walked to the amp, leaned to place his case on the ground and unsnapped it, drawing the instrument out carefully. He slid the strap in place over his shoulder and turned, reaching for the cord he had somehow known would be there, crackling with potential sound from its connection to the amplifier, and the dark, squat stack of speakers beyond.

Turning his back to the amps, and the fire, Brandt tentatively stroked his fingers over the strings, hearing the ripple of rich, deep notes flowing up and outward, the soft sigh of expectancy in the air. The stranger was moving toward him again, oily-bright smile wide.

"Told you *you* could only play the pain, didn't he?"

Brandt hesitated, frowning. "Who?"

"You know who. Old fool told you it was your *responsibility* to play, your *curse*. Said you'd go mad if you didn't play them all free. Been too many times down that road, son, know the pitch. Know the pain, not insane, dig?"

Brandt watched the stranger, not answering. Then, fingers pressed tightly to the strings, not letting them move, or sound, he asked, "Who are you?"

Laughter, deep, dark, penetrating the backdrop of rhythm and sound, echoing off the buildings and shivering with the chill, empty depth of eternity. The man's hand dropped slowly, and drums began to beat, pounding deep and pulsing through the air to tease the hairs standing on the back of Brandt's neck. The rhythm was powerful and insistent. Brandt fought it, pressing his fingers more tightly to the strings. He spun to Syn, but it was too late to speak, or to warn. She was caressing the bass, fingers sliding up and down the polished neck of the instrument, and as she began to pluck those strings, the sound rippled, rich and decadent, catching at Brandt's nerves.

His fingers slipped. He glanced around the clearing. The bodies, none with a face, or name, ornaments on a backsplash of sound and flame, were moving again. Synthia's eyes were closed, and with each roll of the drums she wound her notes more perfectly into that sound. Brandt watched her for a moment—entranced. The grace and hunger masking her features was intoxicating.

Then the itch in his fingers flashed to a burn and his eyes widened.

"Play, boy," the stranger said softly, though that voice carried over and through the song. "Play that pain, new pain, pain no one has ever known. Show us the way beyond, boy. I love a good song."

Brandt felt the sound rip from his heart. His fingers slid over the strings, patterns emerging, chords and discord, melody and harmony. There were others, voices, instruments, but for Brandt, only the strings. The inner voices were still. The pain that had built and wound itself around his heart had faded in that instant, driven back and down by the sound, the clear, dark sound that erupted from the amplifier at his back.

He felt the control slipping from him, felt the notes spiraling down into the blazing pits that had been that stranger's eyes. With an effort beyond any he could recall,

Brandt gripped the strings, tightly, still-birthed notes dying, choked and barren. The sounds around him rose from song to full-throated howl, and from a distance, low and deep, the harmonica played once more.

Brandt shook his head, turning to Synthia. She was not looking. Her eyes were closed, head thrown back, and her fingers flew over the strings of the bass. It was so large, dominating her form in ways that her Fender never could have, stealing her motion and her beauty.

Brandt felt her essence leaking into the polished wood and gleaming metal strings.

"No," Brandt breathed. The notes of the harmonica grew clearer, and the dark stranger turned to him, moving closer, eyes/lips curled into a snarl of rage. Brandt reached back, yanked the guitar cord from the amp, and began to play. He closed his eyes, ignored the stranger, Syn's hypnotic bass, the pounding of dancing feet and the sharp crackle of the bonfire. He concentrated. As the harmonica grew closer and clearer, he dropped his mind and fingers into that sound, drawing the notes from deeper within his heart. The voices, first a murmur, then a roar, surged up and out, dragging his hands and his mind along for the ride.

He felt no heat from the fire, very suddenly. He did not feel the shiver of drums, or the ripple of Synthia's bass. Nothing but his fingers, the notes, Wally's notes, and the voices, their pain shifting from emotion to notes and back again, tears streaming down his cheeks and his fingers, flying now, then slowing, then slurred and broken, then clear again, and still he played. When the rain came, lightning crashing and thunder rolling across the sky, echoing through the streets, he stopped, dropping to his knees. Spent.

It was a long time before he opened his eyes.

SIX

The rain had returned, and wind whipped Brandt's hair about his face, matting the soaked strands across his cheeks. He shivered and opened his eyes. Nothing. No fire. No dancers, and no sound. Not even the harmonica cried out to him. His thoughts grew clearer, and he turned, rising with a stumble and a sharp cry.

"Syn!"

She was lying in the mud a few feet away. Syn's arms and legs were curled tight to her body, a fetal ball of silent negation. Brandt stepped closer, dropping once more to the mud, kneeling at her side. Her eyes were closed, her face drawn back in a death-mask rictus of pain and denial.

"Syn?" Brandt repeated softly. He reached out, trailing his finger over her cheek and down to her throat. Soft pulse, skittering beat as if running from something, too fast for sleep. Brandt slid his arms under her, began to lift, then cursed. Gently laying her back in the mud, he rose quickly.

His guitar still hung from his neck. The wood and strings were soaked, mud splattering the finish and caking the edges. No way he could carry her this way. He staggered back to the case, slid the guitar into place, ignoring the probable damage. His hands worked the snaps, numb and slippery with cold rain. Rising once more, he turned to Syn.

The illumination of a nearby streetlight cut through the now driving rain to paint her features pale white, like death. Harlequin images danced before Brandt's eyes, and for a long, vertiginous moment the past washed over him. The

Ferris wheel loomed, upside-down death-faced clown scowling at him from above. He saw the old woman, and the cards. Brandt covered his eyes.

With a soft curse, he knelt once more, sliding his arms under Synthia and lifting. At first it was too much, and he nearly dropped her, falling to the mud at her side. Brandt closed his eyes, concentrated, and tried again. This time he managed to roll Syn's inert form against his chest, rising unsteadily and snagging the guitar case as he moved. She wasn't so heavy, once he was up, and he turned, making his way back toward 42nd Street.

The rain made it nearly impossible to see, but somehow he crossed Main without incident and made the relative shelter of the buildings lining 42nd Street. He leaned into the arch beneath one of the doorways, blinking to regain some of his sight. Already his arms ached, and he knew he'd never make it to Syn's apartment. Not like this. Syn murmured against his chest and he felt his heart constrict.

Visions of fire, slick polished wood, and flashing fingers filled his mind. He fought them back, humming a tune, any tune, to banish the invading sound. Syn's eyes, her face, the deep-seated hunger as she'd arched to that instrument. Brandt fell against the stone wall at his back, head smacking smartly and a hot flash of pain dragging him back to the moment. Syn murmured, and he watched her face.

"I'll get you home, pretty lady," he whispered. "Somehow, I'll get us both home."

He staggered back into the rain, barely avoiding cracking Syn's head on the wall as he spun. Head lowered, he plowed into the pouring rain. He was concentrating so hard on dragging one foot in front of the next, that he didn't notice the sleek, black limousine as it pulled in just behind him, matching his pace. The lights were dimmed, and beyond the water-streaked windshield, only the dark silhouette of a driver could be made out. Very slowly, the back window began to lower.

Brandt's legs felt like lead. His pants were soaked, his shoes dragged stone-heavy and cold, numbing his toes. It should not be so cold. It was winter, sure, but it was California. Brandt hadn't felt cold like this since his childhood. It sapped his strength, and every few steps he had to hitch back his shoulders and draw Syn closer to him. The ache in his legs spread slowly to his arms, and his teeth chattered crazily.

The nose of the limousine slid slowly forward, moving even with Brandt, then slightly ahead. He didn't notice, not at first. He slogged on, barely making a single step now between shifting and clutching at Syn, fighting gravity and fatigue not to let her slam to the wet concrete beneath his feet. Coal bright eyes watched from the interior of the limo.

"Gettin' heavy, ain't she, boy?"

The words sliced through rain and fatigue. Brandt stopped, Syn clutched to his chest, heart hammering suddenly. He didn't turn, not immediately.

"What the fuck did you do to her?" Brandt asked, still not turning, voice low. He cursed as the cold brought a tremble to his lip. "What the fuck did you try to do to *me?*"

Cold laughter, and the limo started rolling forward again, slowly.

Brandt watched, cold anger gripping his heart. He strode forward, fatigue forgotten.

"Answer me you bastard!" he screamed into the rain. Syn shifted against him, stirring, and he slowed, fighting to compensate for the shift in her weight. The limo didn't slow.

The stranger's face appeared, slipping out the open window to turn, steel-gray eyes locking to Brandt's own. "You need a ride, boy?"

Brandt faltered. He glanced down at Syn. He shivered. It was nearly a mile to her apartment. Syn's face was turning blue from the cold, and her breath was shallow.

Brandt lifted his gaze. The stranger was grinning, and in that empty, emotionless expression, Brandt found his strength. His own gaze hardened, and his shoulders straightened. He stepped forward, turning his eyes to the sidewalk.

"Fuck you," he said. "I'd walk through hell and back before I'd ride with you."

"That can be arranged, boy," the stranger's voice floated back, followed by a flood of dark laughter. "Long walk, son, but it can be *arranged*."

Brandt's gaze snapped up. The limo was gone, but miraculously, a cab slid through the shadows and came to rest against the curb. Brandt lurched to the curb, grabbing the door handle and dragging it open. He slid Syn in carefully, shoulders and arms straining with the effort. Sliding in behind her, he turned to the driver.

"Thanks, man. God, thank you."

"No need to thank me son," Wally chuckled. "Headin' your way anyhow. You take care 'a that one. She's gonna need you like you don' believe. Like you never seen. You don't let her down, hear?"

Brandt didn't speak. He was busy arranging himself, Syn, and the guitar case in the back seat of the cab.

"You could have come a little sooner," he growled at last. "If you're on our side—my side—why is it that you only show up when things are *already* fucked?"

"Don't got to show up at all, boy. Your song. Your pain. You worry 'bout that girl, and forget yourself a while. Be good for you."

Wally drove on in silence, and it was only moments later

that the cab pulled up before the door to Synthia's apartment. Brandt slid out the door, drawing the guitar case after him. Very carefully, he slid in and wrapped an arm around Syn, dragging her from the seat and back over his shoulder. Wally made no move to help.

"You be careful, boy. Every crossroads has four ways to go. Back ain't never been right for anyone, and those two sides can be real temptin'. You keep your eyes pointed forward."

Brandt paid no attention. He turned, gritted his teeth, and lifted Syn to one shoulder and the guitar strap to the other. There was a moment's imbalance where Syn shifted, and Brandt lurched, where he believed either she, the guitar, or both would crash to the wet cement, but with a superhuman effort, he stabilized them all.

The cab pulled away from the curb and Brandt started up the dark stairway, one slow step at a time.

When Shaver slipped out Liz's bedroom door and back into the main room of the apartment, he found Dex stacking again. Coffee cups. At least a dozen, pyramid sequences of white porcelain and colorful logos rising toward the ceiling and then descending, one cup at a time. As Shaver entered, Dex looked up with a grin and shrugged.

"You should see my place, man. Stacks everywhere. Counted, organized. Can't help myself. Sometimes it makes things easier, sometimes it keeps me from losing my lunch over the pressure of just being here. You know?"

"I wish I did," Shaver answered, stepping closer, snagging the top cup and heading for the kitchen. "All I can do to release is play." He paused for a moment, and then continued. "Can't play right now. Don't know what else to do."

The sound of liquid pouring drew Dexter's concentration

from his incomplete pyramid. He rose, grabbing a second cup from the monument to nothing, and joined Shaver in the kitchen.

"It's fresh," he said as he slipped through the door. "I made it, right after I made and drank the last one."

Shaver eyed his friend, poured both cups full, and started laughing. "You don't fucking pile the cups to ease tension. You do it because you'll explode if you don't."

"Well," Dexter grinned, "that too."

A sound from the next room drew both their gazes to the door, and Liz came in, wrapped in a bathrobe, eyes bleary, but smiling. She ran her hand back through her hair slowly, letting it fall over her shoulders.

"There better be enough for me," she said.

Shaver laughed. "You'll have to get a cup from in there," he pointed with the coffee pot. "Dexter was—anxious."

Liz went back into the other room for a cup, and Shaver stared at the pot, held at arm's length. He winced slightly at the pain that grip cost him, but that pain brought a smile. He couldn't have lifted the pot at all the day before. Flexing his fingers and biting his lip against the sharp pain, he held the pot still as he waited for Liz to return. When she did, he very carefully poured her a full cup and set the pot aside. Shaver tried to hide the wince, but not quite.

"Oh." Liz moved quickly, at his side before he could raise a hand to negate the sympathy.

"It's okay," Shaver said. "Really. It's better."

Liz nodded.

Shaver grabbed his cup, lifted it to his lips, and drank quickly. The coffee had cooled enough to allow a long swallow.

"So what now?" Dexter cut in. "You don't want to listen when Brandt calls; what do we do next?"

There was a bitter, hollow emptiness in the question. An emptiness that Shaver wasn't sure he could fill. He poured a second cup of coffee and moved back into the other room, setting it carefully on the table and plopping heavily on the couch.

"It isn't like I told Brandt to fuck off," he said, exhaling the words slowly. "I just want to understand before I make any choices that screw up my life forever. Don't you?" Shaver turned to glare at Dexter. "I mean, *fuck*, he is a drunken asshole most of the time. Why do you all of a sudden see him as some kind of messiah? Why do we *need* a messiah?"

Dexter slid back onto the couch, setting his cup aside and reaching for those that remained, subtracting the three and beginning a new pyramid, shorter and more squat, fingers moving quickly and surely. Shaver watched, mesmerized. The silence spread, broken only by the soft *clink* of porcelain as the cups were carefully placed, meticulously arranged.

"How many?" Liz's voice from the doorway.

"Thirty-five." Dexter never looked up.

Liz stepped closer, swinging and spinning down beside Shaver, curling in close. It was a territorial motion, a question. No words, just emotion. Shaver slid his arm around her shoulders and drew her gently against him. It was all the answer she needed.

"We need a singer," Shaver said. "We need a singer, bass, maybe another guitar."

Dexter looked up very suddenly, almost dropping the cup he was stacking. He met Shaver's gaze for a moment, then looked away, returning to his stacking. After what seemed an eternity, he answered. "Don't know if I can do that. Don't know if I can play with someone else, listen to them gab about contracts and record deals and gigs. Don't even know *what* we would play. You think we could do the old stuff without Brandt? Look at how it ended up with Calvin."

Shaver shrugged. "The old stuff worked for them. They found something, we didn't. I'm not really worried about playing the old stuff."

"What then?" Dexter asked, placing the final cup on the new, shortened version of his pyramid. The cups were aligned perfectly, each exactly the same distance from one as from the others. Patterns.

That pattern clicked in Shaver's mind, synapse-flash burst of inspiration. The clink of the last cup echoed in his mind. Eyes closed and leaning back, he let his mind drift into that sound. He vaguely felt Liz tensing in his grip, realized he had squeezed too hard, ignored it, and drifted deeper. So close. He was so close to—something.

Liz shook him and he tugged away from her. She didn't release, but she didn't shake him again either. Shaver could hear Dexter's voice, far away, drifting. He heard another *clink* and knew the pyramid was unraveling. Something in that was wrong. He lurched, dragging free of Liz, hand outstretched to stop Dexter from undoing what was done, reaching and brushing the cups and then losing his balance.

He felt Liz gripping his arm, leaning back against his motion. He felt the cups, smooth, shifting, tumbling, and bouncing off his wrist and forearm. He heard Dexter's voice, loud, insistent, and incomprehensible. He heard Liz screaming. He heard the clatter of the cups, the shattering, and the reverberating pattern of that sound.

The table was hard, and Shaver landed across it, arm stretched back and held, chest smashing into crushed cups and shattered shards as his mind peaked on a chord and blanked, leaving him to dangle and finally fall into a dark pit of silence.

Shaver woke to new pain. Not his hands, or his fingers. His jaw ached. His lip was puffy, and his shoulder felt at if it had been kicked hard by a steel-toed size nineteen work boot. Both shins were sore. He opened his eyes and, seeing Liz, he smiled.

"Damn you," she breathed, slapping him lightly on his sore chin and eliciting a soft moan. "Stop that, Shaver. No more. Stay with me, or I swear to God I'm out of here."

"Where am I?" Shaver asked, drawing his fingers to his chin, rubbing gingerly and trying to sit up. The room came into slow focus. He was on the couch, dragged/lifted/who knew. The coffee table lay canted on one side, the tower of cups a shattered wreck.

Dexter stood over Shaver, behind Liz and to the side. His eyes were full of questions he couldn't quite form. His fingers were in constant motion, in his pockets, out, slapping lightly on his thighs.

"Sorry I broke the cups," Shaver said. He turned his gaze to Liz. "Sorry because they were yours," turning back to Dexter, "and sorry because you are going insane with nothing to stack."

"I don't care about the cups," Liz said. Her voice broke slightly, and she dropped closer, leaning across his chest and wrapping him in her arms. "Just don't leave me like that again. What *happened*, Shaver?"

Shaver sat up slowly, all the new aches and pains gripping at his arms and legs and face with icy little bug-fingers, distracting his thoughts. "I'm not sure. I heard something, that much I know for certain. And I saw things, patterns." Shaver glanced at the pile of rubble on the floor that had been the coffee cups and frowned. "It was when you started to *un*stack the cups, Dex. Don't know what, but something in the pattern, the numbers, hit me right between the eyes. Then I saw you reaching out to undo it, piece by piece, unraveling the pattern. I needed to see it, to understand. When I tried to stop you, that's when things got crazy."

"They were just cups," Dex said, frowning. "A fucking pile of cups."

Shaver nodded, bringing his hand to his forehead and closing his eyes. "I heard something too. It rose out of the pattern."

"The pyramid?" Dex asked.

"Not sure if that's it, exactly. You were so precise. Every one of those damned cups was exactly the same distance from every other. The designs on the sides blended, the motion of your hand as you placed the last one. Fuck . . . I don't *know,* man."

Liz stood and turned toward the kitchen. Shaver leaned against the back of the couch, his legs sliding off the side. His stomach lurched crazily, and he nearly lost what little coffee he'd managed to retain. Liz came back, broom and dustpan brandished like weapons in a medieval joust. Shaver swung his legs back up, out of the way. Liz attacked the pile of rubble that had been her cups in silence.

Shaver watched her, noting the tight, scrunched muscles in her shoulders and the set of her lip. He slid his legs off the couch again and rose shakily, moving toward her. Carefully making his way around the shattered bits of porcelain and pottery, he moved up behind her, wrapping her in a hug. Liz froze—for a moment Shaver thought she would pull away—then melted back against him with a moan.

"What are we going to do?" she asked. "What if you keep falling, and going away? What if something's wrong with you, Shaver? Have you thought about that?"

Shaver spun her gently, meeting her gaze. "There is nothing like that wrong with me. I am not going anywhere without you. This," he tapped his forehead with one finger, "is fine. We all three know there is some strange shit going down, and this is all part of it. So Brandt finds his peace in a song, and Synthia freaks out on stage, walks out of the bar and the band and our lives. I see things, they hit me harder. Doesn't mean I'm losing it, *or* you."

Liz nodded gently. She tugged herself free of his grip and finished sweeping up the cup fragments, avoiding Shaver's gaze. She brushed the last of the dust and debris into the plastic mouth of the dustpan and turned away again, moving to the kitchen. Shaver took a seat on the couch and watched her, letting his mind drift back. He could see Dexter's hand reaching for the cups, could feel himself shifting and stretching in futile negation. The world shifting.

Deep inside he heard it. The chord. The blending of note over note and back again, winding softly through the sounds of Liz in the kitchen and Dexter, who had found a bag of paperclips, snick-snick-snicking them into a huge chain, winding one to another and blending the chains. Creating a pattern.

Shaver closed his eyes and brought his hands to his ears. The world shimmered around him, wavered, then grew still. He heard Liz returning, her footsteps too loud, reverberating in his head. He fought the nausea and won, rising with a lurch.

"I need more coffee," he said.

Dexter grinned sheepishly, waving his paperclip dream catcher in an arc that dramatically brought the attention of all in the room to the coffee table, where the cups no longer rested.

Shaver started laughing. "Not here," he said. "My treat at the Bean & Buzz. We still have a lot to talk about."

Liz eyed him suspiciously. "You gonna stay with us this time?"

Shaver nodded. "I have to."

Liz left the room then, moving to her bedroom with purposeful strides. Shaver watched, confused, and Dexter returned to his paperclips. The pattern he'd created was circular, growing, concentric ring within concentric ring. Long, trailing chrome-plated feathers dangled. A glittering Christmas tinsel dream catcher, incomplete, as though there was room for things to slip through.

Dexter glanced up at Shaver, shrugging helplessly. "There aren't any more paperclips."

"We'll find some more," Shaver replied.

Liz reentered the room then. She had a small case in her hand. It was black, covered in stickers with the names of bands so closely placed and overlapping that Shaver couldn't make out more than a jumble of letters. Liz's knuckles were white on the handle, but she walked with purpose.

"Let's go get that coffee," she said.

Shaver started to ask her about the case, stopped himself, and nodded, turning toward the door. Dexter moved ahead of them, removing paperclips from one feather of the dream catcher and weaving them carefully into the next, rippling the design around the perimeter of the circles. Shaver stepped in front of his friend, gritted his teeth, and turned the knob on the door. The pain was only a soft ghost of what he'd feared, and he smiled. Already his mind was shifting ahead to his guitar.

SEVEN

Brandt sat in front of the one low window in Syn's apartment, staring through the rain-spattered glass. His fingers slid idly over the strings of his guitar. Syn lay curled on her bed, blanket death-gripped about her. Brandt turned now and then, his gaze tracing her curves beneath the covering and his eyes seeing only what played across the inner tragedy screen theater in his mind.

He played, but was not aware of the notes. His fingers walked pathways of their own, drawing notes in slow, painful strings and rippling eddies of emotion. Beyond the rain-washed window, the sun was rising over the skyline. Brandt couldn't see it through the storm, but the darkness faded by degrees to shades of gray.

He knew he had to sleep. Sometime soon, exhaustion would claim him, and he knew from experience that if he passed out with the guitar in his lap, it was a fifty-fifty proposition whether it would be playable when he woke up. Too much was at stake, and most of it seemed to ride on his fingertips, and where he chose to place them. Here, and the pain subsided to a dull ache; there, and he felt everything shift toward a dark, glowing flame. Silent, and the pressure built swiftly, driving his mind one way or the other without the convenience of thought. There was no middle ground, and in the back of Brandt's mind the upside-down harlequin image grinned at him from the Ferris wheel, taunting.

He slid the guitar from his lap and rose shakily. Too much coffee, no sleep. The case was still open and he leaned, slipping the guitar in and flipping the lid closed with finality. Nothing he could play now would make a difference. The voices had quieted, and he could only hear the faintest echo of laughter.

Told you you had to play the pain, didn't he, son?

The words came back to him, again and again. What had those words meant? Were they an offer of a solution, or another trap? Brandt walked to the bed and rolled in behind Syn, slipping the sheet and blanket over himself and pressing close to her back. Nothing could erase the sight of her and that bass from his mind. Her eyes, the hunger, the beauty of the sound—the empty, vacant sensation in his heart when he'd seen her crumpled in the mud.

Had he caused that? If he'd played what they wanted, would the two of them be together, happy and awake instead of cowering and shivering, hiding from the waking world? Was he a fool? Wally seemed so sincere, but what had he brought to them? Pain. He'd brought pain like Brandt had never known.

Brandt felt Synthia shiver against him, and he wrapped his arm around her, wishing he'd pulled the blinds tight before climbing into the bed. The sun was growing brighter, fighting valiantly through the haze and mist. It would be glaring, soon, high in the sky and sliding across the room to where they lay.

Brandt wondered where Shaver and Dexter were, what they were doing. He let his thoughts slip back. He'd been a fool to try and draw them to him with the music. All he'd ever offered them was pain. So, his solution to reuniting the band? More pain. Personal pain. Pain that had been drawn from somewhere Brandt didn't even understand. He had known it as Shaver's, had known the reaction it would bring. That hadn't mattered at the time. Shaver hadn't mattered. All that had mattered was that Brandt had felt the power flowing through him, had known what to play, how to play it, and that Shaver had come.

That pain had gotten away from Brandt. It wasn't the same as what the voices brought, long dead and filtered through time. Shaver's pain was real, and present, and Brandt hadn't, in the end, known how to play through it. There had been no *ghosts* to guide him, no visions to make him understand what and why he'd played. Brandt had focused on his own selfish desires, and in the end it had fallen short. Shaver needed more than that to answer his pain, needed something real and permanent. Brandt had offered only a return to things past, but without knowing the story, and the conclusion, the song had faltered and died.

Brandt's eyelids fluttered and he drifted.

Could have fixed it, son.

The words slid from the recesses of Brandt's mind, barely registering as sleep slowly claimed him.

Could have taken that pain and owned it, molded it. In the end, pain, no pain, it was always your choice. Depends on the song, boy, only on the song. No past, no future, only you. You are the key.

The words echoed, then drifted away. Brandt fought a futile war with gravity, trying to keep his eyelids propped open long enough to understand, but it was not to be. Darkness claimed him in a rush, drowning memory and thought.

In the chair where Brandt had been sitting, Wally watched the sun rise. The light slipped in over the window sill and ate at his image, but the old man ignored it. He rocked steadily, up and back, chin nodding in time to some hidden rhythm. Moments later, he pulled the harmonica from his pocket and began to play softly. Tears ran down his grizzled cheeks, and he closed his eyes.

On the streets below, the city was coming to life. Cars slid past, leaving a hiss and mist of leftover rain in their wake. Horns honked in the distance, and the roar of city bus traffic rattled the window. On the sidewalk, unheeded, they rose. First one, then another and ten more. Eyes filled with remorse and feet shuffling forward toward the walls of the apartment complex. The music called them, and the sun ate at their existence with relentless fervor, making of them no more than wavering heat-mist hints of human form against a sun-stained backdrop.

Wally shifted the notes, bending his mind to the task. He slipped easily from standard blues progressions into deep country. He reached across the years to one long gone with mental fingers and drew him forth. Robert Johnson, Hank Williams, it was all the same. Those below watched the window, faces upturned, eyes accusing. Wally didn't open his eyes.

There was too much at stake this time, and the boy on the bed behind him was the one in need. The boy, and the girl.

Wally played, and he rocked, and the walls reflected the gray half-light of the morning over and around a host of eerie shadows. The mist rising from the rain-damp streets, no longer a shapeless mass of cloud, teemed with half-seen forms and shivered with intent. They slipped from alleys, stepped from doorways in ghost-buildings that drifted over the real-world facade of the present. The skyline lowered slowly, and the cluttered jumble that was San Valencez crumbled to reveal another city, another San Valencez, or the blend of many. The sounds of automobiles passing faded slowly, then died. In the distance, a dog howled, low and mournful. The sound wailed in counterpoint to the notes of Wally's harmonica.

Wally opened his eyes at last. He didn't quit playing, but now he watched. His eyes misted again, and he blinked back the tears. This was his city now. Again. This was the San Valencez that had given him life and music, love and so much more. As he stopped playing, at last, the image shivered and failed, remaining only as half-seen flashes against the harsh, solid backdrop of time.

Wally rose, slipped the harmonica into his hip pocket, and turned to glance over to where Brandt and Synthia lay, huddled tightly together, sharing warmth.

"Gave you a day, maybe, boy," Wally muttered. "Can still play their pain. Can still make 'em quiet now and again, but not like I used to. Pretty soon, I'll be like them, fading in and out, looking for the one who can set things right and give me rest. You be there for me, blues-boy. You be there when ol' Wally needs another drink."

Wally spun slowly away and moved to the door. As he went, he faded. Not like he walked through the wall, more like the wall faded, changed, and didn't exist by the time his long strides brought him to and through it.

On the bed, Synthia murmured softly, raised her head, and blinked. She couldn't quite bring the room into focus, but something was wrong. The walls were different, the apartment larger. Someone was opening and closing the door, and yet, it wasn't her door, but one several rooms down the hall toward the stairs. She raised herself on one arm, unable to extricate herself from Brandt's grip.

"Wait," she called out, struggling to sit. "Wait, I . . ."

The door closed behind whoever it was with a decisive click. The world skewed violently, and Synthia leaned over the side of the bed dizzily, nearly vomiting from the vertigo. Brandt stirred, trying to draw her closer and she batted at him futilely, managing to roll free and slip off the side of the mattress, dropping painfully to the floor on her hip.

"Shit," she mumbled, rolling to her knees and dropping her head to her hands. Syn heard Brandt sitting up behind her, mumbling sleepily. She wished he'd wait. She couldn't make sense of his words, and the images she'd woken to played through her mind over and over, daring her to open her eyes.

Brandt had swung his legs off the side of the mattress. She felt him close behind her, and she reached back, her palm pressing to his leg, pushing him away, and yet . . . maintaining that contact.

"Wait," she whispered. "Please."

For once in the history of their time together, Brandt listened to her. He grew quiet, and as he did so, the world refocused. Syn remembered the bonfire with a sudden lurch of nausea, nearly losing herself in that image, then drawing back. She could feel the smooth, polished wood of the bass where her fingers had caressed the neck, the cold, stabbing ice that had been the strings, shivering and vibrating at her touch. His eyes, that dark stranger, and the deep rumble of his voice. The music.

Syn opened her eyes with a snap. Her skin was coated in cold, clammy sweat despite the chill in the air. The walls were normal. The door was closed. Brandt stared at her with an expression that hovered between concern and bewilderment.

Syn ignored him, sweeping her gaze around the room. Nothing. Not a bit of anything out of place.

"What's wrong?" Brandt asked at last. "What are you looking for?"

"Someone was here," she answered softly. "Someone

was here, just leaving as I woke. Didn't you hear it?"

Brandt shook his head. "It would have taken a tank breaking through the wall for me to hear it," he said, rubbing his eyes. Rising, he headed for the kitchen. "You got coffee in here?"

Synthia didn't answer. She had slipped to her feet and moved to the wall, running her fingernails gently over the surface and staring intently. Nothing. It was just a wall. No ghosts, no angels . . . nothing.

She turned away, moving to the window. It was still misty outside, but the sun was fighting its way valiantly through the low clouds. Syn stopped. They were everywhere. Hundreds, thousands of them. They stood, lined up in ranks, their necks craned toward her window, eyes closed. Silent. They weren't watching her. They were watching the window.

Behind them, the city wavered. One moment Syn saw the familiar, comfortable surroundings of her apartment, her world; the next she saw other places, more spread out, shorter. She watched as horse-drawn buggies rolled slowly down streets of cobbled stone and dirt, shifted her gaze to find men in austere, black clothing slipping out the doors of dusty saloons. Then it was morning, and the taxicabs honked incessantly at traffic unable to move regardless of the noise, and it was too much. Syn crumpled, falling by sheer luck against the arm of the chair where Brandt, and then Wally, had serenaded the street not long before. She collapsed across it, out before she struck. The sound brought Brandt on the run.

Too late to break her fall, Brandt gathered Synthia up into his arms and carried her quickly to the bed, laying her back softly. Her features were pale, death-white and lifeless. He stroked her cheek with his finger, watching to see if she would stir. Nothing.

Leaving Synthia sprawled across the bed, Brandt moved back to the window. He glanced outside again. There was nothing to see but the damp, gray streets. Traffic moved slowly. The rain was gone, and the sun shone through the spotty cloud cover in bright beams. They shone like spotlights, illuminating small patches of the waking city. Brandt stood and watched for a long time. Something had changed. He felt a release of pressure, as if some burden had lifted, but nothing looked different. He glanced at the guitar case, then back out the window.

The pain wasn't gone, just diminished. Muted. With each passing moment, he felt the infinitesimal expansion of that pain, the synchronization of additional voices complicating the rhythm.

Behind him, Syn stirred and he turned. She had rolled to her back and was moaning, her arm drawing up to flop across her brow and her eyes still closed. Beautiful.

Brandt stepped closer, sitting on the edge of the bed at her side.

"What happened?" she asked, her eyes fluttering open.

"Was hoping you'd tell me," Brandt answered. "I was in the kitchen trying to scare up some coffee."

"I . . ." Syn laid back on the pillow with a soft thump. "I was standing there," pointing, "by the window. I was watching the street, but . . ."

"What?"

"I've never seen so many. They were gathered below us, staring at the window. They weren't watching me, but they saw *something*. And the street was different. Old. There were no cars, and not so many buildings. There was dust. Horses. Brandt," she turned to him, reaching out to lay a hand on his arm, "there were wagons with *horses*."

Brandt watched her eyes. Not bloodshot. Not dilated. "I

just saw the street," he said slowly. "Like always, sun breaking through the clouds."

Syn sat up, catching the way he was examining her to see if she were stoned. "I saw what I fucking *saw*, Brandt. You think I passed out because of a beam of sunshine?"

"I don't know what to think," Brandt answered, turning and rising in a single, fluid motion and walking back to the window. "After last night I'd believe that you saw a regiment of dwarves marching down the block, but I don't *want* to believe it. I don't want . . . *this*."

Brandt swept his arm in an arc that encompassed window, and city, and his guitar case.

"I always wanted to play. I wanted to make people smile. I wanted the whole fucking rock-star-with-an-attitude fling. I wanted a few years of crazy and a lifetime of building toward that point when everyone would say I sold out and I'd know I was growing up." He turned slowly back toward Syn, who was sitting on the edge of the bed now, watching and waiting.

"I wanted you." He said this last very softly, his features losing their edge. "Always wanted you, but figured I wasn't getting anywhere, why drag you nowhere with me? Why even try? Now I've dragged you into this."

Syn rose shakily, stepping up close beside Brandt as he turned to the window once more. "You didn't bring the *angels*, Brandt, they were always there. You helped me start to see them as more, as a truth instead of a private insanity. You helped them see *me* for the first time. I don't know where this will end, but you stayed last night when things got bad. You saw through the darkness and dragged me out of it. You stood up for things you didn't even understand. You might never have had the fame, but for what it's worth, you've got me."

She kissed his cheek softly and leaned in close.

"I just hope someone we didn't count on doesn't have us both," he answered, turning to slide his arm around her shoulder. Syn shivered and snuggled close, and they both stood watching as the sun burst through the clouds at last . . . sliding slowly across the day and glistening off the last of the rain and mist.

Shaver clutched the newspaper clipping tightly as the three of them marched side by side down the street. It was an unfamiliar neighborhood, dark and unfriendly. The buildings were squat and dark, set back from the street and draped in shadow.

"This can't be the place," Dexter said nervously. His hands pattered against the soft denim of his jeans, slapping counterpoint to their every step, making timing work where there was none, matching Liz's shorter strides to Shaver's impatient ones with practiced ease. Blending. Setting a framework, even for their footsteps. Patterns.

Neon letters, some lit, most not, spelled "12 Bar" in crusted pink. The doorway was dark, darker than the streets with their elongated shadows and dim, too-late-for-sunlight, too-early-for-moonlight illumination. Deep inside that darkened pit, light flickered. As the three of them stopped, staring, the sounds of soft laughter and clinking glass emerged.

"This is the place all right."

Just then, as if to punctuate Shaver's words, a single harsh chord rippled from the shadows. There was power in that sound, reverberating through empty alleys and out into the damp night air. Shaver felt a shiver lodge deep in his heart.

"Yeah," he breathed. "This is the place."

He stepped forward into the shadows, and there was nothing for Liz and Dexter to do but to follow. The darkness swallowed them, drawing them into the dimly lit interior hungrily.

There were dozens of low-slung tables, anchored to the floor, some with more than their fair share of damage. Half a dozen of the rough surfaces held drinks, half-empty, glistening with condensation. Dark shapes and darker shadows, dim lights that barely cut the fog of cigarette smoke. In the vague, smoky interior of the club, nothing was more than a vague shadow of reality. Except the music.

Shaver slipped up to the first unattended table and slid into a seat, eyes glued to the stage. Liz melted in behind him, drawing her chair up closer so that her breasts pressed against his back and her arms circled him protectively. Dexter took a seat opposite the two of them. He watched the stage, a half-hopeful, half-distrustful expression warring on his thin features.

The lights were dimmed on the stage, but shadowed figures moved about slowly. The old, dusty speakers hummed, ground-wire loose somewhere deep inside equipment no one cared enough to repair. It was impossible to make out the features of any of the band members. The guitarist had long, waving hair. He might have been black, but again, impossible to tell. The bassist was tall, so tall he looked surreal and out of place, hovering over the others like a giant insect, his instrument hugged tightly to his chest.

Nothing could be seen of the drummer. Every now and then drumsticks fluttered, dim light glittered, and a ripple of rhythm sifted through the smoke-clouded air. No sign of a vocalist. No sign of a waitress, either, for the longest time. Then, lazily, a woman wound her way through the empty chairs and swirling cigarette smoke. She was nearly beside

Dexter before they could make out her features.

Tall, thin, so thin she seemed about to melt back into the smoke, the waitress stood on spindly legs, accented by a skirt no longer than the width of Shaver's hand, fingers pressed tightly together and wobbling atop spiked, five-inch heels. Her hair was teased back carelessly, blonde and streaked with the colors of several different attempts at individuality blended to total anonymity. Her makeup was too heavy, her eyes too vague. She clutched her order pad loosely, an afterthought in a thoughtless appearance.

"Drinks?" she asked. Her voice was lifeless, whispered over double-rouged lips and nearly too soft to hear.

Shaver watched her, shifting his mind and attention from the stage with an effort. Dexter leaned forward, slapping a ten-dollar bill on the table.

"Beer," Dex said. "Three of them, cold." As the girl moved away, he whispered, "In clean glasses, if you *have* any."

The girl turned back and popped gum she had been chewing so listlessly it took them by surprise. Liz clung to Shaver's arm, and Dexter sat up suddenly.

"What kind?" she asked, her expression never changing.

"Cold," Dex answered. "Just cold."

The waitress watched Dex for a few moments longer, deciding if he was kidding, and finally turned, making her way back through the smoke and gloom toward the bar.

"Miss Personality," Liz said softly.

"Hey," Shaver laughed, "if you worked a dive like this, you might not be too cheery either."

Liz didn't answer. She just leaned closer, and Shaver shifted his gaze back to the stage. The harsh tones of instruments and amps being warmed up, tuned, and adjusted echoed from the shadows. It was crazy, in a place this seedy, to anticipate as he did, but something in the air, and the sound, called to him. He was *aching* for the music to start. His fingertips itched and throbbed.

"Why are we here again?" Dexter asked. His fingers drummed nervously on the tabletop, shaking the surface lightly and reverberating through the club.

"Because I heard they were good," Shaver said, "and that they were breaking up. We can't just go for *anyone* if we rebuild the band."

Dexter didn't answer. His own thoughts on "rebuilding the band" had been spoken and spoken again, argued and ignored. Shaver was set in his course, and with Brandt and Synthia lost to the world, the choice was Shaver, or alone. Dexter wasn't going to make it alone. He'd end up counting cracks on the sidewalks from one city to the next, or counting the bubbles in an endless parade of beers until his mind and body rejected him.

The shriek of feedback screeched from the stages as someone stepped too close to the microphone too quickly, amplified instrument in hand. All their eyes shifted and suddenly a single, dim spot was shining on the stage. The man who stood there was tall and slender, his hand wrapped tightly around the mic, cord double-wrapped around his wrist. No way to see his eyes, but his smile managed to glitter in the dim light, as did his hair, white—shimmering and long, falling over his shoulders in silvered waves.

Sometime while their attention had been diverted, the soft shimmer of cymbals had risen to silence the hum of voices from the sparse crowd. Moments later, a deep, throbbing bass line insinuated itself between the ripples, driving the beat, but not distracting from it. The drums grew stronger, shifting to snare, rippling across the snare and into the deeper strung toms.

The guitar bit into the backbone of the music and it was that moment, precisely, that the vocalist chose to laugh softly.

"Welcome, friends." He hesitated, scanning his audience, then continued, "And everyone else. Welcome."

Dexter turned to Shaver, but his friend never flinched. Liz was leaning forward, her chin on Shaver's shoulder, her arms wrapped around him tightly, as if she was afraid he would be pulled away in some direction she couldn't follow. With nothing else to concentrate on, Dexter began slowly, and meticulously, to shred his napkin.

"It is early," the vocalist went on, "but I urge you to lean back, slip a little closer to those already close . . . dig the sound, and enjoy the drinks. Don't forget our lady friends totin' the happy juice, and don't forget, the band is *always* thirsty."

The guitarist, on cue, launched into a flurry of flickering notes, deep minors and shimmering, half-lead, half-rhythm riffs that dragged their attention away from the microphone just long enough to set up the next moment. The drums shivered to silence. The bass, first joining the guitar, then dragging it to a halt, echoed through the room. Nothing. There was no sound, no motion. Everyone in the room was still, captured easily by the perfection of timing and the exquisite "staging" of the moment.

"I feel your pain."

The words were whispered, yet with the amplification, and the reverb, they echoed, reverberating from the walls.

"I *am* your pain."

Shaver wasn't certain he'd even heard the words spoken, because it was that precise moment that the bassist chose to blast into existence, followed like a puppy by the guitar and chased through complicated backbeats by the drums.

The music carried them away, simply and completely. Before they knew what had happened, the vocalist was at the microphone again. He pulled it close, leaning in and reaching up to press a dark, black fedora over his eyes before uttering a sound.

Shaver drifted. He felt Liz pressed tightly against him, clutching his arm and leaning in tight. He sensed that Dexter sat very close beside him, but the sound he heard, the music that invaded his senses, spoke to him alone. Hank. Pure, unadulterated blues, honky-tonk-rhythmed pulse of depression, seeping in deep. Shaver closed his eyes . . . wanted to close his ears. It was too much. Tears streamed slowly down his cheeks, and he blinked, squeezing Liz's hand hard.

Liz heard something wholly different, perfectly harmonious, and deep. The vocals were . . . wrong somehow. The man's voice reached to her soul, drawing out her insecurity and laying it on the table. Liz wanted to withdraw her hand from Shaver's before he felt it too, before he heard. She felt her father's eyes sliding over her, her mother's eyes sliding away, and still she held on.

"No," she whispered.

Dexter was caught up in the beat. His hands were moving, his feet were tapping, harder at each stanza. He could feel the sticks in his hands, the pedals beneath the soles of his boots. The notes sped through his mind, dragging him along in their wake. Faster, deeper, challenging him to keep up, to make the grade and bring the rhythm to life. His hands flew over the table top. The drinks shivered . . . danced. The floor shook.

On the stage, the vocalist stood very still, watching. The music played out around him like a rich, warped tapestry.

His slate gray eyes were fixated on the table where Shaver, Liz, and Dexter sat, transfixed. Everyone in the room was transfixed. Each heard the pain of their heart, the song they least wanted and most needed to hear. There was no interaction, no discussion. Not a word was spoken as the music cascaded off different walls. As worlds played out in parallel agony, and pain that had been bottled in separate containers through the entire spans of separate lives echoed through the room.

The door opened with a soft "Swoosh!" The music, for that one instant, hesitated. No eyes spun to the door, except those of the man behind the microphone. He smiled.

EIGHT

Brandt pushed the door open, and the sudden absence of sound sucked his breath from his lungs like a giant vacuum. Synthia stepped in beside him, pressed close. The smoky interior was dark. Music, loud and powerful, rolled off the stage in waves, shivering through the cigarette smoke that danced serpent-like above the tables and shimmered beneath the low-slung fluorescent lights.

Even the twilight on the streets had been bright in comparison, and the garish glare from the overheads and from the spots backlighting the stage nearly blinded them. Brandt could make out nothing but the nearest tables. Two were empty; at a third, a short, stooped figure leaned in close, hands cupped around a glass.

Stepping closer, Brandt caught a flash of color from the table and turned to look. He stopped, clutching Syn to his side. The hand stretched out flat on that table was aged, withered, and thin. Slender, wrinkled fingers danced across the dingy, water-stained surface, but Brandt ignored them. Beyond their reach, as if forgotten, the cards lay stacked. Brandt drew nearer, all else forgotten, staring. As he neared the table, the old woman turned, gap-toothed filthy grin flashing—ignored.

The Wheel of Fortune. The image on the card mesmerized him, the colors clarifying quickly, symbols. The hook. The ankh. Circles, endless circles. Brandt staggered forward, reaching for the card, Syn staggering in his wake. He leaned into the table, too hard, and it toppled, spilling glass and ice and cards in a whirling dash of color that blended to the shadows of the floor. Syn gripped his arm hard, dragging him back, and Brandt blinked. In that moment, things shifted.

Brandt's gaze flashed to the stage. Locked to those slate-gray, endless orbs, gazing back at him over the top of the microphone. Beyond the stage, the deep, roaring blaze of a fire flickered for just a moment, and the shadowed skeletal nightline of the city replaced the back wall. The world tilted, but somehow Brandt didn't fall. Maybe the counterbalance of Syn leaning on his arm, maybe some inner strength he wasn't familiar with. He swayed, held, took a step forward, and nearly fell again.

Arms grabbed his then, fingers gripping much more tightly than Synthia ever could. Brandt shook his head back and forth, slowly, not letting his gaze waver from the stage. The music swelled, and the vocalist grinned, white teeth sparkling in the darkness. Laughter rolled out to accompany the guitar and the drums.

"Brandt!"

Hearing his name, so close, and so loudly voiced, rocked Brandt back on his heels. Then he turned, eyes wide.

Shaver glared at him. "Watch where the fuck you're going."

Brandt blinked. The music rippled again, tangible, powerful. Brandt stood, and Shaver released him, slowly. Even more slowly, Brandt became aware of his surroundings. His guitar case slapping against his knee. Syn moved up closer, protectively. He felt the eyes of all those at the table he'd nearly trashed. Ignoring it all, he lifted his arm and brought the guitar case up, dragging it across the top of the table, brushing aside the glasses that remained and sending them crashing to the floor. The sound was lost in the pounding of drums and bass, overpowering and impossibly amplified. The vocalist grew taller and more slender, mocked them with his eyes and beckoned with the fingers of one hand in an eerie mockery of Jim Morrison.

Shaver was still glaring at Brandt, but his fingers were flexing.

"Fuck," Dexter interrupted eloquently.

They turned to the stage, all of them. Those still seated, staggered to their feet. The band still played, but it wasn't the band of a few moments past, strange as *those* musicians had been. The vocalist was unchanged. If anything, his sharp, too-handsome features stood out more prominently against the backdrop of those supporting the sound.

They seemed dead. That was the only single word description that fit, and yet, it was more than that: death denied, pain prolonged. Their fingers moved over the strings of their instruments, the drummer's sticks beat intricate patterns on the drum skins, but there was no animation in their eyes. There was desperation, frantic hunger, a madman's expression of helpless creation, but no spark of anything you could call life.

Shaver's hands trembled. He brought them to his chest, trying to still the motion, this bringing the tremble to his heart.

"Fuck," Dexter repeated. His own hands were fisted, clenched so tightly that if anyone had been paying attention to him, they might have feared that he would jam the nails straight through his palms. His foot tapped. Stopped. Tapped again, and trembled to a halt.

Brandt unsnapped the guitar case and flipped open the lid.

The pain rolled from the band in waves. It brought no memories. It dragged nothing from their past. Not like the music Brandt had played. That music had released pain. This music offered it, forced it upon the listeners, and bound it to their minds and hearts. The temperature in the room had dropped several degrees, and all pretense of reality was banished to the shadows.

Brandt hesitated. He wanted to close his hands over his ears. He wanted to slam the case closed, fling one of the empty tumblers at that grinning caricature of a singer's face and drive the smile away, but something held him in check. The guitar. He leaned in, hands caressing the polished wood, and with a quick jerk he dragged the instrument from its case. Somehow, Synthia moved as well, slipping in and wrapping her arms around him to grip the shoulder strap and draw it up and over his head. Brandt felt the familiar weight and his hands caressed the neck—the strings. He concentrated, blocking out the sound.

"What's the matter, *boy?*" the vocalist called out from the stage. "You like to play the *pain*, don't you? You know they don't come to you to dance, or to love, don't you *boy?*"

Brandt stiffened. Long years growing to be a man warred with that subtly-tossed insult. He steadied his hands and closed his eyes, willing the visions of bonfires to the dark recesses of his mind and ignoring the desperate hunger for a connection with his mind that he sensed in the members of the *band.*

Brandt opened his eyes and managed to avoid the stage. He glanced at Shaver. No longer angry, the young guitarist stared, fixated by the wavering, dancing figures on the stage. His fingers clenched and unclenched, and Brandt saw from the bandages and the controlled grimaces of pain that it hurt each time. Shaver didn't seem to notice.

Brandt swept his gaze over the others. Syn had released him and stepped up beside him, standing very still with her hands on the table. Her attention was focused on the bassist. Brandt glanced up, just for a moment, and the stage flickered again. The bass was there, as it had been in the park, glittering and smooth, lacquered surface gleaming in the dim light. Not electric. Not Fender. Upright and old, the musician's fingers flying up and down the neck in intricate counterpoint to the drums.

Drums that were echoed beside Brandt, where Dexter had picked up the beat, his nails rattling across the water-soaked wood of the tabletop, snapping into empty glasses for cymbals and clattering against the edge of Brandt's guitar case. Brandt wanted to stop him, wanted to slap his hands over his friend's, ending that connection, but he knew it would do no good. Dragging Synthia from the park had only been a bandage on a larger wound.

The guitar. Brandt brought his fingers to the strings and closed his eyes. He didn't play. Not at first. He reached deep inside, reached for those who sought him. Synthia could have told him where they were, but she was swaying now, captivated by the sounds from the stage. Wally could have just led them to the club and circled them like Indians at a stagecoach barbeque, but that wasn't happening. Not this time.

The voices were there, faint, but growing, always growing. The music from the stage, deep and raw, paled before the weight of that endless chorus. Years piled upon years of misery, decades of unrequited agony. What the band on the stage played was new, raw and unfocused. It was pain without purpose, seeking an outlet, latching onto anyone or anything close enough to release a bit of its fury. What Brandt felt, welling up in his soul, was ancient, honed and sharp. The images riding those voices were etched into the bedrock of time. The band could scratch at the surface, could promise pain to come and eternities filled with more of the same, but it could not match the depth, the sheer overwhelming power, of what had come before.

Brandt felt it. It wasn't his pain, but he was the channel, the conduit to a million tiny pockets of agony and grief. He rippled his fingers over the strings, checking the tuning. He was in no hurry, despite the intensity of the moment. Wave after wave of anger and hatred washed over him, and he felt the tiny, silver-threads of his friends' lives spinning away from him, winding toward that brilliant, blinking abyss that was the stage. The man. The hell, they faced.

"Hold on," Brandt whispered.

He struck a chord. It rippled through the overwhelming tide of sound, slicing clean and pure. He struck again, letting his fingers slide quickly up and down the strings, sliding, wishing he'd remembered a Bic lighter, or a steel socket. He knew the notes, knew the fluid, half-lazy, half-inspired motions required to blend them and bring them to life. He had only his fingers, a half-dead pick, and the memory of a thousand hours playing the old records again and again.

"Crossroads music, boy?" The man on the stage grinned. "You want to chase me away or call me home?"

Brandt ignored the taunting. He reached for the notes, willing his fingertip smooth, sliding it to the higher E and dragging it down, letting the notes shiver. He felt it tremble deep through the bones of his finger, up his arm, and into his heart. The smoky air rippled and in that instant he saw the vocalist's face clearly. Not handsome. Not powerful. Empty. Eyes like deep pits and a mouth open to howl in insane fury.

The band, no band at all, swayed crazily beside that specter, wisps of red flame, their instruments shadows, the notes they played visible, undulating from the center of the stage like dark serpents, winding through the crowd, choosing targets, rising to strike.

"No," Brandt said simply. He closed his eyes, concentrated, bore down on fingers and pick, drawing out the notes and letting his own thoughts dissolve. The notes were not about him, not part of him. The world slipped away and he felt his hands gripping an older instrument, felt the coarse wood, the rough cat-gut strings. The notes were tinny, clanging with a crude resonance.

Brandt turned, not letting his fingers hesitate. The club was gone. He stood in a clearing. Trees rose above him on all sides, a wooded cathedral, and in the center, a long, low-slung table. Candles lit the scene, flickering and wavering brightly atop four-foot stands. The banjo, rough-hewn and held together as much by love and luck as craftsmanship, rang with the voice of desolation. The sliding blues of Brandt's guitar had faded, and the jangling, discordant notes of death slipped easily into that void. Backwoods minor-chorded dirge, half-gospel, half bluegrass, and all pain. Brandt had never held a banjo, but his fingers floated easily over the ragged strings.

On the table, endless platters of food, roast beef and broiled fish, apple pie and casseroles of all description. The air was alive with the aromas of meat and boiled vegetables, baked goods, and the soft, lingering undercurrent of wine. The lingering, death-sweet scent of lilies hung damp and heavy in the air. The feast was piled high, backed by tacky, hand-crafted horseshoes of roses and carnations in every color of the rainbow.

A plaque leaned against one of those horseshoes. It was etched with deep, burn-cut letters on a backdrop of hard oak.

"Isaiah Johnson. Brother to all, enemy to none. Soldier

of the Lord. May he rest in peace."

Brandt bent the notes double, feeling the emotion embodied in this simple, plaintive display of grief and loss. Isaiah. Such an appropriate name. But the food? The banquet? It was a party with no attendees. A funeral with no deceased. Then Brandt looked closer, and he stopped playing, nearly losing what food he'd eaten earlier in a quick spew of bile.

The feast was centered around a long, lean body, platters piled on its chest, its throat, lining the legs, bread resting in the cleft between the thighs. Flasks of wine and small wooden kegs of beer leaned against the base of the table, and the face was wreathed in an intricate halo of fruit and vegetables.

Footsteps sounded to one side, rustling branches and crushed leaves. Brandt stepped back into the shadows, concentrating on the sound, lacing one note to the next and scanning the clearing carefully.

Stealthy motion to his right. Brandt leaned back against a tree. It wasn't as if he could hide, not with the banjo announcing his presence and insinuating him into the moment, but having the trunk solid at his back bolstered his failing courage. Bright eyes flashed across the table at him, glaring, searching, dropping away. Brandt watched as a tall, slender form melted from the trees and began to circle the table slowly, no longer paying the slightest attention to Brandt, or the music.

A slender hand snaked out to grasp a bit of bread. That bread disappeared, and moments later, long strips of beef were torn free. Consumed. Replaced by chicken and handfuls of radishes. One of the flagons of wine was lifted, tipped . . . drained, washing over thin cheeks and down a narrow throat.

Something rippled through the air. The man made no sound, other than the chewing and swallowing of food. No one else was present, and yet there was something . . . something powerful . . . slipping in and about the shadows of the clearing. Brandt fought the urge to chase those shadow-glimpses. He played, letting his mind and soul flow into the unfamiliar notes of the banjo's bright voice, trying desperately to fight off visions of Deliverance as he gaped at the feasting madman before him.

The candles flickered madly. There was no wind, and yet they danced in eerie time to Brandt's song. Shadows moved just beyond the soft pool of light. Brandt couldn't focus on any of them long enough to make out a shape, and his eyes were drawn, again and again, to the wraith-thin maniac sliding along the table, gripping meat and vegetables, guzzling wine, and stuffing his mouth again and again. Impossible amounts of food disappeared with alarming speed. Brandt caught the man's gaze now and then, those deep, too-white, too-deep eyes.

"That's you, boy."

The voice filtered in through the banjo's wail, whispering from the shadows, familiar and deep. Brandt's skin grew clammy, but he didn't let go of the song.

"That's you, same as the ol' Sineater, boy. Everyone else's sin, everyone else's shadows. You take it in, they let it go, 'round and 'round. Look at him. Go on, look."

Brandt tried not to look. He tried to drag his gaze to his fingers, to follow the intricate dance that drew them from string to string, the glitter of the metal picks that adorned each finger of his right hand. Anything, everything, nothing but that man, and that food, slowly disappearing, nothing but crumbs and droplets of spilled wine left behind. Methodically, the Sineater moved about the dead body, revealing a pale, lifeless thigh, drawing a plate of pork from atop a too-round bulging belly. So much food, so much drink, and disappearing steadily. Impossibly.

"He will take it all in," the voice went on, "all of it, bite by bite and drop by drop. Nothin' spared, boy. Nothing. Every bit of that man's sin is in that feast, every guilty portion his friends and family and priest could dredge from their communal memory. Laid out, open to the world. Nothing between that dead body and me," a wave of soft laughter drifted through the song, "but that skinny-assed *fool* over there. Got so much of what is mine he can't even come to town, don't have a friend in the world, or a love. Nothing but death, and food, and music. Music from boys like you, setting others free and bearing the pain."

The voice fell silent, and Brandt was suddenly aware of the rivulets of sweat running down his face, the taste of salt in the corners of his mouth. His mind raced. The pain hadn't receded, but it flowed smoothly. When he played, it eased. It flowed up and through, out and away. It didn't fill him.

Was it the same? Is that how the man ate and ate and fucking *ate* and never stopped? Never.

Brandt thought, and thought, and tried to stop those thoughts, concentrating on his fingers. No friends. Not able to come to others, or love. Alone with the pain of others. He thought of Wally. Of Synthia, and Shaver and Dexter. Of himself.

The Sineater spun on his heel. The food was gone, all but a single turkey leg, gripped knuckle-white-tight in one thin hand. The man's wild stare tore through Brandt's whirling thoughts and pinned him to the tree like a dead bug in a science project; spread and helpless. Only his fingers felt alive, and they danced to a tune Brandt couldn't even name, let alone control. The man moved away from the table, turkey torn from the bone dangling from his lip. His steps were steady, the gait of a beast stalking prey. Hair, wild and silver-gray, spun out behind him, and wine, gravy, and bits of meat flecked his chin and shirt.

Brandt tried to back away, pushing so tightly to the bark of the tree he felt as if he might sink within that solid surface and fall away, back to reality—his reality. Nothing doing.

That spectral face slipped closer, and closer, soft candle-light illuminating too-sharp features. Those eyes, growing and growing, and that mouth, chewing, teeth yellowed and stained by dish after dish and sin after sin. How many years of living alone and drowning in the evil of others, sending them to a peace you could never claim?

The man was so close now that Brandt could make out thin ribs pressing through the material of a tattered shirt, arms so slender that veins roped his wrists and bones protruded at the elbow. He didn't stop until his worn boots nearly touched, toe to toe, with Brandt's own, until his shirt-tail brushed Brandt's fingers as he played. Until he could lean in and smile so close their eyes could not see beyond the limits of their faces.

"It's you, boy. Look hard. Ol' Wally, he'd like to make you over in this one's image, bet the farm on it, *boy*. Your choice."

The Sineater stared deep into Brandt's eyes. He chewed slowly, swallowing the last of the dark in a dead man's heart. Nothing to wash it down with but fetid breath and eternity.

Brandt felt his hands shiver. Heard a soft ripple in the song. He fought to control it, realized he knew nothing of the song, his efforts jarring the perfection of the flow. Everything wavered.

"No," Brandt whispered.

The Sineater reached out, gripping Brandt by his shirtfront and dragging him closer, silencing the banjo-blending to guitar, bringing pale, bloodless lips too close to Brandt's ear.

As it all faded, as the clearing became the club, overhead lights flashing on bright and hot, the man spoke. "Don't listen. Cycles. It is all cycles. We will meet . . . before . . ."

"Before what?" Brandt muttered the words, then screamed them.

The words faded. Brandt staggered, and for the second time that night, felt strong hands steadying him. This time, there were no harsh words to accompany it. Brandt fought for balance, and with Shaver on one side and Synthia on the other, managed to catch himself before he toppled face-first into the table.

"Brandt!" Synthia's voice was too close, too shrill. She slapped him hard, rocking his head to one side, and Brandt staggered again, this time nearly toppling himself *and* Shaver. "Don't you go away again, you bastard. Don't. You. Go. Away."

Brandt heard the shiver in her voice, the brittle quality, and it snapped into place. Love. He was loved.

Turning to the stage, empty now, completely bare. He glared straight past the microphone center stage and whispered, "Fuck you. Not this time."

Syn reached out and clutched his shirt, and Brandt pushed away from Shaver gently, leaning into that embrace.

"Don't you worry, lady," he said softly. "Not going anywhere. Ever. Not again."

"Where's the band?" Dexter asked.

They all spun to stare at the drummer, then the stage. There was no one else in the club. In fact, it was difficult to believe anyone had been in that place in years. Dust coated the tables and floor, and the lamp over their table hung loosely, dangling from a single chain and creaking in the breeze from a poorly-boarded window. The only light was the soft illumination from streetlights, streaming in through the patchwork of planks.

Dexter's hands stopped their motion. He glanced down. His fingers were empty. There was nothing on the table but Brandt's guitar case. No glasses, spilled or otherwise. No spoons. Nothing.

Brandt shook his head, sweeping his gaze over the table. He couldn't free his mind of that face, those words.

"Before what?" he whispered. His gaze fell on the next table, where Liz was sitting quietly. She had a sheet of paper, God only knew where she'd gotten it, and she was scratching furiously at the paper with a pencil, leaning in close to concentrate in the dim light. The sound of the lead scraping across the paper had grown loud, filling the silent room.

Brandt drew the strap slowly over his head and placed his guitar gently in its case. His gaze never left Liz's hands. The others had begun to move closer, gathering around her as she worked. Brandt pushed away from the table, gaining his balance and stepped to Synthia's side, wrapping his arm around her shoulder.

"Who is that?" Syn asked. "Liz, who is that?"

Brandt leaned in and stared. His arm tightened on Syn's shoulder, his fingers digging in. She squirmed once, then nudged him with her elbow, hard.

"That *hurts*, Brandt. What is wrong with you?"

Brandt loosened his grip, but he was paying no attention to her words. He leaned closer, letting his hand come to rest on Liz's, stopping the motion of the pencil gently. The

Sineater stared back at him from the paper, true to the last detail, eyes haunted and deep.

"Who is it?" Synthia repeated, nudging Brandt again.

"I don't know," he replied, "but I just met him. Somewhere. I was playing a banjo, he was . . . eating."

"You aren't making a lick of sense, man," Dexter commented. "We were all right here," he swept his arm in a wide circle . . . stopped halfway, confused. "We were all somewhere, man, but it wasn't with that guy."

Brandt nodded. Nothing made sense. "I wasn't here," Brandt said simply. "One moment I was playing and staring at that bastard on the stage, and the next, I was somewhere else . . . still playing, just not here."

"Whatever, man," Shaver spat. "Why did you come here?"

Brandt spun suddenly, releasing Liz's hand. "Why did you? I don't fucking know, Shaver. I don't know why I've done a damn thing I've done since that night in the club. I just have to do it." He was silent for a moment, then added, "It hurts."

Shaver nodded.

Brandt turned back to the drawing. Liz had moved her chair away from the table, letting the pencil drop away to the side. The Sineater's face was trapped in a stray beam of street-lamp illumination. His eyes glared at Brandt, and spoke to him at the same time.

"Before what?" Brandt asked softly. They stood there a long time, but there was no answer.

NINE

Brandt sat still on Liz's couch, clutching the sketch tightly and staring into those empty, pencil-shaded eyes.

"Who is he?" Syn leaned in, lifting his hand, and the picture, turning it so she could see.

"I have no idea," Brandt said. They both turned to Liz, who was busily following the swirling cream in her coffee in circles with a hollow, empty stare. She hadn't spoken much since they'd left the dingy, abandoned bar, despite a barrage of questions from all sides that Shaver had finally stopped by pulling her into a tight hug and glaring the others to silence. If Liz had any idea who the man in the drawing was, she wasn't telling. Not yet.

Dexter paced like a caged cat, moving from room to room, picking things up, putting them down, stacking and restacking anything in a quantity of greater than two. Shaver glanced over as the drummer bounced off the frame of the kitchen door, moving toward them.

"For Christ's sake, Dex, you think you could slow down?"

Dexter frowned. "I can't stay in here forever, man. We have to *do* something."

"Like what?" Syn's voice cut like acid. "Go for coffee?"

Brandt stared down at the drawing again. He knew Dex was right. If they didn't get out of that apartment and start sorting out what had become of their lives, they would end up killing one another out of boredom or some warped strain of *Cabin Fever*. But what? Where?

"I don't know what he meant," Brandt said. "I don't know where he meant we would meet, or why. I don't even know which of them was right. Maybe I am just like that, dragging everyone else's bullshit into myself."

"No."

The word was spoken softly, and at first it was difficult to tell who had spoken it. Slowly, the options sifting through their minds, they turned to Liz, who was sitting, gaze still focused on her coffee, hands trembling, and hot, mocha-creamed liquid threatening to spill over her hands and lap. Synthia rose quickly, moving to Liz's side and taking the cup gently from her hands.

"You aren't anything like him, Brandt," she continued. "Not at all."

Everyone was silent. Even Dexter had moved closer, perching on the arm at one end of the sofa.

"How do you know?" Brandt asked.

Liz's gaze flashed from her coffee to Brandt's eyes in that second, brimming with tears. She shook her head, sending the droplets of liquid pain dancing through the light, and straightened her back. "He was my grandfather."

Silence. Dead air. Dexter plopped onto one of the kitchen chairs and began to drum his fingers gently on the table. Brandt let out a long, slow breath. He traced the edges of the drawing, worn and yellowed from too much handling. He lost himself in those deep, too-hungry eyes.

"Tell me," he said.

More silence, then Liz began to speak slowly. The others had to strain, at first, to pick up the words. Then her voice grew more powerful, her sentences more fluid.

"I haven't always lived in cities," she said. "Where I grew up, the nearest 'city' was like a fantasy world, so far out of reach you didn't so much believe in the reality, but soaked up the dreams. We didn't follow the trends, or the newest movie star fads. Our life was the church. Baptist, southern and charismatic. We had a mayor, and a city council, but they wouldn't have done a thing without the say-so of the Minister. The Reverend Forbes, Shane Forbes."

Dexter's fingers drummed a bit more insistently, setting up a rhythm that insinuated itself behind Liz's words. She fell into sync, caught up now in the grip of suppressed memory released.

Brandt closed his eyes, setting the drawing aside and wrapping his arms around Synthia tightly. She leaned in, breathing softly against his neck as they listened.

"I remember the first time I saw him," Liz said, "and the last. I'll never forget."

The church was backlit by a brilliant, orange sunrise. Elizabeth leaned in close against her mother's skirt, thinking how pretty it all would be, if it weren't for the suits, and the dresses, and the veils. Black. All black. It was as if all color had drained from the people of Friendly, California. Even the sun just highlighted the contrast of white church and black-suited men and women.

Elizabeth had asked her mother what was wrong. She'd asked why Mrs. Porter wasn't wearing her pretty yellow dress, and why Mr. Klune didn't have on one of his colorful ties with the big silver clip. Mother had grabbed her by the cheek, an unusual display of quick temper, telling her to shush, and not to ask "unseemly" questions.

Elizabeth hadn't said a word since that moment. Her mother never raised her voice, never denied answers to important questions. Something was wrong. Something that had glittered in her mother's eyes, and shimmered in the slick shine of her father's black boots as they readied themselves for church. Actions that had been habit all their lives had taken on the aura of ritual. Dressing was an art-form, no room for error, or sloppiness. Every crease was perfect, and neither her mother nor her father had touched a bite of their breakfast. Both had stared at their plates, full and brimming with food, and turned away. Liz had poked at her own food, wondering if there was something wrong with it. Something in the attitudes of her parents removed any appetite she'd awakened with.

Her mother had worked late into the night, another oddity. The oven had been fired, and there were biscuits, more than they could eat, and a casserole, as well as a pie that lay cooling in the window. Each of these was gathered carefully, packed and bundled for the walk to church. There had been sit-down dinners at church before, but those had been happy occasions. The cooking had been shared, the baking a lesson. Elizabeth watched as her mother packed that food and wondered why it brought no joy.

Church was a place where Elizabeth was accustomed to feeling a great deal of energy. It wasn't always focused, but it hummed through the pews and shone from the intricate stained-glass windows. She could feel the emotion ripple through those sitting to either side when the Reverend Forbes spoke, could feel the energy, and the love, when they all raised their voices in song.

This day that energy was absent. They passed other families, as always, dressed in dark clothing and eyes turned to the dusty ground beneath their feet. No one spoke, at least not to Elizabeth's parents. Even the other children looked away, though they glanced at her now and then. As they passed the Klunes and their daughter, Chastity, Elizabeth called out gently. Chastity did not answer, though the two of them were only a few feet apart. Chastity had been her best friend for years. The two had been baptized the same day, terrified and trembling in that deep, cold pool, Reverend Forbes towering over them, his eyes flashing and his voice booming out in prayer and song, so loud from where they'd stood that the words warped.

Nothing had seemed normal in those moments. Elizabeth's mother had said it was the Holy Spirit moving inside her. Elizabeth had been too young to know what that meant, or if it was true. She remembered being plunged under the water, remembered large hands sliding over her . . . places she'd never been touched, as she was held down. She remembered the quick, leering smile, there, and then gone, lost in loud prayer and Hallelujahs.

She also remembered Chastity's eyes. Scared, white, and round like big cut-paper parodies of eyes. Cartoon wide, falling off the cliff and staring up at the Road Runner, rocks crumbling beneath your feet and anvil whistling through the air above your scared eyes. Reverend Forbes' hand had slid down the back of Chastity's hair, gripped and drawn her down, gasping, toward the cold water. Again, the words blurred. Again Elizabeth didn't know what to do, what to think. She had stood in that water, freezing and shaking, eyes wide and needing to pee so bad she had to bite her lip and draw blood to prevent it.

The overhead lights had been far too bright to allow her to see her parents, or anyone but Reverend Forbes, who was illuminated like some crazed saint, his eyes bright and the expression on his face somehow falling short of righteous. As Chastity disappeared beneath the rippling surface of the baptismal pool, Elizabeth's gaze had raised. She knew, later, that everyone had thought she was looking to God. She was not.

Far above the pool, the morning sunlight poured in colored brilliance through a stained-glass depiction of Jesus, kneeling in a field, his own eyes upraised. His hands were clasped before him, and his eyes were elongated, too long and sad to be real, radiating a deep, penetrating sorrow. That sorrow permeated the moment and stained Elizabeth's mind.

Chastity broke the surface then, white gown too revealing, eyes wide and terror-stricken, droplets of water catching the brilliant spotlight's gleam and scattering like crystal shards. Elizabeth risked a glance at the Reverend, who grinned down at her in triumph. That glance pinned her in place, stopped the scream she'd been ready to launch mid-throat and choked her to submissive silence. Chastity was thrashing, struggling to free herself, but he held her for a moment longer, then released before the struggle became obvious, making her motion a clumsy stumble from which he caught her effortlessly, turning to the crowd and booming out his prayers and his Hallelujahs in deep, baritone splendor.

The girls had been ushered out of the pool, replaced by others, dried, and led to a room where their clothes awaited. The moment the two were alone, Chastity had dived into her arms, sobbing. No words were exchanged. Nothing could eliminate the moments that had passed, or cleanse them of the filthy sensation of his touch.

They'd dressed and left with their parents, never saying a word. Not to one another, not to their parents. What would they say? He touched me? His hands went . . . there? He was the Reverend, the holy man. He was the representative of God, and the longer the silence prevailed, the more control he stole from their lives, and the more surreal the memory became. Elizabeth avoided Reverend Forbes with a skittish, wide-eyed fear that had annoyed her parents, and embarrassed them more than once.

All of this flashed through Elizabeth's mind as Chastity and her parents passed. That moment, that instant when she realized even the one friend she trusted in the world was not going to smile at her, froze Elizabeth's heart. Alone. She had never felt so alone. Even when the Reverend Forbes had stroked her and dipped her under that frigid water, holding maybe too long, she'd known Chastity was there, watching.

They arrived at the church at last to find that there was a tent erected behind the building, open on all sides, but secure from any weather, and the sun. There were rows and rows of flowers, bunched and grouped along the sides of the small cemetery, and a cluster near the center of the tent, surrounding a long, low-slung table.

Elizabeth's mother shrugged her off and stepped forward toward that tent, her fingers gripping the food she'd prepared so tightly Elizabeth saw the white of her knuckles. When she'd tried to follow, she'd felt her father's hand, gentle but firm, on her shoulder. Her mother's shoulders had shaken visibly, and her steps were erratic and exaggerated. The lump in Elizabeth's throat threatened to choke the breath from her small frame.

"Daddy?" she said.

There was no answer. Her father's grip tightened on her shoulder.

"Daddy," she repeated, "what's wrong?"

"Shhhh."

Only that. No words. No comfort. Elizabeth bit her lip hard and fought the urge to cry. Her mother had nearly reached the table beneath the tent, which flapped over her head like some great bird of prey. As she disappeared beneath it, it seemed to swallow her. Her mother's figure looked smaller in that moment, diminished in some unfathomable way by the unbridled tension of the moment.

She placed the food quickly and carefully along one edge of the table within, spun on her heel, and fled. Her mother's expression gave nothing away, but Elizabeth sensed it—a desperation to be free of something. It had taken eternities for her mother to cross the field to that tent, but seconds later she was back. So quickly that it was difficult for Elizabeth to tell if she'd ever been gone at all. She no longer held the food. Her mother's face was white—ash white and stricken—as if something important had been ripped from her heart.

Elizabeth glanced up to her father's face, seeking support. Nothing. There was no emotion, no twitch of his eye, or turn of lip to set things right. He reached one hand out, letting it come to rest gently on Elizabeth's mother's shoulder, but he didn't speak, and the two did not meet one another's gaze. Elizabeth bit her lip and fought the tremble that started deep in her stomach. She wanted to cry. She wanted to grab her mother's dress and bury her face in that soft fabric and ask over and over what was wrong until she got an answer, but she couldn't.

Her mother wasn't there, not really. Elizabeth could see the tall, slender frame, and the wide, brown eyes, but there was nothing behind them. The lips were pressed too tightly together, the shoulders were set too straight. From somewhere, deep lines had etched themselves over soft features. Elizabeth was afraid to shatter the silence . . . afraid that if she spoke, and this *not* mom answered, her world would crumble away completely.

Reverend Forbes waited for them in the doorway of the church. His eyes were bright, searching. Nothing was missed: no detail, no face, no emotion. Those dark, hungry eyes fixed on Elizabeth for a long, drawn-out eternity of seconds, and she shrank against her father's side. The motion was detected, noted with a curt nod, and passed over. Elizabeth shivered. She wasn't forgotten, but there were other hungers, and other distractions. This was not her day. What she couldn't figure out was whose it was.

As the family passed through the dark doors into the dimly-lit interior of the church, Elizabeth glanced over her shoulder at that white-flapping tent, brilliant now in the bright morning sunlight. Beneath it, shadowed and covered in food and flowers, the odd, low-slung table waited. A feast? A party? Surely this was no party.

The soft whisper of voices kept too low to be overheard echoed too loudly to be ignored. Elizabeth kept close to her parents, allowed herself to be guided and pressed down the narrow space between two pews and seated. She was against one aisle, hard wood tight against one hip and her mother against the other. There was some warmth in that touch, if no emotion showed. Elizabeth felt her mother tremble, and that tiny admission-by-example of emotion cut deep. Nothing was right.

She scanned the pew before her, small shelves lined with hymnals and prayer books, interspersed with Gideon Bibles as far as the eye could see. Above that a line of black-clothed shoulders, jackets, hair pulled back in tight buns, hats jutting this way and that, feathers and veils and lace dangling in a dark, macabre impression of Sunday worship. There was no color anywhere, except in the brilliant scarlet drape that hung over the altar, beneath the candles, and the matching scarlet sash worn by Reverend Forbes, vestments gleaming. He had risen from behind the podium like a shadow, until he was suddenly just—there.

Elizabeth gasped out loud as he spoke, raising his arms suddenly overhead and calling out to those gathered.

"Brethren . . . let us pray."

As Reverend Forbes spoke, and all heads bowed in unison, Elizabeth heard the soft scrape of measured footsteps, robes whispering as the altar boys moved from the rear of the building, long brass-tipped torches gripped too tightly, knuckles white with the effort of concentration, moving to the front of the huge chamber. They passed by the Reverend, moving to the altar, and the array of white candles, touching their twin flames to each side in eerie unison. The candles guttered, then leaped to life, one after the other, backlighting Forbes' tall, slender figure in the dim, stained-glass-tinted light.

Elizabeth shivered and pressed back into the wood of the pew. It was too strange. The warm glow of the candles flickered too brightly. Reverend Forbes loomed over them, unusually intimidating and powerful from where she watched, pressed against her mother's thigh, and wavered in that light. His eyes were too bright, like the candles. The air felt heavy with—something. Something dark and wrong.

The prayer droned on, but the words were lost. All but the last few.

". . . Brother Halprin . . . he will be missed."

Halprin. Elizabeth's eyes widened. Mr. Halprin was the baker. She had been in his shop at least twice a week, picking up loaves of bread, since she was old enough to walk at her mother's side. The scent of bread was sudden and heavy, nearly making her gasp. Then gone. Donuts, fat and running with fresh sugar-frosting, the heady scents of coffee and hot chocolate assaulted her memory.

"Momma?" She whispered the word softly, but it seemed to echo through the church. Elizabeth didn't care.

"Momma?" she repeated, tugging her mother's dress.

"What?" Terse, clipped word. Not a real question, a silencer, blocking the next "Momma" effectively.

Elizabeth didn't let the not-momma voice deter her. "Mr. Halprin. What did he say about Mr. Halprin?"

Silence.

"Momma?" Elizabeth felt her mother's hand drop, felt her mother's fingers gripping her thigh.

"Shhhh. Not now."

Nothing more. Elizabeth wanted to continue. She wanted to press the issue, to lean over her mother and ask her father, but something in the tone of that single "shhhh" stole her courage. The congregation lifted their combined emotion in "The Old Rugged Cross," time lagged, so lethargic it dripped from the air like sticky, too-sweet syrup. Not comforting, but drawing them all from one moment to the next.

Elizabeth clamped her mouth shut and watched, letting it all wash over her, but refusing entry to any words, any emotion. Any song. She concentrated on an image of Mr. Halprin's face, though she didn't really know why. She thought of bread, and coffee, and bulging pies, cherry and blackberry. Anything but Reverend Forbes. Anything but that saccharine voice cutting through to her heart.

The song faded, and Reverend Forbes' voice rose again. This was the time he would launch into his sermon, drawing quotes from the Bible easily and fluidly. Wrongly. All wrong. Elizabeth didn't know why, but his words would drone on and on, and she would know they really came from the big book her mother kept in the hall, but at the same time, they did not say what he said. They did not mean what he said. They were—pure.

The sermon never came. When the prayer ended, the

choir, very austere in robes of crimson and deepest jet, began to sing very low, and slow. Not the hymns Elizabeth was accustomed to, but low, mournful tones, blending into a deep chant. Shoes scuffled up and down the pews, and Elizabeth felt her mother gripping her by the arm—too tightly—and drawing her to her feet.

Again she wanted to ask what was wrong. Again, the expression on her mother's face forbade it. Not her mother at all, some alien-in-mother-form perversion dragging her down to the aisle. The chanting grew louder as they drew nearer to the choir loft, then faded like a passing automobile in the rain as they were pressed toward the huge wooden doors by the crowd. There were bodies everywhere, but none too near to them. Another bit of surreal madness to add to the moment. Hundreds of bodies, pressed together and moving, and one small open pocket with Elizabeth, her mother, and her father in the center. Ahead, the tent waited, somehow more ominous than before.

The congregation filed in under that ceiling of white canvas in solemn silence. Elizabeth's father followed the family ahead of them, Dan Fergusen and his wife Sherry, in stoic silence. No one turned to him. None of the quick, subtle gestures was directed his way. There was a good three feet between her father and the man ahead of him, and another three feet behind Elizabeth, before the Johnsons followed.

Elizabeth couldn't watch the people—her friends, her friends' parents—so she turned her attention to the flowers, and the food, and the table. The air left her lungs, and she swooned, leaning against her mother and stumbling. Only the strong hand, tightening painfully on her shoulder, held her upright. Only the dull, empty glare that met her upturned gaze silenced her.

The food didn't rest on a table. Mr. Halprin lay there, buried in bread from his own bakery, pies and cakes, roasts and fried chicken, casseroles. There was a bunch of grapes dead center on his chest, dangling obscenely to one side, as though he'd been cut open and they'd spilled out. The table was slowly ringed in bodies, all sides closed off from the world.

"Raymond Halprin was a good man," Reverend Forbes' voice rang out. "A *caring* man who did well by his family, and his town. He cared for his children," the Reverend Forbes nodded at the Halprin twins, Betsy and Jason, "and he cared for his wife. He cared for all of us. Who among us hasn't awakened to the scent of fresh bread and smiled?

"Our Lord Jesus broke bread with those who followed and believed. Ray Halprin broke bread with each and every one of us. He was a good man. And he was a sinner."

Silence followed this last announcement, a great, combined out-rush of breath.

"He was a sinner, as you are a sinner." The Reverend's gaze swept the crowd, omitting no one. "He was a sinner as we are all sinners, in the eyes of our Lord. He lived, and he loved, he sinned, and now the Lord has taken him from us. Let all gathered feel that loss . . . and let us pray."

Elizabeth couldn't block out the words this time. Neither could she draw her gaze from the table, and the body, and the food. It was all wrong. Her mind flashed back to the stained-glass, still-frame Apostles and angelic Christ-image surrounding a long table. Food and wine—a feast—laid out before them.

"The Last Supper," Elizabeth whispered.

Her mother turned, yanking on her arm and glaring at her. Elizabeth dropped her eyes to the ground and shook helplessly. There was a soft murmur of voices around her, rising from a whisper. The Reverend Forbes had grown silent, and the air crackled with dark energy.

"There is a way," Reverend Forbes continued. His voice was low now, but the silence of the moment allowed the words to carry as if he screamed. "There is one who can help, one who can take what is rightfully Brother Halprin's and free his soul. There is a *WAY!*"

Softly, those surrounding the table responded. "Amen."

"There is *ONE*," Reverend Forbes continued, "who has the power to take and take and take again as life departs us. One who walks alone in shadow, one who has forsaken that golden road that beckons us. Dark. He is dark as night and hungry. . . ."

The Reverend swirled, his splendid vestments rising behind him like a cloud.

"He walks in places we cannot. He sees things we will never see, and feels those things that can shut the door between our souls and heaven. He holds it in; his hunger sets us free. He will set your brother free. Raymond Halprin will walk the road to *GLORY*, brothers and sisters, and this one dark man is the key. Pray for his soul. He cannot be saved, and yet we pray. He cannot be helped, but we reach out; our food, the bounty of home and hearth, we lay before him.

"He is salvation."

The words died away to a soft murmur of Hallelujahs. Then there was nothing. The wind whipped the tarp over their head. Elizabeth pressed to her mother's thigh—felt that comfort stiffen against her—ignored the sensation and pressed closer still.

A murmur sifted through those gathered, like the rustle of the breeze through leafy trees. A subtle shift, and a break in the circle opened. At first, no more than a single pace, then widening. They slid away from one side of the ring like a door opening to nightmare.

From the trees, his eyes stared at her. Through her. Elizabeth shuddered and tried to slide behind her mother, failed in that iron grip and stood knock-kneed and terrified as the brush parted beyond the circle. He stepped out, hair wild, spreading out around his face like a gray halo. His clothing was filthy and ragged, boots caked in mud, and jeans stained with the road and the trees and the earth.

The crowd began to ripple at the edges. Those closest to the woods wavered, then pulled back slowly, domino-row of wide eyes, hanging on out of fascination—pulling back from disgust, and fear, the disgust and fear winning, drawing them aside like a curtain.

Reverend Forbes held his ground. Elizabeth's mother and father stood rooted, numb and insensitive to those flowing back and around them. At first it was a trickle, a few, here and there, slipping hurriedly and nervously from the tent. Elizabeth watched them out of the corners of her vision, trying to rip her gaze from the man—the *creature* slipping from those trees.

Moments that lingered like years passed and they stood alone. Elizabeth, her mother, her father, Reverend Forbes, and the—man—from the trees. At the head of the table, the good Reverend stood, one hand on each corner, too close to the corpse for propriety, his eyes blazing. Mr. Halprin's expression didn't change, but Elizabeth wanted to cry out to him. To apologize. He looked so—forsaken—laying there.

"You have come," Forbes sang out. "For the sins of the fallen, for the salvation of his *soul*, you have come. Behold." Forbes' arms spread, sweeping wide to encompass the bounty of the feast. "The sins of the flesh, the substance of the flesh . . . the wine, that is His blood."

The man-thing stood and stared, meeting Forbes' gaze easily. The hunger danced in those eyes, but not alone. Emotion rode the surface of each bright orb. Elizabeth watched as that emotion rippled over the man's face. Not a creature . . . definitely a man, very familiar somehow. Those eyes swept the length of the table, took in the food, and the body. Swept up and locked with the Reverend's again. Held.

No words passed. Forbes grinned down the length of the table, the force of that glare withering, righteous and arrogant. He met wild, crazy hunger. He met unrelenting resolve. He met more than he could stomach, and now even Reverend Forbes was turning and staggering away, tripping, falling, and rising once more to run from the tent.

Elizabeth ignored it. She watched now, enraptured. There was an undercurrent of emotion rippling through the tent. She felt her mother stiffen, then sigh softly, shivering. She saw her father take a step forward, and another, saw that huge hand that had so often stroked her hair and gentled her fear, stretching, reaching out. Grasping only air as the thin caricature of a man turned toward the table and moved in.

No hesitation. No further notice paid to Elizabeth, or her family, or the Church, or the world. Food. Only the food, bread and vegetables, washed in endless streams of wine and water and tea, drumsticks devoured in seconds, bones flying in slow-motion arcs as more was grasped, driven between open lips and swallowed in heaving gulps. Too much. One thing to the next, to the next. Elizabeth's mother grew tense as the man reached her casserole, upended it, and pressed it between his lips. Elizabeth thought for a moment her mother would speak, but all that rose was a choked moan as the dish was emptied, tossed aside, replaced by an apple pie and washed away in a torrent of red wine.

Elizabeth's father took another step forward, and that was all it took to break the spell of the moment. Elizabeth's mother lurched after him, and Elizabeth was drawn along in the wake. She cried out, no coherent words, just a strangled, choked cry, but in that sound she packed a lifetime. She clung to her mother's skirt and buried her eyes in that soft material.

The man at the table spun on his heels. In that second, Elizabeth saw her father's eyes staring crazily back at her. She felt her mother jerk, tilting at an odd angle, dragging her forward and down. Somewhere between that moment and the ground her father spun, grabbed them both in arms suddenly wide and strong again. He didn't speak, but Elizabeth felt him *there* as she had not since they'd awakened that morning. He dragged Elizabeth's mother into one strong arm, and Elizabeth into the other, and turned them as a single unit. Away from the table. Away from the insanity.

"Daddy?" Elizabeth glanced up into his eyes, but he shook his head. No answer, as he half-smiled through a sudden trickle of tears. Elizabeth had never seen her father cry. She had never seen him in any way show a weakness that could be attributed to others. When he wrapped her close and turned from that tent, from that table and feast and the crazy man devouring it. When he backed away from those eyes, so like his own, so eerily familiar, she pressed close to his leg and stumbled at his side.

They passed from the shade of the tent, into the bright, mid-morning sun without a word. No glancing back, no turning. Straight down the mountain toward their home.

Behind them, the sounds of crazed feasting echoed.

TEN

Liz grew quiet, and they all stared at her. The story wasn't over, couldn't be over, but none of them wanted to be the one to coax the rest out of her. Dexter rose, letting his fingers come to rest at last, and moved to the kitchen. The sound of running water and the lazy drip of coffee followed moments later, seeming to ease the tension in the room.

"Mother and I were home before I even realized we'd left Daddy behind," Liz went on. "I wanted to go back. Those eyes, the sound of the food being consumed, filled my mind. Thank God for my mother. She changed, once we were out of sight of that tent and the church. It was like she woke up and remembered who she was, who *I* was. She clung to me, her voice low, just talking. I don't remember a thing she said, only that she didn't want me to go. That she wanted me there, very close to her. That she told me everything would be okay, or, that it would be less okay if I didn't stay.

"I can remember clinging to her skirt as if it were yesterday. . . ."

The door was heavy, stained wood with a heavy frame. Elizabeth stared at it, memorizing each crack, tracing the glittering curves of the brass knob with her gaze. She heard her mother speaking, but the words didn't register. Her mind was filled with images, wild images of too-wide, too-wild eyes, long, low-slung tables, and food stacked so high Mr. Halprin's features were hidden, then revealed slowly.

The doorknob turned slowly.

Elizabeth's heartbeat slowed—seemed to stop.

The door opened slowly, creaking as it always did, somehow ominous in this moment of clarity.

Her father stepped through that doorway, and everything shifted. The first thing Elizabeth saw were his eyes. Those eyes. The hunger. She opened her mouth to scream, but no sound came out, and before she quite recalled why she'd wanted to cry out, her father was on the couch beside her, wrapping her in his strong arms, too tightly. She didn't resist. In fact, she leaned into it, pressing her cheek fiercely to his chest.

They rocked that way for a long time. Elizabeth felt her mother melting to her father's back, lending her own support, and strength, to the embrace. Finally, all motion slowed, and her father pulled back. He watched her in silence, gauging the moment.

"Who is he?" Elizabeth heard the words she'd spoken as if from very far away. Detached from her. The answer distanced from hurting.

"He is your grandfather," the words softly spoken.

Elizabeth let this sink in. It fit. The eyes, so like her father's. The stares from the other families as they'd all made their way to the church. The silence, even from her friends. The odd tug at her heart as that man—that *thing*—had met her gaze and held.

Elizabeth's head began to shake back and forth slowly.

Her father's hands, strong and supportive again, the hands of the father she'd expected to walk to church with that morning, gripped her gently by her cheeks and drew her gaze up to his own. His own eyes were deep and pained. Endless, but open. For the first time in years, so open they drew memories from a childhood suddenly faded and withered.

"What was he *doing*, Daddy? Why was he there, eating that food? Why haven't you ever told me about him? Why didn't he know me?"

Her father leaned back; only his arm, draped distractedly over her shoulder, remained of the momentary intimacy.

Dexter broke the mood, setting a large mug of steaming coffee on the table before her. Liz blinked, sat up, and looked around. Brandt was curled up against Synthia. Shaver had his hand on her thigh, resting gently, his arm around her shoulder. Liz started, the similarity to the image in her mind, her father's strong arm, and Shaver's proximity, shivering through her violently.

The room remained silent for a long time. Liz ignored the coffee, regaining her breath and easing the tension Shaver's touch had brought, very suddenly, until she could lean in against his shoulder without shaking.

Synthia spoke softly. "He did know you."

Liz turned, nodded. Her eyes were downcast, and her brow was furrowed with the effort of dragging the memories from deep repression.

"It's okay," Brandt cut in. "We saw."

Liz's gaze whipped up and around this time. Brandt met her eyes steadily. She studied his expression, seeking ridicule, or condescension. Finding none.

Brandt rose, extricating himself from Syn's arms slowly—reluctantly—and moving to the side of the room. His guitar case leaned there, half-forgotten, and he reached for it, laying it flat on the floor and unfastening the hasps with practiced motions.

The strap was around his neck a moment later, his fingers brushing the strings. Everyone was watching him. Everyone except Syn, who looked right past/through him as if she saw some other. Something more. Brandt's fingers pressed more tightly, and he strummed tentatively at the strings, minor-chord vibration of the moment, growing slowly in volume and intensity. He leaned on the corner of the couch, closing his eyes as the music rippled from the strings.

As the notes fell from Brandt's strings, tears rolled down Liz's cheeks. She closed her eyes, breathing deeply to regain control of her voice. When she spoke again, she was quieter, each word deeply entrenched in forgotten, or repressed, emotion. No one in the room moved, except Brandt. Brandt continued to play, softly. His eyes were closed, his head leaned back against the wall, long hair cascading over his shoulders and the guitar resting against his hip, undulating slowly to the rhythm.

"Home was like a dream after all that. As strange as the morning had started, it had become almost normal. Not quite, but close enough that my mother, and my father, were recognizable as themselves. As distant as they had been, now they were close, the expressions on their faces full of some deep, sad emotion I couldn't understand."

The room shifted slowly, the warmth sifting back in, borne by the soft rays of the sun and the tentative smile on her mother's lips. Elizabeth sat on the couch, still shaking. A thousand questions sifted through her mind, but she kept them to herself. She knew what she wanted—what she *needed*—to know, yet somehow it was important that one, or both, of her parents tell her without being prompted.

"He is your grandfather." The words slipped from her father's lips in a whisper. Elizabeth wasn't certain she'd heard them at all. She watched his eyes, waiting.

"It has been a long time, princess," he said at last. Tears welled in the corners of her eyes at that name. He only called her princess when things were very emotional. The best times, and the worst. "I haven't seen him since you were knee-high to a grasshopper. I guess I thought I never would."

"It's that Reverend Forbes," Elizabeth's mother cut in. "He made it happen. Brought poor Hiram back."

"Shhhh . . ." Elizabeth's father soothed. "Papa is what he is. Forbes is maybe not the best man to come down the pike as Reverend, but he made no choices for any other. There are some things no one can control. Papa eats the sin. That is what he does . . . what he has always done. It is what his father did."

There was more to that statement, but it was left unspoken. Elizabeth swallowed, averting her eyes. Images of Mr. Halprin's body, decked out in roasted chicken and fresh fruit, surfaced to haunt her, overshadowed by the deep-set, hungry eyes that had watched her from the woods, and gazed at her from the table.

"It's barbaric," her mother asserted. "It isn't right. There are a thousand churches in this country, Brian, a thousand churches full of righteous women and God-fearing men and not a one of them would stand for this. It is that *Reverend* and I don't understand why you won't stand up for your own." After a moment's silence, she continued, "He is your father."

Elizabeth's father lowered his eyes. His lips grew tight, and she knew he was thinking . . . but also that he wasn't pleased by her mother's words.

"I have lived here all my life," he said at last. "I have seen preachers come, and preachers go. I have seen the church at its finest, and at its worst, but there have always been certain truths that we have lived by. One of those is the Sineater."

Elizabeth's mother looked away. Her features were drawn in a tight frown of disapproval, but she held her tongue.

Elizabeth turned to her father. "Why?"

"It isn't a question of why," her father answered slowly, his expression far away. "It is a question of what is right. There has always been a Sineater. No one ever asks why, or even who. The who is a set thing, and the why is in God's hands."

"I don't understand." The words were soft, whispered, all-inclusive of the moment and so inadequate.

"Men must atone," her father began slowly. "There is a pattern to the universe, and we must conform to it. There is a pattern to the Lord's work—a pattern we too often ignore. It is even more powerful than the pattern that governs your mind. It is more perfect than the best you can do in design, or belief. Perfect. That pattern called out to those who have come before."

Elizabeth's father sounded different, like a recording of some long-practiced speech. The words rang true, but the tone was wrong. Monotonic and forced. Elizabeth glanced at her mother. The expression in those deep blue eyes was more than enough to jar her back to the reality of the moment.

"*Why!*" she leaned in, letting her hands slap down hard on her father's thigh. "Why Daddy? Why Grandpa? Why *you? Why?*"

"Sin." He answered simply, not meeting her gaze. Something had caught at the corners of his lips, drawing them down. His expression was so serious Elizabeth wanted to draw back, pressing to her mother, but she could not. She had to know.

"It is the sin," her father repeated. "It is everywhere.

They tell us to repent, to feel remorse for things we do in the face of the Lord, but who listens? I'll tell you," his gaze swept up to capture Elizabeth's, with a defiant glance at his wife before continuing. "The sin never slows. It is the substance that binds human lives together. It is the core of our hearts. We live. We love. We sin, hoping for forgiveness from a God we fear only in the last moments of our lives."

"We are forgiven." Elizabeth's mother spoke softly. "That is the promise. That is the reason for faith. He died for our sins, that we may live beyond this world."

"Not everyone asks for that gift," came the practiced answer. "Not everyone begs forgiveness before passing."

"You are not your brother's keeper."

"I am my father's son."

Elizabeth started at the sudden sob that broke free of her mother's throat. She turned, but her mother was rising, moving away. Elizabeth started to rise, to follow, but she felt her father's hand dropping gently on her knee, holding her in place.

"It is time," he said softly. "You need to hear what I have to say. Your mother has never understood. You may not either, but you have to hear. He is your grandfather."

"Why," she asked, "hasn't he ever come to see me?"

Her father stopped, shaken somehow by that simple question, his own train of thought derailed.

Elizabeth heard her mother gasp again, turned to that sound and watched the flush spread over those familiar features.

"He can't, Elizabeth," her father said at last. "He never can, never will. Even if he would, I couldn't let him."

Elizabeth frowned. "I don't understand. He's my grandfather, your father. Why can't he come here? What was all that *food*, Daddy? What was the Reverend Forbes talking about?"

"He's the *Sineater*," her mother hissed. "He is *vile*."

Elizabeth's father turned like a snake and growled. "Enough. You don't believe that any more than I do. Don't you *dare* put it in Elizabeth's head."

He turned back to her. "He was there because Reverend Forbes drew him there, Elizabeth. He was there to help Mr. Halprin along his way to heaven." There was a long moment of silence, then he continued. "I have not seen him in a very long time. I thought he would be left in peace."

Elizabeth's mind whirled with emotion and confusion. She started to speak again, but her mother gripped her by the shoulder.

"I never wanted to see him again," her father continued. "No one did. It was to end with him."

"What was to end?" Elizabeth asked.

"He is the Sineater," her mother breathed, repeating herself. "He takes the sin, that the dead may leave us in peace."

Elizabeth's father's eyes dropped. This time he did not silence his wife, only listened as she droned on, words they both seemed to know so well they flowed in a long monotonous chant.

"He takes the sin from those who have passed, consumes it, draws it from their soul. He must finish every bite, nothing to be spared, and the darkness will seek him, abandoning the dead. He carries that sin within him, dark and deep. He walks alone. He sleeps in daylight and each shadow is his brother. He can never return."

"But," Elizabeth whispered, "Why did he *go?* Why did you let him? Where is grandma?"

The soft torrent of questions was too much for her father. He scooped her into his arms and drew her tightly to his chest. Tears flowed down his rugged cheeks, and she felt them dampening her hair, but she didn't pull back. She had never felt such emotion, such . . . pain.

"I was a boy, Elizabeth. I was no older than you are. He went because he had to go, as his father before him went. When the Sineater dies, who will eat that sin? Who will see him home to the heavens, if not his son?"

There was a long silence. Elizabeth had questions, questions that now screamed to be asked. She was not allowed the chance. Her mother spun, rising and stepping away. All that Elizabeth could see was her mother's shoulders, muscles too tight, hands clasped to her breasts. No words, but tension rippled in the air. Elizabeth held her breath.

"My mother, your grandmother, stayed to raise me," Elizabeth's father continued slowly. "She never saw him again, except when there was a death. I haven't seen him in years. When he was gone, no one knew for sure where he went. The mountain. No one wanted to find him. They took him food, people from the church, your grandmother. Others. They brought things to him, but never directly. Always they were left where they could be found, when he walked alone. They were quick to offer him the sins of their loved ones, but where did that leave the sin? Where did that leave him? Alone. The weight of a mountain's sin on his shoulders."

Elizabeth felt tears rolling down her face as her father's voice trembled. "He looks like you," she said. "I want to meet him."

Her mother whirled. Elizabeth had never seen such anger, such absolute shock, on her mother's face. "Never. You may never meet him. He may never come back. Don't you *see*, Elizabeth? Didn't you *hear?*"

Elizabeth's father was up in an instant, moving to calm his wife, but she pulled away, the anger flashing in her eyes.

"He has eaten the *sin!* He walks alone, and he must walk

alone. He is *tainted*. The Reverend Forbes has told us how it must be, how it should always have been. We have been wrong. We have *sinned* and he is our only hope."

"That is enough," her father said quietly. Elizabeth's mother opened her mouth to speak again, but he was there, and she clamped off the words, turning and hurrying from the room.

Elizabeth watched it all with the surreal detachment of a child. She'd heard short arguments, quickly calmed. She'd even seen her mother cry. She had never seen anything to match this. Never felt the shiver of a crack, running up the smooth surface of her family's close-knit love.

Her father took a step to follow her mother's retreat, then stopped. His shoulders crumbled, and he dropped his head to his hands. Elizabeth could see that he was shaking. She rose, moving quickly to hug him, letting her cheek rest on his hip. She wanted to say something, to do something, that would make it better, or even different. She couldn't rid herself of the image, her grandfather, staring at her from the trees. He had known who she was. He must have seen her before—must have watched her.

She felt her father's arm circling her at last, and he turned, drawing her into a tight hug. He held her like that for a long time. Elizabeth felt the thudding echo of his heart in his chest. It was a warm, safe moment. Then it was over. As he pulled back, she glanced up. In that instant, she didn't see her father's face, but her grandfather's.

Patterns shifted and words clicked into proper perspective in her young mind.

I am my father's son.
Who will eat the Sineater's sin?

Her father whispered to her, breaking the spell. "I'm sorry, Elizabeth."

Then he turned, following her mother from the room, and Elizabeth was left in her too-nice Sunday clothes, the room still scented with her mother's perfume and her father's cologne. The door to the kitchen stood open. She could see the dishes left from her mother's baking. The food prepared for the feast that was not a feast. Cooking sin? Was that it? Or did the sin come only from Mr. Halprin, soaked into the food like a sauce?

How could one man eat so much? How was it possible he could do that, be so thin—live in the mountains with no one else there to care for him, to cook for him? How could any man or woman walk alone?

It was a long time before she slipped out of that room and down the hall to her own. She heard the muffled sound of her parents' voices from their own room, but she ignored them. Slowly, Elizabeth unwound the ribbon from her hair, brushed it, tied it back, and began to undress. She slipped into jeans and a t-shirt quickly, leaving the Sunday finery carefully folded on her bed. She knew there would be no attending evening services. She didn't know if she could ever go to that place again. For anything.

Her window opened onto the back yard, opposite her parents' room. The edge of that yard skirted the forest, trees rising and rising in a green blanket as the mountains disappeared above. She couldn't see the church from her window, but it was there. You could just make it out from the porch, gazing off to where the mountain fell away to the road. She felt its presence, felt the Reverend Forbes' eyes on her, accusing. Her mother's voice echoed in her mind.

Never.

Elizabeth gripped the window and shoved it up, the old wood grating slightly. She'd read a thousand books about children sneaking out their windows to avoid the eyes of their parents, but it had never occurred to her she would be one of them. The screen was more difficult, but Elizabeth had seen her father slide it up many times, and eventually she was able to apply enough pressure to the small, corroded catches to press them out and unlock the slides. The air was still warm outside, the sun on the downward slope from noon. It seemed as though lifetimes had passed since they'd fled the church, but it had really not been so long. She was a little hungry, but the memory of the morning's feast nauseated her, and she knew she couldn't eat.

With a quick, nervous glance over her shoulder at the door, she slipped one leg over the sill and slid out onto the grass. The woods beckoned. Had he watched her? Was he watching now? Without taking time to think about it, Elizabeth took off for the tree line, running through the soft grass as quickly as possible. She knew she couldn't allow herself to be seen. There would never be a second chance, but she had to know. Had to see. He was her *grandfather.*

"You went after him?" Shaver's voice cut through the visions. He drew her against his side and circled her in his arms. "God, you were just a kid!"

The room was silent for a moment, except for Brandt. He was playing gently, notes dancing in and around one another. It was a song of the hills, wild, and slow at the same time. Everyone sat back and listened until the notes faded.

Liz turned to watch, curling closer to Shaver. She couldn't recall if Brandt had been playing the whole time she'd spoken. As the notes faded, she whispered, "I had to go. I had to know the truth."

"And what did you find?" Synthia asked. "Did you find your grandfather? What did you do?"

Liz let her head drop to Shaver's shoulder.

"He found me."

The world grew darker as Elizabeth stepped from sunlight to shadow. She had never been far into the woods alone. She and her father had gone there many times, chasing butterflies, hunting nuts and berries, fishing in the stream that came down from the mountain a few hundred yards in.

Elizabeth had never been forbidden to enter them alone; the rule had been an unspoken understanding. When you walked beneath that wide canopy of trees, things began to look the same in every direction. Familiar landmarks repeated themselves on opposite sides of clearings.

Elizabeth kept these lessons in the front of her mind. She was careful. She always listened when her father spoke, and this was one time it came in handy. She took sticks as she walked and propped them up, using the fork of one to point the tip of another, marking her trail. She didn't know where she was going, but common sense told her if he lived in the woods, he had to live near the stream. Logic also told her that if she followed that stream, and marked the place where she started well, she would be less likely to get lost.

It wasn't as dark beside the stream. The trees stretched upward on either side, but that one strip of land was open to the sun and sky. It made her feel a little safer, but still she clutched her arms tightly around her as she walked. She wished her father was there, walking at her side, pointing out the different flowers and trees. She wished her mother was there to sing with her. Elizabeth's voice was thin, and not very loud in the huge expanse of trees, backed up by the rushing of the small stream, and the bright, shrill voices of birds. Still, she sang. Songs from the church. Songs she loved, that she'd shared with her mother as she drifted off to sleep, or as the two of them worked in the kitchen.

She didn't let the image of her mother's face, turning away from her father, intrude on that moment, or on the song. She sang, and she watched the trees, thinking of baking bread, and sewing her first apron, of bright smiles and stories read by the light of her bed-lamp. She saw nothing but trees and more trees, but she didn't let it deter her. The sun was still high in the sky, and she was determined not to return without answers.

The stream bed wound up the side of the mountain, and Elizabeth followed its banks at a slow, steady pace. She had no idea how long she'd walked or how far. The sun had begun to dip on the horizon, and the shadows were lengthening. She knew she'd have to turn back soon, or there was no way she'd find her mark, or her way.

She also knew her parents would be looking for her soon. That thought was comforting, but at the same time it lent an urgency to her search. Her grandfather's eyes haunted her, until each glance at the line of trees beside her, and the matching line across the stream, seemed lined with those eyes. It was this illusion that nearly caused her to miss them when they appeared.

He was leaning out from behind the trunk of one of the larger trees, watching her as she nearly passed him by. Elizabeth caught sight of him in the periphery of her vision and stopped, uncertain she'd seen anything at all. He stood as still as one of the trees, his arms wrapped around the trunk of one, cheek leaning against the bark and his head tilted quizzically, watching her.

Elizabeth turned slowly. She met his gaze and stood there, very still, watching him. She wanted that moment etched in her memory. He might believe as her parents. He might run if she moved toward him, and she wanted at least the memory of being close to him to stick with her. There was no indication that he would move, so she took a tentative step forward, and then another. Elizabeth's heart pounded, but she couldn't stop now. Her steps grew more and more hurried, and before she knew she would do it, she was running to his arms.

He didn't move. He watched her, an expression lost between amazement and reverence etched across every inch of his face. The image of Elizabeth's father imposed itself over his, and she closed her eyes, dropping into her grandfather's arms. He held her carefully, as if afraid she were fragile, that he'd break her or hurt her, or touch somewhere inappropriate. Elizabeth had never been held so lightly, or so completely.

"Why didn't you come to see me?" she asked, not looking up. "Why didn't I know you existed?"

There was no answer. A slight increase in pressure told her he understood, but he didn't speak. He didn't get the chance. There was a crashing in the brush. Her father's voice, loud, hoarse, broke the silence and for one moment, Elizabeth felt her grandfather freeze, gripping her shoulders a bit tighter, his head lifting.

"No," she said. "Don't go. Please. I want to . . ."

Nothing. She gripped nothing. He was gone that quickly, gray hair whipping over his shoulders, flitting from shadow to shadow, lost to her sight as quickly as he'd appeared. Elizabeth reached out, taking a step, then another, trying to follow. Her voice rose now, echoing through the trees.

"No! Come back. Don't go, don't *go!*"

Her words echoed emptily, and moments later, strong arms circled her from behind, scooping her from the ground and into a bear-like hug, scented by her father's tobacco and cologne. Elizabeth struggled for a moment, trying to slip off into those shadows, trying to follow. She got a final glimpse: wide, bright eyes gazing at her, then slipping behind a tree and gone.

"Elizabeth," her father breathed hoarsely, tightening his hug. "God, why did you come here, why?" He was shaking, and though his hug was tight enough to make her squirm uncomfortably, Elizabeth felt the anguish in his voice.

She leaned her head on his shoulder and whispered, "Why did he run, Daddy? I want to know him. Why did he run?"

Her father only rocked her quietly, his own breath heavy from chasing her through the forest. When he found his voice, he ignored the question, turning toward the stream and starting the long walk home, not making a move yet to let her down to her feet.

"I love you," he said simply. "Come home."

Liz grew silent, and they all held their breath, expectant. Disappointed. She did not continue, only laid her head quietly on Shaver's shoulder. He felt her sobbing gently, and drew her closer, leaning so his cheek rested softly on her hair. The silence unfolded slowly, washing over them and quickly driving Dexter past his limits. Only the soft notes of Brandt's guitar trickled over them, and without the story to back him up, he only contributed to that emptiness.

"What happened?" he asked. His voice wasn't as soft as it might have been, his words were a bit too quick. The others glared at him, but Liz didn't move.

Shaver drew her closer. "Not now, Dex," he said.

Dexter blinked, as though just waking up from a long dream. His face flickered from curious to anxious. "I'm sorry," he said quickly. "Just . . . Jesus. Just want to know."

"We all want to know," Synthia said, "but it can wait. I don't know about the rest of you, but my body doesn't function without food. When was the last time we ate?"

Brandt glanced up from where he'd been watching his fingers flicker over the strings of his guitar. He stilled the sound, completing the silence. Then, leaning the guitar against the wall, he moved to the couch, crouching down before Liz and Shaver. He touched her knee lightly, his eyes too bright. "It wasn't your grandfather I met, was it?"

Liz curled tighter against Shaver, tucking her head low. Still, they could all see as she shook her head. Brandt watched her for a moment, then rose. He moved to stand beside Synthia, where she leaned into the corner of the couch, and squatted again, hugging her tightly.

"I know where we have to go," he said softly.

If it had been silent before, the air was *barren* of sound following that remark. They all watched him, waiting. Brandt had turned his gaze to the floor, and was biting at his lip, deep in thought.

"How do you know?" Syn asked. "What did you mean it wasn't Liz's grandfather?"

Brandt didn't answer, and slowly, Liz extricated herself from Shaver's arms and sat up, wiping her eye with the back of her hand.

"Brandt is right," she said. "Grandfather died before I left home."

"Then who . . ." Dexter cut off his question mid-way and cursed. "Oh fuck."

Brandt nodded. "We have to go there. Not today, but soon. I can feel things building."

"Things?" Shaver asked. "What kind of things? I wish to hell I understood what you were talking about. Why would we want to go to a place like that? You feel a sudden urge to join the church? They'll run us out on a rail, if they don't sacrifice us all to some great pagan God. I mean *look* at us, Brandt. What could be waiting there for us?"

"Not what," Brandt answered, turning to grab his guitar again and moving to slip it carefully into its case. "Who."

Shaver growled, but before he could speak again, Liz's hand dropped to his knee.

"I think Brandt is right. I don't know why. I thought I'd never go there again, *swore* I wouldn't set foot on that mountain in this lifetime, but now I know it was all an act. I always knew I'd have to go back and face him. Face her."

"*Who?*" Shaver and Dexter demanded in unison.

"Daddy," she said softly. "And my mother."

ELEVEN

The cottage sat low against a backdrop of heavy foliage and an almost solid line of trees. The windows were open, white curtains bright with lace. The door was open, as well, and a soft trickle of smoke rose from the chimney. Over the front door, a whitewashed wooden sign proclaimed, "He is risen." The letters were red, stark against the virginal white backdrop.

To either side of the door, crude plywood signs had been nailed. One held the 23rd Psalm, carefully lettered with a small black brush. The other was an equally careful rendition of John 3:16.

Crosses lined the porch. Large, small, some ornate—others crude and simple. A few of those that were wide enough bore messages.

"JESUS" vertical and "SAVES" horizontal.

"REPENT" vertical and "BE SAVED" horizontal.

They ringed the porch, cocked at odd angles, and nailed firmly to anything solid. The walls, and to the frames of windows, which also held tracts and biblical paraphernalia pressed tightly to the glass from the inside.

The signs didn't stop at the porch. They stretched into the yard, lined the walk, and circled the fence. There was a single large cross pounded into the dirt in the center of that yard, and from it hung a figure that had been carved poorly from a single fallen log. Its branches stretched to either side, bare arms, and its roots curled to the sides at the base of the cross. At first glance, a tree, but if one stared long enough, the piece took on the life its discoverer, crucifier, had intended. Warped, twisted, the top of the severed stump curling back, bent neck and face staring skyward. In red letters, on the front, were the words, "Why have you forsaken me?"

He watched from the shade of one of the larger trees, taking in each sign, lingering over the scribbled messages. His gaze swept along the front of the house, noting the candles in the windows, the crosses and the biblical verses. Protection? As his gaze swept up and down the twisted tree-corpse sculpture in the center of the yard, he smiled. The morning sunlight glowed on the dark skin of his arms, and glinted too brightly from the flint-gray depths of his eyes. His smile was empty. No emotion, just a wrinkle of lips and a quick flash of white teeth.

Stepping from the shadows, he skirted the fence closely, watching the windows for any sign of motion. There was nothing. The house could have been abandoned, empty for years. The door swung slightly in the breeze, creaking loudly. He stopped for a second, as if he might turn down that walk and enter, then seemed to think better of it and turned toward the trees once more.

In the distance, church bells were ringing. He shifted his attention to that sound, drifting back to the shadows from where he'd appeared. The house remained as he'd left it: the door open, the candles burning, all-but-invisible in the bright morning sun. Inside, the steady creak of a rocking chair echoed softly, keeping perfect time with the bells.

Moments later, the creaking stopped. The curtains of one window were drawn aside with a nervous jerk. Madeline glared out through the dingy glass at the line of trees. She'd seen him. She'd felt his presence, even before he came from the trees and approached her house. She always knew when the dark ones were near. She didn't fear them, but she knew. Her fingers slid up and down the silver chain about her neck, fiddling with the gleaming cross at the end.

There had been a bunch of them over the years. Beggars, demons, men claiming to be preachers, and preachers claiming to be God. Since Reverend Forbes had died, there'd been a slew of pretenders. No one would listen to her. No one understood about the sin. About the one who could cleanse it. The old ways fell steadily aside, and Madeline drew just as steadily back from the town, and the church.

They still met like clockwork: Sunday morning, Sunday evening, and Wednesdays for Bible study. They sang, and they praised the Lord their God with happy, senseless hymns and bingo dinners. They lived, and they loved, and they ignored the lessons of the past.

Madeline's gaze shifted to the shelves along the walls. Amid a small jungle of potted plants and endless rows of tracts and biblical reference books, a single framed photograph stared back at her. His eyes were as deep and caring as they'd been the day she'd married him. Elizabeth's smile was angelic, as though there were no evil in the world. As if it didn't threaten to smother them every moment of every day. As if the Lord would never punish them for spitting in the face of the old ways.

"I knew you would be the one," she whispered, "when I married you, I knew."

There was no answer. There had been no answer in over a decade, and each day he had been gone Madeline had said a prayer in his name, lit another candle, and worked on her "wards." The time was coming when she would need them, every one. There was a strength in the words of the

Bible that many missed, a protection that sealed one away from dangers most never even acknowledged. Madeline saw those dangers every night in her dreams. She knew the words of the Bible to be true; she'd lived them, Genesis to Revelation, night after night.

More often than not she dreamed of the one she loved. She dreamed of feasts, and candlelight. She dreamed of the sins of the community, those who'd died since Reverend Forbes. Those who *he* had not attended. Sometimes she dreamed that it all faded, and he returned, but those dreams ended the same each time. Cold. Alone.

Sometimes, those cold empty mornings, she had visions.

Sometimes she prophesied to those who passed her doors.

Sometimes she cried.

She could still hear the voices of the choir singing low and mournful the night her world crumbled. She could see the candles flickering all along the road that led toward the church. Brian had stood beside her that night, watching. It wasn't a church night, but the bells had begun to ring early on, and had not ceased since.

"What is it Brian?" she asked. "What in the Lord's name is it?"

Elizabeth had crawled out of her bed, sleepy-eyed, creeping down the hall quietly. She knew she wasn't supposed to be up, but this time Madeline allowed it, concentrating on what was happening outside. Between the long, doleful tolling of the bell, the voice of a choir rose gently, pulsing on the breeze.

"I don't know, Madeline," Brian had said. "But you know I have to find out."

She'd shivered, leaning in close against his side. "Don't," she'd whispered. "They will come to us."

Brian had turned then, leaning down and cupping her chin in one strong hand. "I'm an Elder. I have to go. Reverend Forbes will be waiting for me. I should not have waited so long."

Madeline knew she'd shown the weakness of her faith that moment. She'd clung to him, eyes brimming with tears as she turned to kiss his wrist. "They will be fine without you. Please?"

There had been no further words. Brian had kissed her deeply, just once, and turned away. Elizabeth, who'd been watching from the shadows, cried out then, and Brian turned back. Moving quickly, he gathered his daughter into his arms, hugging her tightly.

"Don't worry," he said softly. "The Lord is our strength."

And he'd gone. Just like that. One moment, a family, joined by their faith; the next the world shifting on the Devil's axis. Madeline had wrapped her arm around her daughter's shoulder as the girl moved to her side, but her eyes were locked on Brian's back as he marched resolutely down the road, one moment in shadow, the next backlit by the candles lighting his way, then to shadow again, and finally out of sight.

"Where is he going, Momma?" Elizabeth had asked.

Madeline couldn't answer at first. The lump in her throat was far too large, and the bells were tolling again. "The Reverend is calling him," Madeline choked out at last. "All the Elders must go to such a summons, Elizabeth, you know that."

There was a momentary silence, then Elizabeth said, "There have never been so many candles, Momma. Why do they lead to us?"

Madeline had whispered her answer. "They don't, baby . . . they lead to him."

* * * * *

The vision ended differently, sometimes. Sometimes she was granted images of what had happened in the church that night. Other times she saw things through her daughter's eyes, or through those of one of the ladies who'd once called her friend. Other times she saw nothing but the candles, and Brian's back, through a halo of salty, stinging tears. Prophecy, they said, was a gift. Madeline was uncertain where the line between gift and curse should be drawn. She knew only that, when the time had come to stand at his side and to prove her faith, she'd cowered in their home, falling asleep at last, on the floor beside the bed Brian had left and never returned to, her mother's hand-sewn quilt wrapped tightly around shaking shoulders and stained with her tears.

Now that faith was strong. Years of prayer, and hard work, had seen to that. An empty, accusing bed and thousands of meals with no one to share the sunrise had stiffened her resolve. She missed him, still. At the oddest moments, Brian's face would fill her mind's eye, blocking reality. She'd spoken to him more than once. There was never an answer, but she knew he'd heard.

Others had heard as well. It hadn't taken Madeline long to realize she had to withdraw from everyone. From everything in the world, in fact, except her God. Even Elizabeth, in the end, had turned away. Elizabeth had been there that night. She'd seen her father walk away into those candle flames to never return. The difference was, she'd never made her peace with it. Alternately, Elizabeth had blamed her mother, her father, Reverend Forbes, God, and the world for that night, and none of it had mattered. Each direction she'd turned without finding the answers she'd sought had fed her frustration.

Her friends had shunned her. Reverend Forbes had told her of her father's faith, of his gift to the community, and to the world, while his eyes sparked with a malice borne of nothing akin to any faith other than in himself. The Church couldn't see it. Not then. They heard his words, felt the power behind them, and assumed it to be that of God. When he spoke of sin, and the road to heaven, and the unnamed sacrifice of one they called brother, Elizabeth had to be led from the church.

When Reverend Forbes had attempted to chastise Madeline for her daughter's outburst, they'd had to lead her out as well. Permanently. She'd not set foot in the building since that day, preferring the company of her signs, and her crosses, and the power of her own prayers. It hadn't been enough for Elizabeth, in the end. She'd wanted to leave. She'd wanted Madeline to leave, to go out into the world and find another place, a place with no Sineater, with no church bowing the people under like slaves. A place in a world that seemed real. She'd wanted a life, and that was the one thing Madeline couldn't give her.

She didn't own her life any longer. It belonged to God, as surely as Brian's did, and it belonged to Brian. What she had left was the shell of what should have been his, but she couldn't take that away. As long as he was out there, as long as they didn't know for sure if he lived, or died, she would remain. She would pray. She would offer up her days and her nights on the altar of the love she'd denied. Peter had denied his Lord three times. Madeline intended to stop at one.

The shadow that had passed her window stuck with her, blocking the warmth of the morning sun. No one was in sight, but still she hesitated to move across the plane of the window. It had been a long time since a day had such an effect.

She couldn't get Elizabeth's face from her mind. Elizabeth's face as she'd last seen it, streaked with tears and filled with a pain that would not be denied. Elizabeth's face, turned to Madeline in the supplication only a daughter can bring to bear. Only the weight of guilt, and the surreal tension of the moment, had kept her from drawing her daughter close and fleeing that mountain forever. She'd last seen her daughter through the dust-streaked windows of a Greyhound bus, headed out into a world that might as well not exist. Gone, more surely, even, than Brian. Lost to her, but with one difference. Brian had left because it was his destiny. Elizabeth had left of her own free will. Madeline could understand her daughter abandoning her. She felt the burden of that guilt acutely.

What she could not forgive, or understand, was Elizabeth abandoning her father.

There was no other. No son. No heir. It had never happened in the history of Friendly, in the history of the church that Madeline had searched and learned and loved. There was always another, one to pass the sins along to, to free the *one* from the burden and carry on. Brian was out there, somewhere, alone. He had not been called upon in years.

There had been a movement, Madeline at its head, to plan the feast when Reverend Forbes had died. The church Elders would have none of it. That was part of what they feared and hated in Forbes, and with him gone, they had no intention of letting the traditions continue. They couldn't control it, so they ignored it. Reverend Forbes had been cremated.

Madeline remembered, and she shivered. They had kept it quiet. Elders only in attendance. The crowds had murmured among themselves, grown restless, but in the end, they were only sheep. When the new *shepherd* appeared, they listened, rapt, as they had listened to Reverend Forbes. They wondered—for a time—about Forbes' death, his funeral. They wondered about the feasts, and the shadowy figure who haunted the roadways and the hills, bowed under by the weight of the sins of their fathers. The new Reverend, and his successor, and the next, they helped. They steered thoughts in other directions. They planned things: family cookouts, bingo. When they saw too many sets of eyes trained on the surrounding woods, they changed tactics and held a "revival." When too many wondered about Reverend Forbes, they would bring in a fiery speaker from down the mountain.

In time, it all faded. In time, anything can fade. Anything but faith. The problem with the faith of the masses was that it was collective. Madeline knew her faith intimately. It was all she had, all she dreamed of and strove to sustain.

They could have brought him back. She knew that. They could have sent men and women into those mountains, and they could have brought Brian back. They could have broken the spell cast by centuries of custom. They could have accepted him, brought him home. They did not. They chose to ignore him. To ignore everything that church they worshiped in had been built upon. They had chosen poorly.

Now shadows stalked the roads, moving toward that church, and they worshiped in ignorance. Still he waited. He watched. If they called, he would come. Madeline knew this deep within her soul. He could have come back on his own, but he did not. He knew his place, and he knew his purpose. Sometimes, Madeline believed he knew the future. She wished that she had that gift. It loomed too dark, too lonely, for her own heart to bear.

Finally she moved to the window, staring off down the

road. She could see smoke rising from the cookout barbecue grills. She knew they were gathered, that whatever Reverend of the week had been driven in was railing at them, beseeching them to be generous in the collection and blessed in the meal they were about to receive. There was no sign of the shadowy figure who'd stalked her yard, but she knew where he'd been headed. They would never see him coming.

Madeline nearly went to them. For the first time in years, she had the urge to make her voice heard. There were so few with the true faith. A few, old enough to remember Forbes, and Brian. Even fewer who might answer her warning with anything but scorn. All her life, Madeline had heard stories of the Apostles, of the persecution of those who did the work of the Lord. She'd had an example in Brian's father, and ignored it. Now she knew. She knew that future; she would speak, they would not listen, and then the dark one would know her as a stronger enemy than he'd believed. She wasn't certain she would know him as quickly, despite the sensation his passing had caused.

In the end, she only stared down the road, listening to the voices raised in song, and waited. If he was darkness, she knew he would return. If he stood for death, then his true road was through her—and Brian. He would know that, of course, but he would ally himself with the living. He would find aid among those who had passed, as well. Those who'd passed without Brian's gift. Those who'd believed, and died, and been abandoned by a church that didn't believe in itself. Those who waited.

Brian would have helped them. Madeline would have set the feasts herself, had offered to, each and every time there was a death, until the responses turned from quiet negatives to violent anger. Those she'd once called friend would not give her the time of day. If someone died, they shunned her. If she made one of her infrequent trips to town, they turned away and pretended she was just another bit of sidewalk. They denied the past and Madeline could not escape it.

The sun had risen high above, cutting straight down through the trees to bake the roof of her home. Madeline had only a single, rusted fan, rotating lazily back and forth on her desk, to ward off the heat. Totally overwhelmed, it whirred, and spun, facing the window, then away, moving tepid air about listlessly. Madeline watched it for a moment, empathizing.

With a long, deep sigh, she turned toward the kitchen and slipped into the brighter light provided by wide, open windows that overlooked the back of the home. The grass rolled away toward the tree line. To the left of the kitchen was Elizabeth's room. Madeline hadn't changed a thing in there. It was that window Elizabeth had slipped out, that rolling hill she'd made her way down, breaking the old ways to go to her grandfather. Elizabeth had always been the strong one.

Now Brian was out there, somewhere. Brian, and another. Madeline felt the draw of her husband's presence, but she couldn't go into those woods.

"He walks alone," she whispered to herself, the words no comfort at all against the cold emptiness that was her heart.

Moments later, the stove was lit, and the kettle on to boil. Madeline sat down at the old table, back stiff against the wooden chair and her gaze locked on the line of the forest beyond her safe haven.

"Be careful," she whispered. "Please, God, let him be careful."

Reverend Hiram McKeenan was in rare form. He was

just reaching his stride, just reaching the *meat* of his sermon, when the doors opened. This wasn't a rarity, not at all. Folks wandered in late all the time. Hiram glanced up, nodded to the stranger, and turned his eyes back to the notes he kept on a small note card, hidden on the podium. Except, after he looked back down, he couldn't seem to remember where he'd left off. He could see the words, but they made no sense.

"I . . ." He stopped. Glancing up, he sought those eyes once again, but the stranger had moved, taking a seat and losing himself in the crowd. Reverend McKeenan cleared his throat, eyes watering as if he'd caught a dark whiff of smoke, and reached for his water. The congregation had begun to grow restless at his sudden silence. He gulped the water, closing his eyes and saying a quiet prayer.

When he glanced back to the note card, everything was fine. The room came back into focus, and he felt a sheen of sweat on his forehead that had not been there before.

"The Devil takes many guises," he continued, regaining his voice, but lacking the conviction it had had moments before. "He may appear as an angel of light, or a wolf, in the lily-white skin of a sheep. He may creep up on you by night, or shake your hand in the brilliant light of the sun and smile the smile of the damned. You won't know him, but your faith can preserve you. You can't fight him, but he can never defeat you."

The lights were getting brighter—hotter somehow. Hiram brushed sweat from his eyes with the sleeve of his jacket, knowing it was poor form, but blinded by the stinging invasion of salt. Colored streams of light leaked from the stained glass above and filtered down, confusing his sight as the perspiration formed prismatic halos.

"He will . . ." His throat was parched. Hiram reached for

his glass, missed, toppling it from the podium in a bright glittering trail. The glass shattered loudly on the altar beneath him, and the icy liquid splashed out, reaching those seated in the front row of pews and scattering them. Hiram staggered back, reaching first for the glass, then the podium. He watched in fascination as the crowd parted, slow-motion dives to the side and legs lifted to avoid the water. Then it tilted. Everything, and Hiram gasped in surprise.

"He will come to you," he whispered, "from shadows . . ."

Hiram saw, high above, the stained-glass rendition of Christ hanging from his cross. A bright flash of sunlight glittered through the heart of that image, shattering in a blast of brilliance that stole his breath. In that moment, with that final breath, Hiram tried to scream. The gurgle trickled off to silence, unheard.

Long moments of silence. Feet shuffling, gasped whispers, and a quick settling of those who'd moved to avoid the water. Reverend Hiram McKeenan did not move. He lay on the altar, limbs bent at odd angles and his eyes closed. A thick trickle of drool slid from the corner of his mouth, slowly staining crimson, diluted by saliva and staining the shoulder of his jacket. The cards that had held his words, the words he'd used time and again, drawn out in sequence from the massive files in his office, lay scattered on the floor, forgotten and mute.

Time passed. The low whisper of voices grew to a murmur, then to a low roar. No one moved. No one wanted to be the first to mount that altar, to come to his side and find out the truth. Finally old Martin Kramer rocked himself from his seat. His eyes were wide, and his arms and legs were slow to react, stiff from years and tension. He stumbled his first step, nearly pitching headlong, then catching himself. He looked up.

His near-fall had placed him, one knee to the floor, at the altar. From where he knelt, he could see Hiram's face clearly. The eyes were closed, the slow trickle, now bright red, seeping from his lips had slowed as it thickened. There was no sign of breath, no twitch of arm or leg, to signify life.

Martin rose slowly and moved forward. He started to clamber over the altar, and that movement, that violation of the odd sanctity of the moment, triggered the crowd to motion. Others suddenly crowded in behind him, surging forward, one moment's indecision becoming the next moment's urgency. Martin was lifted, and he fell to his knees beside Reverend McKeenan. They swarmed around him, moving to the body as if there were something there to find, and Martin stayed still. Before him, stuck to the wooden floor in the spilled water from the reverend's glass, shards of which were embedded in Martin's palms, lay one of the cards.

Bright white, blue-ruled lines shimmering through Martin's tears. Tight, dark script in compact lines.

" 'Watch out for false prophets. They come to you in sheep's clothing, but inwardly they are ravening wolves.' "

Martin blinked, closed his eyes, and cried, rocking back on his heels as the congregation slipped around him. Voices cried out. Women screamed. Men shouted for help, for a doctor. For God. Martin wept.

In the distance, the lone howl of a wolf shattered the silence in his mind, but no one seemed to hear.

TWELVE

Geoff Culpepper turned away from the body in silence. He slipped his stethoscope into his pocket absently. He hadn't really needed it. The moment he'd seen Hiram's face, he'd known the truth of it. Hell of a thing. Right there in front of, well, in front of God and everyone. Hell of a thing.

He shook his head as he turned, a signal to his assistant Glenn that it was over. What was needed was the hearse, and those who took things out. Forever. Geoff shivered.

He'd been Doctor, Coroner, Surgeon, and everything medical to the people of Friendly, California for so many years he could barely remember the years that had come before. College drifted through his memories like something he'd read about in a book. And cities? He could barely remember McDonald's, let alone a good restaurant. Now this. It was one thing to pronounce the old and infirm to have passed. He'd seen accidental shootings, sickness that rotted from within. This was the worst. Every eye in the community was boring into his back, waiting for the words they knew he would speak. He knew, though nothing he could have done would have changed a thing, that some among them would blame him. That was how it worked in Friendly. Doctors healed. That was their gift. They were supposed to get it right.

Brushing through those gathered, he made his way to his car and slipped in behind the wheel of the old Buick, the door thankfully cutting him off from the world. He turned on the radio, but before the crackling static of the local country station could snap to life, he slapped his palm into the cassette halfway in, and halfway out of the tape player with a *click!* There was a long, steady hiss as the tape began to slide over the heads. Then the music cut in. Slow, sultry, blues as they hadn't been played in many years. Geoff closed his eyes and concentrated on the sound.

He couldn't rid himself of the image of Reverend McKeenan's face. So void of expression. Geoff had followed the direction of that gaze, glimpsed the face of Christ in that moment. It should have been comforting that Jesus had been watching, but somehow it felt more like being caught by an angry parent. Geoff had turned away, drawing his hand from Hiram's jugular and sighing softly.

Billie Holiday crooned from the speakers, and Geoff breathed deeply, trying to collect his thoughts. He slowly lowered his forehead to the steering wheel, then lifted it again and shifted the car into drive. He had to get clear of the church, out of the influence of his own past. All he could think of was a white flapping tent, dark, hungry eyes. The death had triggered it, as death *always* triggered it.

He smelled the food. He could see their eyes, the parents of his friends, Reverend Forbes swaying at the head of the table. He could see Elizabeth, her eyes blank, empty, and forlorn, her parents too stiff—too intense. Nothing had blocked Geoff's view, and though Elizabeth had never looked his way, he had watched her. He'd seen when her eyes were drawn to the side of the clearing, and he'd followed her gaze with his own, and was trapped, as was she, in the hungry, empty eyes that glared back from the trees.

Geoff shook his head. Wide eyes stared at him through his windshield and he stomped the brakes, honking his horn loudly. Sarah Duponte skittered to the side of the road, directly in front of him, and he swerved, narrowly missing bumping her into the ditch with the Buick's front fender. Geoff slowed and stopped for a moment, glanced into his rear-view to check on Sarah. She was nowhere to be seen, but there was a figure standing in the center of the road, gazing back at him and smiling with teeth too white to be real.

Geoff blinked, and the man was gone, but something else caught the corner of his eye. Three men, moving from the back of the church. Between them they dragged something bulky and white. One edge flapped in the wind.

Geoff gunned it and nearly skidded off the side of the road. Then the tires caught, and the Buick shimmied once, twisting and righting itself with a roar. He took the first curve twenty miles an hour faster than was safe and only slowed a fraction as he raced past the church, skirting the town and veering to the right toward the mountains. He knew he had to get out of there, or lose what sanity remained.

Behind him, the dark man stood to the side of the road, dust swirling around the carefully pleated cuffs of his trousers. He leaned on a cane of polished wood, hands sheathed in skin-tight white leather gloves and wrapped tightly around the top of the mahogany shaft. His expression was contemplative, as if he were considering something important. When he turned back toward the church, his smile widened, and he stepped forward briskly.

The congregation milled about the church grounds, gathering in small groups and muttering among themselves. No one seemed to know what to do. Reverend McKeenan was a large part of their lives, and they were too far up the mountain to expect a replacement any time soon.

"Pardon me," the dark man said, his voice soft, but carrying so that all present turned toward him. "I realize that this is a bad time, but I've come here in search of a dear old friend, come a very long way, in fact. If one of you would direct me to the home of Reverend Forbes, I will be on my way and leave you to your grief."

There was no sound. Even the breeze stilled in that moment. The sun beat down, heat doubled and glare flashing brilliantly from the man's teeth and from his cane, glowing in the depths of his eyes. He shifted his gaze from one side to the other, the quizzical expression returning.

When no one spoke, he continued. "Do none of you know Reverend Forbes? I'd thought he would be here today, it being the Sabbath, but . . ."

"Mister . . ." Helen Saxon began tentatively, "Reverend Forbes—he's dead."

The man grew even more still, a dark statue against the brilliance of the sun, shadow to its light. Unwavering.

"Dead," he repeated, rolling the word off his lips as if tasting something for the first time. "Now, that is a shame," he added, the words a quiet afterthought, all the action imbedded in his eyes. A multitude of expressions scrolled across his features, moving from quiet anguish, through pain, and shifting slowly back to the smile. "Dead."

The second time he spoke it, the word rang with finality. His features shifted, and he leaned in closer. "Who performed the ceremonies for him? Who prepared the feast?"

More silence, and some shuffling of feet, far back in the crowd. The man whipped his gaze toward the sound. He strode forward through the crowd, which parted before him, backing away from the glitter in his eyes. Near the back, he found one old man, bent nearly double from arthritis and leaning on a crooked wooden cane of his own.

"Who prepared the feast?" The question was whispered,

directed at Tom Braddock, who'd been caretaker of the church nigh on fifty years, since he'd hurt his back in high school.

" 'Tweren't no ceremony," Tom mumbled. "Ain't been a feast such as you mean here since the good Reverend passed." Tom's eyes dropped lower, staring at the ground as he repeated words he'd never believed. "Those ain't our ways no more."

The dark man stared. He didn't turn to the others, who were gathering around slowly, but focused on old Tom. There were no words at first, and Tom withered in the heat of that gaze, felt things shifting inside and rising to the surface of his mind. Old things. Things he'd have done better not to forget. Things his Papa had told him. For a moment, Tom closed his eyes, and remembered.

"They said it wasn't right," he said softly. "They said to let it be."

"They?" The man spun on his heel, taking in the crowd, one at a time, studying them. "Who were *they*, Thomas?"

Everyone started. None had spoken that name.

"Who were *they*, Thomas? Who told you it was a good thing to let a man like Reverend Forbes die without his due? Who decided for a dead man how his spirit would reach the heavens?" He spun again, eyes flashing now. "Was there a famine? Was there no food? Were there no strong backs to raise and stake the tent?"

His voice softened. "Does he no longer walk the trees? Alone? Does he not hunger?"

Somewhere in the crowd, a voice whispered hoarsely. "He does."

"Who decided, Thomas?" the man hissed now. "Who chose for that dark one that his days would end in hunger? That his sacrifice would be for nothing? Who will succeed him? Who is going to take *your* sins, Thomas?" The man stepped forward, poking a finger into Thomas' chest. "Who?"

There was no answer, but the man's expression softened in that instant.

"I am sorry," he said, withdrawing his hand. "I have spoken out of line, and in the home of a dear friend. Dear—departed friend. I shall miss him deeply." One last moment of silence.

"I have lost a friend," the man went on. "You have lost a spiritual guide this day. Who will perform the services for Reverend McKeenan?"

"Mister," Wendell Ames said, stepping forward from the crowd. "No disrespect, sir, but just who the hell are you? You come waltzin' in here, giving Tom there what for, and spouting off about Reverend Forbes, who, God rest his soul, has been dead nigh on a full year. I'm sorry to say I don't find you very welcome with your questions and your fifty-dollar suit. No sir."

The man blinked once, leaning on his cane and staring at Wendell, who stood his ground, though there was a twitch at the corner of his eye that hadn't been there moments before. For a long time, nothing was said, and then the man began to speak again.

"Funny you should speak to me about God resting his soul, Wendell."

There was a murmur among those gathered. Again, no name had been offered, and yet this man spoke with familiarity. Wendell took half a step back into the crowd, fighting valiantly to hold his ground.

"Funny you should mention the one thing that you denied him, and that, if I were a betting man, I'd be laying odds you plan to deny the Good Reverend McKeenan as well. Something your fathers and your mothers received in their time. Something your grandfathers received as well. A gift, and a service, a promise of Godspeed to the heavens. God rest his soul indeed.

"I was not raised here, but I know you. I know each and every one of you from letters, and postcards, from long phone calls in the middle of the night. From prayers shared among brothers. I am sorry not to have introduced myself before. I am Reverend Payne. Nathaniel Payne. I attended the seminary with the late Reverend Forbes."

Another long silence. Payne watched them all, and then turned away, staring at the church itself quietly. He started to turn again, toward the road, but again, Wendell Ames stepped forward.

"Reverend?" he said quietly, as if he didn't want to break the silence with his words. "Reverend, I'm sorry. I was out of line. It's just . . . well, it's a hell of a thing when a man dies. Worse when he dies serving the Lord. You've come at a bad time."

Payne nodded. He didn't turn away from the church, but he did begin to speak once more.

"I would be honored," he began, "to assist in your services. I don't know if you've another man of God present. I would be honored to do this thing for Reverend Forbes, and for Reverend McKeenan, but I am a man of certain faith."

Payne turned to face them. "It would have to be the old way. I could not, in good conscience, send them to the afterlife without that. It is the right thing, the *righteous* thing to do. It is what Reverend Forbes would have wanted, and what God demands. There are prices to be paid, in life, and in death. There is hunger, and there is sustenance, and there is faith."

He turned then, not waiting for an answer, and started

to walk off down the driveway of the church, toward the curving road where Geoff Culpepper had fled what seemed hours, and was only moments, before. He took a step, and then another.

On the third step, Wendell called after him. "Where will you be?"

The emotion in his voice, the pain riding just below the surface, brought a sly grin to Payne's lips, though none was in a position to see it. He was not smiling when he turned.

"I will be finding a room in Friendly," he answered. "I'd thought to stay with Reverend Forbes, but as that is no longer an option, I am afraid I have no idea."

Thomas stepped forward, blushing furiously as he cut in. "There's the apartment out back of the rectory," he stammered. "I mean, I've kept it up, since Reverend Forbes . . . it's as he left it, Reverend Payne. If you was his friend, maybe you might ought to stay there?"

Something transited Payne's eyes. He didn't exactly smile, but neither did he frown, or turn away. He thought in silence, and then he nodded. No words, just that quick motion of his head, and everything shifted.

The crowd moved forward, each with a word of condolence, and welcome. Tentative questions were asked about his own parish, how long he would stay. A weight shifted, from their hearts and shoulders to his. Quietly, and without much effort, Reverend Nathaniel Payne moved into the church, and their lives.

As he turned to follow Thomas around back of the church, Helen Saxon called after him. "Shall . . . shall we prepare a feast, Reverend?"

Everyone grew silent. That one question hung in the air, hovering like a cloud. The difference between life under Reverend Forbes' guidance, and that of Reverend

McKeenan, had been night and day. They hovered on that twilight moment, and with a quiet word, he drew them in.

"If you would do that for me," he said softly, "for *them*, and for their souls, it would be an honor to remain for a time, and to serve as God's messenger here in the home of my friend. It is the least I can do, and the most."

Without waiting to see how they would react, Payne turned, and Thomas stumbled around the edge of the church building, leading him away. Invisible strings of pain and doubt unraveled from the hearts of those who watched. Memories clouded reason, memories of earlier times, of stories told by parents long dead and grandparents even longer. White tents flapped in the breezes of each mind, and along the tree line, a shadow stalked. Hungry, and alone.

Before the sun had set, a group of men dressed in dark work clothes arrived at the church, moving with Thomas to the storerooms that had been so long locked. There would be repairs to make, mending and organizing. What once would have taken a day would be at least the full week in preparation. None among them smiled, but they worked as a unit, patching canvas and mending lines, dragging cases of metal stakes from the shadows. In the field, along the edge of the trees, another group worked on the table. Sanded and whitewashed, you could not tell the wood had been so long in disrepair. A very few minor repairs, new nails where the wood had warped. It might have been last week that it had last been used.

As they worked, they watched the trees nervously.

Madeline was back at her window when the candles began to spring into life. The sun had long been set beyond the tree line, and the owls had begun their mournful dirge.

They asked, and Madeline's heart knew the answer.

"Who?"

The candles flickered, a wavering line to each side of the road, winding down the mountain toward the church and curling back into Madeline's past.

Why do the candles lead to us, Mommy?

She shook her head and thought about moving away from the window. Closing the door. She thought about putting water on for tea and turning on the lamp over her desk. She could sit there, back straight in the rough wooden chair, and write to Elizabeth. She could explain things she'd never taken the time to explain, things that mattered. She'd never even explained to her daughter why she had to stay. Why it was so important to her to be there for him. How she felt she'd failed them both.

And now, with the circle closing and those damnable candles springing to life, one after another, drawing nearer with each indrawn breath, Madeline felt the need to confess. She wanted Elizabeth to know and understand. Nothing could mend what had been broken. Nothing could erase the years of pain and solitude and anger. Nothing could give her back her husband, or her daughter, but at least Madeline could, for once in her long life, give something herself. There was no time. The one thing she'd had so much of she could scream, all squandered.

Beyond the crosses littering her lawn, the flicker of soft, yellow light grew closer. Madeline heard the soft chorus of the choir as they marched along the road, and despite the terror threatening to stop her heart, Madeline felt tears in the corners of her eyes. It had been so long since she'd heard a choir. So long since any living being had acknowledged her presence at all without anger, or scorn. Now they wound their way down the road as they had so many times in the past, and she fluttered against the windowsill like a moth—trapped by their light and wanting to flutter away into the shadows. To hide and never come out. To scorn them as they had scorned her.

Instead she watched, and as the shadowed figures placed twin candles on the posts of her gate, swinging it inward and starting down the walk, she moved to the door, opening it slowly. Some things could not be denied. She knew Brian was out there, somewhere. She knew he was watching, and this time she didn't intend to let him down. This time she would do what she could.

And there was the matter of the other. The one who'd passed her home earlier in the day. It was no coincidence that the people came this night. Something had happened, something bad had happened, and for once, they didn't know what to do. If they came to Madeline for assistance, it must have gotten bad.

It was Thomas who stepped forward, Thomas from the church, and at his side walked Wendell Ames. Wendell was turning his hat over and over in his hands, and Madeline thought this was odd, because she could never remember Wendell wearing that hat anywhere but church. He was dressed nicely, as was Thomas, and the two of them had their eyes turned to the ground before them. Madeline couldn't decide if they most resembled shy young men courting or children caught in the act of doing something naughty.

"Evenin' Madeline," Wendell said, as she stood silhouetted against the soft light from the interior of her home. The candlelight didn't quite reach her, sending dancing shadows around the two men's feet, but not quite reaching the frame of the door. Madeline felt as if she were a shadow, conversing with ghosts from her past.

"Hello Wendell," she answered. "Long way from home."

"Reverend McKeenan," Thomas burst in quickly, "he died today, ma'am."

Madeline digested this in silence. "I'm sorry to hear that, Thomas," she said, committing nothing.

"He died in the middle of his service," Wendell added. "Right behind the podium. Hell of a thing."

"I'd imagine," Madeline answered, waiting.

"We've come to ask a favor, Maddy," Wendell said at last, letting loose a long breath and shifting to the familiarity of years long past. "We've come to ask your help, and your forgiveness, if you will offer it."

Madeline allowed herself a small frown. This wasn't what she'd expected at all.

"The Reverend, he was a different sort of man from Reverend Forbes," Wendell went on. "Reverend McKeenan, he knew God, don't get me wrong, but to my way of thinking, he never really took the time to know us. Our ways. Our past.

"To our shame, Maddy. Neither did we. It was the easy road. The safe road, for those of us still living. Brian was a friend of mine. I wanted to be the first to tell you how sorry I am things have come to what they have."

"We got the tent all fixed up," Thomas cut in again. "Fixed the table, too. Took a couple 'a coats of whitewash, mind you." He trailed off to silence.

Madeline wanted to speak. So many things she wanted to say. She wanted to spit in Wendell's face, to scream at him and rail and step out through that doorway to pound the man's chest with her fists. She did what she always did. She stood, and she waited.

"They are planning the feast," Wendell said softly. "For Reverend Forbes, and for Reverend McKeenan. For others as well. All those who've died. It may be too late, but damned if it don't seem the only right thing to do."

Madeline was shaking, and a soft moan gave away the tears that had begun streaming from her eyes. She tried to speak, but only a squeak of sound escaped. Too much at once. Too many images surfacing, too many questions. She bit her lip, concentrated. Thomas and Wendell stood, Wendell still twisting that damned hat, waiting for her to compose herself and answer.

"Who?" she asked at last, forcing the word between quivering lips. "Who will perform the service?"

"His name is Payne," Wendell answered, "Reverend Payne. He was a friend of Reverend Forbes. He'd come here to see him. Hell of a day for visiting, if you take my meaning. Hell of a day no matter what you think. We've come to see if you will forgive us, Maddy. I know we don't deserve it. Hell, I don't even know if Brian is out there. I figured you might know. We all did. You've asked so many times about the ceremony . . ."

The words trailed off. Madeline's mind spun crazily, and she leaned against the doorframe for support.

"They don't remember, ma'am," Thomas cut in. "They don't know what we know, begging your pardon for lumping such as myself together with you. They need your help to get it right. They just don't understand any more."

Madeline gulped down the tears. She straightened her shoulders and breathed deeply.

"That is one *hell* of a lot of sin," she said softly. "What makes you . . . what makes this Reverend *Payne*, think that it should happen all at once? Why? Wendell Ames, when have you *ever* heard of so many deaths and a single feast? Do we know what will happen? Do we know how long is too long? Reverend Forbes could have told us. He always said it had to be soon. Before the soul could slip away tainted. Why is it different now?"

No one spoke at first. Madeline knew her questions must have already occurred to someone, but she waited just the same. It gave her a few extra moments to compose herself. She was trying to force herself beyond the moment, to see the yawning pit she knew was waiting in those shadows. There was a right and a wrong to everything, but somehow she knew the right and wrong to *this* particular moment diverged so completely that they made up the difference between heaven and hell.

And yet they blurred. Madeline wished Brian were there. He had always known. She hadn't believed him, not always, but thinking back—which she'd done again and again and again with tears in her eyes—she had come to the conclusion that Brian had always known. Something in his being had told him when things were right, and when the balance had shifted. Something, the same thing, that had dragged him from her side to give his life willingly to God, had given him that gift. Madeline didn't share it.

She had her mind, and she had her heart. Both had betrayed her again and again, but they were all she had with which to make up her mind.

"Maddy?" Wendell said.

She nodded. "I will come," she said. "Tell them I will come. Not tonight. I will be at the church in the morning."

She stepped back then, before either of the men could speak, and closed the door. The catch sounded with a *click* of finality. Madeline leaned against the inside of the door, sobbing softly.

In the shadows outside, Wendell stood for a moment longer, still turning the hat over and over in his hands. Thomas had closed his eyes as the door clicked shut.

The two turned away at the same moment and trudged out toward the gate and the road beyond. Beyond the shadows, eyes glittered in the light of the candles, deep within the canopy of the trees lining the road. As Wendell and Thomas made their way back toward the church, snuffing the candles, one by one, ritual steps in a pattern as old as time, the eyes slipped back into the shadows. There was no sound, and soon the darkness was complete.

In the small apartment behind the church, there was a fire burning, despite the early summer heat. Smoke curled up and out of the chimney and floated off into the night. There was no other light, but Reverend Payne's silhouette could be made out plainly beyond the single window, if you were standing at the edge of the woods.

Payne shuffled a deck of cards slowly and stared into the flames. All around him, the austere memories, all that remained of Reverend Shane Forbes, cluttered the apartment in random disarray. All but the cards. Payne had found them on the mantel over the fireplace, in a carved cedar case, wrapped in silk. The Thoth deck, Aleister Crowley's contribution to the Tarot. The numbers weren't perfect. The symbols were often warped or rearranged. Payne ignored the faults, concentrating on the moment.

He flipped the cards deftly, cutting them and cutting again. With a smile, he tossed the deck into the wooden box without laying out a spread. That smile faded as the deck caught on the lip of the box, a single card popping free to flutter to the table top, upside down.

Payne stared. It was The Tower. The lightning bolt glimmered, catching in the sudden flare of the fireplace. Payne flipped the card upside down and rose, leaving it where it lay. He stepped to the window, staring up the mountain through the darkness. On the skyline, a single bolt of lightning flashed.

THIRTEEN

The rain had returned, pounding its own intricate rhythms against the walls and windows of Liz's apartment building, counterpoint to the nervous slap of Dexter's hands on his jeans, and the banister, and anything he could reach. He was like a human bolt of energy, waiting to explode. Being cooped up for so long was taking its toll on the young drummer, and the others gave him plenty of room. Caffeine, four walls, and no drums. Bad juju.

For the most part, each of them kept to their thoughts. Liz's story had put an odd twist to things. Brandt was still a major focus, but now there were other considerations as well. What had seemed a localized phenomenon, drawing them in one by one, had spread out and broadened in scope. Others hung in the balance, people most of them had never met. Places they never in a million fucking years would have visited. Balance.

"There's a pattern to it," Dexter kept saying. "I can see it—almost. I can feel it throbbing in the back of my head. Don't you feel it? How can you not *feel* it?"

The others nodded, not really listening. Dexter had been repeating the same thing, variations on a single theme, for days. They knew he was right, in some sense, but since that pattern didn't seem willing to leap right out and slap them in the face, they concentrated on other things.

Shaver, whose fingers were healing nicely, had managed to trade his beat-up Mustang for a two-decades-old Chevy van. There was primer on each fender, and the bumper looked more like a rusty-chrome pretzel than anything that might protect the van in a crash, but it ran. The engine had been rebuilt a scant thirty thousand miles back, and it still burned more gas than oil. Shaver was loathe to part with the Mustang, but somehow, nothing that had mattered in the past carried the same weight.

The one thing they were all certain of was that they had to get out of the city. Friendly, California, one long-assed road trip away, was the target. They had pooled their resources, Shaver packing up what there was of his stuff that didn't need fumigating and donating the rest to Goodwill, Synthia putting her few belongings in a small storage shed, paying for two months in advance, and moving in officially with Liz. They'd tossed their money in a hat and made a journey to Brandt's apartment. After two solid hours of begging, arguing, and finally with Brandt pulling out his guitar and playing on the sidewalk outside her window, they'd convinced his landlady to let them go in and get as much of his stuff as they could carry. Brandt promised to return with the back rent, but he knew, and she saw in his eyes, that he would never return.

None of them would. Not as they were. Synthia was a nervous wreck. What had been a backdrop of unseeing, unemotional *angels* had become a restless, stalking mob. They watched her from street corners, peered out of windows and alleys, following as she and Brandt moved about the city. Nothing she could do removed the cold weight of their constant gaze from her shoulder blades. Synthia became Brandt's shadow. She didn't know if they were watching her or Brandt, but she wasn't about to be alone long enough to find out.

In odd moments, they played. Shaver had finally drawn the first tentative notes from his guitar. He couldn't really bear down, but he could hold chords and notes without screaming. Synthia had produced a tiny, pig-nose amp for her bass, adding a resonant quality to their private "jams" that the Fender itself could not have produced. The instrument was meant for the stage. Syn felt the tremble in the strings, sensed the deep, shivering sound that escaped when more power was applied. She closed her eyes and imagined that sound as she played.

Brandt had slipped to rhythm easily, releasing the faster notes, the chaos, and the abandon to Shaver. Pent up emotion burst from Shaver's fingers in peals of magical notes, flurries and progressions he'd never dreamed of. The song drew it from him. The strings were liquid to his touch. The only thing missing was the drums. Dexter worked at it. He slapped his knees. He tapped pencils and spoons and whatever else he could find on the tables, but there was no room in the small apartment to set up the drum kit, and if they had, they all would have been evicted in moments. Another bit of tension to ripple down Dexter's nerve endings.

The patterns emerged slowly. He sensed the motions, the quick flicks of wrist and snaps of his foot that would draw the sound from the drums. He could see it, all the notes and rhythms and harmony meshing, but he couldn't feel it. Not yet. It slipped away as he reached out, and he ended up, each time, slapping at the table in frustration.

More than once, he'd risen, nearly toppling the coffee table and stalking away from the others, leaving the song to continue, or to peter off, depending on how they all reacted. No matter what they chose, Dexter ignored them. Nothing could console him. He would leave them alone, make his way to the kitchen, and brew yet another pot of the diminishing supply of coffee. As the darkening liquid dripped through the filter, slowly, Dexter would arrange the coffee cups, one row, and then the next, forming a pyramid of empty china, rising, falling, and rising again, his deft fingers working the pattern.

By the time each pot had brewed, Dexter's emotions were under control, but the periods between pots were shrinking.

All of them were restless.

Brandt and Synthia walked the streets each evening, searching for a street corner with enough of a crowd, or a bar with a small stage, anywhere he could play. Each time the pressure began to build, he released it. He no longer fought the images, or the pain. He sought them. He embraced them. Each time it was different. Synthia sat, and she listened, and yearned for her bass—for a four-track recording studio. For an end to the madness and the glaring, staring eyes that would not give her a moment of peace. The music drew her in and pushed her away. Small solace in a crumbling reality.

There was no sign of Wally. The angels gathered, their numbers increasing each time Synthia moved to the streets, but there were no answers forthcoming. Each night, crowds gathered. Brandt had produced an old hat, a weathered fedora so shapeless it was more an eyesore than a piece of head gear, and he kept it on the ground at his feet as he played.

The angels littered the streets and filled the seedy clubs. They milled in and around the crowds of the living, ignoring all but Brandt, and Synthia, as the notes spilled free from his guitar. Each of them heard a different song. Synthia saw it, watched them swaying in different directions, to different rhythms, entranced. When she saw them, when she rose and moved among them, she wondered. She heard Brandt play, felt the way the notes tugged at her heart, felt the harmonies rippling from his fingers. Did they not hear that? Did anyone hear it? Was what she heard played just for her, or did it only work for those already departed?

Brandt never said what he heard. Synthia saw the odd flicker of his eyes, the quivering of his lips as he played, and knew that he was seeing things, just as she was. She knew from his words that he was living pain, another's pain, the pain of nations . . . the pain of those who would not rest. She stayed near his side, and when the hat began to overflow, when those who heard him play felt their own pain ripped free, or that of someone they'd lost, she collected their offerings. Brandt would go on and on, until his fingers could no longer press the strings tightly enough to form the notes, and as long as he played, someone listened.

Once or twice, he played for an audience of nothing but the shimmering angels, but it made no difference to him. Brandt wasn't playing for an audience. He wasn't even playing for the money, though it was part of why he let Synthia lead him to the streets each night. They were going to need some capital to get out of San Valencez, and none of the others was being very productive at the moment. Brandt played because if he didn't, if he let it build up inside him, bits and pieces of his heart and mind melted away, flaking to dust and drifting on the breeze.

The night before they left the city, the others decided to tag along. It was early, not more than seven, but Brandt had broken out in a cold sweat, and Synthia, catching his pallor, had realized it was time. They had little to eat in the apartment. Pizza boxes littered tables and chairs; coffee cans lined the table in an even pyramid, each precisely the same distance from the next. The trash overflowed with whiskey bottles and beer cans and junk-food wrappers.

When they reached the street, they turned inward, toward the older part of the city. Brandt felt the tug of something, an image half-formed and hovering in the recesses of his mind. He walked, and they followed. Synthia kept her eyes glued to the sidewalk, ignoring the glaring eyes of those who watched. The others watched her out of the corner of their eyes, half-convinced she was crazy, half-frightened that she saw things they needed to see. Synthia remained silent, and they walked in a tight group.

Shaver had his own guitar case in hand, gripped tightly, as if it might escape. It had been too long since he could play. Now that his fingers were healed, he had trouble putting the instrument aside. They painted quite the picture, moving slowly down the dingy sidewalks, past empty alleys and abandoned warehouses. Only Brandt seemed unaware of the oddness of the moment. His gaze was fixed, focused on some point ahead of them. He didn't see the stares of those they passed. He didn't see Synthia turning, and staring at the angels that lined the roads.

He followed a trail. It wound through trees, tall trees, multi-colored and full of autumn. He saw a shadowy figure, stumbling ahead. A young girl, clothed only in a white gown. Her breath gasped from tortured lungs, and she glanced again and again over her shoulder. Watching. Not for him, never that, but something. Someone. Turning from Brandt, she staggered off through the trees, and he followed.

They went down a dark, abandoned street and turned into an alley as Brandt plowed ahead, nearly leaving them all behind in his sudden rush.

"Brandt!" Shaver called out. "Brandt, wait . . . where the *fuck* are you going?"

Nothing. Brandt either didn't hear, or didn't care. He

stumbled into the alley, and they plunged in after him, swallowed suddenly in a wall of shadow.

The clearing was dark. Moonlight filtered in through the branches of tall, tall trees, but only in splintered shards of illumination. Nothing that could scatter the shadows. Brandt stopped dead in the center, glancing about himself carefully. There was no sign of the girl, but he saw—with an odd tilt of reality—that the others stood beside him. The bewilderment in Shaver's eyes told him they were there. Really there, not standing at his side and wondering where the fuck he went.

From the shadows, childish laughter drifted across the clearing. Brandt stepped closer. He moved toward the trees lining the clearing on the far side from where they'd entered. Something was piled in a heap. Leaves? Branches? He moved closer, then staggered back and sank to his knees.

"No," he said softly.

Synthia came up behind him, and he moved, trying to block her from that sight, trying to deny what lay before him. His heart ached, dragged inward and twisted like a rag being wrung free of water . . . blood . . . hope.

Synthia stopped at Brandt's arm. Liz was at her side, Shaver and Dexter crowding in behind. All saw as one. Liz choked back a scream. Synthia turned away, her fist crammed *tightly* into her mouth and her teeth clamping down.

They were stacked three high, arms and legs protruding at odd angles. The bodies were entwined in an arcane rotting puzzle. Women. Half a dozen? Ten? More? It was impossible to tell. The arms, legs, and torsos were wrapped and stacked like a pile of firewood. Ordered and tight, like inventory on a hardware store shelf. Dexter's hands slowed and then stopped. He turned to Shaver, wanting to speak, and unable to get the words past his lips.

Shaver didn't see him. Shaver's eyes were locked on the scene before them. His fingers were so tight around the handle of his guitar case that the knuckles went from white to pain-searing red and still he gripped tighter.

Synthia was the one who finally moved. She looked up. She didn't see the bodies. She saw the *angels*. They were creeping closer, every moment closer. They watched Brandt, ignoring the bodies.

Synthia let her knee press into Brandt's shoulder. Nothing. He kept his head down, as if he were praying. She glanced down, kneed him again, then harder.

"Damn it, Brandt," she grated, "play."

Still he didn't move. Synthia watched a moment longer, then she got mad.

"Play, damn you," she screeched, suddenly out of control. "For fuck's sake *play*, Brandt! *Jesus*, why do you think you're here?"

The child's laughter pealed shrilly across the clearing, and Synthia turned. Nothing. Shadows flickered around the perimeter of the clearing. Mocking her attempts to pin them down.

"Boring, boring," a voice called out softly. Peals of laughter rang from the trees.

Synthia whispered hoarsely, lashing out with her Doc-Martin-shod foot. Brandt grunted at the contact.

"Huh?" He glanced up. The bodies flickered on the periphery of his sight, and he focused. The guitar case was on the ground and open in a single fluid motion, and Brandt had the polished wood pressed tightly to his chest moments later. He stared at the bodies now, opening his mind. His fingers slid over the strings, not really playing yet, just preparing for the release, drawing it in like a deep breath.

Images flickered before him. He saw the bodies, and then he didn't. What he did see was an intricate, turning dance. He saw limbs untwining, saw the human puzzle that had stolen his voice and his mind unwinding to bodies. Real bodies. Whole bodies.

They were all young women. Ten, maybe twenty of them, lining up in ranks. They were naked. Long hair, eerily consistent in length, height nearly the same in each case, complexion, even their eye color was consistent. They could have been sisters. Enough sisters to make parents insane.

Brandt dropped his gaze. It was a trap; the images were meant to distract him. It didn't matter if they were all green dwarves from the fifth dimension. He was there for a reason. A release. He let his fingers slide to the strings. In the background, soft blues notes floated on the breeze. Billie Holiday. So soft he could barely make it out. His first instinct was to match the notes, to play in and around them, adding to their depth. He did not.

Another distraction. Another trap. He felt the women gathering around him. He knew they were whole now, and close. Very close to him. He was physical, they were not, and yet he smelled their perfume, and he felt the passage of air as they moved beside him. Brandt ignored it all. He leaned to the side, knowing that the hip he leaned on was Synthia's, and that she saw them. He let his fingers rest silent for a moment, then shifted, pointedly ignoring the deep minor chords that echoed in his head and letting his nails slide across the strings, drawing a G Major from the strings with a flourish. He followed it quickly . . . A, D, G, and C. He didn't play anything he had played before, but he dodged what was shoved in his face. Billie Holiday or not, he knew he couldn't follow that trail. It led to death, something these women knew intimately. It led to madness, and he had come close enough to that, often enough, that he could sense it in the air.

It wasn't about him. Over and over the images played in his mind. Limbs contorted. Bodies in impossible positions, angles all wrong. Billie Holiday crooning in the background. All aimed at Brandt. He played. He slid into the progression, eyes clamped tightly shut, and fingers flowing liquid hot over the strings. He played and he thought of his childhood. He thought of days in bright sunlight, happy days of fun and carefree hours where nothing mattered but the moment.

"He kept us prisoner."

The voices spoke in unison, crazy harmonic clarity.

"He kept us, bound and naked. For a long time. He made us beg to be touched. . . ."

Brandt shook his head and bore down on the strings. "No," he whispered.

"Yes," the voices continued. "He came to us, and he touched us, but only a little, and then he left. Again and again. Alone. When we heard him, we needed—him."

"No," Brandt repeated, louder. He let his fingers fly, releasing them to the song, and he turned away. He didn't want something prodding him to open his eyes and look. He didn't want to be distracted again. Nothing mattered but the connection. He felt the pain. He felt the struggles for individuality, the fight for freedom. He felt chaffed wrists and dry throats. He felt the shame of need. He felt desperation and he felt the slicing, heated cut of the blade.

They'd been awake—bound and helpless—when he'd cut them. Brandt felt himself drawn in. He clamped his eyes tightly shut, but the images surfaced, ignoring him. The woman was spread out on the bed. Her ankles and wrists were bound. Brandt stood over her, watching through eyes he couldn't escape. She wasn't struggling. All the fight was gone from those helplessly tied limbs. Her eyes were blindfolded, and her head turned to one side, as though she were listening carefully.

"Please?" she said softly. "Please touch me. Let me know you are there. Please?"

Brandt shied away; the body he inhabited reached out. Touched. Teased and pulled back. She trembled, arching from the bed. Tears soaked the blindfold at the corners of her eyes.

"Please," she whispered. "Oh God, please, don't go. Don't leave me this way. Please?"

Brandt's pulse raced. She was so helpless. So in need of the touch she craved. So warped in that need and he couldn't draw away.

"No," he whispered a third time. Before he could work to draw back, to cut it all off and play, a flurry of notes cut through his trance.

Shaver. Brandt mouthed the word, but didn't speak. He knew what he heard, and who he heard. That was enough. He was not alone, and very suddenly, the presence that held his gaze released him. Brandt threw every ounce of his concentration to his fingers. He ground the chords from the strings, laying them out like a fine mesh for Shaver to dance his own notes across. Shaver played as if the entire struggle was beyond him. He played as if there was no fucking way Brandt would ever fail to lay that groundwork, as if the rhythm were already set in the firmament of the heavens, and all he had to do was take that plunge, drive his own notes out over that safety net of perfection and watch them fall into place.

Brandt gritted his teeth, opened his eyes, and played.

The others were there. No women, bound to dark beds. No crying, tearful begging. No arched flesh too tempting, so forbidden. Just Synthia slipping in close beside him, Dexter pacing around them all, Liz kneeling with her fingers working, kneading the soft earth at their feet, and Shaver. Shaver's eyes were closed now. No way to tell what he saw, or what he felt—no way to ignore the sound. It was sublime. It drew them all closer, binding them in spirals of sound and drowning out the mocking laughter that had filled the clearing.

Brandt felt the pain uncoiling. He still heard the voices in the recesses of his mind, chiming up as one voice, over and over. The images had faded. He saw only the death. He knew only the pain, and he let it slide through him, hot butter rolling off the edges of the blade that had carved and killed and left them to rot. One by one, their voices rolled free as well. One a little more high-pitched. Another, the patterns of the words shifting. Brandt could no longer make out what they were saying, only random words filtered through.

One thing he did see. The images, as they peeled, one from the other, were eerily similar. The killer had taken them all for a reason. A single reason. They all were the same. They looked the same. He saw them as the same woman. One after another, whirling away, freed by the notes that were reaching a crescendo and shimmering back down like warm rain.

And then there was one. The girl they'd followed in the first place. The catalyst. She gazed at Brandt as the notes trailed away, first in anger, then in puzzlement. Finally, she dropped her eyes, and the clearing grew silent. Everything shimmered, the cohesion of the "vision" slipping away. Still, she stood, and she watched.

"He will not be pleased," she said at last. The words were so soft, a whisper like wind through the trees overhead. "He will come for you."

"I am going to him," Brandt replied without thought. "There is no hiding." He stood for a moment in silence, then added, "The one who sent you to me is not the one who . . ." Brandt's eyes flickered to where the women's corpses still sprawled on the carpet of dead leaves and soft grass. "Not the one who did this."

"No," she said. Her own gaze trailed after his. "No, he is not. He is much darker. This . . ." her hand swept out in a slow arc, gesturing to the carnage, the girls piled high and cold and gone, "this is my brother's work."

Warring emotions flickered across the surface of her eyes. She couldn't quite meet Brandt's gaze now.

"He wanted me. I used to sit on the end of his bed, when we were alive. When we were young. I used to slip in, in the middle of the night when Ma and Dad were asleep, pull my nightgown over my head and sit on the end of his bed.

"It was fun. He used to do things for me. Anything I asked, if I let him touch me. Used to beg to touch me. I had to tell him to be quiet, to lay still. Told him if he was my good little boy, I'd let him touch more, but I never did. I liked it too much, the touching. I was afraid if I let him touch me more, I'd like it more, and I wouldn't be able to control him. I was right, in the end.

"I didn't control him. He caught me one night slipping out my window to go out with some friends. I never made it past the edge of the yard before he had me. Didn't know he could hit so hard. He got me in the back of the head. I was down, half-conscious, and he had me tied, gagged, and was dragging me into the woods. These woods. He was only sixteen, but he was very thorough. He even brought my nightshirt.

"He tied me out there that night. He took my clothes, made me dress in the nightshirt, and tied me to a tree. He left me there."

There was a sharp intake of breath. Synthia. Brandt felt her reacting, and he turned to her, silencing her with a glance. His fingers were pressed tightly to the strings of his guitar, painfully. He listened, and the girl continued.

"He came back the next night. He touched me, but only once . . . very softly. Lingering. He didn't speak at all. He gave me a piece of bread, and some water . . . and left again.

"It was the third night I begged. I couldn't help it. He was going to go again, to leave me there. I begged him not to. I begged him to touch me, and he did. Again, and again, and I was so relieved. I was so sore, and so tired. Then, when he had his fill of it, he killed me. I remember when father gave him that knife."

The images were flickering now, strobing like an old movie nearing the end of the reel. Flecks of what Brandt saw, and heard, shivered away from him.

"It is over now," he said softly.

"No," she answered, as she slipped away. "It is over for me—for them," her arm waved across the clearing. "He is not dead."

They stood alone, in the alley. No trees. No bodies. Only the softest trickle of moonlight seeped between the walls of the buildings that walled them in. Brandt saw it flicker off the strings of Shaver's guitar, felt Synthia leaning in even closer. He closed his eyes again. In the distance, very faintly, he could still hear Billie Holiday.

"What the hell was that?" Dexter asked at last. "Jesus."

"I think that is just what it was," Brandt said, shaking his head from side to side to clear the cobwebs. "Or very close to it. Hell. Never thought I'd be the one to help people avoid it."

"Did you hear her?" Liz asked. She was kneeling still, on the concrete floor of the alley. Between her legs, something rested on the ground.

Brandt nodded in answer, turning and leaning down to place his guitar back in the case. The aching need to play was stilled, but he couldn't keep himself from staring over at Liz, wondering what it was she had. He remembered her fingers, working the soil, remembered that she'd been working as the girl had talked.

He snapped the case closed and lifted it, turning and stepping closer to her.

As the object came into focus, he frowned. It was a cross. The cross-arms were formed of sticks, bits of wood, bound by an old length of string. It wasn't the cross that caught his eye. Bound to it, warped and twisted, was what might have been a body. It was a third stick, twisted and knotted, broken to a length that fit on the cross neatly. The shape was that of a body, bent double by pain, helpless to ward off that anguish.

There was a bit of the girls they'd seen in the image. There was a bit of the man who'd bound them, and the sister who'd brought it on them all. There was the Christ, something Brandt could see, and yet, that meant so little to him. Too much.

He staggered back, turning away. More images assaulted him: trees, mountains, fiery, hungry eyes that he recognized only too well.

"Fuck," he whispered. He felt Synthia wrapping her arms around him, holding him, once again, from a fall.

Liz rose quickly, gathering the small "sculpture" up as she did. She seemed embarrassed, somehow, to be on the ground, and upset by Brandt's reaction.

"Let's get out of here," Dexter said. "We have a mountain to climb, and music to make."

Brandt shivered once, hard, nearly slipping from Synthia's grip, then nodded and stood up straight. "There isn't much time," he said softly.

They walked from the alley and into the brilliant moonlight bathing the street beyond, each lost in their own thoughts. For the moment, the music had silenced.

FOURTEEN

The five of them, their instruments, what bags and clothes they figured they could get by on, and a massive stack of beat-up cassette tapes bounced down the freeway, just outside San Valencez. The van wasn't really designed for the comfort of five, but with some creative packing, they'd managed to make it bearable. Dexter was firmly planted behind the wheel, a twenty-ounce black coffee steaming beside him and his fingers tapping rhythms on the steering wheel. They'd known he would never make it through the trip sane if they didn't give him something to occupy himself with. Road maps and traffic patterns seemed the perfect answer.

Beside him, Shaver rode shotgun. He had his guitar in his lap, and Synthia's pig-nose amp, turned low and wailing like a tiny Marshall stack on the console between the seats. He ran through progressions randomly, piecing them together and watching the pattern of Dexter's fingers tapping on the wheel.

Liz had turned, facing the back, and made a backrest of that console. Beside her on the floor were her pads, and a freshly sharpened pack of pencils. She'd been sketching the others to pass the time. Just that moment, she was resting, her head leaning against where Shaver's elbow rested, her eyes closed, listening to the music. The top pad held a sketch of both Brandt and Synthia, but not your average photo-realism. Brandt held his guitar, facing some unknown menace just to one side. Synthia was wrapped around him, literally, like some giant, dark serpent. She rose to blonde hair that peaked in the shape of a fender bass, her arms, elongated, curled around Brandt's chest.

It was an eerie caricature, quickly drawn with deep, powerful strokes. The most striking thing about it was a small reflection in Brandt's eye. You could only make it out if you concentrated, and yet it was impossible to miss. Shaver had stared at it for a long time without speaking, pulling it closer, shoving it out to arm's length, squinting.

"What is it?" he'd asked at last, handing the pad back. Liz had stared at it, an odd expression on her face.

"I'm not sure," she answered. "Don't even remember drawing it." She took the pad back, turning it sideways, then upside down. Then she'd passed it back to Brandt and Synthia, who were curled on the ample back seat in the space left beside Dexter's drum kit.

Brandt took it and held it for them both. Synthia was sprawled sideways, her head curled into the crook of his shoulder. Nothing was said for a long time. Brandt stared at the image of himself carefully, and he felt Synthia pressing back more tightly against him as she studied the sketch of herself, and Brandt's careful reaction to it.

"It looks as if I'm smothering you," she'd said.

"No," Brandt's answer had been contemplative and certain. "It is a metaphor, I think, of the music. You are weaving yourself in and around me, but here," he pointed to the base of the image in the drawing, "is the support. It is you, strong coils holding me up as I play. See the way your hair is the neck of your bass?"

Brandt had turned to Liz then, handing back the picture and smiling. "I'd like to see how the rest of the band would fit into that, if you get the notion."

Liz had smiled, her secret shared and understood, nodding in silence and moving closer to Shaver, who turned then, leaning back to catch Brandt's gaze.

"But what is that thing reflected in the eye?"

"That's what we're going to find out," Brandt answered with a quick shrug. "That," he added thoughtfully, "is the key to the pattern."

There hadn't been much conversation since that initial burst. Shaver played, the others listened, Dexter wove the old van in and out of the moderately heavy out-bound traffic. They left San Valencez behind quickly, and turned toward the mountains, barely visible in the distance. No one spoke, and Liz refused to rise high enough from the floor to see the mountains at all. They had at least a day's journey ahead of them, and the consensus was that they'd stop early on, not push themselves, find a room or two somewhere and crash hard. No telling what they were about to face off with on that mountain, so why be exhausted when they found out?

Dexter drove on through the growing darkness as if he could go forever. The coffee was drained, then filled from the Thermos he and Shaver shared. When the Thermos was nearly empty, they had traveled a few hours, a couple of hundred miles, and had begun to take note of the glowing signs and offerings of food, lodging, and relaxation that lined the sides of the road.

"Man," Shaver said, "the rooms get cheaper the closer we get to this place. When we left the city, every sign was saying at least $39.99 a night. Now we're down to $19.99, and the offer of 'adult entertainment' and 'special' rooms with vibrating beds. What planet are we traveling to?"

"You haven't seen anything yet," Liz cut in. "You wait until we're close enough for the signs Reverend Forbes paid for to start showing up. You'll think you're driving into some sort of snake-handling circus. He was not shy about spreading 'the word of the Lord' far and wide. He was also not shy about what sort of folks would be welcome in Friendly, California. You'll see."

They chose an exit that proclaimed "Home Cooking, Just Like Ma Used to Fix," and double rooms for $19.99 a night with free HBO. Dexter swerved gently onto the ramp and rolled down to the single traffic light swinging at the end. He turned right, following the signs. To the left there was a dimly lit gas station, and a convenience store, stark against the deep black of the night.

As they started down the road, the glow of a small town lit the skyline. The signs were closely placed, one after the other, proclaiming all the worldly delights of South Haven, California. They rounded a bend in the road, and the signs began to show life. Color, neon lit and blinking:

BEER

LIQUOR

SOUTH HAVEN MOTOR-LODGE

"That must be the place," Dexter grunted, signaling the turn to no one, as they were alone on the road, and wheeling the van into the gravel parking lot. The "Vacancy" sign was lit, half of the "V" broken, and the sign hissing and spitting into the utter silence that fell as Dexter killed the engine.

The office sported a patched screen door with a big "OPEN" sign dangling from wire in its center.

There was a dim light from somewhere deep in the interior, but no other signs of life.

"Jesus," Shaver said, "it's only ten o'clock."

Dexter popped open his door and slid out onto the gravel. Shaver did the same, and the two advanced on the old wood-framed door slowly.

There was a bell "For Service" to the right of it, and Dexter punched it without hesitation. A high-pitched buzz sounded, like a bug-zapper at the dinner table, and a light flashed on in the back, brighter than before.

Muffled footsteps, the heavy scent of a cigar, burning past its prime, and the latch on the inside of the door was being unfastened.

The woman was old. No way of telling how old. All distinguishing features had been erased by time, total disregard for health, and the worst fashion-police disaster Shaver had seen since his Aunt Mable had come to "visit" when he was a child.

"Um," Shaver said at last, feeling that ancient, withered gaze sliding up and down him in distaste, distrust, and what bordered on anger. "Do you have three rooms?"

The woman blinked at him, inhaling and drawing enough air through the cigar butt to bring the embers at the tip to glowing life.

"Might have," she spat the words, rolling the cigar to the corner of her mouth. This allowed her to speak, but slurred the words. "Might be I'd be more likely to say if you was to tell me why you two need three rooms?"

Dexter blinked once, then smiled. "Ma'am, you see that van over yonder?" He was drawling his words, not his voice at all, but somehow, some way . . . it was working. Shaver bit his lip and forced back the smile.

The woman glared at him, but nodded, the motion almost imperceptible.

"Well," Dexter leaned in, his eye glittering and his head turned, conspiratorially, "there's a band in there, ma'am. Finest blues band to ride these roads in goin' on forty years. See, me and my buddy here, we can't let on to folks what we know, cuz they'd be gatherin' around and raisin' all sort of hell, you get my drift?"

"Who is they?" the woman spat again. "I been hearin' ever' band through here for nigh on twenty of those forty years yer talkin' about, boy."

"You probably wouldn't have heard about us way out here, ma'am," Shaver cut in. He'd considered adding the drawl to his own voice, then thought better of it. He had no idea how Dex had pulled that off, but now was *not* the time to ask.

The woman swiveled to appraise Shaver. "You don't look like much to me, boy," she grated. "Don't look like you'd remember the day of a good blues band, let alone be in one."

Dexter cut in again. "His . . . *father* brought him to music, ma'am. He's a young one, but a good one. The band is 'Channel Blue,' like on the TV?"

She watched them both for a moment, then nodded. "Catchy handle," she commented, turning and drawing the screen door inward. "Been a bit of time since any music worth hearin' came through South Haven. Been a long time since I heard anything *not* on the TV."

Dexter winked at Shaver as they passed inside to the counter. Shaver just shook his head and grinned, though he was quick to kill that expression as the woman slid around behind the desk.

"I'm Mae," she said, "Mae DeLucas. Been runnin' this here place since my Donald died; expect I'll be runnin' it for some time to come. I don't take to no loud music; you get the remote for the TV when you get your key. Cash in advance, and no pets."

Dexter nodded, reaching for his wallet and peeling off three twenties and a five. He dropped all of that on the counter and took the register that Mae slowly turned toward him. He carefully penned in each of their God-given names, ignoring nicknames and making each letter as legible as possible. His handwriting, like everything else about him, was sharp and precise.

"Don't suppose you'd care to give me a listen to some of that music, seeing as how you're here, and all?" Mae's voice had softened a little, and there was a hint of the wistful in her tone.

Dexter glanced over his shoulder at the van, then turned back, smiling. "I'll see what I can do," he said. "Should we dial '0' to get you, ma'am?"

"You call me Mae," she said, reaching across the counter and pressing her gnarled fingers into his arm. "You call me Mae, and yes, it is '0' if you boys need anything."

"Thank you," Shaver said.

Mae nodded. "Hell," she chuckled, spinning the cigar deftly to the other side of her mouth, "I'd have rented the rooms to anyone, really. Good to know an old girl can still charm the fellers."

Shaver nearly groaned, but Dexter laughed.

"I knew you would, Mae," he said, winking at her. "I can never resist the opportunity to be charmed."

Mae might have blushed at that. It was hard to tell with her rough complexion, and she turned away just at that moment. Then she was sliding three keys and three television remotes across the counter. "You give me a call," she said, turning and disappearing into the back.

Dexter snagged the keys, and the two of them banged back out through the screen door, sliding into either side of the van with a triumphant flourish.

"Three 'roadside cottages fit for a king,' " Dexter announced.

Shaver stared at him. "What the hell was that in there,

Dex? I mean, who the fuck *was* that guy? How'd you know she'd believe you?"

"She didn't believe a word of that," Dexter laughed. "You forget man, I didn't grow up in any city. I saw that cigar, and I knew I was home."

Shaver shook his head and mimicked the tones his friend had used moments before, "Best blues band to pass this way in nigh on forty years." Then he laughed.

Liz had turned, her hands now on the console, and she glanced from one to the other of them quizzically. "What *are* you talking about?"

"Never mind," Shaver answered, leaning down to kiss her, still chuckling. "I'll give you the whole story while we set up for the 'concert.' "

Liz stared back at him, returning the kiss, but watching him as if he had lost his mind.

"Concert?" Brandt called from the back.

"Wait," Dexter answered, waving a hand at them. "I have to find the right rooms first."

He backed out of the parking place in a crunch of gravel and turned into the shadowy lot. There was a single dim light with a tin-shade, funneling illumination into a yellowed circle in the center of the parking lot. Dexter had to come at the line of rooms from an angle, so the headlights illuminated the numbers. They had numbers 11, 12, and 13. Not that it would have mattered which keys Mae had grabbed. There was one other vehicle in the lot, parked near the office. An old truck, rounded fenders and bowed hood speaking of days when gas wasn't a precious commodity, sat leaning slightly to one side like it had a limp.

"Popular place," Liz commented.

Dexter pulled in directly in front of room number 12, and killed the engine. He slid out quickly, moving to the door and fumbling the key out to get the door open. Moments later, he disappeared inside, and a light flickered to life, leaking out through the door and onto the parking lot. As he reappeared in the doorway, silhouetted, the others piled out in a rush. By the time Dexter had tossed one key to Shaver and moved to room 11, they were all standing in a closely huddled group, staring at their surroundings as if they'd landed on some alien planet.

When the lights had been turned on in all three rooms, there was a little more reality to the scene, but only a little.

"It's so quiet," Synthia said, shivering.

"You've been in the city too long," Dexter commented. "Listen for a while. You'll hear things you would never hear back home. Real things. Things that are alive. The sound is just another pattern, and it is the backdrop for everything you see."

"Pretty profound for a fucking coffee addict," Shaver commented.

Dexter smacked him on the arm, but they all did as Dexter suggested. The silence that had seemed so complete moments before came alive with soft buzzing, and low hoots. They could hear the hum from the transformer that ran the parking lot's lone light, and back the way they'd come, the passing of traffic ebbed and flowed gently.

Brandt finally tore himself loose from it and turned back to the van, opening the side doors fully and reaching for the first of the bags.

"Plenty of time to commune with Mother Nature once we get settled in," he said, heading for the center room.

The others shuffled behind him, handing bags back and forth and sorting through the debris of junk food and coffee cups in silence. No one seemed willing to speak and break the mood of the moment. It took a surprisingly short time to empty the van and split it all three ways. Shaver and Liz moved into the first room, Brandt and Synthia to the second, and Dexter piled his drums and his small pile of "essentials" just inside the door of the third, flopping back on the bed.

The rooms were surprisingly clean and dust free. Each was equipped with a small, one cup coffee maker, and a nineteen-inch color television. They'd just gotten their clothing semi-unpacked and had a chance to rifle through the drawers and comment on the complimentary Gideon Bibles, when there was a metallic scrape out in the parking lot.

Dexter bounced off his bed and moved quickly to the door to investigate. It was Mae. She was standing, looking a bit sheepish, in the gravel just outside. In her hands, bouncing against each hip, were about six aluminum lawn chairs.

"Well," she said, the intake of breath reddening the cherry of a fresh cigar, "don't just stand there, son, give me a hand here."

Dexter laughed and slipped out into the shadows, taking the chairs from her with a gentlemanly flourish.

Mae watched him, her hands dropping straight to her hips, or the point in her short, shapeless form that appeared to be her hips.

"Don't you get fancy with me, sonny. I thought maybe I wouldn't wait for you to call me. Might miss out on some pretty fine music that way. Thought to myself, Mae, you go out and you fetch them into the parking lot, bring out some of that good corn whiskey you got stashed for somethin' special, and you plunk yourself in one of those chairs until it happens."

The others had wandered out of their rooms to see what all the commotion was, and Dexter waved at them.

"Seems we have an audience," he said with a chuckle,

his voice dropping easily into the country twang he'd affected when they signed in. "Shaver, you want to help a friend with some chairs?"

Everyone but Shaver stood stupefied by the scene before them, but the young guitarist took his cue easily and with grace. He took half the offered chairs and he and Dexter aligned them carefully, two in the audience (so there was a place for Liz to sit) and the rest arranged for the band. Mae had returned to her own quarters, and now was back with a heavy-duty extension cord over one shoulder and a stoneware jug in her free hand.

"Thought you might could use some power," she grinned. "You ain't the first musicians to visit South Haven, you know." She smiled and let the cords fall in a heap at her feet, the trailing end snaking back to some unseen source.

Dexter had finished with the chairs and made his way to where Brandt and Synthia were still staring, openmouthed.

"You were complaining about the silence, a minute ago," he said. "Let's see what we can do about that? You up for it?"

Brandt thought about it, but only for a moment. The voices inside were anything but silent, and he knew he'd have to play soon, probably that evening, somewhere. Why not here? Why not with the others? Why not see what would happen? They hadn't played together since that night, so long ago, when he'd walked out and not come back. He stepped out into the night and nodded.

Synthia wasn't so quick to move. She looked past the chairs, past Mae, at those who gathered. Maybe fifty of them, dragging along, some old and some much younger, eyes locked on Brandt as he stepped from the room.

Synthia felt their need, their desperation, and she nearly moaned at the sudden onslaught of emotion.

Brandt sensed something was wrong and turned, but Mae was faster. She plunked the jug of whiskey in the gravel and scuttled over to where Synthia had swooned against the wall. Mae's stout shoulder was under Syn's taller, more slender arm, supporting her.

"You seen 'em, didn't you, honey?" the older woman said, a tinge of amazement in the tone of her voice.

Syn raised her eyes, shaking her head and getting her bearings. Without thought, she answered. "I always see them," she whispered. "Always. I have never felt them before."

Everyone had gathered closer, and Mae turned, shooing them away with one chubby hand. "You give her room to breathe," she said with a grunt. Turning, Mae eyed the lot beyond the chairs. "You too. You got no call comin' in so close, scarin' folks.

"It's me, you know," she said. "It's me who feels them, have for nigh on seventy years. No one ever listened, so I quit talkin' about it. My mother told me 'twas the Devil in me, and I should pray. I prayed plenty, let me tell you." Mae turned back to Synthia, capturing the younger woman's gaze with her own.

"None of them listen. I don't know if they are the dead, or the almost dead, or the damned all-ghost-choir. I can tell you one thing, and that is that prayer don't mean a tinker's damn to a one of 'em. Never seen 'em pay a bit of attention to a living soul, until now."

"You said you felt them?" Synthia asked. "All that pain? Always? That hunger?"

Mae nodded. "Every bit of it, hon. You be damn glad all you do is see 'em. I guess you picked those feelings off of me, and I'm right sorry for it."

"Or me," Brandt cut in, offering Mae his hand.

"And who might you be?" she asked, taking the hand, but

looking him up and down skeptically. "You see 'em too?"

"I don't see them, but they are here to see me," Brandt answered gently. "They are bringing me their pain, their stories. I'll see those stories tonight. Likely, if you listen, you'll see them too. Share that pain. Live it again, and let it loose. I have to play it, have to live it with them, through music, or it builds up inside. You feel it when they are here. I feel it, always. Sometimes it's just a low ache. Sometimes it's a slow burn, and other times a raging fire, but the one thing it always *is* is there."

Mae watched Brandt's eyes as he spoke, then turned out to watch the gathering host of angels. "Don't know why, son, but I believe you. Got no reason to lie to an old woman. I'll tell you this. I've been here a long long time. I've seen them born and dead and I know faces in that crowd. A right many of them, to be truthful. You say you'll be setting that pain free tonight?"

"That is what happens when I play," Brandt replied. "I don't know if it's me, the music, a blessing, or a curse, but I'll play, and they'll listen. What happens next is out of my hands."

Mae nodded. "Let's do it then. I'm gonna plop in that chair over there," she pointed across the parking lot, "and I'm guessin' one of you is joining me, from the arrangements. I'm going to open that jug, and toss back a few gulps. You get ready to play, then ol' Mae will tell you a secret before you start."

Brandt smiled. "I love secrets," he said, turning back to the room, and his guitar.

The others moved too, Synthia regaining her bearings and following Brandt slowly. Each of them was lost in thoughts of their own. They remembered. It hadn't been so long for any of them since the night it had all began, and for all those but Brandt, there had been the second night, the night Synthia had joined him. It wasn't something to be hurried into, this music.

They'd practiced a little, but not all of them together. Dexter was rolling his drum kit out, unpacking slowly and carefully and placing each stand gently in the gravel, testing for balance. He was the key, somehow. They knew it as they watched him, though not one of them could have told you why. Even his setup was methodical. Rhythmic. He tested each drum, tuning carefully, teased the cymbals and adjusted the high hat with practiced ease and symmetrical precision.

The others had little to do. The stage amps were hauled out and Mae's multi-plug extension brought to bear. Everything was juiced up and humming with power within a very short span of time. Each moment added to the anticipation, and the electricity.

"Won't it be too loud?" Synthia wondered.

"Hon," Mae laughed. "There ain't a soul within a country mile of here, and if there were, they'd be hightailing it over here for this. Hasn't been a damn thing new in this town since my Donald died, nigh on twenty years ago. You go on and play, and don't you worry about the noise. You let ol' Mae handle that."

She laughed then, turning up the jug and taking a deep swig.

"And don't think for a moment," she called out, "that you'll be playing without sampling this. I been saving it a long time."

Dexter looked up at that, laughing. He made a final adjustment to his snare, nodded, and turned away. "I'm up for that," he said, dropping his accent. "I've had more coffee than a fleet of redneck truck drivers. If I don't cut the edge, you girls," he winked then at Brandt and Shaver, "will never keep up."

They all laughed at that, and moved toward Mae as a group. The old proprietress grinned up at them, passing the jug and watching intently to be certain that none of them shirked on their "swaller."

"Does my heart good," she said at last, taking the jug back and smiling at Liz, who'd taken the chair beside her, pad and pencil in hand. "Held onto this for so long I'd given up hope on a proper moment to finish it." Mae squinted over at Liz's pad. "You got enough light, honey?"

Liz nodded. "I don't really need to see that well to draw," she answered. "Sometimes I don't even remember doing it."

Mae nodded. "Figures," she grunted. "Hangin' out with a pack of hooligans like this." Then she saluted Brandt with the jug and took another swig.

Brandt nodded in answer, sliding the strap of his guitar over his shoulder and giving the strings a last second tuning. Synthia did the same. Shaver seemed content to hold his fingers tightly on his strings, feeling the power in the amp, hissing in an undercurrent of controlled fury.

Dexter held his sticks tightly. He appeared motionless, but it was deceiving. There was a shimmer of sound from the head of the snare, just the hint of what was to come. His fingers and hands literally vibrated with potential energy, waiting for the spark. It had been far too long since he'd really played. Slapping his finger and tapping spoons was a distraction, but this was his world. His reality.

He glanced at Mae, and winked.

Raising the drumsticks over his head with a flourish, he cracked them together loudly, and called out to the others.

"Ready? A one . . . a two . . . a three . . ."

FIFTEEN

The light above them flickered when Brandt and Shaver hit the strings of their instruments simultaneously, but the power held. Mae only spared the power line a single glance before leveling her concentration on the band. That is what they were again, a band. Weeks, even months, had passed between sessions, and yet, in that instant, no time had passed at all. They rolled into action, warming up with the same old blues. Familiar riffs and quick rolls fell from their fingers, and rippled off Dexter's drumsticks. It was tight, tighter than it had ever been.

Still, it wasn't the same. They all felt it. The moment that Brandt began to play, things shifted, internally and externally. The parking lot, formerly shadowy and empty, shimmered. The single bulb above them flickered as if caught in the eye of a powerful storm, rocking so hard it nearly came loose from its mounting.

The desert slid inward, erasing the line of dingy rooms to a blank slate, endless and glimmering in the light of a suddenly full moon. The angels lined up in ranks, an army of the desperate and the dead, not surging forward, or retreating—listening. It wasn't like anything any of them had experienced before. Brandt had expected a vision, a quick shift of reality to the memory of a single man or woman or child. It didn't happen, not right away. They gathered, and they waited.

As the ringing echo of Brandt's and Shaver's dancing notes hung, crisp and full in the air, the drums shimmered, opalescent heat rising from the gravel and sand in mockery of the long, cold day. The sound rippled through the crowd, and Synthia's bass slid in tight and easy, deep throbbing notes that lingered, sustaining just long enough for the transition to the next chord. The ground shook as her strings vibrated. The air rushed around them, roaring as she thumped her fingers heavily up the neck, and back down.

Brandt watched the crowd and waited. No one had stepped from those ranks, and yet, even the endless lines of faces and pale limbs formed a pattern. He knew the game. He knew that there was one in that multitude who would be the key to the notes. Someone would funnel that pain, building and hanging over him like a tidal wave. His fingers lingered, shifting through a slow blues progression easily, waiting for a focus.

Nothing. He felt Shaver hovering at his shoulder, felt the control, the elegant mastery of sound that was Shaver's talent, held in check and waiting. They were all waiting, waiting for his lead. The last time he had taken them all by surprise, stunning them to perfection, and then, at last, to silence. This time they knew it was coming. This time it would be more powerful.

The pain itched out from Brandt's heart, burning down the tendons of both arms and sliding icy fingers up into the back of his skull. He needed to find the release. Needed it so badly that the music threatened to spill out, wasted and without purpose, just so he could move his fingers. Just so that he could focus and not pass out from the searing agony.

Brandt started at the sound of Mae's voice. He nearly lost the soft rhythm he'd been playing. The desert rippled again, and a sensation much like a sigh, though silent, suffused the air. Brandt gritted his teeth and bore down on the strings. The chord shimmered and held, and Shaver wound around it easily, saving the moment.

"You come outta there, Clem," Mae repeated her outburst. "You come outta there now, you hear? I didn't carry my old ass out into the parking lot in the middle of the night to watch you snivel."

The crowd wavered, then parted, and a slender, gawky youth wound his way free, standing just beyond the ranks, which closed quickly behind him, and wavering like a candle flame in a stiff breeze.

Brandt watched him, reaching out with his mind, and his heart. The pain had reacted to Mae's words, but Brandt couldn't yet be certain this boy was the catalyst. Clem sauntered forward another few careful feet and stopped, eyes to the ground. Nothing to read. Nothing that called out to Brandt, and the pain began to slip over its boundaries. The young face was obscured in shadow.

"Clem!" Mae's voice cracked out this time, and the boy's head snapped back, eyes wide.

Brandt caught the expression this time, the guilt, and the denial and the weight that drew the boy's gaze to the ground at his feet. He caught the interplay of mind to mind and family to family and the hatred that simmered, deep within and well-checked by the forced semblance of love.

The music washed over and through him with no warning, nearly driving Brandt to his knees. He felt the purity of the sound, the unerring dagger-to-the heart agony of release, shifting quickly to release, and completion.

"Yes," he hissed.

Shaver hit the groove with the accuracy of a circus-act dagger, slicing through the grinding rhythm and cleanly dissecting the pattern. Brandt blinked, nearly losing it again. He felt the pain ebb, flowing up and through him, but there was more this time. It flowed out and coalesced into—something. Something held in place by the shimmering notes of Dexter's drumbeat and pounded into intricate designs by Shaver's notes.

Then the shift. Not subtle, or slow, but sudden and distinct. Brandt would have sworn he heard the mellow tone of a bell tolling in the distance, and the desert slipped away.

They were gathered around a bright yellow Formica table, screaming "fifties" with all their breath. Mae stood across from them, only not the Mae they had met. Younger, not so stout or round, but full-figured, curving gently from a motherly, almost pretty smile.

She was turned to face them, hand gripping a large wooden spoon and stirring a steaming pot on the stove before her. There were several others gathered around the table. One of them was Clem. The boy was even younger, and even thinner, but there was no mistaking those downturned eyes and that sallow complexion. He was bordered by a girl on his left who must have been his twin, and a boy on the right that favored Mae, stouter with freckles and deep laugh lines.

None of the kids could have been more than eleven or twelve, and from the difference in Mae's figure and complexion, this was a mid-twenties mother, "her Donald" the tall thin man at the head of the table, eyes stern, but with the corner of his lips twitching into a smile he couldn't quite contain.

Mae was carrying the pot from the stove to the table when the door burst open and the pain washed through Brandt again, erasing the happy scene in a wave of pure, white-hot agony. Mae tripped, falling forward with a cry. The pot, steaming chicken stew, canted wildly, and she couldn't hold it. Donald tried to leap in front of that scalding splash, but only managed to press his arm to the side of the pot, skin sticking and flaking.

The room was liquid with screams. The hot soup hung in the air. Brandt wanted to close his eyes. He felt the wave of pain shivering up and through and his fingers lurched into the strings, creating the sound that wound each image to the next.

The first splash of stew caught the girl beside Clem flush in the face, washing over her and obscuring her features. She had no time to move before the searing wave hit Clem, but Brandt and the others could see her face drawing open, eyes and mouth wide, rictus of pain unvoiced.

Clem was already screaming. He had time, time to see the danger, time to take in the agony on his sister's face and know it as his own. The world shifted and Donald crashed over both children, pushing Clem back and, rather than blocking the stew, allowing it to splash directly over the boy, coating his face and driving him back and down toward the floor. Clem's chair shot back, cracking into the solid wood planks, and Donald rolled over him and away, trying not to fall on top and make things worse.

"Where's that lazy ass *boy!*" Words too loud, too gruff to be human slashing through the screams as the door swung on its hinge and spring and slammed back into its frame. The room shook with the words. For just one long, tepid breath the screaming stopped, cowed by the onrush of sudden, mindless terror.

"You hear me Don? Mae? Where the hell is my boy?"

Another crunching boot step closer and the huge, grizzled face appeared.

Mae moaned, fighting to right the pot and back away at the same time. Her eyes flashed with terror, and yet, she didn't really back away. Not far. She lifted the pot and held it, fingers knuckle-white on the handles, ignoring the sting of the heat.

"*Where?*" the monster growled.

Donald had rolled back to his feet, and he rose now, tall and slender, nearly the height of the intruder, but less than half his girth, and still, standing stiff as a board, one arm clutched to his side tightly.

Mae took a step forward, steady, but shaking.

The big man hesitated, as if taking in the scene before him for the first time. He glanced down, and there at his feet were Clem and his sister, hands clutched to their faces, writhing on the floor.

"They may be blinded, Sam," Donald said dully. "They're scalded, sure as blazes. I think maybe you should call Doc Nutman."

Brandt felt the notes shifting again, felt the balance of energy failing and reached out, trying to steady it, only to find the notes trailing down and away, awash and trapped in the moment. Shaver's lead rippled suddenly, almost ripping free of the rhythm, and the room began to shake. Pounding, slamming thunder. Synthia.

Everything shook. The image blurred, lost focus, and then steadied in a low thrum of pounding. Now the room didn't so much shake as it swayed. Each motion slowed, and speeded, and slowed again, and Brandt caught, riding the wave and fighting to hold it all together. The rhythm focused. The drumbeats grew deeper, primal, sucking the chaos from the music and reapplying it to the moment.

Brandt gasped. The pain that had been steadily trickling from him washed out in a flood. The cohesive bond between the members of the band worked like an amplifier. Everything laid bare, and his eyes locked now to the panorama before him, captured and held by the sound and the screams.

The monster had leaned down, and now he towered over the table. From each hand, a young battered and burned child dangled limply, and his head was thrown back in rage. Mae became a blur. First she stood, crouched, a cornered animal with nothing but rage in her eyes, and then she launched. Donald launched, as well, but again, he was too late. The pot rose high in the air, glittered with the light of the sun, trickling in the window.

Brandt leaned in. He wanted to toss the guitar aside. He wanted to reach out and stop her, to cry out and scream along with the children, but he did not. He played. His fingers were locked to the strings and the tears streamed down his cheeks as pain ground through him, out and away. Too much, too fast. More than he could bear and still that gigantic form danced a St. Vitus waltz of rage, crashing into the table, toppling it with a surge of huge, tree-trunk thighs and turning toward the door.

Too late to escape.

Just in time to meet Mae's crashing stew-pot equalizer of focused rage, temple first, blood and flesh and brain splattering and still he was turning, young hair gripped knuckles white-tight, slamming Clem into Mae and Donald, very suddenly wrapping his arms around the girl, the silent, sad-eyed sister, trying to tear her free.

Mae raised the pot again and brought it down, this time both hands gripping the handle, and her stout, short form nearly leaving the floor, shaking from the beating of the drum, caught in the power of the moment and unable to break free. The monster's head broke, showering the room with blood. There was no struggle, no dance. He toppled, like a tree, felled with a single mighty stroke. The girl broke loose into Donald's arms, who could only stand and hold and stare.

Brandt watched the girl turn in Donald's grip. Her eyes were swollen closed, horribly, her skin blistered, and her lips had to be forced apart. Brandt played, tears streaming down his cheeks, and those cracked lips parted. She spoke.

"Daddy."

Brandt reeled. He wanted to scream now.

"Monster," he mouthed, and his fingers played.

"Jesus, he is no *Daddy*," and the music shivered around him like a shroud.

His eyes closed. He couldn't stand this blind-eyed wraith of a girl screaming for a Daddy who lay dead on the floor and Mae's broken features, hands clutched to her cheeks and eyes and tears rolling out and around clutching fingers. Donald standing, stupefied, holding the girl as his wife sobbed and Clem, poor forgotten Clem, writhing at his father's feet, Mae's son wrapped over him like a protective blanket of flesh, wide-eyed and ready to be his shield, too late, all too late and too crazy.

The shimmer of cymbals drew Brandt back. The throbbing grind of the bass, slipping to a dull roar, and subsiding to a heartbeat Thump! Thump! Thump! of low tones and deep resonance dragged his eyes wide once again.

And again, everything had changed. Mae sat at one end of the table, knees drawn up to her chin and arms tight-wrapped around herself. Her eyes were swollen and closed and dry, but raw from the rubbing and rubbing of tears on her shoulder until no more would come, and then rubbing some more.

Donald stood, back to Brandt, shoulders bowed. On the table, lain out as if it were a bed, two slender forms, Clem and his sister, very still. Donald's shoulders shook. He was silent, and another figure, slender, white lab-coat shimmer of doctor examining the obvious, head shaking the entire

time as he worked, and the pain shivering up through and out of Brandt like a geyser. Too much. Too fast, and still he played. His fingers wouldn't pry loose from the strings. Brandt saw the doctor shake his head again. Brandt's head swung back. He screamed with the rest of them, drowned them with the volume of the sound as his fingers danced, slave to a sound he could no longer hear.

Everything shook. The world skewed and Brandt screamed again, releasing the guitar and gripping his head, hands tight in his hair and eyes clamped shut. The sound had just . . . stopped. Brandt trembled. Every inch of his frame shook, so violently that his teeth chattered and he had to force his mouth/throat open to breathe. He was clutching the guitar to his gut, pressing into it to try and relieve the taut, rippling tension in his gut.

Nothing helped. It rang and echoed against the insides of his brain, screamed for release and was denied each time, caroming off another nerve and skittering back inside. Without the music, the pain seeped from him like blood from an open wound, and he couldn't stop it. Nothing could stop it.

Clem's face—his sister's face—that monster, storming and raging over them like something from a B-grade monster movie, only with A-grade special effects and that word. "Daddy." That single, misplaced, horrifying revelation of *wrong* as the girl spoke.

Brandt rocked, up and back, and he whispered to himself, over and over. "Not Daddy. Not Daddy. No fucking way, not *Daddy*."

Arms wrapped around him tightly. He heard the crack of wood on wood and knew it was Synthia, and that she'd not waited to slip free of her bass, that the guitars were fencing dangerously, threatening to end the sound and he couldn't bring himself to care. Brandt wrapped his arms tightly around her neck, drawing her close and leaning over her shoulder, pressing his eyes down into her hair, clamping them shut against images that required no vision, that defied the ability of his eyelids to deny them.

"No," he mouthed, no sound escaping, just the intent of the words. "Not Daddy."

The world skewed suddenly. The air, which had been warm and too close, scented with chicken stew and fresh blood, shifted. It was cool. A breeze rippled through Brandt's hair and cooled his face. He heard the murmur of voices, though he could make out few of the words. The wood of his guitar was driven into his ribs, and gently, very gently, he pulled away from that physical discomfort, without extricating himself from Synthia's death-grip support.

"Jesus," Shaver whispered. His arms hung limp at his sides, his guitar dangling from his neck like an overgrown peace-bead necklace. Helpless in the aftermath. He almost felt the urge to raise his hands, fingers splayed. "Jesus."

"That isn't the end."

The words dropped over them, Hiroshimaesque in their impact and simple in their presentation.

"That isn't how it ended, and that isn't where I'll let it rest, begging your pardon."

It was Mae. She'd risen from the chair, her cigar tossed and forgotten, eyes awash in tears and red. So red that it showed, even in the dim light of the one overhead bulb. Brandt lifted his head, watching Mae move closer. He clung to Synthia, the position painful for them both, fighting not to damage their instruments and unwilling to slip even a moment from one another's arms.

"That ain't the end by a long shot," Mae continued.

"Guess it's time I told it, though. Guess I couldn't find an audience, other than you all, that would even understand what I was talking about. Too late for Clem to tell, or Eave. Too late for their Dad. Too late for Donald too."

Her voice broke a little then, and Brandt was finally able to move. He uncurled slowly, being careful to maintain contact with Synthia, equally conscious, suddenly, of the instruments. Without them, they would be at the mercy of the pain, or *he* would be. Synthia moved with him, and they were free, though their hips brushed, and their legs touched, and their eyes flickered from Mae, to one another, and back again.

The drums had shivered to silence. Dexter sat, eyes glued to Mae's face, hands trembling. He felt her pain most acutely. He felt as if he knew her, had lived her life inside and out and wrapped it around his soul. A pattern, half blended from his past and half from hers, backdrop to a story he couldn't know. A past they did and didn't share.

Shaver very carefully slid his guitar from his shoulder and moved to lay it in its case. Of them all, he was the only one focused on anything but Mae. The muscles in his arms were taut, and he gripped the guitar too tightly. His brow, furrowed and running with glistening rivulets of sweat, was a map of concentration.

As the guitar gently slid into the case, he released it, eyes closing, and fell back, collapsing in the gravel, arms clutched to his stomach.

Dexter caught the motion from the corner of his eye and gasped, starting to rise, but Shaver rolled up, sitting with an effort and shaking his head. He nodded at Mae, and, reluctantly, Dexter turned back. Mae had fallen silent, watching and waiting. The expression on her face said clearly that if Shaver had keeled over unconscious, she'd have sat there still and told her story. If none had listened, she'd have talked to the angels, gathered around them now, silent. Watching and waiting like the crowd for some huge production. Like they'd been waiting there for years, just for this story. For this moment.

Liz had slid from her seat behind and beside Mae quietly, skirting the older woman and moving quickly to kneel beside Shaver, wrapping him in her arms. She tried to ask what was wrong but he shook his head, and again nodded toward Mae. Liz met his gaze for a moment, searching, and found no answers, so she settled in behind him, drawing him back against her as Mae began to speak.

"Clem was a good boy," Mae said softly. "Was some said he was touched, but I knew the truth of it. That dad. That damned Sam Tanner was the one was touched. Touched by too many bottles." Mae's gaze swung down to the jug at her side. She frowned, and then lifted it to her lips, drinking deeply, and stepping forward to offer it to Brandt.

At first he couldn't move to accept it. He could only stand, and watch, wondering what was the right thing to do and knowing that no matter how right a thing might be it couldn't change a second of what he'd just seen . . . what had been released. Hand trembling, hooking the jug quickly, he brought it up and tipped it, drinking deep. He coughed, nearly choking, then gulped again before lowering the stoneware vessel, eyes closing for a second, and feeling Syn prying the jug from his hand.

"Touched by the bottle," Mae went on, "and so many devils you couldn't have beaten them out of him with a hammer. Just mean. You ever know a boy," she turned to Dexter, common ground easing the pain of the moment, "who'd hurt a dog? Who'd laugh and stone it and whip it with sticks and lure it back with a bit of meat, just to beat it again?"

Dexter blinked. Then, slowly, he nodded. "Or hang a litter of puppies in a gunny sack, shoot the bag with buckshot, and keep the one that lived, because it was a 'fighter?' Yes."

Mae nodded. "Like that. Mean. Started a long time before he was old enough to be fathering children he had no business within miles of, but here, out here in South Haven, well, things get overlooked. You live far enough from the spit-hole they call town square, you live in your own world. Stay clear of the freeways and don't shoot nobody, you got yourself a safe home. God save America.

"Sam was a survivor. Emma, the girl he stole away from her ma over by the tracks, she wasn't a survivor, but she was lucky, in some ways. Sam, he would beat a dog for walkin' on the same side of the street he did, but he wouldn't tolerate anything wrong for Emma. She was his one treasure. Not bright, mind you, but what use did that man have of a bright woman? She could stew meat and brew coffee, and knew enough to keep her mouth shut when he was drinkin', which was most of the time.

"Then there came Clem and Eave, and everything went to hell in a hand basket. That Sam, he never counted on kids. He had him a dog, old bitch coon hound, that he loved. I saw that animal heavy with pups so many times I can't count. Never saw a pup. Sam had a limit, one per species, and all his. When Doc Nutman told him it was to be twins, there was a storm brewing in the depths of those cold eyes before the words was dead in the air.

"Only thing Sam never counted on was that girl Emma. 'Tweren't for her, I suspect we'd have never seen those twins. I don't believe they'd have ever breathed or walked an hour in their lives, but she saved them. Don't know how. She kept them alive, and she kept them at her side, day and night. In church, they were front pew. The moment services ended, they was gone, but they was there every week like a Swiss clock.

"Clem and Eave was ten when Emma died. No one knows what happened, really. Sam came walkin' into town one day, Emma in his arms, already passed, his eyes as dead as two lumps of coal. He didn't say a word. He brought her to the church, laid her on the steps out front, so gentle you'd have thought he was a child playing with a kitten, and then he turned on his heel and marched off, pretty as you please. No one said a word.

"Local sheriff wanted no part of that man. No one did.

"That left the children. Clem and Eave still came in every Sunday for services. Don't know how they got Sam to allow that. They came, and they sat, quiet as you please, right where they'd sat every week of their lives when their mother was with them. Their eyes would be on the floor, as if there was something to be ashamed of, but they listened, and when the hymn-time came you could hear them singing together softly."

"Why did you bring them to your home?" Dexter asked, breaking into the moment. "Why?"

"They was hungry," Mae answered. For just that moment, her animated voice dulled. "I wanted to feed them, one solid meal. They were so . . . naive, and pretty. So needy. I remember asking them, you know?" Mae's head lifted and her eyes flashed. "You know what that girl child said to me?"

I don't think we should, Mae ma'am. My daddy, he needs me. I'm the mommy now, and dinner will be late.

"All the while that girl is speakin', her brother Clem is

nodding. Nodding like a plum empty-headed fool. You can see in his eyes these are words he's heard, again and again. You can see in his eyes that he's hungry, and believes she should be cookin'. You can see in *her* eyes that when she says, 'I'm the mommy,' she doesn't just mean she cooks.

"It's then I see her for the first time as a young woman, a young woman so like her mama you couldn't tell the image of the one gone from the one before you, quiet and mouse-like and eyes turned to the floor. The same glow when you mentioned that Sam's name and all the while, Clem noddin' like a village idiot.

"You know I took those babies home. I took them home and Donald was standin' there at the door as we came, his eyes wide as saucers and his head shaking before he said a word."

Mae, you're askin' for trouble. You're beggin' for it. Sam ain't goin' to take to this no way.

"And I didn't listen. I brought them in. I set that Eave to dicing the potatoes and I snapped the pole beans. We had chicken a'plenty and fixin's to make it go a long ways. Plenty of food. I just wanted to see them eat.

"What I should have done was to call the sheriff. If he'd high-tailed it, he might have gotten there in time. If I'd failed to mention who I was calling about, he might have done it, too. Never did.

"And those two children—those babies, all burned and ruined on the table, Eave crying for her 'daddy,' and Clem moaning. I fell in the corner, just fell, flat on my ass and hands to my eyes. I couldn't look at what was left of Sam on the floor, couldn't bear to see any of it, so I cried. I was like that when I heard the screams, ripping through the air and slicing at my ears and heart. I knew the voice, you see. I knew it from whispered soft words in my ear at night and the first things spoken over coffee in the morning. I knew it from forever-vows and long-whispered 'I love you, Mae's on the porch swing.

"Donald was screaming, louder than I would have believed possible, and there was another sound, higher pitched still, a keening, wailing voice that rose and fell like a siren. I was up quick, on my feet and shaking my head to clear the cobwebs, but it was too late. Donald was falling toward me. His eyes were wide. So wide. He reached for me, and there was no accusation in that gaze, nothing but love—regret. He reached for me and I stood there like a bump on a dead log as he fell, face first. He'd hit the floor before I saw the blood, streaming and pumping from his back.

"And there behind him stood Clem. He was nodding, still nodding, as if Eave were telling him it was time for her to cook dinner for Daddy because she was the mommy now. The blood was splattered over every inch of him, coating his arm and drenching the white shirt he wore each Sunday. That boy was weaving back and forth and back and forth like a snake, his lips moving without a sound to be heard.

"I screamed then. I screamed, my hands slipping up to grip my hair and my eyes locked to him like I was hypnotized. The world was crashing down around me, tumbling and falling to pieces, and he didn't see it at all. He didn't see Donald, bleeding to death on the floor, or his father, smashed beyond recognition. His sister.

"I looked to the girl then, desperate, and I saw where all that blood had come from. Not from Donald. Not from my Donald at all. Eave was torn open. Not a slice. Not a clean wound, but torn, throat to belly, one long ragged rip and another, and another; each time momentum stopped he must have dragged that blade free and dug it in again. The table ran red. Clem rocked. The world rocked, and I fell. My head caught the kitchen counter hard, and I don't really know what happened much after that.

"I know when I woke, he was still rocking. I know when I called the doctor, for what reason I'm still not certain, and when I called the Sheriff, he never moved except slowly up and back. I went to him and I took that knife."

Mae stopped for the first time since she'd started, glaring at them all in defiance.

"I took that knife, and I washed it, and I dried it. I stepped around Donald and I gritted my teeth, blinked through the tears, and found a way to slide it into Sam's hand before they arrived. I took a kitchen towel, and I soaked it in Eave's blood, twisting it and wringing it over Sam until he was a spattered wreck of gore.

"Then I washed up, just a little, and I took that boy and sat him in the corner. He was still hungry. I don't think he saw a bit of it. I don't think he knew what he'd done."

"They believed Sam did it?" Brandt asked softly, breaking in finally, and drawing Synthia closer.

Mae nodded, lowering her old eyes toward the gravel. "They'd have believed anything in the world that took someone like Sam away forever. I kept Clem with me. For years."

"What happened?" Liz asked very suddenly. "Why is Clem . . . here tonight?"

"He walked out the door one night," Mae said slowly, "like he did every night of his life. He walked down there to that freeway, and he took a stroll into the front end of a big rig. Not even a warning, or a horn. One moment in the shadows, and the next . . ."

"An angel," Synthia finished, her voice broken and

small. "An angel," she repeated.

Mae dropped her eyes again, without comment. The sounds of the countryside intruded gently. The crickets echoed, magnified by the void Mae's voice had left. Brandt turned to Synthia, hugging her, and the motion broke the last of the spell.

"You kids better get some sleep," Mae said, hardly more than a broken whisper.

Dexter rose from his seat, moving to Brandt and Synthia and retrieving the jug. He took a long swig, and then walked to Shaver. Shaver looked up, and as Dexter started to hand him the jug, the drummer stopped, caught by something in those eyes. Dexter glanced down to where Shaver clutched his hands to his belly.

"Again?" he asked.

Shaver shook his head. "Not like that. Too much, too soon, but I'll be okay."

Dexter nodded, then tipped the jug to Shaver's lips and held it as his friend swallowed. Liz shook her head, eyes red, as Dexter offered it to her next. She helped Shaver to his feet, being very careful of his hands.

Dexter turned to Mae. He walked to the old woman slowly, the jug swinging easily in his hand. As he reached her, he swung it up and took another long belt before handing it back. Mae took it, immediately turning away, but he stopped her with a hand placed gently on her shoulder.

"It isn't a bad thing, Mae," Dexter said. "There are those who deserve our love and consideration, and there are those who deserve nothing. There are those who would have cheerfully killed Clem for what happened. You chose to care for him. He has waited a long time for tonight. You owe him this. You know what he is waiting for."

Mae stopped cold. She turned to Dexter, her face slack and pale, and her eyes wide. "I can't."

Dexter slid an arm around her back, turning her away from the building and back toward the parking lot. "You can, and you will. We can't be stopping by here every time you think you *might* be ready, you know. Got a lot of *pressing* engagements."

Mae listened, and yet she didn't. As she turned, the humming of the overhead light grew impossibly loud. They all turned, watching as she watched. The parking lot was gone again. The desert stretched, endless and desolate, and they littered that plain. Row upon row, silent and staring, waiting. Watching.

Brandt closed his eyes. The pain had subsided, and yet, the scene shifted. The dull ache was nothing more than that. He didn't need to play. There was no more to be released. Not here, not now. Synthia moved closer in his arms, and he held her, his eyes opening once more to watch as Dexter and Mae stepped toward that silent crowd.

As the two stepped forward, a single slender figure melted from the gathered angels. His eyes were turned to the ground. His features were obscured, but they all knew him. They all knew him now and could not have forgotten with all the tequila and Jack Daniel's in the world.

Mae stopped. Dexter stood beside her, his arm still firmly around her shoulder, and at last she lifted her gaze.

"It wasn't your fault, Clem. None of it. Wasn't your fault you was born with the damned Devil as your daddy, and not your fault I brought you home that day. That I had to be the one to help you. Not your fault I took the blame and let you walk in front of a truck. Not sure there's a bit of fault in any of it, but I'm sorry. So sorry."

Mae moved forward then, breaking free of Dexter's arm

and reaching out, wrapping herself around the wraith-Clem in what would have been a tight, tight hug. Would have been, if that moment, that very second she moved, it hadn't faded to nothing. All of it. They stood, watching Mae hug the air in the center of an empty, poorly lit parking lot, and they cried. Every one of them, tears streaming and breath gasping. Mae hugged herself, and Dexter moved in closer, wrapping his own slender arms around the woman's shoulders.

The others moved forward as if on cue, joining the hug. One, then another of them wrapping around the others and laying their heads on the shoulder of the person before them. It was a long time before they broke and slipped into their separate rooms, different hugs blending to embraces and heat and in other rooms to deep sleep.

In a distant place, the candles burned up and down the road and a table waited, squat and low, long and endless, bordering the woods where one walked—hungry and alone.

SIXTEEN

Madeline carefully aligned the candles along her walk, watching the road, and the woods, and the mountain in quick succession. The sidewalk shimmered with the flickering light of dozens of white candles. She moved to the sides, carefully placing each votive in alignment with the last, forming the cross with symmetrical precision.

Eight to one side, three up, and eight back, moving slowly. One thing Brian had taught her was precision. Each thing in its place.

With a soft shiver, Madeline moved to stand at the center of the crucifix. She didn't know what had moved her, but somehow it seemed the right way to face what was to come. The candles reminded her of days when the church had been her life. They reminded her of Brian, and of Elizabeth, and of Reverend Forbes and his deep, resonant voice.

The brush rustled at the edge of the trees. Madeline shivered and snuffed the long fireplace match she'd been holding, letting it drop to the ground. She had a leather-bound edition of the Bible in the pocket of her blouse, and she pulled that free, clutching it to her breast tightly.

No candles lined the road from the church this night, but she knew he was coming. She'd known since that day he slid past the front of her house, not stopping, really, but watching her, that something was wrong. Now, with all the attention from the congregation, and the town fathers, and with the reformation of the old covenants, Madeline was doubly wary.

And she was worried. Worried for Brian. Worried if Brian would even respond, or if he were watching. She could feel him, sense him, but that meant nothing in the face of what was to come. None had acknowledged his sacrifice for so long—would he? Did he hunger for his sacrifice, or did he merely hunger for retribution?

Madeline turned to the bent and twisted bit of wood dangling from the cross in the center of her yard. Brian had left it. She hadn't seen him. He had left no note, nor a sign, and yet one day, it had been there, leaning gently against that cross, looking like nothing so much as a visitation from the heavens—a reminder of mortality.

Madeline had left it as it was for days, watching it, thinking about it. Wondering what to do. In the end, there had been but one thing she could do. She'd found Brian's old hammer, a pile of half-rusted nails, and she'd raised the twisted wood to the center of the cross, propped on a base of old bricks and stones, to be hammered into its rightful place.

Madeline remembered that day as if it had happened within hours, and not a decade in the past. She remembered how the tears had streamed as she'd placed the first nail, irrational tears that hadn't ended until hours after the final stroke had implanted that "idol" on her cross. She remembered kneeling for hours, the hammer long forgotten and her brow pressed to the knot at the center of the log.

There had been a strange comfort in that. No one had seen. No one ever came to visit her, and there was nothing further along the road up the mountain than her home. Madeline had had the log, and her yard, and her mind to herself that day. She felt in her heart that Brian had been watching, that it had all happened according to a plan he'd set in motion, but there was no way to be certain. Brian had been gone so long that if she hadn't had the pictures, Madeline might not have even remembered what he looked like.

There was a rustling at the tree line, and she shifted her attention, slipping a bit closer to the center of the candle-lit cross. At first there was nothing. She stood, and she watched, heart hammering, as the shadows continued to be shadows, and the night grew progressively chillier, despite the season. Madeline strained her vision, forcing the darkness to part, searching each nook and cranny of darkness, but she might as well have stood in the desert in the middle of the night and screamed.

No one was there. Nothing moved, not really, only shadows that danced in and out of the periphery of her vision, speeding her heart and slipping back to darkness.

"Who's there?" she called out, her voice more shrill than she'd intended, and without the force. "Who's there, I say? Come out and face me in the light."

At first, nothing. She coughed, wavering on shaky legs, and nearly turned back to the house, feeling foolish for standing there alone.

As her gaze flickered from the tree line, he stepped forward. When he spoke, low and deep, Madeline nearly leaped from the cross and ran.

"Hello Maddy," the man said softly. "I have been waiting to meet you for some time."

She turned back.

He stood, nearly as dark as the shadows that bordered his slender form, black hat tipped down over one eye, silver hair streaming out over his shoulder, the other eye glittering like the moon itself. Mesmerizing. Cold. Madeline curled her arms around over her breasts and clutched herself, shivering.

"Who are you?" she asked. As an afterthought, "Don't

call me 'Maddy.' No one has had the right to call me that for a very long time, and surely not you."

"I'm sorry, Madeline. I feel as though I've known you forever—from the words of your neighbors. They call you Maddy, and if that is an offense, then let me apologize. No offense was meant."

"Who are you?" Madeline whispered. "You were here before. I felt you, saw your shadow. You came here before you ever went there. Why?"

"So many questions." The man's one visible eye glittered. His lips twisted into a smile that was nothing of the sort and Madeline felt herself begin to shake, slowly. "So many answers I could give you, lady, and none you would understand, fewer still you'd accept."

"Why have you come?" She knew she had to remain strong. No way she could appear anything but terrified, and yet, within the flames of the candle-cross, she didn't really *fear* him, so much as loathe him.

Stepping closer, the man tilted his hat back further, exposing smooth, dark skin and a second eye as cold as the first, completing that snake's gaze she'd expected, and never seen.

"Who are you?" Madeline breathed the words this time. Almost no sound, and yet she knew he heard, knew he'd anticipated the question before she'd known she would form the words. She waited, still clutching herself in a death-grip hug.

"They call me Payne," he answered at last, voice smooth and slick as quicksilver. "Reverend Payne. That isn't important. Not to you, Maddy, or to Brian." He hesitated then, letting his words sink in. "What is important, well, that would be my past. I know people, Maddy. I knew your Reverend Forbes, and I knew your Brian's daddy. I know about the feast, and I know about the hunger.

"You know that hunger, don't you Maddy? You've felt it, through him. You've known the need. How do you think he feels, your Brian? How do you think he's been this past year, since Shane—Reverend Forbes, passed? You think time has been kind to him, Maddy? You think he's one with the forest, maybe? You think he started his own little commune of *love* out there?"

Shifting his gaze, the man stepped toward the wooden cross, and its symbolic, warped wooden tenant.

"I think not," he went on, whipping his gaze back to hers, lashing her and pinning her in place, all in that single motion.

"He's hungry, Maddy. He's so hungry his mind is going, slowly, and there is only one thing you, or anyone, can do for him. He has to feed. They have to pass. It is the way it has always been, the way it always will be, for Brian. You know that. You knew that when you met him. They told you to stay away, didn't they? Told you he was to be left alone, but you couldn't do it. Now he is hungry, Maddy, hungrier than any have been in the span of years of your mothers and grandmothers, and the weight of that hunger is yours to bear. The others, they remember, but they don't know. They don't know what to bring to the feast, or how to react once they are there. They don't know why they do it, nor do they have anyone to turn to but you.

"You know those answers. You know what will bring him home. Only you."

"You know." Madeline whispered the words. She didn't even know how she knew them as truth, but she did, and they were, and she waited.

He watched her, eyes blazing for a moment, and then softening. His lip twisted again, that smile that was no smile, but that smile cracked as well and melted to laughter that rippled and rolled from his too-tight lips, echoing up and down the side of the mountain. The man's features rippled oddly, his body bending nearly double with the effort of regaining his self-control. Then, as if it had never wavered, he stood, facing her again, leaning on his cane.

"They will not listen to me alone, Madeline," he said at last. "They will listen to you. They trust my knowledge of the old ways, as they trusted Reverend Forbes before me, but they trust *your* knowledge of he who walks alone. They trust you when it comes to his hunger."

Turning to her yard once more, sweeping his gaze over the small army of crosses, their hand-lettered messages, largely ignored, but timeless in their vigilance.

"You are the only one, Maddy, who has kept that faith. You are the only one, through all of this, who still believes. They remember. They know what they believed before, but it has been stolen from them, packed away and 'washed in the blood of the Lamb' by watered-down men of some other God. Not our God, eh Maddy? Not He who watches over us, or over you. Not He who demands the feast and the hunger."

Payne turned then, gazing directly at the wooden parody of Christ, dangling from its rickety cross. A quick nod of his head, eyes flashing, and Madeline gasped as the gnarled, twisted wood burst into flame. She took a step back, nearly burning herself on the votives, eyes locked to that burning wood. Deep within the flame, something moved. Imperceptibly at first, difficult to focus on, too bright and suddenly hot enough that the sweat poured down her brow and soaked her blouse.

A face, wizened by age and lined with the creases of infinite sorrow, pain she could not fathom, so deep and pervasive that Madeline's legs gave out, and she fell, painfully, to her knees, trapped there in that gaze. His gaze.

"No," Madeline whispered. "Dear God, no."

Brian watched her as white-heat licked at the features of his face, dancing and blazing where hair and beard should have shielded him from the elements. The wood shifted, moving and writhing in time with the flames. Limbs formed, reformed, and disappeared once again into the tangle of twisted wood. Acrid smoke permeated the yard, floating around her, clouding the trees and the road and even dimming the light of that flame. Only his eyes pierced that gloom, and breathing became more and more difficult.

Madeline toppled forward, arms reaching out toward him, forgetting the candle-flame cross and he who had watched her moments before. She forgot everything but those eyes, focused on them and crawled. The candles lit her blouse, and still she crawled, trying to roll side to side and quench the now-too-close flames, but not stopping her forward motion for it, even when the heat seared. Even when the flames began to lick their way up toward her hair.

"Brian," she whispered. "Brian, I'm so sorry."

There was a roaring sound from above, a roaring she first confused with that of the flames, but Madeline ignored it. She concentrated, sliding another couple of feet toward the cross, toward Brian. She didn't know why, didn't know what she would do, or why, but she had to try.

The pain grew and she rolled over and over in misery, flames eating away her clothing and searing her flesh, threatening ever closer to her hair, and only a few scant feet remained. A distance she could have covered in a matter of a few steps, that she couldn't seem to crawl, that she couldn't pass through, and all that while his eyes, downturned and tracking her as she moved. As she failed.

The roaring grew, and very suddenly, Madeline grew afraid. She was not only outside the cross she'd so carefully formed, but her flesh screamed from the searing heat, and no matter how many times she rolled over and over on what should have been cool grass, the flames danced higher.

It was loud, like a tornado, a freight-train of air crashing down from the mountain, and dark, so dark that with the flames, it made an ebony curtain back-dropping the flaming cross. Madeline shifted her gaze to the sky, watching, trying not to, trying to retain her grip on the image of Brian, to roll over and finish her journey, drag him out of that fire and . . .

Sudden crash of air, chill, driving thought and sight from her in an instant, washing over flame and cross and yard and trees, blacking it out completely. One moment the skies opened, spilling darkness and whirling, faster and faster, a vortex drawing Madeline's sanity up and away and then . . .

Nothing.

Madeline lay on the soft earth, eyes clenched shut and arm wrapped tightly to her chest. Her dress was plastered to her, clammy-sweat causing it to cling to her thin frame. Her hair fanned out behind her, bedraggled and full of leaves and pine needles. There was no breeze. No heat. The burning had snuffed quickly and completely.

With a soft moan, she opened her eyes and turned, lifting her head weakly. The cross stood, as it had stood since the day she'd erected it. The gnarled wooden image, not Brian, not resembling Brian, but left by his hand, hung in its place. Untouched. No scorch marks. No burning. No face.

Madeline collapsed, inhaling a long, gasping breath and fighting to still the trembling that shook her frame. Slowly, she managed to rise to a sitting position. The road was empty. The trees held no shadowed figures, nor did she catch the white flash of eyes from the shadows. Alone.

She turned to the ruined cross on the sidewalk. The candle-drawn symbol was the only evidence of the reality she'd faced. No one would believe. She didn't know what she believed. She saw where she'd toppled over the flames. She felt that heat, searing her flesh, and yet her blouse and skirt were intact. Her skin, a bit scuffed and scraped, was unscathed. Her mind whirled.

From the woods, so soft it might have been mountain wind and hoot owls, though she knew it was not, that too-slick voice floated back to her.

"He is hungry, Maddy. So hungry."

Madeline shook her head and blocked that voice out. With painful determination, she turned, kneeling in the yard, alone, as the hour grew later and the moon's illumination became an eerie silver blanket over the scene. Inch by inch, she moved forward, feeling the small branches, pine needles, and stones jabbing her knees as she went. To the cross. This time, she made that short pilgrimage slowly, but with no resistance.

Madeline knelt before the cross, and laid her cheek against the center of the twisted wooden Christ-image. Her arms wrapped around that, and the cross, and her shoulders heaved with sudden release as the tears began to roll down her face, wetting the wood, trickling down and running with the dirt from the yard to stain her collar and her sleeves. Madeline didn't see it, nor did she hear, as the tires of the van slowly crunched their way up the road from the church below.

"Jesus," Shaver commented, as the van continued the bouncing, painful climb up the mountain, leaving the church, and the small community of Friendly, California behind. "You didn't tell us it was a fucking expedition into Deliverance."

Liz would have laughed, maybe, had she not been lost in a cloud of painful memories. Nothing much had changed. There were a few new homes, a few buildings not where she remembered them being. Not progress, really, but change.

As they had driven through the streets, and on past the church, the few locals they'd passed had watched them closely, trying to peer through the dingy windows of the van and figure out who, or what, was invading their little world.

"I'm betting they don't get a lot of out-of-towners here," Brandt said softly.

"Almost never," Liz said, answering at last. They were only a few curves in the road from the home she'd once shared with a father and a mother she only vaguely recalled. "No one ever came here. Almost no one ever left."

Shaver leaned down from the front seat and kissed her on the forehead. "That time is over now," he said. "We're here, you're here, and right now the important thing is that we find your mom and see what she knows about your dad."

"If she'll talk to us," Liz replied, her voice breaking slightly. "If she doesn't hate me now for leaving her here, alone. Just like Daddy did, only he didn't really leave. At least he had a reason beyond his own selfish needs."

"It isn't selfish to want a life," Synthia said from the back seat. "It isn't selfish to want your parents to see that you have your own mind, or your own visions. It isn't selfish to want them to listen."

Synthia's words silenced them all, and the only sound that accompanied the last few hundred yards of their journey was the soft crunch of gravel.

The trees continued on in a straight line as they rounded the bend, but to the right, the ground was open and grassy, stretching up in back until the tree line started again. Nestled at the base of that slope, the small home glittered in the moonlight, white against a backdrop of shadow. The entire scene was eerie, silver-white light brighter than anything most of them had ever seen.

"It's the city that steals it," Dexter said. "In the city, there are so many lights, you never really see this. Night and day, they hide the way it's supposed to be."

Liz nodded, but didn't speak. Her breath was stolen by that first sight of her home. It was odd to think of it as such, but now that she was there, and could see it, she knew.

"What's that in the yard?" Shaver asked, leaning to the windshield and squinting as they drove nearer. The headlights of the van cut an odd, yellowish swath through the already well-lit yard, glaring off white signs, and the white house, and something else. Something tall and odd in the center of the yard. And moving.

"It's a cross," Liz said softly. Then, even more softly, "Mother?"

Dexter pulled in and killed the engine, leaving the lights on for just a moment, spotlighting Madeline, who froze, trapped like a deer by the brilliant light. Her face registered shock, and then a mingling of fear and anger. She looked like someone who'd been intruded on during a very private moment.

The others waited as Liz yanked open the side door and clambered out, stumbling a little at first as her stiff limbs stretched out. She leaned against the van for a moment. Madeline stood very still in the center of the sidewalk, as if deciding whether to wait to see who it was, or turn and bolt inside.

"Mama?" Liz said.

Madeline started at that, turning back slightly, though looking no less frightened. "Liz?"

The two were moving, probably as they inhaled the same breath, slowly at first, then more quickly until they were flying down the walk and then together, clinging and wrapped tight, swaying in the breeze that had blown in again. Shaver and Dexter watched in silence as two generations embraced.

"Seems as if she's welcome," Dexter observed. "Hope the rest of us are as well received."

He was silent for a moment, then he slapped his knee, turned to his door, and opened it slowly. "I hope she has coffee."

They were gathered around the small table in Madeline's kitchen, coffee hot and steaming in each cup and more brewing. There wasn't much light inside.

"I use the candles, mostly," Madeline had apologized. "Sometimes I forget when the bulbs are gone."

The truth was, she rarely went to town for anything, and electric light wasn't high on her list of priorities. Not nearly as high as privacy. Her nerves were completely on edge with so many young strangers in her home, but the sight of Liz, after all the months and years, held her together.

Liz sat beside the window, staring out toward the forested mountain beyond. "Is he still out there, Mama?" she asked softly. "Will he come?"

"I don't rightly know that, as a fact," Madeline replied, choosing her words carefully, "and yet, I do know. There is something between your father and I, something I can't quite explain. I believe I'd know if he were gone. I don't believe, if I knew that he were gone, that I could go on."

Liz didn't answer that, but neither did she turn her gaze

from the line of trees across the long, sweeping yard from them. Her mind was lost in the past, wandering memories she'd tried very hard to suppress. Memories that Brandt and the others had dragged from her so easily. When she finally turned, her eyes were wide.

"Is it right, Mama? Should we go through with it? I know he is chosen. I know it is his destiny, and I know he will never come home—but should we put this burden on him? Reverend Forbes? So much sin."

Her words trailed off, and her mother's chin drooped to her chest.

"I don't know that the choice is ours, Liz," Madeline said at last. "I think he made the choice himself that night, so long ago, and it would be disrespectful of us to not take that into account. He did it for us. He did it for everyone on this mountain. How can we not prepare the way?"

"Begging your pardon, ma'am," Brandt cut in softly, "but Synthia and I have met the man you talked to out front, and we've all seen him. I have to say, I don't think he would be promoting anything that was going to be good for anyone. Question is, why does he want this to happen?"

"I don't know," Madeline answered, turning slowly to stare out the window. "I don't know the answers to that sort of question, though I've prayed to know day in and day out most of my adult life. What I do know is that I've always counted on Brian to know what was important. He never let me down, not in our life together, and certainly not since. If there is something wrong, he will let us know. He will stop it, if he can."

Brandt thought about this for a few moments. "I will stop it, if I can," he said. "I don't know why I've been drawn to this place, at this time, but I do know who drew me."

He stood and moved to his bags, piled alongside those of the others along one wall in the front hall, and drew forth a folder. From within that folder, he pulled Liz's drawing, carefully pressed between thicker pages. Without speaking, Brandt crossed the room to where Madeline stood and offered the paper.

She took it, not turning to meet his gaze. She scanned the drawing, one hand holding the paper and the index finger of the other stroking the lines of the drawing, tracing the deeply etched lines of the face. Tears crept slowly from the corners of Madeline's eyes, and Liz, watching her mother's reaction, rose, moving to wrap her arms around her mother, comforting her.

"Where did you get this?" Madeline asked at last.

Brandt nodded at Liz. "Liz drew it. I met this man, in a vision. I saw the table, and the sacrifice. I shared his hunger, saw it seeping from his eyes. He told me that 'it' was not over. He told me that we would meet again, but before he could tell me why, or when, or how, he was gone."

"He called you then," Madeline said, nodding with sudden conviction. "He knows what is to come, knows more than any of us. Whatever it is, one thing is certain. We must prepare the feast. We must call Brian from the shadows and prepare the sacrifice. God moves in mysterious ways."

"Still have to wonder which God," Dexter commented dryly. "That guy seemed to think you and he share one. I remember some strange things from where and when I grew up. Saw some *bizarre* fucking . . ." he hesitated, lowering his eyes sheepishly. "I'm sorry," he continued, "some strange things. Snakes. You would be surprised what a sane man or woman will do with a live snake. You would be shocked, I think, to hear how well a trailer-park-dwelling matron who never graduated sixth grade can recite in Latin. There was a power to all of it, and a pattern, but I could never convince myself there was an ounce of *good* in it. It drew me in and spit me out more than once. Wild shit."

Dexter clamped his mouth shut, nearly biting through his tongue as his language slipped again.

"That must have been a long time ago," Shaver grinned. "You seem to have lost some of your humility along the way."

Dexter sipped his coffee. "Whatever. All I'm saying is, there's an awful lot of 'Gods' involved in all of this, and I hope to Jesus, no offense intended, we find the right one."

"There is only one," Madeline asserted, turning away from the window and fixing Dexter with a stern gaze. "There are a lot of things in this world that we don't understand, and a great many of those I expect we were never intended to understand. You have seen those who saw His grace in the eyes and sharp tongue of a serpent, and you have heard His voice in languages that meant nothing to you. I have seen His grace in the sacrifice of one great man to the sins of another. The willingness to take on a burden not your own, to allow a soul entrance to Heaven. There may be other powers at work here, but make no mistake, God is watching, and Brian is watching, and as long as the two of them are our focus, we will see our way through this."

Brandt nodded, leaning back and wrapping his arm tightly around Synthia, who'd been brooding and silent through it all. There was a long period of deeper quiet, each lost in the scent and taste of the coffee, and their own thoughts.

"Dex," Synthia said, "you know where Brandt comes from, we all do. You know my life now, the angels watching me morning to night every day of my life, and you know all about Shaver's father, and Liz's father. What about you? You drop all these hints, all these bits and pieces of," she thought for a moment, "of a pattern. All you talk about is music, *the* song, and patterns."

Dexter wasn't watching her. His gaze was focused on his coffee, and he was trembling visibly, as if he knew what was to come.

Synthia continued. "I just want to know *your* pattern. I want to know you like you know us. Hell, I don't want to face the Devil without knowing everyone on my team, and where the hell, no pun intended, they come from, you know?"

The room grew silent. No one even seemed willing to breathe into that moment. Synthia's words had the ring of a challenge, and though it was tinged with love and respect, it was a challenge still. Tension spilled into a room already overflowing with nervous fear.

"You know we'll listen, bro," Shaver said. "You know we care."

Dexter nodded. He expelled a long, even breath, gathering his thoughts, and then he rose and moved to the coffee pot and refilled his cup. His fingers danced nervously over the rim, as if seeking something to count, or stack. Instead, he returned to the table, took a quick sip of the hot coffee, and began to speak, never once raising his eyes from the Formica tabletop.

"I wasn't raised by my parents," he began softly. "I never knew them. Let's say I was a foster-child of God. Here's the story. . . ."

SEVENTEEN

"I was left on the doorstep of the Church of the Holy Light when I was small enough not to know the difference. Light was light, food was food. I probably missed my parents. I probably knew they weren't there, but after a while, as a baby, food, and light, warm and happy, and nothing else matters. That's how it started.

"I was raised by the church. I never really had a family, though I lived in Reverend Bob Sanders' home most of my young life. They took turns. I was 'the miracle baby, brought to them by God to watch over and protect.' For Sanders, it was probably a gimmick, though he was good enough as pseudo-fathers go. Even then, I was fascinated with patterns.

"I painted, worked in the garden, and I listened. Always, I listened, because there was something, just beyond what I could understand, that itched at me. Reverend Sanders said it was my 'calling' to the Church, but I knew pretty early on that whatever was calling me, it was *not* a fuc . . . not a church."

The fumble over his language brought Dexter's hands to the tabletop, where he unerringly reached out and snagged a spoon, and a knife, left over from some earlier meal. He flipped them nervously in his fingers, tapping the tips on the table in an odd, intricate rhythm as he talked. It was mesmerizing. Dexter didn't even seem aware he was doing it. His words were in sync, and yet, they were not.

Synthia was staring at the silverware, unable to draw her

gaze from the near-magical motion, blurring the plate-steel across the table.

"My family," Dexter went on, weaving the words into the rhythm, "was the church. I spent weekends with different families. I did homework with one group of kids each night, different homes, but all the 'brethren' of Holy Light. It wasn't a bad life. Hell, at times, it was the best of all worlds. Was never in one place long enough to really piss anyone off, and I had all the support and love a kid could want.

"I guess if it hadn't been for Sundays, that life would have rocked."

Dexter fell silent. Madeline moved closer, pouring more coffee into his cup. The sound revived his hands, and the rhythm returned, slowed only for the moment it took him to take a long, hot sip of the coffee and close his eyes.

"The Church of the Holy Light," he said softly, "was a slice of reality that just didn't fit. No matter how you cut it, it came out crooked, malformed, and odd. I don't know how to explain it. The world would sort of warp as you walked through those doors. Perfectly normal people would stare at you with an intensity that shifted their features completely. Sunlight, warm and comfortable on your skin, wove through the images on the stained-glass windows of that church and nothing was ever the same in that light.

"The women's features sharpened, and the men grew tall, brooding, and dark. No smiles. No joy, really, but intensity. So much intensity, belief, like an addiction to them all. On Sunday, I was the 'miracle child' in ways that barely made sense the other six days of the week.

"They showed me the pattern first. In that church, every Sunday, I got a glimpse of it. I saw, and I was pressed closer, and I slid my hands in, and through it, rearranging and shifting each line and shape. Writhing and twisting, turning and sliding, line over line and design over design, but all *one* big pattern.

"They pushed me to it, at first, but it drew me in. Each time I didn't die. Each time they chanted, and danced, and cried out, it drew me deeper."

"Snakes?" Liz whispered the word, question and statement in one, her eyes very wide.

Dexter nodded. "Snakes. Hundreds of them. They were Sanders' passion, after God, and the Church. He kept them in a series of large, glass aquariums. Somehow he always had plenty of food for them, mice, rats; he would trap them carefully and save them in separate feeder cages.

"The congregation never saw that side of him. They saw this tall, imposing man in dark robes, his eyes full of fire and his voice like some kind of controlled thunderclap. That was the 'Reverend Sanders.' I knew Bob Sanders, too, and he liked those snakes. On Sunday he'd spout how they were the symbol of Satan, how the serpent had tempted Eve. He'd tell you how the sins and redemption of men swirled in that tank, and how faith, and faith alone, could bring one through that dark embrace unscathed.

"Sounds like a joke, I know. Sounds like something out of a B-grade horror flick, but it wasn't. Not at all. It was powerful, compelling. All eyes in that church were locked on that tank and the swirling mass of motion it contained. They couldn't really see them. They could sense them. They could see the movement, and could feel the tension drop over the room like a shroud, but to them it was no different, say, than the choir launching into 'Amazing Grace,' or Reverend Sanders calling for the Communion.

"Most of them never took that stage. Most of them never got close enough to a snake to know if it were a garter snake, or a rattler. Might have been f . . . freaking gummy worms for all they knew, or cared.

"Now that I'm out of there, and can look back on it, it reminds me of watching professional wrestling, or a NASCAR race. I was a naive kid. I was the 'golden boy' of the church, the miracle child. That is what they told me, and for the longest time, I believed it. Now I know. I was the 'Jerry Springer Show' of the Church of Holy Light.

"They weren't watching for me to pluck the serpents from the tank, hold them aloft, and be praised for my righteousness. They were there for that one slip-up. They were there to see a sinner taken by the poison and to dance hallelujahs all over his grave. They came up disappointed each time, but the power was there, the draw of danger and the knowledge that it could be next Sunday, or the next.

"I never felt the tension at all. I watched those sliding bodies, those shifting patterns of stripes and triangles, bands and colors, eyes glittering but not really registering me as I watched. It was always the same. Sanders would start with a prayer, every head bowed, and his words would flow with the sinuous motion of those snakes. His mind would link, somehow, with their minds.

"I never closed my eyes. I never prayed with them. I watched, and I waited, and as I did, I used to drum on the tanks. At first, I kept it quiet. No one wanted Reverend Sanders staring at them during a service for any reason, and damn *certain* not for making noise as he prayed. This was different. I watched those serpents, and my fingers worked over the glass, tapping, thrumming, sometimes moving so quickly they vibrated and the glass hummed, other times more subtle, less distinct, but still there.

"They reacted. The snakes reacted, and the congregation reacted. Even Reverend Sanders reacted. I thought he would be angry with me, but he never said a word. He watched those snakes, and he watched how they moved when I 'played' on the glass, and he kept his peace.

"When the time came in each sermon where he talked about those snakes, the eyes in the room were already focused on me. I never saw them, but I felt them. My own gaze was trapped by the pattern. It would slip through and around and out of those twisting, turning bodies each time. Never the same twice, never the same for more than an instant, and yet, I knew deep inside that it was always the same. I knew that if I could just pluck the truth from those slipping, sliding bodies and live it, if I could find the pattern with my fingers and play it back to them, they would form it a final time and stay that way. I knew it. I felt it so strongly it stole my reason, and each time this happened, I would wake to the sound of voices, crying out, screaming, praying, and to the sight of bodies writhing in the aisles of the church.

"Each time I opened my eyes to find that I'd plucked two bits from the puzzle, that two of the serpents dangled from my hands and my head was thrown back, eyes to heaven. I was never bitten. I must have slid my hands into that sea of moving death thousands of times, and never once did I even come close. It was a pattern, and I could see it clearly. Every time they shifted, I anticipated it. They moved to the rhythm I tapped on their glass, and that rhythm drew my hands in, and out, and though it preserved me—though I didn't die like the dumbass I was, sticking my hands in a pile of poisonous snakes—it was never enough. Each time I ended up in tears, feeling that small bit of the puzzle I'd dragged free, and unable to piece it back together. Unable to see the whole of it.

"Reverend Sanders said I had a gift, but there were Sundays when I thought it would be better if the damned snakes would just take me, make me one with that pattern and drag me down.

"I don't play with snakes any more," Dexter said at last, "but I'm stuck with the patterns. They're everywhere. I find them, I work to recreate what I remember, stacking and counting, and none of it works. It isn't the same. I see pieces, just like with the snakes, only now they are all pulled free. I don't have just two parts, but all the parts, and there are times I believe that if I don't get them all together, I'll just sit in a corner and scream. If it weren't for the drums, and the music, that might have happened already.

"Then you," Dexter's gaze flashed up to capture Brandt's, holding steady, "you had to bring it all back. You had to waltz in there and play that . . . that song, that pain, that pattern flowing from your fingers like a squirming tank of snakes. I was part of it again. I was part of what held it all together, and I felt it like I'd never felt it before, and then it stopped. Just stopped. You walked away. No one even yanked a piece out that time; it walked away, and all I could do was stand, and watch as it all unraveled. I didn't know what the f . . . didn't know what to do, man, but I'll tell you honestly, I was leaning toward following you and just kicking your ass."

They all burst into laughter at that, even Madeline, and a few moments later Dexter joined them, grinning sheepishly.

Then he turned to Shaver. "I wanted you to know most of all, bro. You put up with me when no one else would. You listened to me go on and on and on about that perfect song. Well, it isn't just a song. There is so much more to it, but that song is our ticket in, you know? I heard you play the first time, I knew you could open the door. Still know it."

"I had no idea," Brandt said. "The pain. I don't know

how to describe that to you. It was all I could think of, and that night I saw things I have not seen since, and that I hope I never see again. I was barely aware the rest of you were there, once it started, and at the end? I was empty."

"Not your fault," Dexter said quickly. "Not trying to lay the blame on you. Not anyone's fault. We all saw what went on that night, Brandt. No idea how, no idea who all those people were. I felt that pain, not like you did, but felt it ebbing and flowing, felt how you channeled it. The pattern, all part of the pattern. That is what I saw. That is what I lost. Synthia, she was staring off into the back of the bar like we were being watched by some ghost-patrol, and damned if I don't believe we were. Not sure what happened then, but it touched her, and it touched them, and I wish you could have been there the night *that* pattern unfolded."

"I wish I could have been too," Brandt said, turning to Synthia and drawing her closer. "Wish a lot of things might have been different, but then, who knows what that might have caused? If we are here as part of a pattern, then everything happened as it was supposed to happen.

"The best we can hope for now is to figure that pattern out. There has to be something here that has drawn our evil friend along, something in this 'pattern' that is potentially wrong. On the other hand, I was drawn here as well, as were we all, bit by bit, and piece by piece, and I know it isn't all his doing. There are deeper powers and stronger forces than any of us here involved in all of this. I wish Wally were here."

"The old guy?" Shaver asked.

Brandt nodded. "Wally is the one who showed me the pain. He is the one who told me not to ask for things I didn't really want, and the one to guide me to safety the few times I was too far over the edge. I think he was even in

Syn's apartment the other morning when things were too much. I have no way to contact him, no way to know if he is with us, against us, or unaware, but I know that he pushed us here as certainly as Madeline's Brian drew us.

"I don't know why we are here, but somehow I know it *is* where we belong. All we can do is blend into," he turned and glanced at Dexter, then smiled, "the pattern, and hope that what we've heard since we were all children is true . . . that good will conquer all."

"Amen," Madeline said. The others echoed her, and even that soft echo formed a pattern, sifting off into the silence and the shadows.

"How do we do that?" Synthia asked suddenly. "How do we blend into something we aren't a part of?"

"I can help," Madeline answered before anyone else could speak. "In a way, Payne was right. They'll come to me, I expect. They'll wonder what to make, and how much, how to lay out the table, and what to do with the candles and the flowers. Most of them have been to the ceremony, but few of them were ever involved in it.

"We always had music. When Reverend Forbes was alive, there was the choir. There was something about the singing at those times, something powerful that would draw you in and mesmerize you, turning your mind from the moment at hand. Since they will come to me, and since Liz has come home with you," Madeline turned to her daughter and smiled then, the most genuine smile they'd seen from her since they arrived, "I will suggest that they defer to you for the music. I trust you know a few things that would be appropriate?"

Brandt and Shaver and Dexter laughed in unison.

"I'm sure we can work it out," Brandt said at last. "Hell, if Shaver here can get me to play Hank Williams Senior, I guess almost anything is possible."

Synthia rose and moved closer to Dexter. She watched him carefully, and slowly the others quieted. Dexter frowned, but didn't speak, as Synthia moved closer. Her eyes were wide, and she was staring, as if terrified, though she kept moving closer.

"What is it, Syn?" Brandt asked quietly. "What do you see?"

She shook her head, stepping right in front of Dexter and waving her arms over his hands slowly. Dexter's eyes cleared, and he shook his head.

"They aren't really there, Synthia," he said softly. "You know that."

Synthia stared again, then took Dexter's hands and gazed into his eyes. "They *are* there. They are waiting. Two pieces of the pattern. I don't know why I never saw them before. I have the feeling they've always been with you. Maybe . . ." Synthia hesitated for a long breath. "Maybe they are trying to find their way back to where you took them from? Maybe they are the draw, the reason the pattern pulls at you so hard. We have to take them home."

"We're a long way from where they would have come from," Dexter answered, staring at his hands, only half-believing. "A very long way."

"Maybe not," Shaver cut in. "You're the one always talking about the pattern, and the song. *The* song. The one you and I are going to find, the one that will make it whole, and bring us to where these two," Shaver waved a hand toward Brandt and Synthia, "already went. Don't tell me you don't believe it anymore? I think we can find a place or two to slap those snakes if we concentrate. I know they look like drumsticks when you play, but if you start to see snakes in the song, dude, you put them back."

Dexter nodded, not smiling. "Maybe so," he said. "Maybe this is it. Maybe we're all here for some reason, finally, and I just had to wait. Hell." He grew silent for a moment, and then his grin returned. "I might have been putting the pattern back together all along. I tried to get you to follow Brandt way back. I came after you even when your fingers were mush and you couldn't play a lick. I even took you to the coffee shop where Liz was, because I thought she might put some energy back into your sorry . . . um . . . butt."

"You saying this is all your fault?" Shaver's eyes were sparkling.

"Could have done worse," Dexter answered. "You finally got rid of that dog of a Mustang."

They all laughed again, though Madeline was a bit baffled by their banter, though it was stilted by their almost comical efforts to modify their language for her benefit. It was a moment of hope, and in that moment, Brandt moved as he always moved, toward the case that held the old guitar. For the first time since meeting Wally in the alley, he didn't feel the all-consuming draw of the pain. No one called out to him, and yet he needed to play. He felt it welling up inside of him, and there was only one release. Always, that one way out.

The others followed his lead. Dexter didn't drag out his drum kit, but he leaned in, making himself comfortable with Madeline as he had with old Mae. "Where do you keep the spoons?" he asked.

Madeline turned and pulled open a drawer.

Dexter grinned, snagging a handful, choosing four, and dropping the rest back into place with a clatter. "Learned to improvise," he whispered conspiratorially. "They kept me locked in an apartment for *days*."

Liz rolled her eyes and slid into one of the chairs surrounding the table. She had one of her sketch pads open, and she watched Dexter with mild amusement as he slapped the spoons experimentally, adjusting his grip and tapping them against his thighs.

Shaver had his guitar free of its case and slid the strap over his neck. Without an amplifier, it wouldn't have much volume, but somehow, it didn't seem to matter at that moment.

Syn had her pig-nose amp, but she adjusted it so low that the soft thump of the base didn't drown out the rest of the sound.

"What are you going to play?" Madeline asked, smiling almost girlishly. "I haven't heard a bit of music since Reverend Forbes passed, and that wasn't too cheerful."

Brandt grinned sheepishly. "I'm afraid that most of what we have played in the past isn't going to be—appropriate. I just felt like playing. I guess we'll just start with what we do best, and see what comes of it."

He pressed his fingers to the strings and drew the pick down in a quick jangle of notes. E. Solid and tingling with promise. Brandt broke into a simple blues progression, drawing the notes, one to the next, with sliding strokes of his fingers that twisted and tortured the strings. The others waited, letting him play a quick interlude, catching both rhythm and sequence easily. Shaver was the first to join in, catching up on the third time through, second bar, with a soft flurry of notes that shifted between Brandt's chords and wound up and away. Synthia settled in with a quiet, but solid back-beat, closing her eyes and swaying from side to side.

Dexter wasn't as quick as the others. He waited. He let the rhythm settle, though he would usually be the backbone of that. He let the melody soar, and settle, and soar again, and still he waited. He closed his eyes until the sound gripped him. His hands twitched, but he controlled the urge to release the energy. Finally, as the third chorus rushed past, he felt an opening, a hole in the sound that was unacceptable, and he slid into it. The spoons vibrated, clapping together and slipping apart with an easy rhythm. Dexter didn't try to become the rhythm section. He didn't try to force his own beat to the music, but flowed instead to that of the bass, letting Synthia be the backdrop. Instead, he let the clatter of metal on metal dive between Shaver's notes. He let Brandt's steady, heavy chords drive through him and transferred each to his fingertips, letting the emotion and the melody sift through his mind and translate to those spoons.

His hands vibrated. He brought it all to the front of his mind, concentrated, and shifted it through and out. Vaguely, Dexter was aware that Brandt had begun to sing. He felt the words, felt the softer vibration of Brandt's voice, but he couldn't make any of it out. He was focused too deeply.

The room had begun fading slowly from the moment Dexter first slapped the spoons to his thigh. He hadn't really been with the others for some time. The memories had drawn him in, and the visions of his past were powerful. He'd buried those visions deep, and now they had returned, haunting him. Try as he might, as the notes slipped over and around him and his own rhythms danced into the mix, the visions were too powerful to deny. He watched helplessly as the room disappeared around him.

The altar loomed, a million miles away, down the aisle and up behind an oak railing. Dexter felt the size of an ant as he began the slow walk down the aisle and up those heavily carpeted stairs. Voices echoed all around him, whispered words, questions, and even a few bets. Dexter ignored them, keeping his steps even as Reverend Sanders had instructed him. It was all part of the "show," as Sanders called it.

Dexter had walked that aisle a thousand times, and yet, something was different. Something was wrong. He heard the soft music in the background, not exactly as he remembered it, but close. He stepped into the aisle, but no heads turned. No eyes bored in through his skull to try and steal the secret, or the pattern. No one seemed to know he was there at all.

Every head was turned forward. Every gaze was locked on the altar, and the tank beyond. Dexter shifted his attention and stopped, standing very still. The music rose around him, loud, much louder than he had ever heard it, and the congregation had begun to stand. First one, then a couple more, a slow trickle of rising human flesh that swayed in the grip of that deep, pulsing sound. Dexter took a step forward, raising his arm and opening his mouth, as if to speak. He said nothing.

The man staring back at him from the other side of the tank was familiar. The face they all stared at was young, maybe early twenties, and intense. His eyes glowed with reflected light from the colored spotlights Reverend Sanders had had installed for the "rite."

In the background, through the music, Dexter heard Sanders' voice, crooning, coaxing the crowd and the moment to a frenzy. He'd heard those words too many times, felt the effect they had on the people, the insidious hypnotic blur they induced, combined with the voices of the choir. Only there was no choir this time. The music was richer, full and resonant. There were guitars, and bass, and on one level, Dexter knew what that music was, where it was. He could feel the quick slapping of the spoons against his thighs, could unwind the bass from the lead and back.

He took another step closer.

"And the Lord our *God* shall protect us, one and all," Sanders intoned. "He shall send His *angels* to lift us up, that we not fall and be hurt. He shall send His *spirit* to fill our hearts with love and drag us from the mouths of demons and the pits of hell, and He shall give us His *courage* in the face of that which challenges our *faith*. The Devil shall not have us brethren, and The Lord our God shall protect us, even in the face of the serpent's poison, even in the presence of the *tempter's* true form, and all it portends, shall He sustain us. Forever, and ever . . . *amen.*"

Dexter stepped closer, slowly, lifting each foot with an effort and planting it a little closer. His gaze was fixed on the young man's hands. He knew this moment, felt it tingling up and down his nerve endings. The room shifted, and the light dimmed. The bodies swaying and dancing to both sides of him, between the heavy oak pews, drew long, twisting shadows across the red carpeted floor. Dexter watched them from the corners of his eyes. Watched the bodies, and watched the shadows, letting his gaze flicker from one to the other, to the altar, to the young man, whose head was thrown back now, eyes to heaven and his arms, sliding down, and in.

Dexter felt the motion all around him, forming, reforming, the pattern swallowing slowly. The shadows had elongated until they wound in and around one another, knotting and slipping free, and still Dexter moved through them, slipping closer, fighting for a closer look. That man.

He wanted to call out, to make them stop. Whoever that

man was, he shouldn't be there. It was Dexter's place, his reason for being, that tank of serpents. Dexter stumbled, and then righted himself, his steps blending to the pattern, drawing him forward and in, down and across the room.

Dexter glanced to the left, and he caught a glimpse of Madeline, swaying with the others, but her eyes were clear, and they were not aimed at the stage, but at him. She smiled, a smile so filled with love and compassion that Dexter's eyes clouded with tears. Behind Madeline, Liz writhed, caught in the grip of the song and stretching, reaching out toward the stage, elongating.

Dexter turned away again. This time his head spun the other way and he caught sight of Brandt, Synthia, and Shaver. They stood back-to-back in a triangle of extended guitar necks and cords, impossibly thick cords that wound down and around their legs, binding them to one another as they played. Brandt's eyes were closed. Synthia stared right through Dexter as if he weren't there at all, and Shaver, who turned the triangle slowly as they caught Dexter's attention, stared directly into his friend's eyes. Shaver's face was taut with concentration. His fingers flew; the tendons on his arms stood out like cords, looking for all the world as if you might pluck one and get a tone. There was a madness in those eyes, and a hunger. He caught Dexter's gaze, and he held, just long enough, just long enough to convey—strength, support, long enough to remind Dexter of the rhythm in his hands and the spoons, of the small cottage and the mountain, of the man on the altar.

He turned, and he moved forward, more swiftly now, winding between shadows and sliding bodies, as the congregation moved from the pews and filled the aisles. Dexter's foot pressed lightly to the first step, and he lifted himself, feeling a long, slender leg slide over his smoothly, and away, moving between two other figures, slipping lower to the floor and back up. Winding and drawing himself upward. Second step, and third, dropping away behind and the world glowing red now: no candles, no dim overhead lighting, but flame, deep and burning, somewhere in the distance.

He stood atop the altar, and he saw that the young man had drawn free two of the serpents. The snakes coiled tightly around slender arms as they were lifted, as the chorus followed, as Reverend Sanders began a low, rumbling "Hallelujah." Dexter stepped closer, standing directly across the tank from the young man who'd taken that place of power and death, who'd slipped his arms into the pattern and drawn the serpents free. The pattern had not slowed, it moved all around them, drifting from one image to the next and dragging tendrils of shadow over and around the altar.

"Who are you?" Dexter asked, voice low. "Why are you here?"

Sanders had turned, and his eyes were pure evil as he seemed to only just realize Dexter was there. "You should not be here," the Reverend said, voice still a low chant. "You should not be here, you will disrupt it all."

Then that face shifted. Dexter nearly stepped back as Sanders' face melted to the leering, too-bright smile the young drummer had seen on only one other occasion. The bar. The bar where Brandt and Synthia had found them, where Liz had drawn her father/grandfather, and the music had drawn them in.

"I *should* be here," Dexter said, ignoring the shift, ignoring everything but the pattern surrounding him, the sound and the images, and the voices whispering in and out of his mind. "No other can do as I can do. No one can find the pattern."

"I can," the young man's chin lowered, and his eyes came level with Dexter's. In that moment, Dexter knew him. In that moment, everything whirled, and he fought the sudden attack of vertigo to remain upright. He stared into his own face, his own face in years to come, and not so many years. A face that could *not* be staring across that tank at him.

"How . . ."

The man's eyes grew sad, so sad that tears flowed suddenly down Dexter's cheeks.

"I tried," the man whispered. "I tried to put them back."

Sanders was Payne was Reverend Forbes, was Sanders again and his laughter rocked the small church on its foundations, drowning thought and speech. Dexter lurched forward, but he was too late. The young man with Dexter's face drove his hands back into the tank, the serpents still clutched tightly, and his face twisted in agony, immediate and desperate, as Sanders moved behind, pressing him close and holding him there as the serpents drove their fangs in deep, again and again, more and more of them, turning, and twisting, the pattern fallen to pain, and anger, and Dexter was falling forward, toward the tank, determined to stop it . . . to drive it all over on top of the bastard who wouldn't stop *laughing*, but he fell, and fell, and nothing, hit nothing, until the floor, curling into a tight ball as Madeline's kitchen shifted into place around him.

Brandt slid from the guitar strap and leaned the instrument against the wall. It started to fall, but Synthia reached out and gripped it, and with a quick and silent "thank you," Brandt slipped from her side and was on the floor, kneeling over Dexter in seconds. Liz was there, as well, and Shaver not far behind. Madeline sat, stunned, staring at them all as if she saw nothing, her hand clutched to her breast.

"Dex," Brandt said softly, shaking the drummer by his shoulder. Liz gathered up the spoons, laying them to both sides, and Shaver came up on the far side from where Brandt was kneeling. The two of them managed to gently turn Dexter over to his back. Liz handed Shaver a small glass of water, and Shaver dipped his fingers into it, splashing the cool liquid over his friend's face.

"Hey," Shaver said. "Wake the hell up."

Dexter blinked slowly. His eyes flickered once, and then opened, and his hand slipped up to rub gingerly at a red spot on his forehead.

"Wha . . ." Then his gaze cleared, and he fought to sit up, Brandt and Shaver forcing him to move more slowly, and then lifting him to his feet and into one of the chairs.

Liz had moved to her mother's side, leaning down and wrapping her in a hug.

"It's all right, dear," Madeline said at last, blinking. "You make sure that young man is okay."

"I'll live, ma'am," Dexter said shakily. He turned to Brandt. "Did you see him?"

"Which him?" Brandt asked. "I saw 'Reverend Payne,' and I saw another Reverend—was that Sanders? I saw a young man who looked a lot like you, staring back at you over that tank."

"That him," Dexter nodded. His voice dulled, and he glanced at the floor. "I'm thinking I just learned something important. I'm thinking, maybe, that I wasn't left on the doorstep of the church, or that my parents didn't abandon me at all. Not one of them, anyway. I think I know how Sanders knew I'd be able to see the pattern. I think that was my father."

They all grew silent then. Brandt, Synthia, and Shaver moved to put their instruments away, and Liz set yet another pot of coffee on to brew. Outside, the wind picked up slowly, until it was whistling through the trees, ushering in a heavy storm. Rain splashed against the windows, and they all gathered more closely around the table.

"Well," Madeline said at last. "I hope you young folks won't take this wrong, but I think that will be enough music for tonight."

They all laughed at that, and as Liz poured the coffee, and the wind rose to a roar beyond the walls of the small home, they fell into a comfortable silence, waiting, and wondering for what.

EIGHTEEN

Sunlight filtered in through the blinds, painting the kitchen in zebra-striped brilliance. The table was littered with empty coffee cups and the remnant of a half-eaten muffin on a paper plate. Dexter snored lightly, his head sideways on a pillow of arms, chair scooted back from the table.

The others had wandered off to various corners of the home to try and rest. Madeline had watched them all in silence, smiling despite all that had happened as Liz and Shaver slipped off together. It had been too long since she'd felt like a mother. A woman. Too long since she'd felt at all. The group of them, full of energy, and so—powerful—had energized her as well.

She and Dexter had been the only ones left, he sitting, hands clasped tightly around a final cup of coffee and she seated at the far end of the table, reading a passage from her Bible. They'd spoken quietly for a bit, but the words had trailed off. There wasn't much left to say. Something was happening, something that was drawing them all in deeper and more fully with each passing moment.

When Dexter's head had finally dropped, Madeline had risen, removed the half-full coffee cup from his grip, and rinsed it quietly. With a quick puff of breath, she'd doused the last of the candles, and walked slowly to her own room, and her bed. There was a comfort in the house not being empty, an air of warmth and caring that had been missing, despite her faith.

Now the morning sun crept across the tiled kitchen

floor, the only motion dust-motes floating in those bright beams. Then something—a shadow—moved across the window. Just an eclipse-flicker blocking the sunlight, then gone. A scrape of sound on the porch beyond the window made Dexter shiver, groaning softly and shifting on his arm, but he didn't awaken.

The window darkened again, and a face rose slowly, filling a single pane of the window on the back door. Deep, haunted eyes gazed into the room, sweeping left, then right, taking in everything at once. Long, gnarled fingers slipped up to press against the glass, not really trying to enter, but feeling. Sensing the home, and the moment—savoring it.

Then another shift, and a soft gasp. Madeline was in the doorway, wrapped only in a white terrycloth robe, now clutched to her with knuckle-white fingers. The face disappeared in a flash: there, and then gone. Madeline tried to catch her breath, tried to take a step forward, but found that she had to lean against the doorframe for support.

Dexter raised his head groggily, and was on his feet in seconds as he took in her pallor and the expression of shock on her face. He rounded the table quickly, sliding an arm around her back for support.

"Madeline?" he said, "what is it? What did you see?"

She shook her head, then raised an arm and pointed weakly at the door. "He was here," she whispered. "Oh God in Heaven, he was here."

Dexter helped her to a chair and moved quickly to the door, glancing out across the grass toward the trees. Nothing moved. The morning was in full bloom, flowers swaying gently in the breeze and the sun glittering off the tops of the trees and glistening in the dew on the grass.

"I don't see anyone," Dexter said. "Who did you see? Who was there?"

Madeline was silent for a few moments, gathering her courage. "Brian," she said softly. "I haven't seen him in years—so many years—but it was my Brian. He looked so much like his father."

Madeline dropped her face to her hands and her shoulders began to shake gently. Dexter stood his ground, letting her let it go. He turned back to the trees again, searching, looking for any sign of motion. He saw nothing, and was about to turn from the window when a flock of birds, flushed from the comfort of the trees off to his left, took to the sky in a flurry of motion and color. Dexter stared at those birds for a long time, wondering. Wondering who had startled them. Remembering the bar, and the vision Brandt had dragged them through. Remembering the snakes, and another man, glimpsed that one time and etched into his mind.

Dexter turned from the window almost violently, moving along the counter and reaching for the coffee maker. He stumbled and nearly knocked the glass carafe from its base, but recovered just in time, gripping the handle tightly.

"You saw him?" Madeline asked softly.

"I don't know," Dexter answered. "Saw someone, something, in the trees. A flock of birds took flight. Startled."

"What is wrong, then?"

Dexter stared at his hand for a while, then slowly released his grip and began to make the coffee, thinking. "I've been searching for—something—for a very, very long time," he said at last. "I thought I knew what that thing was, though I didn't really know how or where to find it. Now, everything has shifted. Everything.

"Seems like only a few days ago I was at Shaver's apartment, dragging him back into the world. I was in charge, the guy who was going to make things happen. Brandt had taken off, and Synthia went right behind him. They brought us right to that edge, right where I was all those days in front of that damned . . ." he glanced at her sheepishly, shrugged, and went on, ". . . damned tank of snakes. The pattern was there. I was part of it, sucked in and whole for just that long.

"Then it was just me again. Me, and Shaver, and after I dragged him out of that apartment and back into the world, Liz."

The coffee was brewing, and Dexter turned, spinning one of the chairs at the table so he could straddle it and watch Madeline as he spoke.

"The thing was," he continued, "things kept getting stranger and stranger, and the more I thought I knew what would fix them, the more I was proven wrong. The less control I had, the less certain I was that I'd ever find the answers to any of it."

Madeline nodded. "Well, you are all here now. So strange. Every one of you, myself included, with a piece of this. Every one of you from a very different place, with a very different gift, and yet, the Lord brought you together."

Dexter watched her, his eyes gentle, but his mouth curved into a slightly bitter smile. "I'm not sure I agree who's behind it. Not sure I have any faith in a God, or salvation. I can say that I've seen some very bad things, and some incredibly wonderful things, and most of them in a short span of time, in the company of those four hooligans in the other room. I have experienced—something—power, I guess, beyond what most of the world will ever see. I have been part of it—am part of it.

"I don't know if this 'Payne' is the Devil. I don't know if Brandt and Wally and your Brian are the emissaries of a higher power, or just more pieces of the same puzzle—bigger pieces.

"What I do know, or, what I believe, is that something very important is about to happen. I don't know what, or exactly when, but I feel it. It's in the air. It was in that vision last night. In each and every step along the weird road that brought us all here. I think Payne believes he is controlling it. I don't believe that. There are too many 'powers' at work, and not necessarily working in the same direction at the same time. I don't think any one of them knows who is right, and who is wrong, necessarily, and I'm damned certain they don't know which way the scales will tip.

"So," he trailed off sheepishly, realizing he'd been nearly ranting, "I guess I'm hoping you are right. I'd feel a whole lot better about all of this if I knew I was on the good guys' side, and that we were going to win."

"What if there aren't winners and losers?" Brandt asked from the doorway, entering slowly. Dexter nearly blushed when he realized his friend had been leaning on the doorframe for some time. "What if it's a balance? What if you can't have a Wally, or a Brandt, without a Payne, or a Forbes? What if you can't have good without the bad to judge it against?"

"One big cycle?" Synthia asked sleepily.

"Or pattern," Dexter said, nodding.

Coffee poured, the conversation wore on, and would likely have continued through the morning into the afternoon, if it hadn't been for the voices from the front of the house, and the sharp knock on the door.

Madeline set her coffee down and rose, moving from the kitchen. Liz rose and joined her mother, the others slipping up behind, so that when the door swung wide, they were gathered around Madeline in a semi-circle of support.

It was a small group they faced, eyes turned to the

ground beneath their feet. Helen Saxon stood in front, flanked close behind on either side by Wendell Ames and Tom Braddock. Tom had his hat in his hand and was twisting it, one way, then the other, as if he was on the brink of ripping it in half.

"Yes, Helen?" Madeline asked, her voice steady.

"Maddy," Helen Saxon spoke softly, the name unfamiliar after all the years, "Maddy, I don't know no other way to say it, but that it's to be today. This very evening. The others, they talked among themselves, and we just don't think we can wait another week. It bein' Sunday and all, and Reverend Payne not bein' here for much longer."

"It was always a morning thing," Madeline said. "You know that, Helen, and you—Tom, you know it better than any, you having carried that tent in and out of your shed more times than I'd care to count. It's a morning thing."

"We know that, Madeline," Wendell cut in. His chin was set, and his eyes narrow, as if he'd been in this argument too long already. "We told them all that. Hell, I near to told them I wouldn't have a part in it, but what can we do?"

"The Reverend Forbes, Maddy, we let him down," Helen said. "We let him down, and we turned from him, and our own ways. It was shameful, and we have a chance, now, to set it right. Will you help?"

Madeline hovered between yes and no—between flight and courage. Helen's eyes dropped again, waiting, and Wendell glanced off toward the trees. Only Tom, old Tom Braddock, held her gaze steadily, waiting. He would do what she said. In that moment, Madeline saw this. He wanted to set the Reverend Forbes free. It didn't matter how bad that man might have been, how much pain he might have caused, Tom wanted to do what was right, and in his mind, there was only one such thing.

"It's a hell of a thing," Wendell mumbled.

Madeline nodded. "That it is," she answered. "That it is. My daughter is here, Tom, did you know that? Helen? Wendell? It's funny, I haven't seen her in almost as long as it's been since any of you spoke a civil word to me. Here you all are, though.

"She and these young folks," Madeline turned, letting her visitors see the band gathered behind her, "understand more of what is to come than any of you ever will."

Madeline turned then, following Wendell's silent gaze with her own, scanning the line of trees beyond the road.

"Is he out there, Maddy?" Wendell asked softly.

"He is," she said, "and God help us, but I know we have to do this thing. I will be there, I will do my part. The youngsters," she turned back to the doorway again, "will be our music. Our choir."

"But, we have a choir," Wendell started to protest. He stopped when he met Madeline's gaze.

"I've said my piece, Wendell. You do this my way, or I don't do it at all, and I wish you Godspeed."

Madeline turned away and started back through the doorway. Brandt and Liz and Shaver stepped aside, to let her pass.

"Whatever you say, Maddy," Wendell called out. "Whatever you say. Nothing about this will be the same, and maybe that's as it should be."

Before he could say more, there was the crunch of tires on gravel, invasive on that near-deserted stretch of road. They all turned, and Madeline stopped, spinning on her heel. The sound of the engine died, and the heavy slam of a door announced the arrival of George Culpepper. He stood for a long moment beside his Buick, taking in the scene at the door with a scowl.

"George," Wendell said, nodding slightly.

"Morning, Wendell," George answered, stepping away from the car and making his way down the walk slowly. "I reckon you all came to tell Madeline about the ceremony?"

"We did," Wendell answered, with the tone of someone girding himself for a fight.

"Don't suppose you mentioned that there were those opposed to such nonsense," George stated, tipping his hat deferentially to Madeline, who'd returned to her place in the center of the doorframe. "Hello, Madeline," Culpepper said quietly. "I hope the day finds you well?"

"I don't know as I can say 'well,' George," Madeline answered, "but I've been worse. Yourself?"

"I won't beat around the bush, Madeline," George said. "I feel like hell about all this. I don't mind telling you, it's an odd thing this Reverend Payne waltzes into town, and into the church, and that very sermon Reverend McKeenan keels over and dies. Has anyone told you what I told them about that, Madeline? I'm guessing not, because I see them up here, dragging you into this thing, and I don't see them fighting or pleading."

"They've not mentioned you or Reverend McKeenan at all." Madeline spoke the late Reverend's name with something akin to contempt.

"I don't expect they did," Culpepper replied. "Madeline, I don't trust that man, Payne, and I don't like what is happening to us one bit. We are all being dragged back into something we left of our own free will, and why? Because some man, claiming to be a man of God, walked into our town, watched our minister die, and decided he should be in charge. Doesn't that seem just a little bit odd to you?"

Madeline watched Culpepper for a long time. No one

spoke, and Wendell had begun to fidget before she finally answered. "There are a lot of 'odd' things about what has happened to our town, George," she said at last. "There are a lot of odd things we have done, in the name of God, and in our own interests. I understand what you are saying, and it is a terrible thing when a man dies, but you have come to the wrong place if you plan to preach the new ways. Look at what has become of us, and tell me they are better. Tell me that Reverend McKeenan was making a difference, that things were changing for the good while he was alive. Go on, that's what you think. I know it, have known it for years, but don't expect me to agree with it.

"Things weren't better for *me*, George. You didn't care for Reverend Forbes. A lot of folks didn't. Most feared him, some even hated him, but I'll tell you one thing, George Culpepper, Reverend Shane Forbes understood the sacrifice my husband made. He may have played against that, used it to his own gain. He may well have been a very evil man, but he understood. He knew things you will never understand."

"I understand that a man lies dead," Culpepper replied. "I understand that a man we called our Reverend Father until a few short days ago has breathed his last breath. I *also* understand that, rather than follow that man's wishes after his death, his remains are about to be subjected to something I thought we'd left behind us, alongside of the remains of another man he fought very hard to replace.

"That wasn't a natural death, Madeline. I don't care what they say, or what you have heard or seen. I have been following death on this mountain so long I can hardly remember the days I didn't, and I'm telling you. No man dies like that. There is no physical reason. There is no history of weakness in the heart, or the body. McKeenan was a healthy, happy man looking at another twenty years of life and the ministry, and he is now dead.

"I want this all to stop. I want his body taken down the mountain to his own people. You all do as you want with those ashes, that bottle of dirt that used to be Forbes, but leave McKeenan out of it."

"That's not my call," Madeline answered, "and you know it. I will tell you this, George Culpepper. I know you went to a lot of fancy schools before you came here. I know you have all sorts of well-learned facts and memorized histories to back you up. I know a few other things as well.

"I know this mountain. I know what has gone before, and in large part, I know why. I know my husband. Brian was a good man. You say what you want about Reverend Forbes, but he wasn't the first preacher on this mountain, and he won't be the last, nor will Payne. Brian is out there, and he hungers. He hungers to do what is his gift, and his lot, and his curse in life to do. You would deny that. You would push it all neatly back into a history book and find some nicely dressed city-bred man of God to tell us it is all legend, and heresy, and fantasy. You know what I think? I think you are afraid of what you'll see tonight, Mr. Culpepper. I think you've been afraid of what goes on here since the first day you set foot on the mountain. I think you feel it deep in your heart and that you fear, as well.

"I will be spending the day at my stove. I will be preparing my portion of the feast, and I will be praying. If you were a smart, God-fearing man, you would be doing the same. The rest is out of our hands. For good, or for ill, the hunger will be sated. He will walk among us."

"Amen," chorused Wendell, and Helen, and Tom.

Madeline turned away again, and this time she disappeared into the house without a word. Brandt stood for a long moment, staring into Culpepper's angry, frustrated gaze. Then he too turned away, and the others followed. Dexter slowly shut the door behind them. There was nothing more to say.

Slowly, those gathered beyond the door turned and headed down the walk, Culpepper to his car, and the others to the road, not bothering to ask for a ride. Lines had been drawn, and decisions written in silence. The sound of gravel shooting from beneath the old Buick's tires echoed long after the lot of them disappeared down the mountain.

Only hours remained.

NINETEEN

Liz and her mother stood side by side and watched as the procession made its way up the mountain toward their home. Years melted away in a matter of seconds, and they wrapped one another in a tight embrace, both, in their own way, wishing the years away and another at their side. It had begun. The candles lined the road, flickering their eerie light against the backdrop of the trees.

"I wish he was here," Liz said softly, leaning her head on her mother's shoulder. "I wish I could talk to him before this starts."

"I know honey," Madeline said, wrapping her daughter in one arm and squeezing tightly. "I know. I wish he was here too. Brian would know what to do, what to say."

"It will come to you," Dexter said, stepping up behind them. "That is the way it works. Everything is a pattern. Besides," he added, "they didn't seem to have a clue what to do, or say, when they were here earlier. I suspect they will do whatever you tell them and be glad for someone to make the decision."

Madeline didn't answer. They all watched as the townsfolk approached once more. Brandt and the others were making last minute preparations and tuning their instruments. Dexter had chosen to bring only a small portion of his drum kit, and those pieces were already stowed in the van. He'd been drinking coffee straight through the day, as the others worked. Madeline, Liz, and surprisingly enough, Synthia, had been cooking since their visitors had left that morning. Under Madeline's supervision, the tiny home had come alive with the clatter of dishes and the pungent aromas of baking bread and roasting meat.

The food had stacked and stacked, but none of them had the least bit of appetite. There were a few nibbled crumbs near the sink, but for the most part, the knowledge of why, and for whom, the food was prepared was enough to keep them away. The tension, and the coffee, did the rest.

Madeline and Liz moved to the kitchen, each taking up a large platter of well-wrapped food and walking back to the door. The walk outside was lined with pale, moonlit faces, flickering in and out of focus as the breeze coaxed the candles into a soft dance. No one spoke, there was nothing left to be said. The two, mother and daughter, stepped through the door and onto the walk, heading to the road with long, steady steps. As they moved away from the house, those lining the walk closed in behind them.

Brandt, Synthia, Dexter, and Shaver watched as the strange parade moved away, and down the road, leaving the candles wavering as they passed. They knew it wouldn't be prudent to start the van so soon, so they waited, not moving from the doorway until the odd procession was completely out of sight.

"I guess this is it," Brandt said softly. He turned from the door and moved into the room, to his guitar case.

No one answered him. They retrieved their equipment, and they walked to the van. None of them hurried. No one wanted to turn that key, or drive down that hill. Dexter slipped in behind the wheel, and they all took their places, just as they had on the ride there, minus Liz.

The air was charged with energy. Every motion, every sound, took on meaning and scope. With a quick twist of his wrist, Dexter brought the van to life and backed slowly down the drive, turning carefully to avoid the line of burning candles to each side. He spun around slowly, aimed the headlights' glaring beam at the church below, and kicked the old vehicle into gear. Very, very slowly, he inched down the mountain. Near the bottom, he turned to the side, heading into the parking lot beside the church and away from the soft, flaming bonfire-light that had flared up along the tree line, near the old tent.

Dexter parked and cut the lights, and they sat for what seemed a very long time without moving. Finally, Brandt opened the side door and stepped out into the night. The pain had begun to build again, not as slowly as usual, but in quick, agonizing stabs that made him wince and lean on the van for support.

"Brandt," Synthia said, "what is it?" She sounded sincere, but Brandt could see that her gaze slipped on around and beyond him, and he turned, trying to see what she saw.

"Just feeling it," he said. "It's different. Stronger. I guess I should have expected that."

Synthia nodded.

"What do you see?" Brandt whispered.

"So many," she replied. "So many, Brandt. I can barely see the tent. They are gathered in big circles. We have to walk through them to get to the tent."

"Will you be okay?"

It wasn't really a question. There was no choice remaining but to move forward.

Dexter had come up behind them. "Time to do it," he said. "I can feel it. I can feel that pattern, just like before. Just like with the snakes, and the church. I can't see it yet, but it's there, waiting."

"We'd better not disappoint it, then," Shaver whispered, stepping up from the other side. The four of them started toward the tent at a slow walk.

Synthia stayed close to Brandt's side, guiding him right, then left, avoiding what he could see and feel only as a soft ripple in the air. Dexter and Shaver walked to either side. Dexter had his drums by the handles, sticks tucked carefully up under one arm. Shaver had his guitar case, as did Brandt. Synthia had her case, and dangling from her hand, the pig-nose amp. The four of them cast lengthening shadows as they approached the tent, and the fire.

"I don't remember there being a fire," Brandt said softly. "I remember early morning, sunlight, and those eyes," his voice trailed off, then returned. "I don't think there is supposed to be a fire."

"I remember a fire," Synthia said, "but it didn't have anything to do with this place."

They stopped, just at the outer ring of the townspeople. The fire was off to one side, and they could see that there was a small line of people carrying more wood for that blaze, tossing their burdens into the flames and moving on. No faces could be made out, only dark silhouettes against the darker backdrop of the night.

Brandt stepped forward, moving between those gathered silently. They parted to let him pass. Synthia and the others followed, single file, making their way slowly toward the center of the circle.

Low voices surrounded them, whispering, under-breath comments, some positive, others questioning. Brandt felt the others—those speaking beyond the circle, directly to him—growing in strength. He felt them clutching at him with ghost-fingers of pain, driving their images between his thoughts. He concentrated.

In the center of the circle, beside the table, Payne stood, leaning on his cane and watching as they approached. Nearby, Madeline stood as well, and Liz. They were watching Payne, as well.

The dark man didn't speak as Brandt broke free and entered the circle. He nodded, as if to an old acquaintance. As his gaze brushed over Synthia, he smiled. Just for an instant, the cane in his hand grew, and shifted. It was a bass, shining and polished, leaning in against his shoulder. The bass Synthia had played that night in the city. Then it was gone again, and only the moment remained.

The food was piled high on the low-slung table. Reverend McKeenan's body was barely visible, covered in platters and draped with napkins holding fruits and bread. At the very head of the table, beside a large flask of wine, sat the urn. Reverend Forbes' ashes. There was a bunch of green grapes draped over the handles, and a small loaf of French bread leaned against the side.

Not an inch of space was wasted. There was enough food to feed a small army, and the dancing shadows brought to life by the bonfire rippled over them all, lending an air of surreality that even the feast itself couldn't have provided. The flames reflected in Payne's eyes, but there was more. There were figures, moving, and the sound of wailing deep and far away. Brandt watched, mesmerized, then shook his head and turned away, toward Madeline.

Payne laughed.

Madeline didn't speak, but she nodded, and then inclined her head to one side. Away from the fire. Brandt returned the nod and started forward. They filed past Payne, who had now shifted his countenance to an expression of serious contemplation. With Brandt no longer blocking him from the view of the townsfolk, the "Reverend" Payne was back at the pulpit.

Brandt moved in behind Madeline, and Liz, who smiled weakly at him. He placed his guitar case on the ground, and opened the snaps, as Synthia and Shaver did the same. Dexter placed himself a bit further back, behind them all. He had only three drums, the snare and two toms, and he set them up quickly, seating himself cross-legged behind them—waiting.

Brandt chose to stand, the guitar strapped over his shoulder, Shaver to one side and Synthia on the other. Synthia snapped the cord into the tiny amp, but didn't flick the switch on. They all waited now, watching, as Payne stepped to the head of the table and the whispered, mumbled comments died to silence.

"Brothers and sisters," he began, his voice carrying easily, though he did not seem to strain for volume, "welcome. Welcome, and praise the Lord for your lives, for tonight we gather to mourn those who have passed. Those who no longer call this world home, and yet, have ties that bind them to us, and to this place. Ties we can sever, through faith, and through sacrifice. That sacrifice, brothers and sisters, can send them home."

Brandt heard the murmur of voices again, and he scanned the crowd. No one spoke. No lips moved, all eyes were locked on Payne's smooth, dark features. Still, the voices grew in volume, and though he fought it, Brandt began to listen.

Synthia moved closer again, and turned her back toward him, facing the crowd, and the circle. This time, when Brandt followed her gaze, he saw flickers of motion, just beyond those gathered—shadows that slipped from one place to the next, then weren't there. Motion that wasn't quite motion, because all that moved was a blur, a shift in the firelight that may or may not have ever existed, and was quickly gone. Brandt knew that Synthia saw more than that, but he couldn't concentrate. The voices had risen to a roar, none distinct enough to be understood over the crushing weight of sound from the others.

DEEP BLUE

All that was clear was the pain. It seeped up from deep within Brandt's soul, first a dull ache near the base of his spine, then ice-fingers climbing through his nerve endings, each ripple blending with the tail-end of the last. Brandt's hands shook, and he gripped the neck of the guitar, pressing his fingers so tightly to the strings that all the blood ran from his hands and he was forced to bite his lip to keep from crying out.

Shaver's face was a wash of concentration. His fingers quivered on the strings, and it was obvious that only an act of extreme self-control was keeping him from playing. The music rolled, just beneath the surface, and he held it in check. He watched Brandt, and he watched Payne, and he waited, wondering how much longer he could hold out.

Only Dexter was calm. His eyes were closed. The drumsticks rested gently in his fingers, their tips lying motionless on the skin of the snare. There was no way to tell what he might be hearing, or seeing. There was no way to tell if he was aware of his surroundings at all.

In front of the four of them, Liz and her mother stood side by side. They were listening to the Reverend Payne, who still spoke, though his words had slipped away to those who sought them, becoming a part of the blur of sound to Brandt and the others. Madeline's gaze kept shifting, one moment fixed on Payne, the next the table, and the next the line of trees beyond the fire. Her shoulders were tense, and her arm around Liz's shoulder was too tight, too stiff.

"Brothers and sisters," Payne's voice broke through suddenly, clear as a bell and resonating across the circle, and into the night, "let us pray."

That was all Brandt could stand. The voices, the pain, washed up and through him. He slid his fingers high on the neck of the guitar, not playing a chord, but a single note, sliding it, letting it wail from his finger, deepening and echoing through the shadows. Brandt's back arched, and his head dropped back as that first wave of pain slipped up and away, and for just that single moment, nothing existed but the note. The voices stilled. Payne's voice fell away to nothing, and the fire gave way to the soft wash of moonlight.

Then it began. Brandt's hand slid down and rippled across the strings, and like magic, Shaver was there. He didn't intrude. His notes were quiet, carrying, much like Payne's voice had moments before, but not drowning Brandt, or the voices, or the pain. Shaver wove into it, becoming one with the emotion and sifting it out through his fingers as Synthia tapped into the pulse, the ebb and flow that bound the moment, and became that beat, that heart-pump regular backdrop of sound that Brandt and Shaver could hang their notes on.

Dexter remained silent. His breathing was even and calm. His eyes never flickered open, never took in the swaying of the crowd, or the dancing of the flames. Never slipped up and down the length of Reverend McKeenan's body, or the food, though the scent of the feast permeated the air like incense.

There was singing. Voices blended with the music, a slow, harmonic hymn that resonated through shadows and firelight, that drew voices from reluctant throats and set even the most steadfast "believer" swaying in time. Payne paced through the circle now, his moment of "prayer" stolen. He stalked from one end of McKeenan's body to the other, a hungry predator, stalking his prey. Payne paid no attention to Brandt, or the others. His concentration was fixed on the line of the trees, and on the line of shadowy, faceless figures tossing fuel on his fire.

Slowly the circle faded. The night shifted. The faces and voices surrounding them fell away until Brandt stood on the edge of a cliff. Below him, waves crashed against the stone base like distant thunder. The spray drifted up and splashed across his face, and he blinked his eyes, not wanting to be blinded, but unwilling to stop playing to brush the moisture away. He knew the song he was playing. He remembered it from an album his father had played for him lifetimes in the past, except that when Charlie Parker had played it, there had been a saxophone, and now there was Shaver, only Shaver to drive the pain through the notes, nails through solid planks of sound and drawing the blood of the world. So perfect. So bittersweet, and changing, ever changing, until it wasn't Charlie Parker any more at all, just blue.

Synthia played the motion of the crowd. Her notes reverberated, and the bodies swayed, one entity, blended to the melody, and the harmony, syncopating the world. Brandt felt them near, though he saw only the ocean, and the cliff. Syn played the pounding of the surf, Shaver played the mist. Brandt was the steady ebb and flow of the waves.

Out over the water, the mist parted, and a shadowy hulk took shape, plowing slowly through the waves, bound for the rocks below. Brandt strained his eyes, half-blind from the spray and mist. It was a boat, a ship, wooden prow breaking the waves and sails, ratty and torn, dangling from broken masts. Figures moved about on the deck, chalk-white in the sudden flare of lightning, stark against the backdrop of the sea.

Brandt heard voices, wailing, crying out to the heavens, and he wanted to warn them, bent his notes to their ears and played as if he might become a beacon, a lighthouse, to warn them from the shore. They could not have listened, had they wanted. There was no way to steer the broken craft, no way to turn from the wicked rocks below, and as Brandt watched, more figures poured onto the deck. The first was tall, wild hair blowing about his shoulders, and the others followed too closely to one another. Something was wrong. Something kept them from walking normally.

Chains. The lightning flashed again, not white hot and instantaneous as it should have been, but red and gold, a firelight slash of brilliance across the darkened sky, lingering and bringing the deck of that ship to life. Slaves. They were bound together in a coffle, led to the deck, only in time for the ship to lurch. The man who'd led them from below fought valiantly, but waves crashed over the side, and with a mournful, plaintive cry, the entire chain was gone. One second there, the next a frothing splash and nothing, mist in moonlight, glowing emptily—the man standing, one hand clutching the door of the cabin, leading down and in, and the other grasping empty air.

Brandt cried out. He closed his eyes and willed that moment from his mind as his fingers slid lower, drawing raw, heavy sound from the strings as his pick hand ground hard. He wanted to break the strings. He wanted to snap the neck of the guitar and smash it, heave it to the rocks below and leap in after, but he did not. He played. He played as he'd never played before, and slowly the sound of the waves faded. The image of those men, and women, sliding over the side of the ship strobed in his mind.

He saw them, forcing their way through the waves, first one, then all of them sliding under that cruel surf, only to bob up again, caught helplessly and slammed toward the rocks, and the shore. On the deck of the ship, more and more, pouring from the hold, tied tightly, unable to dive to safety, only finding the freedom of the fresh air in time to find Death hovering in the mist.

"Yes," a voice whispered. "Take their pain, Brandt. Take it and set it free, concentrate."

Brandt shook his head. He knew the voice. It jarred his thoughts. Payne.

"Don't let them suffer alone," Payne whispered. "Don't leave them, boy."

It was wrong. The pain flowed up and out, slipping away. Brandt felt the release, the freedom the notes brought, and he reached for that, the only shield against the horror of it all. He clutched those notes, dragged them from the guitar and sent them soaring. But he couldn't hold it. He couldn't concentrate. What had Payne said? *Why* had Payne wanted him to play? To help?

The last of the image of cliffs and sea faded with a glimpse of wide, staring, haunted eyes, dragged under by the pull of the surf. The bonfire focused clearly over the heads of the circled townsfolk. They parted, like the waves had parted before the prow of that ship. They slid to the right, and to the left. Beyond them, striding through the trees, he came.

His eyes appeared first. Bright, wild eyes that shone like beacons, trapping the brilliance of the fire and reflecting them back, glowing coals that lit a gaunt, lined face. Skeletal, tall and emaciated beyond reality, the Sineater stalked the table. The crowd rolled back, flowed away skittishly, silent now. Only the music floated across that clearing.

Payne had stopped, standing at the head of the table, his arms outstretched to both sides, as if welcoming their "guest." He swayed with the sound for a moment, as if trapped by it, and then slipped free. His steps were mincing, an intricate dance that drew him from the table, into the crowd, and back again. The Sineater turned, taking in that discordant, disruptive motion. His concentration wavered.

Brandt caught this just in time, and shifted the sound. The blues bent, and the notes deepened. The echo of organs whispered against the trees and shivered through the leaves, and the eerie light of the fire lent a stained-glass aura to the backdrop of trees and night. Shaking his head, clearing it, Brian turned back to the table, and stepped forward.

Payne slipped nearer, and then to the side, dancing around the wild-man, so close their skin must nearly have brushed. There was no reaction. Brian had focused, and he reached for the first of the food, drawing a loaf of bread to his lips ravenously. Payne snarled, but the sound didn't carry. Brandt forced it away, fingers sliding now in an old, dark progression, minor chords and deep, slippery notes that stretched from one to the next without a break. Shaver's notes danced down that ripple in a flood of sound. Brian ate. Slowly, then more quickly, moving along the table.

"You let them drown, boy," Payne's voice insinuated itself into Brandt's thoughts, though the man's lips never moved. "You let them down."

Brandt ignored it, almost smiling in answer as he bore down on the strings.

Around them, the people picked up the beat, caught by the deep resonance of Synthia's pounding notes, forced to move, and to join, hand meeting hand in a syncopated back-beat rhythm. It was primal. The feel of the jungle filled the air, and the mood. The motion of the crowd became more sultry, speeding and losing sync with the music.

It was Payne. He moved among them, whispering, cajoling, his dance a winding path of discord threatening to tear the seam of the moment and let it spill out in tragedy. Brandt caught the man's eyes, heard the soft flow of laughter, the confidence, and the dark threat.

"Not today, pal," Brandt whispered. He shifted again. He let his mind drift, back to Dexter's church. He remembered the sound, the rhythm that had drawn Dexter down the aisle, that had stood that congregation on their feet and drawn their attention to the altar.

Brian, and the table, they were the altar this night. There were no snakes, but there was a meal, a very special meal, and for some reason, Payne had gone to a lot of trouble to see that the table was set, only to turn and do his best to see the moment ruined. Brandt kicked up the tempo, and Shaver and Synthia followed easily. Shaver turned, just an instant, and winked at Brandt, understanding somehow, and he stepped forward. The notes flowed less quickly, but with sudden, deep intensity. Shaver was throwing a lifeline of sound to those gathered, and sensing this, Synthia pounded in behind him, the new song, tempo, and rhythm shivering out from her bass and through the tiny amplifier, the only electronic addition to their sound, the only thing with a power not generated in their minds and their fingers.

Liz glanced back suddenly. She caught Shaver's eye, clutched her mother's arm tightly, and turned away, back to where her father, steadily, and with no concern nor attention for those gathered, slowly ate his way around the table, laying the late Reverend McKeenan's corpse bare to the night. Payne hadn't slowed Brian's efforts.

The shifting of the sound seemed to have maddened Payne, and his gyrating, off-kilter dance took on new power. Bursting from the crowd, he whirled to the table, leaping up on one end, balancing there, and nimbly leaping across to the other side, shaking the framework and nearly toppling it all.

Payne passed in front of Brandt very closely. The tails of his long coat whipped in the breeze and flicked out like long fingers, reaching to still Brandt's fingers. Brandt closed his eyes and ignored the distraction, playing easily now, instinctively. He felt the low chorus of voices trapped deep within him, humming the melody and strengthening his notes. Even without their amplifiers, Brandt and the others were filling the clearing with sound.

It wasn't enough. Payne slipped out through the crowd, to the bonfire, and he turned, letting the jacket flare out to the sides and up, cheap stage-magician cape to bat-wing proportion in seconds, and his laughter rang out, deep and powerful. The fire shifted, nearly snuffed by the force of that sound, and the music dimmed. Brandt played, desperately, but the sound had reverted to the weak, tinny notes of unamplified electric guitars.

Those who'd been feeding the fire turned as well, moving in just behind Payne. They shifted, growing taller, more gaunt. They held instruments. One stood tall, the polished bass leaning in close against his chin and his wrist bent just so, angled to pluck the deep, vibrating sound free. There were guitars, three of them, each glazed and glittering, polished to a high sheen. There was a sax, and a lone dancer, swaying and beautiful, tambourine held high and shaking softly.

They didn't play. They stood, and Payne stood before them, and then began to walk forward. He paid no attention as Brian slipped around the final corner of the table, where the wine and the final helpings of Reverend McKeenan's sin, stacked on plates and cooled in baking pans, were waiting for consumption and redemption. He moved straight toward Brandt with confident, fluid strides that covered the distance with deceptive speed.

Madeline stepped forward and planted herself between Payne and the band.

"Move aside, woman," Payne growled. "This isn't your game."

"It isn't a game at all," she answered, her voice wavering, but strong. "It isn't a game, and it isn't *your* place." She looked Payne up and down once, and then actually smiled. "Judging from your fancy dress, 'Reverend,' this isn't your *time* either."

"All times are mine," he answered with an arrogant smirk. "All pain is mine. Pain, and time, are both relative. Do you believe in the afterlife, Maddy?"

"You know I do," she replied. As an afterthought, "Don't you call me Maddy."

Payne laughed again, but Madeline held her ground.

"You aren't welcome here," she said softly. "Leave us in peace."

As she spoke, the music swelled, rising in volume and picking up power. Payne laughed again, a bit less confidently, and spun away.

"I don't think so, *Maddy*," he hissed. "Don't think so at all. I must say, I'm a little disappointed in this evening's—festivities. Maybe it's the music."

Payne raised his hands dramatically, stalking around the end of the table toward Brian. Brian held the wine flask. The last of it, the last of the food and the drink, the bread and the meat, gone. Impossibly, gone. Miraculously gone. But he held the wine, and before he could lift it to his lips, Payne was there, dancing closer, too-white teeth gleaming in the firelight.

"You don't want that, Brian," Payne whispered. "You don't want to drain that man's evil into you—it's his, don't you see? It isn't your burden. Let it go. Pour it out, and walk away."

Brian backed toward the crowd, and the fire. They parted before him, as they'd parted when he arrived. His eyes, if anything, were wider—wilder than before. They no longer shone with hunger, but with another light. A deeper light. His hand gripped the flask tightly, and he brought the brim to his lips. He spoke no word, but there was a strength in his silence. Payne took a step back, and he brought his arms down in wide arcs to his side.

Those standing by the fire . . . Payne's band . . . began to play. It was a sultry sound, emanating from deep within the flames. It leaped to life as Payne's arms dropped, and Brian staggered. Something in that sound, something running wild in the notes, dragged at his arms, pulling the flask from his lips. He cried out softly and steadied himself, the effort a horrible struggle that strained muscles and coated his brow in sweat. He shook, fighting an inward battle outwardly displayed. Payne laughed again, and this time the tones of that laughter had deepened, and strengthened.

Brandt gritted his teeth and played. He could barely make out the sound from his own guitar, so intrusive and all-encompassing was the music of Payne's minions. He felt it weighing on his soul, pressing him back, and down, yet still he played.

Crossroads, or the cross-hairs, boy, ain't no in-between.

Wally's words floated to him through his mind. Brandt closed his eyes. He saw that alley, fires burning in the trash barrels and he heard the music. The solo, lonesome voice of that mouth harp, drawing him in. He flashed on the image of the old woman, the cards. He glanced down, and there she was as he stepped forward, in wonderment.

Toothless grin and a flick of the wrist and a card sent sailing into the breeze. Brandt tried to focus on the image, tried to see what it could be. He played, and he stepped forward, following that twisting, wavering image with his eyes and his soul. Yellows and greens. Something curved and twisting.

A gnarled hand whipped from the shadows, snatching the card and turning it face-to Brandt, holding it very still. He stared. Shock prevented him from glancing to the hand, or the arm, and focused his attention on that card.

The Universe. A naked woman, fighting a snake, twisting in an oddly symmetrical figure-eight pattern. Masks at the four corners, looking inward. Balance. Brandt stood straighter. He turned, gaze shifting down the arm, the tattered shirt. Meeting those familiar eyes as the sound washed over him, pure and clean.

Wally stood there. The old man tossed the card again, and it floated in the mist above them as ancient, callused fingers wrapped around the harmonica, and the sound swelled. Brandt rode that wave, became that wave, slipping beneath the notes and lifted them higher. At his back, he felt Shaver, felt the sudden adrenalin rush and exaltation of sound as the lead raced to catch Wally, and to dance, subtly, between the notes.

The music grew, and washed over the clearing, and for that instant, Payne backed away, toward his fire. His eyes glowed, but the sound of his *band* had dwindled to a hum, and he no longer loomed so large. Payne's toothy grin had become a snarl, and he slipped back through the crowd quickly.

Brian watched, and tilted the flask, letting the first of the wine trickle over his lips. Head thrown back, he gulped slowly, eyes closed.

Payne roared. The sound shattered the music, splintering it and sending the shards bursting from the clearing. He moved forward again, making straight for Brandt, and Wally, eyes blazing, and the smile slowly curling back across his lips. The card shimmered in the air, and Brandt concentrated on it, brow furrowed and fingers burning like fire. Like they'd not burned since that first night. He felt those within him screaming for the release, begging him, saw the old man and his violin, playing a dirge to millions as black-booted, goose-stepping devils kept cadence. He saw the girl, and the endless parade of Cherokee dying, marching to oblivion, heard the tinny, whistling song of the flute as they moved. Felt Wally sliding closer, blending more firmly with his own notes. Felt it all fading, and flickering, and failing.

Payne was nearly upon them, and the card was drifting down, slowly, caught in the breeze and slipping side to side as it descended. Too much. The weight of those eyes, and the relentless, pounding beat from the band, and the pulsing flames, pressed against Brandt. He felt the heat, felt his skin reddening, near to blistering. He felt the strings so warm—hot—they nearly glowed. He gritted his teeth, tears streaming down his face, and he played.

Beyond Payne, over one shoulder, he saw Brian, the flask still tilted, his throat working slowly, as that sin, and that pain, flowed down and in and away.

Then it happened.

Slowly, a shimmer of sound like sandpaper whisked over wood, brisk and clean. It started low, a misty, rain-soaked sound that grew steadily, and powerfully. The mist became a shimmer, became a downpour of sound, rolling and twisting, shifting and driving into Payne's shocked features. Too close. The man had come too close, and now, as the sound grew and the strings cooled, as Brandt felt the pain shifting, and exploding up and out and away, Payne could not escape. He could not retreat to his fire, or his band. He couldn't smile, or frown, but only stare, and slowly—ever so slowly—diminish.

And the rhythm grew. It danced, and it rippled, growing

in strength and speed, impossibly intricate and delicately balanced.

Dexter. Dexter had finally drawn himself from his reverie, lifting the drumsticks and letting them dance, his wrists moving so quickly they blurred in the firelight, and the beat, the pounding rhythm *so* perfect that it dragged Brandt, and Shaver, Wally, and Synthia into its depths and molded them to the sound in an instant.

Payne mouthed a word. A negation, but the sound died, stillborn. He tried to back away, but as he took the steps backward, he shrank. As he moved, his features sank inward, and the air shimmered brightly. The vibration was palpable—visible and pummeling Payne toward the table. It danced in time with Brian's Adam's apple as he gulped a final time, draining the flask and smashing it to the table, even that sound engulfed in the music.

As that last drop was drained and the flask shattered, the fire grew with a sudden rush, becoming a single, brilliant pillar of flame, reaching toward the heavens. The band that had stood before it was gone, swept up and away in that burst, and Payne, stretching now, his face a rictus of pain and anger, was drawn in as well, slowly. He fought it. He held his ground and reached out, trying to grasp Brandt, trying to rip at Wally's throat, trying to put a single discordant beat into Dexter's onslaught. Failing.

He grew, taller, thinner, drawn up and into that column of flame as if it were a tornado of fire. He screamed, but even that sound was silent in the face of the music, and suddenly, Dexter moved forward. He no longer played, and he no longer held the drumsticks. Twin serpents dangled from his arms, and his head was thrown back in the ecstasy of the moment.

The air shimmered, and where Payne had stood, a

ghostly image grew. A woman, arched in the air, twisted and reaching toward Dexter as he moved forward. Dexter never saw, never needed to see. He stepped forward with certainty and thrust his arms toward the apparition, the snakes growing, elongating and taking on a shimmering glow of their own.

The serpents stretched upward, blended with the woman, and Brandt cried out softly, seeing it. The card, The Universe. The image flared, trapped in the mist and darkness, strobing so brightly it stole their sight and flickered in bright after-images.

The images whirled, shifted away, leaving Dexter standing with his empty hands and arms outstretched. The scene whirled, vertiginous shift of light and dark and suddenly it was Brandt, and the woman, and the serpents, and Brandt turned away, toward the cliff. He glanced out into the waves, saw the groping hands of those on the coffle, stretched . . . and felt his fingers grasp another's.

It went dark. Everything, pitch black and empty. No sound, no light, only the whisper of soft breeze, dancing through the leaves and limbs of the trees.

Brandt staggered, dropping to one knee. He managed, somehow, to cup the guitar in close, not damaging it. He heard the others, one by one, indrawn breaths and soft cries. He heard the moans of the townspeople as they gained their senses, as the darkness and the moment faded slowly to solid reality.

There were no voices. That was the first thing he knew. There was nothing, just the night, crickets chirping softly, and the sound of the others around him. He glanced to where Wally had stood, listened carefully, but again, nothing. The night, and the silence, and already the voices of those around him, softly denying, wondering, praying.

He rose, turned, and caught Synthia in his arms as she fell toward him. Shaver and Dexter were moving in from the side, and Madeline had turned, as Liz watched, and moved toward the table, now devoid of the impossible feast, bearing only the body, and the urn.

Brian stood there, watching her approach. He didn't flee, nor did he flinch from her as she ran the last few steps and threw herself into his arms. The two were so tightly embraced they scarcely noticed when Liz added herself to that tight mix, or when Shaver moved up and wrapped himself tightly around her.

They stood that way, the group of them, as the people of Friendly, California faded into the shadows, one by one, leaving them to their peace. As the moon's glow bathed the clearing, a single harmonica sounded in the distance, low and clear, and Brandt smiled, hugging Synthia even closer.

They turned toward the van, and as they stepped away from the clearing, Brandt stopped. He leaned down, and there, in the dirt of the clearing, he saw a brilliantly colored card. The Universe card. Up, and to the side of that, he saw a card with a young man, stepping off a cliff, oblivious to the danger, a dog attached firmly to his ass.

Brandt picked them both up, staring, and he laughed. He tossed The Universe card to the night breeze, slipping The Fool into his pocket.

Dexter stepped up beside him. With a grin, the drummer snatched the drifting Universe card deftly from the air.

Brandt asked, "What happened to the snakes?"

"I put them back," he said softly. "Wonder if there's any coffee left?"

Laughing, the band was swallowed in silence and moonlight.

ABOUT THE AUTHOR

DAVID NIALL WILSON has been writing and publishing horror, dark fantasy, and science fiction since the mid-eighties. His novels include the Grails Covenant Trilogy, *Star Trek Voyager: Chrysalis*, *Except You Go Through Shadow*, *This is My Blood*, and the *Dark Ages Vampire* clan novel *Lasombra*. He has over 100 short stories published in two collections and various anthologies and magazines. David lives and loves with Patricia Lee Macomber in the historic William R. White House in Hertford, NC with their children, Billy and Stephanie, occasionally his boys Zach and Zane, a psychotic cat, a dwarf bunny who continues to belie his "dwarfness"—and a pit bull named Elvis.